YEARS

SIMON &
SCHUSTER
PAPERBACKS

Also by Elizabeth Fremantle

The Tudor Trilogy
Queen's Gambit
Sisters of Treason
Watch the Lady

The Girl in the Glass Tower
The Poison Bed
The Honey and the Sting
Disobedient

FIREBRAND

Elizabeth Fremantle

Simon & Schuster Paperbacks
New York   London   Toronto   Sydney   New Delhi

100 YEARS

**SIMON &
SCHUSTER
PAPERBACKS**

An Imprint of Simon & Schuster, LLC
1230 Avenue of the Americas
New York, NY 10020

This book is a work of fiction. Any references to historical events,
real people, or real places are used fictitiously. Other names, characters, places,
and events are products of the author's imagination, and any resemblance
to actual events or places or persons, living or dead, is entirely coincidental.

Copyright © 2013 by Elizabeth Fremantle
Originally published in Great Britain in 2013 by Penguin Books as *Queen's Gambit*

All rights reserved, including the right to reproduce this book or portions
thereof in any form whatsoever. For information, address Simon & Schuster
Subsidiary Rights Department, 1230 Avenue of the Americas, New York, NY 10020.

First Simon & Schuster trade paperback edition June 2024

SIMON & SCHUSTER PAPERBACKS and colophon are registered trademarks
of Simon & Schuster, LLC

Simon & Schuster: Celebrating 100 Years of Publishing in 2024

For information about special discounts for bulk purchases, please contact Simon &
Schuster Special Sales at 1-866-506-1949 or business@simonandschuster.com.

The Simon & Schuster Speakers Bureau can bring authors to your live event.
For more information or to book an event, contact the Simon & Schuster Speakers Bureau
at 1-866-248-3049 or visit our website at www.simonspeakers.com.

Manufactured in the United States of America

1 3 5 7 9 10 8 6 4 2

ISBN 978-1-6680-0536-1
ISBN 978-1-6680-4362-2 (ebook)

For Alice and Raffi

Author's note to this edition

Firebrand was first published in 2013 as *Queen's Gambit*. It was my debut novel. At that time the screen rights were optioned, but my expectations were small, as many books are optioned and infinitesimally few end up in cinemas.

Imagine my delight then, when almost a decade later I learned that not only was the film to be made, but that Alicia Vikander—an actor of extraordinary talent and luminosity—was to play the lead. I could not have imagined a better person to bring the Katherine Parr of my novel to life, nor that Jude Law would be cast to play my aging and monstrous Henry. I cannot describe the thrill of seeing my characters brought to life on the screen.

As a result, I was given the opportunity to create a new edit of *Queen's Gambit*. It has been an illuminating process to revisit work conceived a decade ago and to encounter, once more, the extraordinary woman who inspired me to write historical fiction: Katherine Parr.

I was originally drawn to Henry VIII's last queen, as she was the first woman to publish an original work in the English language. I felt her fight for survival, her struggle to be heard and her shrewdness in negotiating the stifling patriarchy of the Tudor period would resonate with modern women.

Perhaps this is even more the case now. As I write, women in Afghanistan are being denied an education and their freedom has been snatched from them. There remain many, many parts of the world where young girls are forced to marry elderly strangers, where women suffer violence at the hands of men and are as far from sharing equal rights as were the women of Tudor England. Even here in Britain, approximately three women a week are murdered by men. So, for me, Katherine Parr's fearless voice continues to sound out down the centuries.

For this new edition—*Firebrand*—I have not altered my original narrative, rather I have polished it, tidied the writing and honed the style. I have also given the text room to breathe by separating it into more chapters and dividing the whole into four parts. Since *Queen's Gambit* was published, I have written six more historical novels and my craft has developed as my knowledge as a writer has broadened. So, I hope this editorial work has added clarity and fluency.

The result is not a response to the screenplay, which has taken its own brilliant direction and covers a specific period of Katherine Parr's life, but a more refined iteration of my original text. I sincerely hope that those who have enjoyed *Firebrand*, the film, will relish engaging with the longer story of an exceptional and courageous Tudor queen.

Prologue

The notary smells of dust and ink. How is it, Latymer wonders, that when one sense blunts another sharpens.

He can pick up the scent of everything, the reek of ale on the man's breath, the yeasty whiff of bread baking in the kitchens below, the wet-dog stink of the spaniel curled up by the hearth. But he can see precious little. The room swims and the man is a vague dark shape leaning over the bed with a grimace of a smile.

"Make your mark here, my lord." He enunciates as if talking to a child or an idiot.

A waft of violets sweeps over him. It is Katherine—his dear, dear Kit.

"Let me help you up, John." Katherine shifts his body forward and slips a pillow behind him.

She lifts him so easily. He must have wasted quite away these last months. It is no wonder with the lump in his gut, hard and round as a Spanish grapefruit. The movement starts something off—an excruciating wave that rises through his body, forcing an inhuman groan from him.

"My love." Katherine strokes his forehead.

Her touch is cool. The pain twists deeper.

He can hear the clink of her preparing a tincture. The spoon flashes as it catches the light. The chill of metal touches his lips, and a trickle of liquid pools in his mouth. Its loamy scent brings back a distant memory of riding through woods and with it a sadness, for his riding days are over.

His gullet feels too thick to swallow and he fears setting off the pain again. It has receded but hovers, as does the notary who shifts from one foot to the other in an embarrassed shuffle. Latymer wonders why the man is not more used to this kind of thing, given that wills are his living.

Katherine strokes his throat and the tincture slides down.

Soon it will take effect. His wife has a gift with remedies. He has thought about what kind of potion she could concoct to set him free from this useless carcass of his. She'd know exactly what it would take. After all, any one of the plants she uses to deaden his pain could kill a man if the dose were right—a little more of this or that and it would be done.

But how can he ask such a thing of her?

A quill is placed between his fingers and his hand is guided to the papers so he can make his mark. His scrawl will make Katherine a woman of considerable means. He hopes it will not bring the curse of fortune-hunters to her door.

She is still young enough, just past thirty, and her charisma that made him—already an elderly widower—fall so deeply still hangs over her like a halo.

She never had the ordinary beauty of other men's wives. No, her attraction is complicated and has blossomed with age.

But Katherine is too sharp to be taken in by some silver-tongued seducer with his eye on a widow's fortune. He owes her too much. When he thinks of how she has suffered in his name, it makes him want to weep, but his body is incapable of even that.

He has not left her Snape Castle, his Yorkshire seat. She wouldn't want it. She would be happy, she has said often, were she never to set foot in Snape again. Snape will go to Young John.

Latymer's son did not turn out quite the man he'd hoped and he has often wondered what kind of child he might have had with Katherine. But that thought is always shadowed with the memory of the dead baby, the damned infant that was made when the Catholic rebels ransacked Snape. He cannot bear to imagine how that baby came about, fathered by, of all people, Murgatroyd, whom he used to take out hunting hares as a boy. He was a sweet lad, showed no sign of the brute he would become.

Latymer curses the day he left his young wife alone with his children to go to court and seek pardon from the King, curses the weakness that got him involved with the rebels in the first place. Six years have passed since, but the events of that time are carved into his family like an epitaph on a tomb.

Katherine is straightening the bedcovers, humming a tune he doesn't recognize, or can't remember. A surge of love rises in him. His marriage to her was a love match—for him, anyway. But he hadn't done what husbands are supposed to do. He hadn't protected her.

Katherine had never spoken of it. He'd wanted her to scream and rage at him—to hate him, blame him. But she remained poised and contained, as if nothing had changed. And her belly grew large, taunting him. Only when that baby came, and died within the hour, did he see the smudge of tears on her face. Yet still, nothing was ever said.

This tumor, swelling in his own belly in gruesome mimicry, is his punishment. All he can do to atone is make her rich. How can he ask one more thing of her? If she could inhabit his wracked body even for an instant she would do his bidding without question. It would be an act of mercy, and there is no sin in that, surely.

She is by the door, seeing the notary out, before floating back to his side. She pulls her hood off, discarding it at the foot of the bed, rubbing her temples with the tips of her fingers and shaking out her russet hair. Its dried-flower scent drifts over, making him yearn to bury his face in it as he used to do.

Taking a book, she begins to read quietly, the Latin tripping easily off her tongue. It is Erasmus. His own Latin is too rusty to get the sense of it. He should remember this book but he doesn't. She was always better learned than him, though pretended otherwise.

A timid knock interrupts them. It is his Meg holding the hand of that gawky maid, whose name escapes him. Poor little Meg, who, since Murgatroyd and his men came, has been jumpy as a colt. It made him wonder what might have been done to her too. The little spaniel comes to life with a frenzied wagging and wriggling about the girls' feet.

"Father," Meg whispers, placing a spring-meadow kiss on his forehead. "How do you?"

He lifts his hand, a great dead lump of driftwood, placing it over hers and attempts a smile.

She turns to Katherine. "Mother, Huicke is here."

"Dot," Katherine says to the maid, "will you see the doctor in."

"Yes, my lady." With a swish of skirts the girl makes for the door.

"And Dot . . ." adds Katherine.

The maid stops in the doorway.

". . . ask one of the lads to bring more wood for the fire. We are down to the last log."

The girl bobs, with a nod.

"It is Meg's birthday today, John," says Katherine. "She is seventeen."

He feels clogged up, wants to see his girl properly, read the expression in her nut-brown eyes, but the detail of her is blurred. "My little Margaret Neville, a woman . . . seventeen." His voice is a croak. "Someone will want to marry you. A fine young man." It strikes him like a slap in the face—he will never know his daughter's husband.

Meg's hand wipes at her eye.

Huicke slips into the chamber. He has come each day this week. Latymer wonders why it is that the King sends one of his own physicians to care for an almost disgraced northern lord such as he. Katherine says it is a sign that he is truly pardoned. But it doesn't make sense and he knows the King enough to suspect that there is an ulterior purpose to this gesture—although what it is, he's not sure.

The doctor is a thin black shadow approaching the bed.

Meg takes her leave with another kiss.

Huicke draws back the covers. A rancid stench escapes. He begins to palpate the lump with butterfly fingers. Latymer hates those kid-clad hands. He has never known Huicke to remove his gloves, which are fine and buff like human skin. He wears a ring set with a garnet the size of an eye over them. Latymer loathes the man disproportionately for those gloves, the deceit of them pretending to be hands, and the way they make him feel unclean.

Sharp bursts of pain peck at him, making his breath come fast and shallow. Huicke sniffs at a vial of something, holding it up to the light while talking quietly with Katherine. She glows in the proximity of this young doctor.

He is too fey and girlish to be a threat at least, but Latymer hates him anew for his youth and his promise, not just for his gloved hands. He must be quite brilliant to be in the King's service and still so young. Huicke's future is laid out before him like a feast, while his own is all used up. Latymer drifts off, the hushed voices washing over him.

"I have given him something new for the pain," she is saying. "White-willow bark and motherwort."

"You have a physician's touch," Huicke replies. "I would not have thought to put those together."

"I am interested in herbals. I have a little physic garden of my own . . ." She pauses. "I like to see things grow. And I have Bankes's book."

"*Bankes's Herbal*, that is the best of them. Well, I think so, but it is rather scorned by the academics."

"I suppose they think it a woman's book."

"They do." He smiles with a lift of the eyebrows. "And that is precisely what recommends it to me. In my opinion women know more about healing than all the scholars in Oxford and Cambridge together, though I generally keep that to myself."

A new bolt of pain shoots through Latymer, sharper this time, folding him in half. He hears a scream, barely recognizing it as his own. He is dying of guilt. The spasm wanes slowly, as if something is being unscrewed from his gut, leaving just a dull ache.

Huicke has gone. He must have been asleep. He is struck with a sudden, overwhelming sense of urgency. He must ask her before speech deserts him, but how to phrase it?

He grabs his wife's wrist, surprised by his own strength. "Give me more tincture."

"I cannot, John. I have already given you the limit. More would . . ." Her words hang.

He grips her more tightly. "It is what I want, Kit."

She looks at him, straight on, saying nothing.

He thinks he can see her thoughts like the workings of a clock, wondering where in the Bible she might find justification for this; how to reconcile her soul with such an act; that it could send her to the gallows; that if he were a pheasant got at by the dog, she would think nothing of a merciful twist of his neck.

"What you ask of me will damn us both." Her whisper is filled with resignation.

"I know," he replies.

PART ONE

Better to be his mistress than his wife.
Katherine Parr

I

There has been a late snowfall and the dusted turrets of Whitehall Palace are indistinct against the pallid sky.

The courtyard is deep in slush. In spite of the sawdust that has been strewn in a makeshift path across the cobbles, Katherine can feel the wet chill soaking through her shoes and the damp edges of her skirts flick bitterly at her ankles. She shivers, hugging her thick cloak tightly about her as the groom helps Meg dismount.

"Here we are," she says brightly, though bright is the last thing she feels, holding out her hand for Meg to take.

Her stepdaughter's cheeks are flushed. She has the sweet, slightly startled look of a woodland animal but Katherine can see the effort she is making to hold off more tears. Her father's death has hit her hard.

"Come," says Katherine, "let's get inside."

Two grooms have unsaddled the horses and are brushing them down briskly with handfuls of straw. Katherine's gray gelding Pewter throws his head about with a jingle of tack and snorts, billowing trails of steam like a dragon.

"Easy, boy," says Katherine, taking his bridle and stroking his velvet nose, allowing him to snuffle at her neck. "He needs a drink," she says to the groom, handing him the reins. "It's Rafe, isn't it?"

"Yes, m'lady." A hot blush rushes over his cheeks. "I remember Pewter, I gave him a poultice once."

"Yes, he was lame. You did a fine job with him."

The boy's face breaks into a grin. "Thank you, m'lady."

"It is I who should thank *you*." As Rafe leads Pewter towards the stable block, she clasps her stepdaughter's elbow and makes for the great doors.

She has been numb with grief for weeks and would rather not have to come to court so soon after her husband's death. But she has been summoned—Meg, too—and a summons from the King's daughter is not something one is able to refuse.

Besides, Katherine likes Lady Mary. They knew one another as girls, even shared a tutor for a while when Katherine's mother was serving Mary's mother—Queen Catherine of Aragon—before the King cast her off. None of that is ever to be spoken of, at court or elsewhere.

Things were simpler in the days before the whole world was turned on its head, the country rent in two. But she won't be commanded to stay at court just yet. Mary will respect her period of mourning.

When she thinks of Latymer, how she helped his passing, shame rises through her like milk on the boil. She has to remember the horror of it all in order to reconcile herself to her actions: his anguished screams, the way his own body had turned on him, his desperate request. She has searched the Bible since for a precedent, but there is no story of merciful killing there, nothing to give hope for her blighted soul. There's no denying it—she killed her husband.

Katherine and Meg enter the Great Hall. It smells of wet wool and woodsmoke and is teeming with people, busy as a market square. They mill in the alcoves and strut in the galleries, showing off their best clothes. Groups gather in corners to play cards or dice, throwing down bets. Occasionally a whoop goes up when someone has won or lost.

Katherine watches Meg, wide-eyed at it all. She has never been to court. She's barely been anywhere, and after the deathly quiet of Charterhouse, all cloaked in black, this must be a rude awakening.

They make a somber pair in their mourning garb among the flocks of bright-clad ladies floating by, bubbling with chatter. Their dresses swing as they move, as if they are dancing and eyes are cast about to see who has noticed how fine they look. There is a fashion for little dogs, bundled in their arms like muffs or trotting obediently at heel.

Even Meg manages a laugh to see one that has hitched a ride on its mistress's train.

Pages run back and forth and pairs of servants move through, burdened with baskets of logs, one between two, destined to stoke the fires in the public rooms. Long tables are being laid for dinner in the Great Hall by an army of kitchen boys clanking by, balancing precarious stacks of dishes.

A group of musicians tunes up, the dissonant chords eventually transforming into something like a melody. To hear music at last, thinks Katherine, imagining herself caught up in the sound, whirling and spinning until she can hardly breathe with joy. She stops that thought. She will not be dancing just yet—not while she is mourning her husband.

They step aside to allow a band of guards to march past and she wonders if they might be on their way to arrest someone, reminding her of how little she wants to be in this place. But a summons is a summons. She gasps as a pair of hands comes from nowhere, clapping themselves over her eyes, catapulting her heart into her throat.

"Will Parr," she laughs.

"How could you tell?" Will drops his hands.

"I would know your smell anywhere, brother." She pinches her nose in mock disgust, turning to face him where he stands with a group of men. He beams like a small boy, his brassy hair sticking up where he has removed his cap, his mismatched eyes—one gray, one hazel—flashing.

"Lady Latymer. I can hardly remember the last time I clapped eyes on you." A man steps forward. Everything about him is long: long nose, long face, long legs and bloodhound eyes. But somehow nature has conspired to make him quite becoming in spite of his oddness. Perhaps it has something to do with the unassailable confidence that comes with being the eldest of the Howard boys, and next Duke of Norfolk.

"Surrey!" A smile invades her face. Perhaps it will not be so bad at court with these familiar faces about. "You still scribbling verse?"

"Indeed I am. You will be pleased to know my style has improved greatly."

He had once penned her a sonnet when they were little more than children. They had often laughed about it since—"virtue" rhymed with "hurt too." The memory causes a laugh to bubble up in her. One of his "juvenile embarrassments," as he had described it.

"I am sorry to see you in mourning," he continues, serious now. "But I heard how your husband suffered. Perhaps it is a mercy that he has finally passed."

She nods, her smile dropping away, unable to find words to reply, wondering if he suspects her, scrutinizing his face for signs of condemnation.

Have the circumstances of Latymer's death been discovered?

Is it spreading through the corridors of the palace?

Perhaps the embalmers had spotted something irregular—her sin written into her dead husband's guts.

She dismisses the thought. What she gave him leaves no trace and there is no accusation in Surrey's tone, she is sure of it. If it shows on her face, they will think her distraught with grief, but nevertheless her heart is hammering.

"Let me present my stepdaughter, Margaret Neville," she says, gathering herself.

Meg shrinks back wearing a barely disguised look of horror. Since those cursed events at Snape Katherine has kept her away from the company of men as much as possible, but now there is no choice. Besides, the girl will have to marry eventually. Katherine will be expected to arrange it, but God knows, Meg is far from ready.

"Margaret." Surrey takes Meg's hand. "I knew your father. He was a remarkable man."

"He was." Her voice is small.

"Are you not going to present *me* to your sister?" A man has stepped up, tall, almost as tall as Surrey. Slapping her brother on the back with one hand, he waves a velvet cap with the other. It is adorned with an ostrich feather the size of a hearth brush, bobbing and dancing as he gives it an unnecessary flourish.

Katherine stifles a laugh. He is got up spectacularly, in a doublet of black velvet with crimson satin spilling out of its slashes and finished with a sable collar. He seems to see her notice the sable, bringing a hand up to stroke it.

Trying to place him, she tries to remember the sumptuary laws and who is entitled to wear sable. His hands are weighed down with rings—too many for good taste—but his fingers are fine and tapered and they wander from the sable to his mouth. He draws his middle finger over his bottom lip slowly and deliberately, not smiling. But his eyes, a startling blue, and his disarmingly direct gaze are making her feel hot. She meets his gaze only momentarily, catching the briefest flutter, before dropping her look to the floor.

Did he wink at her? The insolence. He winked at her. No, it must have been her imagination. But then why in heaven's name is she imagining this overdressed ninny winking at her?

"Thomas Seymour, this is my sister Lady Latymer." Will seems amused by whatever it is that has just passed between them.

She should have known. Thomas Seymour is bearer of the dubious accolade of "comliest man at court"—the object of incessant gossip, youthful crushes, broken hearts, marital discord. She concedes inwardly to his looks. He is a beauty, that is indisputable, but she is not foolish enough to be drawn under his spell.

"It is an honor, my lady," he says in a voice as smooth as churned butter, "to finally meet you at last."

Surrey rolls his eyes.

So there's no love lost there, she thinks. "Finally *and* at last!" It trips off her tongue before she can stop it. She can't help herself wanting to put this man in his place. "Goodness!" She places a hand to her breast affecting exaggerated surprise.

"Indeed, my lady, I have heard of your charms," he continues, unprovoked, "and to be confronted with them makes me tongue-tied."

By charms she wonders if he means her recently acquired wealth. News of her inheritance must be out. Will for one can't keep his mouth shut. She feels a little surge of anger for her brother and his blabbering.

"Tongue-tied?" She searches for a witty retort and keeps her look firmly directed at his mouth, not daring to meet his eyes again, but his wet pink tongue catches the light disturbingly. "Surrey, what think you? Seymour here has got his tongue in a knot."

Surrey and Will don't hide their amusement as she racks her brain for something more. "And it might be his undoing."

The three men burst into laughter simultaneously. Katherine feels triumphant. Her wit has not deserted her, even in the face of this unsettling creature.

Meg stares at her stepmother aghast. She has not had much opportunity to see this Katherine, the sharp-witted courtly one. Katherine throws her a reassuring smile while Will introduces her to Seymour, who looks at her as if she is made of sugar.

Katherine takes her hand, saying, "Come, Meg, we will be late for Lady Mary."

"So brief but yet so sweet," simpers Seymour.

Katherine ignores him, placing a kiss on Surrey's cheek. As she walks away, she half turns back to vaguely dip her head in the general direction of Seymour for the sake of politeness.

"I shall walk with you." Will puts himself between the two of them.

When they are up the stairs and out of earshot, Katherine quietly admonishes her brother. "I would prefer it if you would refrain from discussing my inheritance with your friends."

"You're too quick to accuse, sister. I've said nothing. It's got out. It was bound to, but—"

"What was all that about my so-called charms then?" Irritation makes her tone shrill.

"Have you considered he might really have been referring to your charms?"

She emits a peeved snort.

"Do you always have to be the disgruntled elder sister?"

"I'm sorry, Will. You're right, it's not *your* fault that people talk."

"No, it is *I* who should apologize. Things have been hard for you." He pinches the black silk of her skirts between his fingers. "You're in mourning. I should be more sensitive."

As they walk down the long gallery towards Lady Mary's rooms, Will mutters under his breath, "I wish it were I in mourning."

"You don't mean that."

He scowls in response.

Will and his wife loathed each other from the moment they met. Anne Bourchier, the sole heir of the elderly Earl of Essex, was the prize their mother had almost beggared herself to catch for her only son. With Anne Bourchier came great expectations, not least the Essex title to hitch the Parrs back up a notch or two. But the marriage had brought poor Will nothing, no children, no title, no happiness—nothing but disgrace, for the King gave Cromwell the earldom while Anne eloped with some country cleric.

Will couldn't shake off the scandal, was ever beset by jibes of "clerical errors" and "priests' holes" and "parsons' noses." He didn't see the funny side and, try as he might, he hadn't managed to persuade the King to sanction a divorce.

"When I think of the hopes Mother had for my marriage, all she did to arrange it."

"She never lived to see its failure. Perhaps that is as well."

"It was her greatest wish to see we Parrs on the rise again."

"Our blood is good enough without her." Katherine is firm. "Father served the old King and his father served Edward IV, Mother served Queen Catherine." She counts them off on her fingers. "Do you want me to go on?"

"That's ancient history." Will sounds like a petulant child. "I don't even *remember* Father."

"Nor me, really." She does remember clearly the day their father was laid to rest. How indignant she'd felt at being deemed too young, at six years old, to attend the funeral. "Besides, Anne has served all five Queens and now serves the King's daughter—and it is likely I shall, too, once more."

She's irritated by her brother's grasping ambition, wants to tell him that if he cares so greatly to raise the Parrs, then he should start currying favor with the right people instead of that Seymour fellow. Seymour may be Prince Edward's uncle but it is his elder brother Hertford who has the King's ear.

Will begins his grumbling again but seems to think better of it and they fall to silence once more, weaving through the crowd outside the King's chambers.

Then he squeezes her arm. "What think you of Seymour?"

"Seymour?"

"Yes, Seymour . . ."

"Not much." Her voice is clipped.

"Do you not find him splendid?"

"Not particularly."

"I thought we might try to make a match for him with Meg."

"With Meg?" she blurts. "Have you lost your senses?"

The color has fallen from Meg's face.

Seymour would eat the poor girl alive. "Meg will not be marrying anyone just yet. Not while her father is barely cold."

"It was only—"

"A ridiculous idea." She is sharp.

"He is not what you think, Kit." He lowers his voice. "Seymour's one of us."

By that she supposes he means he's for the new religion. She doesn't like to be packaged up with the court reformers, prefers to keep her thoughts on the matter close to her chest. She has learned over the years that it's safer to cultivate an opaqueness at court.

"Surrey doesn't like him," she says.

"Oh, that's nothing but a family thing, not even about religion. The Howards think the Seymours upstarts. It has no bearing on Thomas."

Katherine huffs.

Will leaves them to admire the new painting of the King that hangs in the gallery. It is so fresh she can smell the paint and its colors are vivid, with all the detail picked out in gold.

"Is that the last Queen?" Meg points to the somber woman in a gable hood beside the King.

"No, Meg." She presses a finger to her lips, whispering, "Best not mention Catherine Howard here. It is Queen Jane, the sister of Thomas Seymour whom you just met."

"But if it is a new painting, why is it of Queen Jane, when there have been two Queens since?"

"Queen Jane is the one who gave him the heir." She omits adding that Jane Seymour was the one who died before the King could tire of her.

"So that is Prince Edward." Meg points to the boy, a pocket version of his father, mirroring his stance.

"It is, and they," she indicates the two girls hovering about at the edges of the picture like a pair of butterflies with nowhere to alight, "are Ladies Mary and Elizabeth."

"I see you are admiring my portrait," comes a man's voice from behind.

The women turn, startled.

"Will Sommers!" Katherine says. "*Your* portrait?"

"Do you not see me?" He points to the back of the image.

"There you are. I hadn't noticed." She turns to her stepdaughter. "Meg, this is Will Sommers, the King's fool, the most honest man at court."

Sommers stretches out a hand and pulls a copper coin from behind Meg's ear, provoking a rare delighted laugh from her.

"How did you do that?" Meg stares at the coin in wonder.

"Magic."

"I don't believe in magic," says Katherine. "But I know a good trick when I see it."

2

Susan Clarencieux, in egg-yolk yellow, looms over the door to Lady Mary's inner rooms, shushing them like an adder as they arrive.

"She has one of her headaches." Susan smiles tightly. "So keep the noise down." Looking Katherine up and down, as if totting up the cost of her dress and finding it wanting, she adds, "So very dull and dark. Lady Mary will not approve." Then her hand swoops to cover her mouth. "Forgive me, I forgot you were in mourning."

"It is forgotten," replies Katherine.

"You will find your sister in the privy chamber. Excuse me, I must deal with . . ." She doesn't finish and slips back into the bedchamber, closing the door silently behind her.

The privy chamber is scattered with ladies quietly concentrating on their needlework. Katherine nods at them in greeting before spotting her sister, Anne, in a window alcove.

"Kit!" Anne stands, drawing her older sister into an embrace. "What a pleasure to see you at last. And Meg." She kisses Meg warmly on both cheeks.

The girl has relaxed visibly now they are in the women's rooms.

Anne suggests Meg go and look at the tapestries on the far wall. "I believe your father is depicted in one. See if you can find him."

Anne leads her sister away from the other women, to a bench in the window.

"So, what's the occasion? Why do you think I have been summoned?" Katherine can hardly tear her gaze away from Anne, her easy smile, the translucent glow of her skin, the pale tendrils of hair escaping from her coif, the perfect oval of her face.

"Lady Mary is to stand godmother. Quite a few have been asked to attend."

"Not just me then . . . I am glad of that. So who is to be baptized?"

"It is a Wriothesley baby. A daughter called . . ."

"Mary," they say simultaneously, smirking.

"Oh Anne, how good it is to see you. My house is a gloomy place indeed."

"I shall visit you at Charterhouse when Prin—" She cups both her hands over her mouth with an intake of breath, eyes searching the room for eavesdroppers. "When Lady Mary gives me leave." She leans right into Katherine's ear and whispers, "Lady Hussey was sent to the Tower for addressing her as Princess."

"I remember that," says Katherine. "But that was years ago and she was making a stand. It was different. A slip of the tongue wouldn't be punished like that, surely."

"You've been long away from this place." Anne looks suddenly serious. "Have you forgotten what it is like?"

"Nest of snakes," Katherine murmurs.

"I hear the King sent Huicke to attend your husband."

"He did. I don't know why."

"Latymer was certainly pardoned then."

"I suppose so."

Katherine had never fully understood Latymer's part in the uprising. The Pilgrimage of Grace, they'd called it, when the whole of the North—forty thousand Catholic men it was said—rose up against Cromwell's reformation. Some of the leaders had arrived at Snape armed to the hilt. There had been heated discussions in the hall and a good deal of shouting but Katherine couldn't get the gist of what was being said. The next thing she knew Latymer was preparing to leave, reluctantly, he told her: they needed men like him to lead them.

She wondered what kind of threats they'd made, for Latymer was not the sort to be easily coerced even though he thought their cause justified. The monasteries had been razed, the monks strung from the trees and a way of life destroyed with them—not forgetting the beloved Queen cast aside and the Boleyn girl turning their great King about her finger like a toy. That was how Latymer described it.

But to take arms up against his King—that was not the husband she knew.

"You have never talked of it." Anne picks at a loose thread on her dress. "The uprising, I mean. What happened at Snape."

"It is something I'd rather forget." Katherine snaps shut the conversation.

A version of events had spread around the court at the time. It was common knowledge that when the King's army had the rebels on the back foot, Latymer had left for Westminster to seek the King's pardon. The rebels thought he'd turned coat, sending Murgatroyd and his men to hold Katherine and Meg hostage, ransacking Snape—it made a good story for the gossips.

But that was not the half of it. Even her sister knew nothing of the dead baby, Murgatroyd's bastard son. Nor that she'd given herself to the brute in desperation, to save Meg and Dot from his clutches—the darkest secret of them all. She did save the girls but doesn't know what God thinks of that, for adultery is adultery, whatever the motive.

Katherine has often wondered why it was that all the other leaders had swung, and Murgatroyd too—two and a half hundred put to death in the name of the King when the uprising failed—but not Latymer. Perhaps he *had* betrayed them. Murgatroyd had certainly assumed so. She prefers to believe that Latymer was loyal, as he'd maintained, otherwise what was it all for? But she will never know the truth.

"Did you ever hear anything," she asks Anne, "about Latymer and why he was pardoned? Were there any rumors at court?"

"Nothing reached my ears." Anne rests her hand on Katherine's sleeve. "Don't dwell on it. The past is past."

Katherine nods but she can't help thinking of the way the past erodes the present like a canker in an apple.

She looks across the chamber at Meg intently searching the tapestry for her father's likeness. At least his image has not been stitched over like some.

She returns her attention to Anne—sweet, loyal, uncomplicated Anne. There is something about her, a freshness, as if she has more life in her than she can possibly contain. It strikes Katherine suddenly why this is.

Her heart gutters and, leaning forward, she puts a hand to Anne's stomacher. "Is there something you're keeping from me?" She wonders if her smile hides the surge of jealousy that comes in the face of her sister's fertility. It is written all over her, the flush and bloom of pregnancy that Katherine has wanted so very much for herself.

Anne reddens. "How is it you know everything, Kit?"

"That is wonderful news." The words stick in her throat. Her widowhood is a hard unassailable fact. The possibility of a child is nothing but a distant fantasy now at her age, with not a single living infant to her name, only the dead baby that is never spoken of.

Her thoughts must have seeped through her surface, for Anne squeezes her hand with the words, "There is still a chance for you, sister. You will surely marry again."

"I think two husbands are enough," Katherine replies, firmly. "I'm so very happy for you. Unlike the Wriothesley baby, I know *this* one won't be a little Catholic with Lady Mary as its godmother."

Anne brings a finger to her lips with a "shhh" and the sisters share a secret smile. She stretches out a hand to the pendant that hangs from Katherine's neck. "Mother's diamond cross," she says, holding it up so it catches the light. "I remember it bigger than this."

"It is you who was smaller."

"It is a long time since Mother left us."

All Katherine can think of is the length of her mother's widowhood.

"And these pearls," Anne is still fingering the cross, "they are almost pink. I'd forgotten. Oh dear, one of the links is loose." She leans in closer. "Let me see if I can mend it." Her brow knits in concentration as she presses the open ends of the link between her thumb and forefinger.

Katherine can smell her scent. It is sweet and comforting, like ripe apples. She turns a little towards the paneling so Anne may better get to her throat. On the wood she can clearly see where the initials CH have been scraped away. Poor little Catherine Howard, the most recent Queen, these must have been her rooms briefly. Of course they were, they are the best in the palace, save for those of the King.

"There." Anne releases the cross. "You wouldn't want to lose one of Mother's pearls."

"How was it, Anne, with the last Queen? You have been quite silent about it." Katherine's voice has dropped to a whisper and her fingers absently stroke the scraped place on the paneling.

"Catherine Howard?" she mouths.

Katherine nods in reply.

"She was so young, younger than Meg even."

They both look towards Meg, seeming barely out of girlhood herself.

"She hadn't been raised to hold high position. Norfolk dredged her out of the further reaches of the Howard tribe to serve his own needs. Her manners!" She frowns. "You can't imagine how crude she was or how shallow. But she was a pretty little thing and the King was utterly unmanned in the face of her . . ." She pauses, searching for the right word. ". . . her attractions. It was her appetite that was her undoing."

"For men?" Katherine further drops her whisper.

The sisters' heads are close together now and their faces are half turned towards the window so as not to be overheard.

"A compulsion almost."

"Did you like her?"

"No . . . I suppose not. She was insufferably vain. But I wouldn't have wished *that* fate on anyone. To go to the block like that and so young. It was dreadful." There is a wobble in Anne's voice. "Her ladies—we were all questioned one by one. I had no idea what was happening. Some must have known what she'd been up to, carrying on like that with Culpepper, under the King's nose."

"She was just a girl. She should never have been put in the bed of such an old man, King or not."

They sit in silence for a while. Through the window Katherine watches a skein of geese fly high above the river. "Who questioned you?" she asks eventually.

"Bishop Gardiner."

"Were you afraid?"

"Petrified." Her face crumples. "He's a monster. Not a man to cross. I once saw him dislocate a choirboy's finger for missing a note. I knew nothing, so there was little he could do with me. But we all had the Boleyn business in our minds."

"Of course, Anne Boleyn." Katherine's hand moves instinctively to her neck. "It turned out the same for little Catherine Howard."

"Just the same. The King withdrew, refused to see her, just as he had with Anne. The poor girl was mad with fear. Ran howling down the long gallery in just her kirtle. Her screams stay with me still. The gallery was teeming with people but no one so much as looked at her, not even her uncle Norfolk. Can you imagine?" She tugs the loose thread in her dress right away. "Thank heavens I wasn't chosen to serve her in the Tower. I couldn't have borne it, Kit. Standing by to watch her step up to the scaffold. Untie her hood for her. Bare her neck." She shudders.

"Poor child."

"And rumor has it he seeks a sixth wife."

"Who do they talk of?"

"The rumors fly as usual. Every unmarried woman has had her name bandied, even you."

Katherine snorts. "Better to be his mistress than his wife."

"Everyone's putting their money on Anne Bassett. She's younger even than the last one. I can't imagine him taking another young maid like that. Catherine Howard shook him to the core. But little Anne's family are pushing her forward nonetheless. She has a whole new wardrobe to flaunt."

"This place." Katherine sighs. "Did you know Will suggested a match between Meg and that awful man Seymour?"

"That doesn't surprise me in the least." Anne rolls her eyes. "They are thick as thieves, Will and he."

"It won't happen."

"You weren't taken with the palace charmer then?"

"Not one bit. Found him . . ." She can't find the words, is too distracted by the fact that Seymour has been tapping at the edge of her mind this last hour. "Oh, you know."

"This lot wouldn't agree with you." Anne nods towards a group of younger maids strewn about the hearth chatting and pretending to sew. "You should see how they flutter as he passes, like birds in a net."

Katherine tells herself that she is not one of those birds. "Has he never been married? He must be, what, twenty-nine?"

"Thirty-four!"

"He carries the years well. Something wrong with him if he's never been married at that age." But the thought that is foremost in her mind is that Thomas Seymour is older than she.

"I seem to remember talk of him and the Duchess of Richmond once." Anne is warming to the topic.

"What, Mary Howard? I thought the Howards and the Seymours were . . ."

"Not friendly . . . yes, that's likely why it never came to anything. Personally, I think he's holding out for an even more illustrious match."

"Well then, Meg wouldn't be suitable."

"She *is* full of Plantagenet blood." Anne lifts her brows.

"That may be, but I'd call her a *good* match, not illustrious."

"True."

Meg breaks away from the tapestries. The group of maids looks her up and down as she passes, a few whispers hissing around them.

"Did you see your father, Meg?" asks Anne.

"I did. I'm sure it was him, on the battlefield beside the King."

There is a commotion as Susan Clarencieux appears from Mary's bedchamber, to announce in that bossy yet quiet way particular to her, "She will be dressed now." And to Katherine she says, "She has asked that *you* choose her outfit."

Katherine, seeing immediately that Susan's nose is put out of joint, replies, "What would you suggest? You know her better than me. Something sober?"

Susan's face softens. "Oh no, I think something to cheer her."

"You are quite right, of course. Something bright it is then."

Susan's face stretches itself into an uncomfortable smile. Katherine knows how to deal with these slippery courtiers and their insecurities. She learned it from her mother.

"And," adds Susan as Katherine is smoothing down her dress and straightening her hood, "she wants the girl presented."

Katherine takes her stepdaughter by the hand. "Come, Meg. We can't keep her waiting."

"Must I come?" she mumbles.

"You must, yes." She pulls the girl towards the door rather more brusquely than she means to. "She may be the King's daughter but she is nothing to be scared of. You shall see." Stroking Meg's back she notices how thin she has become, the bones of her shoulders protruding like the nubs of wings.

Lady Mary is cocooned in a fur-lined robe. Katherine has to hide her shock at the other woman's appearance. Mary is four years her junior yet she is frail and puffy about the face with a feverish glaze to her eyes—the legacy of the treatment she has received at her father's hands.

At least now she has been welcomed back to court where she belongs, no longer hidden away in some dank distant place. Her position remains tenuous, though, and since her father tore the country apart to prove he wasn't ever truly wed to her mother, poor Mary still has the blot of illegitimacy hanging over her. No wonder she clings to the old faith. It is her only hope of legitimacy and a good marriage.

"Katherine Parr." Her thin mouth twists into a smile of greeting. "Oh, how glad I am to have you back."

"It is a privilege to be here indeed, my lady." Katherine curtsies. "But I am only here for the baptism. I am told you are to stand godmother to the Wriothesley infant."

"Only today? That is a disappointment."

"I must respect a period of mourning for my late husband."

"Yes, of course." Mary closes her eyes, lifting a hand to press the place between her brows.

"Are you in pain? I can mix you something." Katherine bends to stroke a hand over Mary's brow.

"No no, I have tinctures—more than enough." She draws herself upright, with an intake of breath.

"If I rub your temples that might ease it."

Mary nods her assent, so Katherine stands behind her and gently massages Mary's temples in a circular motion. The skin there is parchment thin, revealing a delta of blue veins. Mary closes her eyes and leans her head back against Katherine's stomacher.

"I was sorry to hear about the loss of your husband," she says. "Truly sorry."

"That is kind, my lady."

"But Katherine, you will come back soon to serve in my chambers . . . I am in need of friends. I only fully trust your dear sister and my Susan. There are so many ladies in my rooms—I don't even know who they are. You and I shared a tutor as children, Katherine, your mother served my mother. I feel we are almost kin."

"I am honored that you consider me so." Katherine realizes only now how lonely life must be for a woman like Mary. By rights she should have been married long ago to some magnificent foreign prince, borne him a flock of princelings and allied England to some great land. Instead she has been pushed from pillar to post, in favor, out of favor, legitimate, illegitimate. No one knows what to do with her, least of all her father.

"Are you still of the true faith, Katherine?" Mary asks, dropping her voice to a whisper though there is no one else in the room save for Meg, hovering awkwardly behind her stepmother. "I know your brother is committed to reform, your sister and her husband too. But you, Katherine—tell me you are not also lost to the truth. You have been long wed to a northern lord and the old faith holds sway up there still."

"I follow the King's faith." Katherine hopes nothing is assumed from her vagueness. She knows only too well how things go in the North when it comes to faith. She cannot think of it without feeling Murgatroyd's rough hands on her, the unwashed stink of him. She tries to push the thought away but it persists.

"My father's faith?" Mary looks sad. "He is still a Catholic at heart, though he broke with Rome. Is that not right, Katherine?"

Katherine has barely heard her, can't help herself from remembering her dead baby, the moment his black eyes popped open, his disquieting gaze reminding her from whence he came. She collects herself. "It is, my lady. Matters of faith are no longer straightforward as they used to be."

She hates her own ambiguity, feels no better than all the other perfidious courtiers. She cannot bring herself to say to what extent she has taken up the new faith. She couldn't face Mary's disappointment. This is a woman whose life has been a series of great disappointments and Katherine cannot bear to add to that, even in a small way, by telling the truth.

"Would that they were," Mary murmurs. "Would that they were." She fiddles absently with a rosary, its beads clicking as she moves them along the silk string. "And this is your stepdaughter?" It is as if she has only just noticed Meg's spectral presence.

"Yes, my lady. Allow me to present Margaret Neville."

Meg makes a tentative step forward and drops into a deep curtsy as she has been taught.

"Come closer, Margaret," Mary beckons, "and sit, sit." She waves towards a stool beside her. "Now, tell me your age."

"I am seventeen, my lady."

"Seventeen. And you are promised to someone, I suppose?"

"I was, my lady, but the Lord took him."

Katherine has told her to say this. It wouldn't do to publicize the fact that her betrothed was one of those hanged for treason after the Pilgrimage of Grace.

"Well, we shall have to find you a replacement."

Katherine's heart wants to break to see the doomed expression shadow Meg's face.

3

The Mass is endless. Meg fidgets and Katherine's mind wanders unwittingly to Seymour. The thought of him disturbs her. She remembers the bouncing feather, everything about him overdone, and forces her attention back to the dull service.

Lady Mary, at the font, seems so fragile it's a wonder she can hold the infant, which is round and robust with a pair of lungs that would scare the Devil himself. Bishop Gardiner presides, full of self-importance. He drags things out, his voice, slow and interminable, rendering the Latin ugly. Katherine can't help but think of him questioning her sister, terrifying her—that and the poor choirboy's finger. There is a cruel look in those dark eyes, their lids saggy as melted wax.

They say Gardiner has maneuvered himself closer and closer to the King in recent years, that the King seeks his counsel at least as much as the Archbishop's. The child wails without let-up, until the holy water is poured on her head. From that instant she is completely silent, as if Satan has been chased from her, and Gardiner carries a smug look as if to say it is his doing rather than the Lord's.

The King does not attend. Wriothesley, the infant's father, is perturbed. He is a ferrety man—russet beard, russet hair, russet eyes—with a permanent look of apology and a tendency to sniff. He is Lord Privy Seal and some say he holds the reins of all England along with Gardiner. You wouldn't think it to look at him. Katherine notices his frequent anxious glances towards the door as he absently cracks his knuckles, so that an occasional soft gristly clack punctuates Gardiner's drone.

A slight such as this could mean anything with a King whose

fancies change on a whim. The Lord Privy Seal may hold the reins of England but that means nothing without the King's favor. Wriothesley should know all about the King's whims. After all, he was Cromwell's man once, but managed to slip and slide out of that association as soon as the tide turned—another one to beware of.

Once it is done they all file out behind Lady Mary, who holds tight on to Susan Clarencieux's canary-yellow arm as if she is unable to walk without help. Her ladies follow through a scrum of courtiers in the long gallery, who part as she approaches.

Seymour is among them. Two of the younger girls giggle stupidly when he smiles and doffs that ludicrous feather their way. Katherine looks away, pretending to be fascinated by old Lady Buttes's commentary on her many ailments. She vaguely hears Seymour say her name along with some insincere flattery about her jewels. She offers him a brief, unsmiling nod before turning back to Lady Buttes's string of complaints.

Once back in the relative calm of Lady Mary's chambers Susan Clarencieux hustles them all through to the outer rooms and helps Mary, who seems on the brink of collapse, into her bedchamber.

The younger girls, now they are in private, start to pull off their hoods and loosen their gowns, chattering and giggling. The women mill about in quiet groups, settling eventually to their reading or needlework, and spiced wine is handed around.

Katherine is about to take her leave when a commotion starts up outside, a drumming and singing accompanied by a lute and a great stamping of feet. The girls all reach for their hoods, hurriedly shoving them back on their heads again, helping each other to tie them on, stuffing stray tendrils of hair away, pinching their cheeks and biting their lips.

The doors fly open and a band of masked minstrels dances into the room to a cacophony of clapping and cheering. They jig about in a reel, twirling in figures of eight, pushing the ladies out to the sides. Katherine steps onto a stool, pulling Meg up with her, in order to see over the heads. The atmosphere in the room heightens to a contained frenzy, like the strange crackle of air before a storm.

Anne grabs one of the girls and says, "Quickly, fetch Susan. Tell her Lady Mary must come out. Tell her there is a visit."

Katherine sees now, with a barely concealed gasp, what all the fuss was for. There at the center of the circling minstrels, limping and hefting his huge form about, is the King, preposterous in his minstrel garb, one leg black and the other white.

She remembers him doing this years ago. He believed himself completely disguised, and the whole court colluded in the dumbshow. He wanted desperately to know if people were as delighted by the man as they were by the King, unable to see the impossibility of his aim. He burst in then as now, surrounded by his finest courtiers, and he, a head taller than them all, agile, muscular, vigorous, was an impressive sight indeed. The effect was utterly disarming, particularly to Katherine, who was then just a girl.

But to be cavorting in such a way still, barely able to stand without the support of a man either side of him, his minstrel's doublet stretched around his girth, straining at its laces, reeks of desperation. And to surround himself with such well-formed specimens, his fine ushers and chamberers, young and bursting with life, fit from the hunt, makes the whole charade infinitely worse.

Meg is open-mouthed.

"It's the King," whispers Katherine. "When he removes his mask you must feign surprise."

"But why?" Her face is a picture of bewilderment.

Katherine shrugs. What can she say? The entire court must collude in an illusion that makes the King feel young and beloved for himself, when all he inspires truly these days is fear. "This is court, Meg. Things here often defy explanation."

The men are now cantering in a circle and at its center is little Anne Bassett. Her mother, Lady Lisle, is practically salivating, as her ripe sixteen-year-old daughter is twirled about among the men under His Majesty's acquisitive gaze.

"I fear history is repeating itself." Anne doesn't need to explain in what way. The whole room is thinking of Catherine Howard, except perhaps Lady Lisle, whose sense is doubtless clouded by ambition.

The circle breaks and Anne Bassett is spun out to the edge of the crowd. The music dies and the King whips off his mask to a great gasp of counterfeit surprise, as the room drops to its knees.

"Who would have believed it—the King!" cries someone.

Katherine keeps her eyes down, inspecting the grain of the floorboards, resisting the temptation to nudge her sister for fear of the giggles. The whole thing is more ludicrous than an Italian comedy.

"Come," booms the King. "This is an informal visit. Rise, rise. Now let us see who is among you. Where is our daughter?"

Lady Mary steps forward. A rare smile casts itself over her face and the years seem to drop away from her as if a crumb of her father's attention has collapsed time.

A few other men have arrived and are milling about.

"Will is here," Anne says. "With his crowd."

Katherine catches sight of that feather bucking and bobbing about the room. She drags Meg sharply away, only to find herself standing before the King.

"Ah, is that my Lady Latymer we see lurking? Why do you lurk, my lady?"

A waft of fetid breath engulfs her. It is all she can do to prevent herself from reaching for the pomander that hangs from her girdle. "Not lurking, Your Majesty, just a little overwhelmed." She holds her gaze on his chest.

His tightly laced black and white doublet is encrusted with pearls. Rolls of him spill from its edges, giving the impression that were he to remove it he would lose his form altogether.

"We offer our condolences for your husband's passing," he says, holding out his hand for her to kiss the ring embedded in the flesh of his middle finger.

"That is most thoughtful, Your Majesty." She dares a glance towards his large face, square and doughy with raisin eyes sunk into it, wondering what became of the magnificent man he once was.

"I am told that you cared well for him. You are quite known for your nursing skills. An old man needs to be cared for." Then, before she has a chance to respond, he leans in towards her ear, close enough for her to hear the wheeze of his breath and get a whiff of ambergris perfume. "It is good to see you back at court. You look appetizing even in a widow's weeds."

Inwardly cringing, she struggles to respond, managing a few mumbled words of gratitude.

"And who is this?" The moment of intimacy is thankfully over. He is waving a hand towards Meg, who drops into a deep curtsy.

"This is my stepdaughter, Margaret Neville."

"Get up, girl," the King says. "We want to see you properly."

Meg does as she is told. Katherine notices her hands are trembling.

"And turn about." He watches her carefully as she turns for him like a mare at auction. Suddenly he cries, "BOO!" causing her to jump back, terrified. "Nervy little thing, isn't she." He laughs and one or two of his men join in as if he has made a particularly good joke.

"She has been sheltered, Your Majesty," Katherine says.

"Needs a fellow to break her in." He is rubbing his hands and asks Meg, "Anyone here take your fancy?"

Seymour saunters by and Meg looks momentarily towards him.

"Ah! We see you have an eye for Seymour." The King seems amused by this. "A handsome fellow, don't you think?"

"N-n-no . . ." Meg cannot control her stutter.

Katherine kicks her sharply on the ankle. "I think what she is trying to say is that Seymour is nothing when compared to Your Majesty." Katherine's tone is slick as oil. She barely believes herself capable of such easy disingenuity.

"But he is talked of as the handsomest man at court," says the King.

"Hmmm." Katherine tips her head to one side, thinking how best to form her response. "That is a matter of opinion. Some prefer greater maturity."

The King emits a loud guffaw. "I think we will arrange a match between your Margaret Neville and Thomas Seymour. My brother-in-law to your stepdaughter . . . It has a nice ring to it."

Clasping both women firmly by the elbow, he steers them across the room to a gaming table. Katherine can think of no way of discouraging the match without causing offense, so she remains silent.

Two chairs are brought by a scurry of staff. The King heaves himself into one, indicating that Katherine take the other. A chessboard is magicked from nowhere and the King beckons Seymour to set out the pieces. Katherine dares not even glance his way, for fear of the confusion of feelings that twists about inside her seeping to the surface.

She is aware of Lady Lisle's darting glances from where she stands with her daughter. She can almost hear the woman's machinating thoughts of how better to push her girl, school her, groom her, to catch the biggest fish in the sea. She must be happy with the fact that Katherine is no competition, twice widowed, past thirty and not a surviving child to her name. Beside pretty Anne Bassett in the full flush of her youth she is nothing. If he wants sons he will choose Anne Bassett or one like her. And he does want sons, everyone knows that.

She makes her play.

"Queen's gambit accepted." The King takes her white pawn, rolling it between fat fingers. "You mean to rout me at the center of the board." He looks at her, sunken eyes flashing, his breath wheezing as if there is no space for air in him.

They make their moves back and forth, swiftly and in silence.

He takes a sweetmeat from a platter, popping it into his mouth, smacking his lips, then picks up a rook, placing it, blocking her move with an "Aha!" Then he leans in towards her to say, "*You* will want a husband as well as your stepdaughter."

She runs the little white knight over the pad of her thumb. "I am in mourning. My husband is barely cold."

"I could make you Queen."

She feels droplets of his spit land next to her ear. "You tease, Your Majesty." She forces a tinkle of laughter out.

"Perhaps," he growls. "Perhaps not."

He wants sons. All the world knows he wants sons. Anne Bassett would give him a score of infants—or a Talbot girl, or a Percy, or a Howard. No, not a Howard—he has had two Howard Queens and sent both to the block. He wants sons and Katherine has had nothing in two marriages save for a secret infant that died within a half hour of birth.

The thought hits her, suddenly and devastatingly, like cannon shot—the thought of making a child with Seymour, beautiful Seymour, a man in his prime. It would be a sin for such a man not to procreate.

She silently admonishes herself for entertaining such a thought. But it refuses to be quashed and sits there germinating at the back of her mind.

She has to employ every last shred of her willpower to keep her eyes off Seymour, to focus on the game and on amusing the King.

Katherine wins.

"Checkmate!" The small gathering of spectators shrinks back a little, as if anticipating an explosion.

"That is what we like about you, Katherine Parr." The King laughs. The gathering relaxes.

"You do not humor us by losing, as all the others do, who think it pleases us always to win." He takes hold of her hand. "You are honest." He pulls her towards him, stroking her cheek with waxy fingertips. The room watches and Katherine is aware of her brother's grin as the King cups a hand for secrecy, presses his wet mouth to her ear and murmurs, "Attend us in private later."

Katherine flails for some kind of response. "Your Majesty, I am honored," she says. "Deeply honored that you would choose to spend time alone with me. But with my husband so recently gone I—"

He places a finger over her lips to hush her, saying, "No need to explain. Your loyalty shines from you. We admire that. You need time. You shall have time to mourn your husband." And with that he beckons one of his ushers to help hoist him from his chair and, leaning heavily on the young man, limps towards the door, followed by his entourage.

Katherine sees the usher stumble on the royal foot. The King's arm flies out in a sharp slap across the man's face, fast as a frog's tongue to a fly. The hubbub of conversation dies.

"Out of my sight, idiot. Want to have your foot cut off for clumsiness?" the King bellows, sending the poor cowed usher scuttling off. Another takes his place and everyone continues as before. It is as if nothing has happened—no one remarks on it.

As Katherine seeks out her sister she can feel the atmosphere of the room has shifted, turned towards her. People part to let her pass, throwing compliments like flowers in her wake. All but Anne Bassett and her mother, who look sideways at her across the room. Katherine feels queasy. Her sister is like an island in this dissimulating sea.

"I need to get away from this place, Anne."

"Lady Mary has retired, no one will mind if you go," her sister replies. "Besides," she adds with a playful nudge, "it appears you can do no wrong."

"This is no joke. There is a price for this kind of favor."

"You are right." Anne is serious. They are both thinking of all those miserable Queens.

"He was only flirting. He *is* the King ... Entitled to that, I suppose ... not serious ..." Katherine is gabbling. "Best I keep away from court for a time, though."

Anne nods. "I'll see you out."

4

It is almost dark in the courtyard and fine flakes of snow are caught hanging in the light from the torches under the arcades. Much of the sludge has frozen over now and the grooms tread carefully over the treacherous cobbles.

A large party arrives, dismounting noisily, and the flurry of pages and ushers receiving them suggests they must be of some note. Katherine notices the goggle eyes and thin-lipped sneer of Nan Stanhope, whom she knows from childhood, a spiteful and self-important girl who had sometimes shared the royal schoolroom all those years ago.

The woman swans past, nose aloft, shoving Anne with her shoulder as she passes, as if she hasn't seen her, not acknowledging either of the Parr sisters.

"I see some things never change," Katherine says.

"She's been insufferable since she married Edward Seymour and became the Countess of Hertford," says Anne. "You'd think she was the Queen the way she goes about."

"But she *is* descended directly from Edward III." Katherine rolls her eyes.

"As if we didn't know that." Anne groans.

"As if she'd let us forget."

A page brings their furs, which Katherine and her stepdaughter fold themselves into against the cold. They bid goodbye to Anne, who disappears up the stone steps. Katherine will miss the easy familiarity she has with her sister. The gloom of Charterhouse is not appealing, though she will be glad to be away from this nest of vipers.

They wait for the horses on an alcove bench. Meg looks drawn. Katherine closes her eyes, letting her head drop back to the cold stone wall, thinking of Latymer's prolonged agony, of how difficult it must have been for the girl.

"My Lady Latymer," says a voice, drawing her out of her thoughts. She opens her eyes to find Thomas Seymour standing over her. Her stomach lurches.

"Margaret," he says to Meg, smiling like a man who always gets what he wants. "Would you be very kind and make my excuses to your uncle. He waits for me in the Great Hall and I have some business to discuss with Lady Latymer before she leaves."

"Business?" questions Katherine as Meg disappears up the steps. "If you're intending to ask for Margaret's hand—"

He interrupts. "Not at all. No ... though she is a lovely girl ... and with Plantagenet blood to boot. Rather timid for my taste." He is garbling as if slightly disarmed.

This surprises Katherine, for she is feeling the same, confronted by this man alone. He stands a little too close to her, closer than is correct. The planes of his face all seem to agree with one another, his jaw defined, his cheekbones high, his forehead lofty with his hairline gathering into a point of hair at the center, like an arrow saying, "Look at me."

He smells male and musky and is looking at her intently. Her belly feels liquid and she would run if she could, but she is at bay to her good manners and those eyes have paralyzed her.

He is holding something in the outstretched palm of his hand. "Yours, I believe."

She looks. It is a pearl.

"I think not." As she says it her fingers reach to her mother's cross, feeling an empty place where the central pearl should be and the jagged ends of the broken link.

How did it come to be lying in this man's palm?

She is bewildered, as if he has performed some kind of sleight-of-hand on her, like the copper Will Sommers pulled from behind Meg's ear. She stares at it for some time, angry with him, as if he'd ripped it from her throat deliberately.

"How did you get your hands on it?" Her voice is clipped and cross and she's annoyed with herself for revealing too much in her tone. His eyes continue to bore into her. Her breath sounds loud in the silence.

"I saw it drop from your pendant in the long gallery and tried to get your attention. And then again in Lady Mary's rooms but the King . . ." He stops.

"The King," she repeats. She had all but forgotten about the King's approach.

"I'm so glad I found you before you left." His face opens up into a wide, beguiling smile with his eyes creasing at the corners. In an instant they are no longer menacing but bright and captivating.

She doesn't return his smile but neither does she take the pearl, which still sits in his palm waiting to be claimed. She can't get away from the feeling that she has been tricked.

He sits down on the stone bench beside her, saying, "Take it."

But she doesn't move.

"Or better still," he adds, "give me the necklace and I shall have my goldsmith mend it for you."

She turns to look at him, wanting to find fault. Everything is so perfectly put into place, the careful ruffle of his silk shirt, the neatly clipped beard, the way his cap sits firmly over one ear, and that infernal feather, so showy.

The crimson satin spilling from the slashes in his doublet makes her think of bloodied mouths. She wants to reach out and scuff him up a little. The snow has spotted his velvet shoulders and the tip of his nose is red. She smiles and turns her back, surprising herself, lifting the lappets of her hood to expose the nape of her neck. He slips the loose pearl into her hand while he unclasps her necklace. She had not intended to do that, but something in this man's open smile and the sweet ruddy tip of his nose makes her feel, in spite of herself, that she has misjudged him.

He takes the necklace, bringing it briefly to his lips before stashing it somewhere inside his robe. A melting sensation passes through her as if it had been her throat he'd kissed rather than the necklace.

"Take care of it. It was my mother's and is very precious to me."

She has managed to gather the drifting bits of herself together and injected her voice with its usual straightness.

"I can assure you, my lady, I shall." He pauses a moment before adding, "I am truly sorry for your husband's passing. Will tells me he suffered greatly."

She doesn't like the idea of her brother discussing her or her husband with this man, wonders what else might have been said. "He *did* suffer."

"It must have been unbearable for you to see that."

"Yes." She is still looking at him and his face seems to register genuine concern. A curl has escaped above the whorl of his ear and it is all she can do to resist stretching out her hand and tucking it away. "Unbearable."

"He was a lucky man to have you to take care of him."

"You think he was lucky? He wasn't lucky. Not lucky to be struck down like that." Her voice is sharp. She can't help it.

Seymour looks chastened. "I didn't mean to—"

"I know you meant no harm." She can see Meg descending the steps. "Meg is back, it's time to go."

She gets to her feet, noticing Rafe outside, with the horses. Meg goes straight to him and Katherine wonders if she is avoiding Seymour after all that talk of a match.

"And the pearl," Seymour says.

Momentarily confused, she opens her hand and finds the pearl nestled there. She feels tricked again, can't remember taking it from him. "Oh yes, the pearl." She hands it over.

"Do you know how a pearl is made?"

"Of course I do." She is suddenly angry with herself at being taken in by this man with his sweet talk and platitudes, imagining all those giggling maids hanging on to his every word as he describes the making of a pearl, twisting and turning the metaphor for them until they are talked into bed and into revealing their own oysters. "And *you* are a grain of sand in my shell."

She turns to leave.

Seymour will not be rebuffed so easily and snatches up her hand, to plant a kiss on it. "But perhaps in time I will become a pearl."

He mounts the steps two at a time, his gown swaying from his broad shoulders.

She wipes the back of her hand on her dress, wishing she'd made it clear that if he's after a tumble with a widow, she wouldn't be that widow for a thousand gold pieces.

She is struck with a sense of loneliness, feels unmoored without her husband, misses him desperately, wishes she were going back to him.

There is a commotion on the stairs, a clatter and a gust of laughter. She looks up to see one of the young pages on the floor with an up-turned plate of tarts that are scattered everywhere.

People pass, kicking the tarts about, treading them into the floor, taunting the boy. She can see the humiliation in his crimson little-boy cheeks. She moves to help him but, as she does so, she sees Seymour drop to the floor on his silk-clad knees and begin to gather up the tarts.

This silences the wags, who drift away shiftily for they know Seymour is the King's brother-in-law and that they all ought to be scraping to him. You'd think by the looks on their faces that he'd turned the world on its head by getting down on his white-stockinged knees to help this nobody.

He pats the boy on the back, teasing a smile from him and Katherine hears him say, "Don't you worry. I'll talk to the cook."

As they ride away Katherine wonders if she should have given her mother's cross over to Seymour so lightly when she barely knows him, cursing the confusion of contradicting emotions the man seems to have kindled in her. He is Will's friend, surely that is enough to recommend his honesty, and how kind he was to the page with the tarts. Perhaps, beyond that showy exterior, there lies a tenderness that doesn't deserve her antipathy. She has come to distrust most men since Murgatroyd did his damage.

"Mother," says Meg. "Look what Uncle Will gave me." She pulls a book from beneath her cloak, handing it to Katherine.

She is suddenly angered with her brother yet again, thinking it one of the banned books, Zwingli or Calvin, and that he is trying to draw Meg into something she's too unworldly to understand. The intrigue of religious factions at court is dangerous indeed. But she looks at the title, finding it is only *Le Morte d'Arthur*.

"That is lovely, Meg." Katherine hands it back, thinking how suspicious she has become. She kicks Pewter into a trot, reassured by the strength of him beneath her, wanting to get back home to Charterhouse all the sooner. Gloomy it may be, but at least she knows what goes on within its walls.

"I can't wait to show it to Dot." Meg and her maid Dot have become close as sisters since the business at Snape, and Katherine is grateful for it. "She likes me to read the romances to her."

5

Meg warms her frozen feet by the hearth in her bedchamber with the spaniel puppy Rig on her lap, while Dot combs out her damp hair for her.

"Aren't you going to tell me what it was like there?" says Dot, her curiosity almost too much to contain. "Did you see the King?"

"I did."

"What was he like? Is he really as big as they say?"

"Bigger." Meg stretches out her arms to indicate the size of his girth, which makes Dot giggle but Meg is not amused. "He was terrifying." The fire spits an ember onto the stone floor. Dot stamps on it. "It was all so confusing there, Dot. The King was disguised as a minstrel, and though everybody knew who he was, they all pretended they didn't."

"I wouldn't think the King given to games like that. I'd have thought him more ..." Dot searches for the right word. Dot hasn't much considered that the King might be a real man. He is more like some monster from an old story, who chops off the heads of his wives. "I'd have thought him more serious."

The comb snags causing Meg to cry out.

"Hold still. You're making it worse." Dot carefully unpicks a tangled knot of hair.

"No one says what they mean there, even Mother talks in riddles. And all anyone had to say to me was to ask me when I am to marry and to whom." She pulls a grimace, hugging the puppy tightly. "If I had it my way I'd never marry."

"You'll have to, whether you want it or not. And you know it."

"I wish I had your life, Dot."

"You wouldn't last an hour being me—all the skivvying I have to do. See your beautiful hands." She holds her own calloused hand up to Meg's, which is smooth and white, her nails perfectly oval. "Yours aren't made for scrubbing." She kisses the top of Meg's head, then begins to plait her long hair, twisting the strands deftly and pinning them in place before slipping a nightcap over them.

Meg falls silent for a while before saying, "But *you* can marry whom you please."

"Fine choice I have. Have you seen the kitchen lads . . ."

"There's the new squillery boy."

"What, Jethro? He's more trouble than a bad tooth, that one." Dot doesn't mention the fumble she's had with Jethro in the stables. She never talks of those things with Meg.

"Uncle Will would have me marry his friend Thomas Seymour."

"What's he like then, this Seymour?"

Meg grabs Dot's wrist, so tight her knuckles blanch. "He reminds me of . . ." Her breath is short and shallow, as if she is choking on the word, her eyes dark. Dot pulls her to her feet, scattering Rig, to take her in her arms, holding her tight.

"You mean Murgatroyd," Dot says. "You mustn't be afraid to say it out loud. That way it is out, and out is better than left in to fester." It's what Dot's ma used to tell her to do: *name your fears.*

Meg feels half wasted away. Dot has seen how little she eats, as if she wants to starve herself back to childhood. Perhaps that is the point.

Though only a single year separates them, Dot feels older by far in spite of Meg's cleverness: the reading, the Latin, the French. She has a tutor, a pale man dressed in black who feeds her all that knowledge.

Dot's head floods suddenly with unbidden memories of sitting in the stone corridor outside the turret chamber at Snape, cupping her hands over her ears so as to block out Murgatroyd's grunts and Meg's muffled cries. He had locked the door and Dot could do nothing.

The poor child, for she was a child back then, was lacerated down there when he'd finished with her. No wonder she doesn't want to marry. That is the secret that binds Dot to Meg, and it is a heavy one indeed. Even Lady Latymer doesn't know what truly happened.

Meg swore Dot to secrecy—and one thing Dot is good at is keeping a secret.

"Mother was arranging the match." Meg chews at her thumbnail. "I'm sure of it. She had a private conversation with Seymour."

"You can delay it. Tell her you are not yet ready."

"But I'm seventeen. Most well-born girls my age have been married two years and are cooking a second infant already." She breaks out of Dot's embrace to sit on the bed.

"Your father has just passed away. I'm sure Lady Latymer will not make you marry while you are mourning."

"But then . . ." Meg's voice drags off to silence and she flops back with a sigh.

Dot wishes she could tell her that there's nothing to worry about, that she can stay unmarried, and that she, Dot, will be there for her always. But she won't lie to Meg, and heaven only knows where she will be sent next. All the servants are wondering what will become of them now Lord Latymer is gone and everything is in flux.

"What's this then?" Dot wants to change the subject and picks up the book Meg brought back from court.

It is covered in dun calfskin and tooled with a pattern of ivy. She brings it up to her nose, breathing in the leather scent. It smells faintly of home, the little place in Stanstead Abbotts where she grew up. The cottage stood next to a tanner's yard and that smell got itself into the very walls. She remembers how, in the summer, when the hides were stretched out in the sun and brightly dyed, big splashes of color, the smell was at its most intense. It was too strong to be a pleasant scent—it was why the rent was cheap—but they were accustomed to it.

She wonders what her ma is doing now, imagines her sweeping snow off the stoop, making a picture of it in her head: Ma's sleeves rolled up, capable hands holding the broom. Her sister Little Min helps, spreading grit on the path. Her brother Robbie, with thatch dust in his hair like Pa always had, is cracking the ice in the water butt.

But she knows that picture is all wrong, that Little Min is not so little any more and Ma's face is a map of lines. She feels the heart-tug of missing them, but it's so long ago and she has grown into the wrong shape for that life, couldn't fit herself back into it.

She was twelve when she left for Snape Castle all the way up in Yorkshire, to work for Lady Latymer, whom her ma's ma had wet-nursed as a baby. The Parr family at Rye House more or less kept the entire village of Stanstead Abbotts employed back then, when Ma's ma was still alive, or so it was said.

Dot left at the time when Pa had fallen off a roof thatching and broke his neck. Ma started taking in washing, but there was never enough to go round even with Robbie taking over Pa's work. Dot re-members the hunger pangs at night, when all there'd been was a half ladle of pottage each for the girls and a whole one for Robbie, who needed his strength for climbing on roofs and hauling great sheaves of thatch about. They had to count their lucky stars that there was a position for Dot at Snape, for that left one less mouth to feed at home.

Ma had given her a silver penny as a keepsake, which is still stitched into the hem of her dress for good luck. She remembers say-ing goodbye to her best friends, Letty and Binny, who seemed not to realize that Yorkshire was almost as far as the moon, for they kept talking about what they would do when she came back to visit.

There was a tearful moment with Harry Dent too, a handful of a lad she was sweet on and whom it was generally assumed she would marry in the end. He said he'd wait for her for ever. She wonders at the heartache she had over Harry Dent when she can hardly even picture his face now. Dot thought she might never return, but she didn't say so for they seemed so very sad about it all as it was.

She did go back to Stanstead Abbotts, though, on the journey down to London from Snape. Lady Latymer had given her a couple of days off to spend with her family. But Letty had passed away from the sweats and Binny had married a farmer from Ware. Harry Dent had got a girl in the family way and had scarpered—so much for him. Robbie was drinking more than he should and everyone was think-ing he'd fall off a roof and go the way of Pa, though no one said it.

Everything was different but most of all it was she who had changed. She felt out of place in the cottage, kept banging her head on the beams and the stench was overwhelming. She'd got used to a different kind of life.

"It's a book Uncle Will gave to me. *Le Morte d'Arthur*," says Meg, jolting Dot back to the present.

"That is not English. What tongue is it?"

"The title is in French, but the rest is English."

"Shall we read it?" Dot really means for Meg to do the reading and she to do the listening. She runs her fingers over the embossed letters of the title, whispering "*Le Morte d'Arthur*," trying to get her tongue around the strange sounds. She wishes she could understand how these lines and squiggles transformed into words, thinking it all a kind of alchemy.

"Oh let's!" Meg's mood thankfully seems to lift at the thought of it, and it strikes Dot that she—plain Dorothy Fownten, a thatcher's daughter from Stanstead Abbotts—is having romances read to her by the daughter of one of the great lords. That is the extent to which she has changed.

Dot gathers all the candles she can find so Meg has enough light to read by, and piles some cushions and furs beside the fire, where they snuggle up with the book. Closing her eyes, Dot lets the story wind itself around her, making pictures in her head of Arthur and Lancelot and the giant warrior knight Gawain, imagining herself as one of the fair maidens, forgetting for a moment her too-big, calloused hands and her clumsiness and the indelible fact of the tar-black hair and sallow skin that make her look more like a Romany than one of the lily-skinned, flaxen-haired ladies of Camelot.

A couple of the candles start to gutter and Dot gets up to look in the box for replacements.

"What do you want most in the world, Dot?" asks Meg.

"You say first."

"I want a sword like Excalibur." Meg's eyes gleam. "Imagine how you would never feel scared." She strikes her thin arm through the air, gripping the imagined hilt. "Now you, Dot—what is your wish?"

Without even having to think about it Dot says, "I should like a husband who can read," and then she laughs, for it sounds so very silly when she says it out loud and more impossible even than Meg getting her hands on a magic sword. She feels she has broken the spell of the story by saying it.

Meg doesn't say anything, seems lost in her own thoughts.

Dot leans over to look in the candle box. "There are none left. Shall I go down and fetch some?"

"It's late. We should sleep." Meg rises with a stretch and picking up one of the furs, drags it over to the bed.

Dot goes to pull the truckle bed from where it tucks neatly under the tester.

"Sleep in here with me." Meg pats the place beside her. "It will be warmer."

Dot tidies the hearth, breaking up the embers with the poker, and places the mesh guard carefully in front of it, then climbs onto the bed, drawing the hangings tight, making a small safe place for them. Rig scrabbles up too, scratching and fussing and turning in circles before settling into a tight little ball. Dot slides between the cold covers, rubbing her feet back and forth to generate some warmth.

"You are as bad as Rig," says Meg.

"Some of us don't have the warming pan."

Dot feels a feather hand reach out for her, and she shifts across the vast expanse of cold bed. Meg grips on to her, as if to let go would unmoor her completely. Her nightgown smells of woodsmoke from sitting by the fire and Dot is reminded of cuddling up to Little Min in the truckle they used to share. It seems like someone else's life she has found herself in.

"If we could shape-shift like Morgan le Fey," whispers Meg, "you could become me, Dot, and marry Thomas Seymour. He would read to you till the cows came home.'"

"And what of you?" asks Dot.

"I would be you, of course . . ."

"You'd have to empty the piss pots every morning. And what would *I* do with a fine nobleman like this Seymour? I don't think he'd fancy my dancing. I have two left feet at the best of times."

They both laugh at the thought of it and press themselves closer together for warmth like a pair of spoons.

"Thank goodness for you, Dorothy Fownten," Meg murmurs.

6

Katherine can hear the clatter of hooves in the yard. She looks out of her chamber window, supposing it to be one of the King's pages. She had hoped that her absence from court this last month might have put her out of the King's mind but that has not been the case.

Each day a delivery has come: a brooch with two good diamonds and four rubies; a marten collar and matching sleeves; an overskirt of cloth of gold; a pair of lovebirds; a side of venison. The meat was divvied out to the poor of the parish, for her household is so diminished (with Meg's brother and his wife, the new Lord and Lady Latymer, gone to run the Yorkshire estates and most of the staff with them) that they would have struggled to eat it before the maggots invaded.

These are the gifts of a man who wants something, but the idea of becoming the King's mistress doesn't bear thinking about. Besides, there is no space in her mind. The part of it that is not filled with grieving for her husband is filled with Thomas Seymour. Against her better judgment she allows thoughts of him to wander freely about her head.

She can't help but long to find a page clad in the red and gold Seymour colors in the courtyard below, with a letter, a token, the return of her necklace. But daily disappointment comes with a delivery boy in the green and white Tudor livery, bearing more unwanted and seemingly endless offerings.

She has tried to send them back but the page politely informed her that the King would punish him for failing in his duties. So she has kept them, reluctantly, each one making her feel a little emptier, as if she is an hourglass and her sand is almost run through.

She would exchange them all for the slightest token—a dandelion, a thimbleful of thin ale, a glass bead—brought by a Seymour page. She can't take control of her feelings. Why is she waiting like a lovesick girl for some petty gift from that shallow man? But he has embedded himself deeply at the core of her, and he will not be excised by reason.

She tells herself it is her mother's cross she longs for, but she knows it is self-delusion. It is *him* she wants. He skits through her thoughts with that infernal bouncing plume, and she cannot eject him.

She opens the casement, craning her neck to see who is dismounting. It is not the King's boy but Dr. Huicke, the physician who cared for her husband, returned from Antwerp. If not a Seymour page, then Huicke is who she would have hoped for. She wants to shout to him from the window, realizing how lonely she has been in her mourning.

She has itched for company and here is Huicke, one of the few, aside from family, she feels entirely herself with. She had felt an inexplicable affinity with Huicke from the outset. He had come each day to tend Latymer and they had become close over those months. He had been a support to her. It is not often in life, she thinks, that one encounters a true friend—once in a decade, perhaps.

She dashes down the steps, excited like a girl, arriving in the hall just as Huicke is shown in. She wants to fling herself into his arms but Cousins, the steward, is standing by and decorum won't allow it.

"So glad to see you." She is slightly breathless from rushing.

His look dances over her and his face opens into a smile. He appears, with his dark eyes shining like two fat drops of molasses and his thick inky curls, as if he might have walked out of an Italian painting. "The world is dull indeed without you, my lady."

"I think we know one another well enough now to dispense with the formalities. Call me Kit, then I can pretend we are brother and sister."

"Kit." He seems to taste the word as one might a French wine.

"But I shall continue to call you Huicke," she adds. "I know far too many Roberts."

He nods with another smile.

"So, tell me about Antwerp." She leads him to a seat in the window where the April sun washes in. "Did you learn anything?"

"The place is brimming with life. All the talk is of the reformation. The printing presses are churning out books. It is a city of great ideas."

"Reform has become a force for reason. When you think of all the horrors that have been committed in the name of the old Church." She cannot help but think of all that has been done, to her and to her family in particular, in the name of Catholicism. She would never say it aloud, not even to Huicke. The idea of reform pleases her. It seems embedded in reason. "And did you meet this Lusitanus fellow?"

"He has such notions, Kit." His eyes are shining. "Ideas about the way blood circulates. I sometimes think our generation, more than any yet, stands on the brink of change. Our sciences, our beliefs, all is in such a state of flux. It excites me."

Katherine watches him speak, animated, mimicking with his gloved hands Lusitanus slicing open a cadaver to expose its intricate workings, talking fervently all the while. She has never seen Huicke ungloved, even when he came to examine her husband.

She reaches out, catching his fingers in mid-air.

"Why do you never take these off?"

Huicke silently begins to peel back the lip of his glove, exposing a sliver of skin that is covered with raised, red welts. He looks at her, watching, waiting for her to turn away in disgust. But she doesn't. She takes his hand and strokes the deformed skin with the tip of her finger.

"What is it?"

"I haven't a name for it. It is not contagious but all who see it are disgusted. They think me leprous."

"Poor you." She bends down to press a feather-light kiss on his ravaged skin. "Poor, poor you."

He can feel the prick of tears behind his eyes. It is not that he has never been touched, for he has. Lovers have touched him in all sorts of ways, but even in the thrall of Eros he can see revulsion in the set of their mouths and their squeezed-shut eyes. What he sees in Katherine is something else, something entirely sympathetic.

"It is everywhere, save for my face."

She grabs both his hands and, standing, pulls him to his feet too. "Let's go to the still room. We can concoct a balm." There is a spark in her. "There must be something that will cure it."

"Nothing I have found yet. Though it can be soothed a little with certain unguents."

They walk arm-in-arm through the dark paneled corridors that wind to the rear of the house.

"Who would have imagined friendship arising from such adversity," she says.

"True friendship is rare indeed." She doesn't notice the flaw in his voice. He feels disingenuous. There is a secret he is keeping from her, a subterfuge he fears would break their bond. He has come to see her as more than a friend, could not bear to lose her. He cares for her in the way he imagines caring for a sister, though as an only child he has no measure for that.

His deceit prods at him. "Particularly," he adds, "when most of one's time is spent at court."

It is true there is no such thing as friendship at court with everyone vying for position. Even the King's physicians play a constant game of one-upmanship. He knows they don't particularly like him, for he is a good decade younger than most of them and a better doctor already.

He wants to make things even with her, give her a hold over him in return for his deception. "In Antwerp—" he begins, but stops abruptly.

"In Antwerp what?"

"I have become . . ." He doesn't know how to phrase it. "I m-met . . ." He stammers. "I fell in love." But that is only the half of it.

"Huicke." She grips his hand, seeming to enjoy his confession. "Who is the lady?"

"It is not a lady."

There, he has said it, and she is not reeling in shock.

"Ah!" she says. "I had suspected as much."

"How so?"

"I have known men before who prefer the intimacies of . . ." She pauses, dropping her voice. ". . . their own kind."

He has given her something that will bind him to her. This

information in the wrong ear could see him hang. He feels a comfort in having redressed the balance.

"My first husband," she continues, "Edward Borough. We were both so very young, no more than children really."

A servant lad passes with an armful of freesias. Their spring scent hangs in the air.

"Are those for my bedchamber, Jethro?" she asks him.

"Yes, my lady."

"Give them to Dot, she will see they are arranged."

He dips in a little bow and moves on past them.

"Edward Borough was completely unaroused by me." She picks up where she left off. "I thought it was inexperience. Neither of us were prepared really. But there was a tutor in the household, a serious young man, Eustace Ives. He had a beautiful mouth, a permanent solemn smile. It was when I saw how Edward blushed as he talked to Eustace Ives that it began to dawn on me . . . How little I knew then."

"What became of Edward Borough?" Huicke is captivated by this nugget of his friend's past.

"He was taken by the sweating sickness. Slipped out of his life in an afternoon. Poor Edward. He was such a gentle soul." She has a faraway look talking of the past as if she has gone back there and left just her ghost in the present. "Then I married John Latymer." A little shiver seems to bring her back. "But tell me about you. This man is from Antwerp?"

"No, he is an Englishman. A writer, a thinker. He is quite remarkable, Kit." Huicke feels a little thrill run through him as he speaks of Nicholas Udall. "And wild . . ." He pauses. "Excessively wild."

"Sounds dangerous."

He laughs. "Only in the best kind of way."

"And your wife?" Katherine asks. "Is she understanding?"

"We are virtually estranged. Have been for some years." He is reluctant to talk of his wife, feels too guilty. Instead he changes the subject. "There is much love in the air these days. And much talk of the King and a certain someone."

Her face drops. "I suppose that someone is me." They have stopped walking and she turns to him, big-eyed, shot through with worry.

"Why me, Huicke? There are plenty of willing young beauties at court. The place is overflowing with them."

"Perhaps it is your very unwillingness that encourages him." Huicke knows only too well what a spur indifference can be to desire. All those pretty youths he's fallen for, who were revolted by his skin. "The King is accustomed to getting what he wants. You are different in that respect."

"Different, pah." She heaves out a sigh. "What would you have me do? Throw myself at him? Would that cool his ardor?" She marches off down the corridor.

"He talks of your kindness," Huicke calls out to her receding back. "And how tenderly you cared for your husband."

He couldn't begin to tell her how the King has plumbed him for information. How was she with her husband? Did she tend him kindly? Did she mix her own physic?

"And how would he know that?" She turns to catch his eye with a flash of indignation.

They walk on in a brooding silence, he slightly behind her. She swings open the still-room door. A resinous smell envelops them and at last her frustration seems to abate. She begins to pull out jars, uncorking them, sniffing at their contents, tipping a few herbs out into a mortar, beginning to crush them with a pestle.

"Goldenseal," she says, before taking several more pots from a shelf, arranging them on the bench. She selects one, reading its label, removing its cork and holding it up for him to smell.

"Myrrh?" It is pungent and ecclesiastical, reminding him of a cleric he once fell for.

She grinds a little of it with the goldenseal, then lights a burner beneath a copper dish, dropping in a hard glob of wax and leaving it to melt while she continues pounding. She adds some almond oil then drips in the hot wax, stirring fast until it stiffens.

"There," she says eventually. "Now, give me your hands."

He removes his gloves, feeling entirely naked without them, and she massages the salve into his poor angry skin. He is quite overwhelmed again, to be touched in this way.

"This is why people think of you as kind."

"No more than most," she says. "The goldenseal works like magic."

"You are gifted with herbs. Your tinctures for Lord Latymer were little short of miraculous."

She looks at him strangely and he thinks he sees a fleeting hint of fear, or something like it, cross her features.

"Did you notice anything unusual in my husband after he passed?"

There it is again, the look of a beast at bay.

He wonders what it is that's getting at her. "Only that the tumor had eaten his guts away. It was a wonder he survived as long as he did. I shouldn't say it, but it would have been better if he'd died sooner."

The look dissolves to nothing.

"The Lord's way is not always easy to understand," she says.

"How is Meg? How has she taken her father's death?"

"Not well really. I worry for her."

"Have you tried a few drops of St. John's wort?"

"I hadn't thought of that. I shall try it. But I fear Meg's worries run deep."

"The King is adamant that she marry Thomas Seymour," Huicke says. "Not a bad match for her, I'd say."

"Not Seymour." She is sharp. "Meg will never marry Seymour."

"*You* like Seymour?"

"I didn't say that."

"No, but it is written all over you."

It is—it is woven into her like the pattern in a carpet. And Seymour of all people. The King would never sanction it. It doesn't even bear thinking about.

"I don't want to like him. I am so very confused by it all."

"You must forget him."

"I know I must. And you," they are talking in whispers now, "you won't say anything, will you?"

"You have my word."

He can see that she doesn't fully trust him. She is weighing up his honesty. He is the King's physician, after all. The King put him in her house.

"Why did the King send you to attend my husband?" It is as if she can read his thoughts.

FIREBRAND

"I cannot keep the truth from you." He brings his hands up to cover his face, to cover his shame. "The King asked me to report back about you. He has long had you in his sights, since you were at court a year ago. He *commanded* it, Kit."

There it is, out, his shame displayed for her to see.

"You, Huicke, a spy?" She narrows her eyes.

He can feel her slipping away, her friendship taken back. "I was, maybe, but not now. I am *your* man now."

He can't look at her, looks instead at the rows of labeled jars and pots on the shelves behind her. She turns her back to him. He reads off the names in his head: figwort, meadowsweet, wood spurge, milkwort, cocklebur, elecampane, burdock . . . The silence between them is unbearably heavy, suffocating.

"Kit," he says, eventually, "you *can* trust me." His voice has a supplicant's tone.

"How can I?"

"I didn't know you then . . . I know you now."

"Yes, and I know you."

Is she thinking of the shared secrets that bind them together? He hopes it is so and not that she knows him to be a traitor.

She picks up his gloves and hands them to him. "Do your hands feel soothed?"

"They do. The itch has lessened already."

"Come." She moves to the door. "My sister is due. I shall have your horse brought round?" She is dismissing him.

He feels hollow, wants to prostrate himself on the flagstones and beg her forgiveness. But her polite coolness has rendered him incapable. He follows her back through the dark passages to the hall where she calls her steward.

"Doctor Huicke is leaving, Cousins, will you let the groom know and see him out." She lifts the back of her hand for him to kiss.

"Friends?" he asks.

"Friends." She offers a vague inscrutable smile.

7

Katherine strolls in the Charterhouse gardens with her sister. Anne's usually luminous skin is gray and the milky bloom of a month ago has gone. She has lost the baby but is sanguine. "There will be others," she'd said, when Katherine offered her sympathy.

It had rained earlier, a brief fine spray, leaving the new leaves sparkling. The sky has now cleared completely of cloud, now that intense after-rain blue, and the spring sun flares against it, an early herald of summer.

"I have had no one but lawyers for a month and then two dear visitors in one day," Katherine is saying.

"I'm sorry to have stayed away so long, was laid low with this miscarriage." Anne has the light behind her and the tendrils of pale hair that have escaped from her coif are lit up like a halo.

The sun catches at the edge of everything, making the courtyard seem touched by God. The cobbles gleam and the windows shimmer, winking as they pass. Katherine opens the gate to her physic garden, leading the way through. The pear trees in the orchard beyond are in full blossom, billows of white against the blue sky, and the yew hedges around the perimeter are impossibly green. There is a circular pond at the center where silver carp slip and shimmy just beneath the surface.

"Who else was here?"

"Doctor Huicke." Katherine is still feeling uneasy about Huicke and his spying mission.

"You two have become very close."

Katherine changes the subject, telling her sister about the garden.

Her herb beds set around the pond have been newly dug, the earth fresh red, and the hopeful young plants are carefully labeled with carved rounds of wood set on stakes. The sisters sit on a shady stone bench but stick their damp feet out into a pool of warm sun to dry.

"Will you stay here?" asks Anne.

"I don't know. I don't know what is best. I'm trying to stay away from court. All this business with the King."

"He does seem to have a bee in his bonnet."

"I don't understand it, Anne. He barely knows me and—"

"Knowing has never been a necessity for marriage."

"*Marriage!* You don't really think it is *marriage* he wants from me?"

"It is common knowledge he seeks a new Queen. And after the Anne of Cleves blunder he won't look abroad."

The bell of St. Bartholomew's rings out three times, with echoes of more distant church bells behind it.

"Why not you, Kit?" Anne continues. "You are perfect. You have never put a foot wrong."

Katherine's secrets press down on her. "I wouldn't be so sure. Huicke thinks the King only desires me because I am unwilling and he's used to getting everything he wants. I am a novelty." An acid laugh escapes from her. "Think of all those young maids he could have, their sap rising."

"Don't you see? That's what he had last time, and look what happened. Your attraction is precisely that you are *not* like Catherine Howard. You are her opposite. The King could not stand to be cuckolded again."

Katherine's heart sinks. "How am I going to avoid it?"

"I don't know. If you stay away, you risk fanning the embers. And besides, Lady Mary will call for you soon. She wants you back."

Katherine rests her forehead on her palm, closing her eyes, imagining taking Pewter and galloping off, finding another life for herself, another person to be.

"Think how happy Mother would be were she still alive ... you being courted by the King himself."

"Our ambitious mother! Why can't I do as you did, Anne, and marry for love?"

"But to be Queen, Kit—would you truly not want that?"

"I should have thought you of all people would know what it means to be *his* Queen." Anger is leaking from her—anger and fear. "You were there. You saw what happened to them all. Catherine of Aragon cast out to meet her end in a damp castle in the middle of no-where, estranged even from her daughter. Anne Boleyn—need I even say it? Jane Seymour not properly tended in her childbed—"

"Many women succumb to childbed fever. You can hardly blame the King for that."

It is true—death stalks pregnant women.

"Well, perhaps not, but then look at Anne of Cleves, who only escaped with her head because she agreed to an annulment, *and* what about little Catherine Howard . . . ?" She pauses. "You were there, all the way through, all of them, you served them all—you saw it all." She has the urge to slap her sister.

"You are not like *them*. You are sensible and good."

Katherine is wondering what Anne would think if she knew that her sensible sister had whored herself with a Catholic rebel and ad-ministered a lethal tincture to her husband. "Sensible?"

"What I mean is you are not driven by your passions."

"No, indeed." But Katherine's head is suddenly full of Seymour again.

"Do you remember when we used to play queens at Rye?"

Katherine's anger disperses in the face of her sister's disarming sweetness. "Yes. With me all wrapped up in a bed sheet and married off to the dog."

"And the paper crowns that wouldn't stay on . . . What was the name of that dog? Was it Dulcie?"

"No, I don't remember Dulcie. She must have been after I left to marry Edward Borough. That one must have been Leo."

"You're right. Leo was the one that bit the barber's son."

"I'd forgotten that . . . Leo was Will's dog."

"No wonder it was a biter," says Katherine. "I'm sure Will teased that poor animal something rotten."

"Do you remember Will in Mother's fine red damask stuffed with a pillow, playing the Cardinal, when he dropped the silver cross from the chapel?" Anne is laughing. "It was never the same after that, always a bit skewed. I didn't dare look at it during prayers for fear of the giggles."

"And when you stumbled on my bed-sheet train and knocked into the steward with a pitcher of wine that went flying."

Anne's good humor is infectious. They were always laughing back then, when they didn't have to be at court and on their best behavior.

"I nearly forgot." Anne digs about in the folds of her gown, pulling out a little leather pouch, which she drops into Katherine's hand. "From Will."

Katherine knows what it is without looking. It is their mother's cross. Her throat is blocked as if she's swallowed a stone.

"Why did Will have it?" Anne is asking.

"It was being mended." Katherine stands and saunters to the herb beds with her face turned away so as not to reveal her disappointment.

Why did Thomas Seymour not bring it himself? He was simply toying then. Flirting with the idea of bedding a widow. Pull yourself together, she demands inwardly. You barely know him.

"And there is a letter." Anne hands her a fold of sealed paper. "Why does it have the Seymour stamp?"

"I have no idea, Anne." She tucks the letter away in her sleeve.

"Will you not open it?"

"It is not important, just a goldsmith's bill, I expect." She feels the letter might burn a hole in her gown.

"Why would a goldsmith's bill have the—"

Katherine cuts her off before she can ask again. "Let me show you what I have planted. Here is mandrake for earaches and gout. See, I have labeled them all." She imagines the mandrake roots as little buried bodies putting out feelers into the dark earth. "They say witches make love potions from it."

"Can it make *anyone* fall in love?" Anne is wide-eyed.

"It's claptrap, of course," says Katherine bluntly.

"And digitalis?" Anne points to one of the markers. "What is that?"

"Foxglove." Katherine feels a pressure around her neck as if her husband's ghost is squeezing the breath from her. "Pains of the liver and spleen." Her tone is brusque.

"They call it dead men's bells, don't they?"

"They do." Katherine's impatience is building with her sister's infernal questioning.

"Why?"

"Because it will kill a man if the dose is large enough," she snaps. "Poison! They are all poison, Anne. See this . . . henbane will cure a toothache if you burn it and inhale the smoke." She is almost shouting now and can't stop. "And hemlock here," she snaps off a twig and waves it in front of Anne's face, "will calm a raving lunatic if mixed with betony and fennel seed. And a drop too much of either will send a grown man to his grave . . ."

"Kit, what's got into you?"

Katherine feels her sister's hand on her back, rubbing, soothing.

"I don't know, Anne, I don't know." She can feel the letter in her sleeve against her skin, has the sense it might give her a rash or scald her or leave some kind of indelible stain like a devil's mark. "I don't feel myself."

"You're grieving. It is no surprise. And all this business with the King."

Katherine says nothing.

When Anne has taken her leave Katherine pulls the letter out, holding it between the very tips of her fingers as if she fears the paper might be impregnated with one or other of the poisons she knows so well. There are Italians who understand how to do such a thing.

She is tempted to throw it in the fire, never know its contents, pretend never to have met Thomas Seymour, not have this inner throb that is set off by the merest thought of him. She runs her fingers over the seal, the conjoined wings of the Seymours, dreading that it might contain just a polite note, but dreading equally something more.

She breaks the wax, brittle red shards scattering, and unfolds the paper. His hand is an untidy scrawl, at odds with the way she sees him, nothing-out-of-place. It makes her wonder about him, whether he is the man he seems to be at all. But what does he seem to be? Why is it that she, who usually knows exactly what she thinks, is so very confounded by this man? The word "admiration" leaps out of the spidery text, the sight of it making her heart palpitate as if a bird is trapped in her breast.

My Lady Latymer,

Firstly I tender my most sincere apologies for the length of time it has taken for me to return this. I have deliberated so on whether to bring it to you myself but dared not for fear that you would find me too forward. I felt I carried a little piece of you about my person but what small comfort that was. God knows I wanted an excuse to lay my eyes on you, but feared that on seeing your sweet face I would not find a way to check the feelings of admiration that have taken root in me, growing and flourishing beneath my surface. I feared you would turn me out. I fear it still.

There is no more distressing thing to me than the knowledge of the King's plans—he talks to me often of his wish that I should marry your dear Margaret. If he commands it, I will be a lost man. His intentions to you, the rumors of which fly about the palace like a murmuration of starlings, leave me utterly hopeless and I only pray that his desire will alight elsewhere before long.

You have not given me cause to believe my feelings reciprocated but I felt compelled to declare myself, for to not do so would be to live my life in the knowledge that I had not been honest to the only woman who has ever truly stirred my heart. I must see you or I fear I shall wither to nothing. I beg you to entertain this single wish.

I await your word.

Forever your humble servant,
Thomas Seymour

She exhales deeply, standing motionless, save for the hammering of her heart, its frantic rhythm reaching the furthest outposts of her body—her fingertips alive with it, her belly fizzing. She barely recognizes herself. How can he feel this way after a single meeting? But her own feelings are making themselves known—unfamiliar and enticing—against her better judgment.

She hears footsteps in the corridor and, almost before she realizes, the letter is balled in her hand and tossed on the fire. She watches it blaze then curl and blacken before the last bright wisps of it float up and away.

8

Jethro heaves a carton onto the kitchen table. "From the palace, for Lady Latymer. Smells fishy." He makes a grimace.

"Open it then," says Cook.

Dot, her curiosity lit, stops what she is doing, melting down candle stubs, and, getting to her feet, sends the pot of hot wax flying. Under her breath she curses her clumsiness.

"Dot." Cook doesn't hide his anger. "Not again. Clean that lot up."

Dot grabs a knife and drops to the floor, scraping at the spill of warm wax and trying to ignore two of the lads who are having a joke at her expense.

"Butterfingers," one of them says, his eyes narrowed and flashing. A goose hangs limply from his hand.

She pokes her tongue out at him. The wax comes up onto the knife easily in pretty ripples. She scrapes them back into the pot, which she leaves on the shelf for the chandler.

Jethro wrenches the lid off the carton to reveal a vast number of oysters packed in sawdust and ice. They smell strong and briny, a female scent that Dot supposes must be the smell of the sea.

She has never seen the sea, but ever since she heard the story of Tristan and Isolde, how they fell in love aboard ship, the idea of it has fixed itself in her head. She has sometimes stood by the Thames listening to the cark of the gulls and tried to imagine what it might be like, all that water stretching away to the horizon in every direction. But she cannot quite manage to make a picture of it.

"What in the Lord's name am I to do with all these?" says Cook.

"She will want them given to St. Bart's to distribute to the poor,

I suppose," says Cousins, the steward. "She gave me a stock of ointments to take over there. They are ridden with scurvy, apparently. I shall take the oysters too, when you have removed what you need for the household, Cook. Jethro, you can help me."

"I'll make a stew of them for Friday, the rest you can have." Cook begins prizing some of the oysters from the box and flinging them into a bowl.

Dot picks one up. It is rough and cold.

"Put it down," barks Cook. "We don't want the whole lot scattered." She drops it back into the dish.

"What about all these gifts from the palace, Cousins?" Cook lowers his voice. "Do you think the King really wants to—"

"It is not for us to speculate," cuts in Cousins.

"But we've got our livelihoods to think of. She'll not be keeping this place going if she marries the King."

"Lady Latymer would never have us starve," says Cousins. "She'll see us all right. She's not the sort to leave people wanting."

"I've put word out that I'm looking for a new position anyway," says the squillery lad, who has started to pluck the goose and now stands in a cloud of feathers. "The kitchen clerk at Bermondsey Court says they'll be needing a pot scrubber. I'd rather do that than end up queuing for alms with that scurvy lot outside St. Bart's—"

"She won't marry the King." Dot doesn't let him finish. "It's nothing but gossip. The King gives gifts to everyone all the time." Dot knows only too well that people, even great ladies like Lady Latymer, don't become Queen. That only happens in stories.

"And what would *you* know anyway, Dorothy Fownten? The whole of London talks of it, so why would they be wrong and you right? I've a wager on it." The lad spits a feather off his lip. "Besides, you'll be all right. She'll take you with her."

"There are others talked about, that Anne Bassett for one." Dot is repeating what she has overheard. "What I *do* know is that she'll marry some lord or other in a year or two and we'll be off to another castle in the middle of nowhere."

She slips out into the yard for a moment alone, sitting herself on an upturned bucket in the sun, closing her eyes and leaning back against the hot brick wall. She is surprised that none of the servants seem to have got wind of the match that is in the offing for Meg. They're too busy harping on about Lady Latymer becoming Queen, as if it's all signed and sealed.

There is definitely something afoot. The Seymour page seems to be about the place constantly, letters are passing back and forth, sometimes three or four in a day—arrangements, Dot supposes, though how much arranging can there be for a wedding?

And Seymour himself arrived today, or Dot supposed it was Seymour, for his page—who, if she half opens her eyes, she can see lounging about outside the stables, slurping on a cup of beer—is the same one who delivers the letters. She got a glimpse of the man himself dismounting from a beauty of a horse, red-brown and shiny as a conker with a long, crimped mane and hooves oiled to a sheen. She didn't see his face but he was kitted out in enough velvet and fur to sink one of the King's great warships, and his hose were whiter than virgin snow, which made her wonder about the poor maid who has to keep them that way.

"I've been looking for you!" It is Meg, crossing the yard towards her with Rig in her arms. "You'll ruin your complexion sitting in the sun like that."

"Who cares about having lily-white skin when the sun feels so good."

"But you have freckles on your nose." Meg looks quite horrified. "People will think you coarse."

"Since when did it matter to me what anyone thinks—besides, I *am* coarse." Dot laughs.

"*I* don't think so."

"No one's ever going to mistake me for a lady."

"Will you walk with me?" Lines of worry scrunch Meg's brow. "I'm escaping from Mother's visitor." She drops her voice. "It's *him*."

Dot stands, hitching her skirts up and bolting towards the orchard gate, calling out, "Last one to the back wall earns a forfeit."

The puppy scrambles from Meg's arms, caught up in the excitement. Meg follows, encumbered by her heavy gown.

It is cool and shady at the bottom of the orchard where the blossom has carpeted the ground thickly in drifts. Dot pulls her coif off and throws it aside, shaking her head so her hair flies out. Scooping up an armful of blossom, she tosses it into the air allowing it to fall over her, watching the pale petals spin and float in the shafts of light that speckle the ground.

"You will never get all that off you." Meg is out of breath.

"Try it." Dot laughs, tugging at the ties of Meg's hood, pulling it off.

She scoops up a pile of petals and holds them above Meg's head, and, ignoring her protestations, slowly releases them until her brown hair is smattered with white.

Soon they are flinging great handfuls at each other, a blizzard of petals, and laughing so much they can barely breathe. It is everywhere, clinging to their skirts, in the folds of their sleeves, stuck to their skin, in their ears, down the fronts of their kirtles. They collapse to the ground in a billow of laughter and lie flat, looking up through the branches of the apple trees at the sky beyond.

"Sometimes I wonder if Father is watching me." Meg tugs at a frond of grass. "And when I have too much fun I fear he might think I've forgotten him."

"Oh Meg, you are such a worrier. If your father thought you were spending your life on your knees praying for his soul I have no doubt it would make him sadder than anything. He would be glad to know that you are happy."

But Meg is never truly happy.

Dot sometimes wonders what happens when people die. It is a thought too big to fit into her head. Where is Heaven and why are there no glimpses of angels and cherubs sitting up in the clouds? How difficult it is to believe when there is no proof. That is what they mean by faith, she supposes.

If she is good, which she tries to be, she will find out soon enough about Heaven. And if she is not good . . . She wonders about Hell. If it is a lake of fire, as it is said to be, how does it burn with all the water? How much does it hurt? Do you not get used to it? She burned her finger, quite badly, once and that hurt a good deal.

She *will* be good—though it's hard to tell what is good when some say one thing and some another, and both think they are right.

When she was very small, before the great changes, it was more straightforward. If you did something bad, had wicked thoughts or swiped a dried fig from a merchant's cart when his back was turned, then you would confess. Penance would be a string of prayers and Hail Marys and that would be that, the sin rubbed out.

If you were rich and sinned really badly you could buy a pardon from the Pope and even that really bad sin would be rubbed out. She knew she would never sin that badly for it would be stuck to her for good—she could never afford a pardon. Like when their neighbor's brother in Stanstead Abbotts killed a man in a fight. He knew he was headed for Hell and that was that.

Some still believe in that, but many don't. Many think they have to carry every single one of their sins around with them until they are judged. That is what Lady Latymer and Meg think, though it is not to be talked about. If Lord Latymer was of the old faith, does that mean he has gone to Hell? She doesn't say it, for it would upset Meg all the more to think of that.

"There just seems so much to worry about in life," says Meg.

"But if you dwell too much on it all, you will make life even harder." A single petal has stuck itself to Meg's cheek and Dot stretches out to pluck it away.

"You're right. I just wish . . ." Meg's sentence drifts off into silence.

Dot doesn't know what she thinks about religion, doesn't care whether the gospels are in English or Latin—she can't read anyway and never really bothers to listen to the chaplain droning on in chapel. She remembers learning about transubstantiation, when the wine is supposed to actually, literally, turn into the blood of Christ. And the bread actually, literally, becomes his body.

The whole idea of it is quite disgusting when you think too hard about it. Once, when no one was watching, she'd spat it back out into her hand at Mass. It was nothing but a gob of guck and crumbs in her palm, which she wiped on the underside of the pew. There was nothing fleshy about it at all. Doing that must have been a sin, she supposes.

The new religion doesn't believe in that either. They say it's symbolic and that if you believe enough you get God's grace just by pretending. Nor do the reformers think it's right about the Pope's pardons, they get their hackles up about that too, and there's always someone standing on a box and going on about it at Smithfield.

She thinks the reformers have got a point. Besides, Murgatroyd and his lynch mob were fighting for the old ways and it can hardly be God's work when you're brutalizing and raping young girls. But she has no idea if disagreeing with the old religion makes her a reformer. None of it makes any sense. If truth be told, she doesn't care much, for God hasn't a good deal of time for people like her, and besides, life is for living, not wasting it all worrying about what's going to happen when you're dead.

"Which would you rather," Dot changes the subject with a familiar game, "only ever eat turnips or only ever eat cauliflower?"

"Yuk to both." Meg laughs. "Cauliflower, I suppose. Which would *you* rather be, a poor man or a rich woman?"

"That's a tricky one—"

They are interrupted by the sound of voices beyond the yew hedge in the physic garden.

"Shhh," breathes Dot, placing a finger over Meg's mouth. "Listen, it is your mother and Seymour. They will be arranging your marriage."

Meg grimaces. "Can you hear anything? I can't hear them," she whispers.

"Come." Dot crawls into a hollow at the base of the hedge. "Bring Rig, or he'll give us away."

Meg grabs the puppy and squeezes in beside her where they have a view of the physic garden unseen. Lady Latymer and Seymour are standing beside the fishpond, deep in conversation, but they are a good twenty yards away, too far to be overheard.

"At least he's good-looking," Dot whispers.

Meg doesn't say anything.

They watch in puzzled silence as he lifts a hand to stroke Lady Latymer's cheek. She smiles, grabbing it, kissing it. Why?

Then, with a sudden swipe, he pulls away her hood so it hangs down her back, still attached by its strings at her throat, and takes a hank of her hair, twisting it tight.

Meg gasps. Her eyes are round with shock and her mouth gapes like a baby bird waiting for a worm. Seymour has pushed Lady

Latymer up against the hard stone of the sundial, one hand still clasping her hair, the other rummaging beneath her skirts.

"No," cries Meg, too loud, but they don't hear—they are completely enthralled in each other. "He's hurting her. We must stop him . . ."

Dot claps a hand over Meg's mouth, whispering, "They'll discover us."

Dot knows she should stop watching, but she can't seem to turn away. He is kissing her now, on the mouth, on the neck, on the breast. She can see how he rubs and presses up against her. Dot looks over at Meg. Tears are streaming down her cheeks, catching the light.

"What about Father?" she sobs.

Time has stopped.

Katherine is melting. Her mind empties of everything but the touch of him, his smell, a woody, musky male tang. She cannot contain herself in the face of him, her decorum abandoned entirely by the sweep of his smile, the shine of his eye. She is helpless, would do anything he asked of her.

His sharp tooth catches her lip, biting down, flooding her mouth with the taste of copper. His rough beard scrapes over her skin. It is so long since she has felt a man on her. He has rendered her awash with desire. She could eat him alive, pull him into her depths, swallow him, digest him, make him part of her.

All those thoughts, doubts, anxieties over his intentions—was she just another conquest, the convenience of a widow's experience, the allure of her new wealth?—have dissolved to nothing. She is Eve and he Adam and they are wallowing in exquisite sin.

She doesn't know this woman. Sensible Katherine Parr, who never puts a foot wrong, is nowhere to be found.

His hand searches among the folds of her dress. There is a moan. She can't tell whose mouth it comes from. She sucks on the salt skin of his neck. She would suffer an eternity in Hell's fire for a moment of this.

Her fingers are propelled to his laces, finding the knot, unraveling it.

He lifts her slightly onto the sundial and he is in, pushing to her very core, lost in her.

She is lost too.

9

The Seymour Barge, May 1543

Katherine is light as air. She is one of the paper lanterns that are lit for celebrations and take to the sky, flying up until they are indistinguishable from the stars.

"Thomas." His name is honey in her mouth.

"Sweetheart." He folds her into him, her face pressed tightly against the satin of his doublet.

Her belly unravels, a snake uncoiling inside her.

In these last weeks, six weeks of snatched secret moments, she has become engulfed by desire; barely able to think of anything but him. But this is more than desire, it is something unrecognizable.

She has considered her first impression of him, the disdain she'd felt and how quick it was to change. Has she been ambushed by love? If so, love has no logic. It can appear out of animosity as a flower might miraculously push itself through a crack in a brick.

Her brother was right—*he is not what you think*. But in a sense, he *is* exactly what she thought. He *is* flamboyant. He *is* self-regarding. But she has discovered that those things she found so loathsome are the very things she now finds endearing. Does his flamboyance not point to an originality of spirit? And his self-regard, is it not an ebullient confidence, a belief in himself? And she had misinterpreted his lightness for shallowness.

He says it again. "Sweetheart." The word liquefies her.

"How is it words have such power to move?"

"What are we if we are not words?"

The barge rocks and lulls. The drapes are drawn around them for privacy, curtaining them from the world. He twines his fingers with hers. She nuzzles his neck, breathing him in.

All else has receded. She has forgotten her guilt about Latymer's death, forgotten her worries about Meg. Snape is nothing but a story once told by someone and now mostly unrecalled. The King, the rumors, the gifts, are all dissolved to nothing. All her cares have slipped away to the recesses of her, and there is no past, no future, just a glorious, endless now.

She has been used to the slow-growing affection of a marriage that is an arrangement. But this is not that. This is a terrifying and glorious compulsion.

She has read Surrey's poetry. He has tried to describe it. She remembers him reading in Lady Mary's chambers. His long, serious face and dark, hooded eyes. "Description of the Fickle Affections, Pangs and Slights of Love" was his title, and when he said it the whole room sighed in recognition. Only now does Katherine understand.

The bells of St. Paul's peal as they pass as if to announce them. She has forgotten her husband is buried there. The river noises are a serenade: the roar of the Lambeth bear pits, the prattle of the gulls, the shouts of the rivermen, the cries of the Southwark mollies touting for trade, the thunk of the rudder, the wet skim of the oars, and the coxswain calling out the time like a heartbeat.

He leans down for a kiss. The slippery wetness of his tongue uproots her, makes her want him desperately. He breaks away slightly, close still, so close his two eyes become one.

"Cyclops," she says, laughing and pulling back further so as to see him better. The sight of him grips her like a good story.

"Your one-eyed monster."

"The language of love is nonsense," she says.

He blows in her face. His breath smells of aniseed.

"Hard to port," calls one of the oarsmen.

The boat lurches and veers to the side. She peeps out to look. The water is grimy, teeming with flotsam. A flotilla of small boats surrounds something white and bloated in the water. Men stand to catch a glimpse, wobbling as their little crafts bob and sway.

"What the hell is it?" shouts one.

"Floater."

"Poor soul."

"Don't look." Seymour gently guides her face away with a light touch to her cheek, too late to prevent her from seeing the saturated corpse, its face mutilated, entrails spilling.

Her worries crowd back, filling her head. What would happen if the King found out about this? They have not been careful enough. That first time in the garden was reckless—anyone could have seen them. But they have been so very careful since. She feels screwed down with a sudden fear of the consequences.

He peels away her glove and kisses each of her fingers. "Is this what love feels like, Kit?"

She tries to ignore the dread that is twisting into her. "How would I know?" she says, trying to keep her voice light, keep the concern out of it.

"You are the twice-married one."

"And what has marriage to do with love?" She pushes out a light laugh, but the screw burrows deeper. "It is *you*, Mister Seymour, who has all the experience of love, if court tittle-tattle is anything to go by." She prods him gently. "All those heartbroken maids."

He is serious now and looking straight at her, looking into her. "All that was youthful folly. And they were just girls. *You* are a woman. A real woman."

"And why would that make me a greater prize?" She wants to ask him if he's not worried too, but can't bring herself to burst the bubble.

"It is not that you are a woman. It is that you are you. I cannot explain it. Even the poets cannot explain love. But you." He seems embarrassed, dropping his gaze. "You make sense of my world."

How is that possible, she wonders, when *she* cannot find sense anywhere?

She is summoned to court tomorrow into the service of Lady Mary. She shivers, becoming aware of how far the river chill has seeped into her.

"I am ordered to court," she says, hating that she has killed his pleasure.

His jaw tightens, giving him the look of a petulant boy, and she wants to take him in her arms and make it perfect for him again.

"Did the King command it?" His tone is serrated with upset.

Katherine wonders if Thomas has talked about this with her brother. "This is the best opportunity in the history of the Parrs," Will had said. "The *royal family*, Kit. We'd have our place in history."

"Your ambition is too much, Will." She'd hated him in that moment.

"It's what I was raised to," he'd reminded her, "we all were."

It is true. Their class were raised to lift their families as high as they could—a perpetual game of snakes and ladders. She wonders if she is now at the foot of a ladder or the head of a snake. Impossible to know.

"And besides, whoever said anything about marriage?" she'd added. "The King is likely just toying with me until he tires of it. His attentions will move on. Just you wait."

What would her brother think if he knew his friend Seymour was standing in the way of his shot at the heavens?

If she married Seymour she wouldn't be free for the King. She reprimands herself for even thinking it—marrying Seymour. But she thinks of it all the time. It is a wild thought indeed. But why not? Why shouldn't she have her love match?

There are many reasons why not, the least of them being that, as brother-in-law to the King, Seymour would need royal permission. Without consent it could be deemed treason. Anything can be construed as treason nowadays, anything that upsets the order of things. And the King dictates the order of things. The thought of it is a tangle in her head, impossible to undo, tightening constantly.

"No, it is Lady Mary who has asked for me." She tries to keep her voice calm as if there isn't a great confusion of thoughts clogging her up.

"I'd wager the King is behind it." He snatches his hand from hers.

"Are you sulking, Thomas Seymour?"

He glowers.

"You're jealous." Her heart gives a little jump of joy at this proof of love, and all those thoughts of the King are banished, gone, like magic. She laughs.

Thomas doesn't laugh with her, though. He can barely manage a smile.

"Time, Thomas. Give it a little time. Once the King has tired of—"

"I don't want to talk of the King." He cuts off her words.

"You have nothing to worry about. He'll marry that Bassett girl. Everyone is saying it. You'll see." She fails even to convince herself.

"*I* want you. I want you just for me."

"A little time. That is all. Be patient."

"Must you go to court?"

"I must. You know that."

"And will you take your stepdaughter?"

"She has been requested."

"People are talking of her as a match for me. I don't want those flames fanned." His eyes flit about.

"Just more nonsense. Meg will not marry anyone without my word."

"But if the King wishes it?"

"The King has more important things on his mind, I'm sure, than the marriage of Margaret Neville. It was just a momentary whim that the gossips have got hold of."

His gaze meets hers. "If I marry anyone, it will be you." Her heart lurches. His grip on her has become unassailable.

IO

Whitehall Palace, June 1543

Dot had tried to imagine what Whitehall Palace would be like.

She has seen the Tower that squats with the Thames lapping at its skirts, slits for windows, fetid moat, iron gray. It is an ancient place, fortified, turning in on itself, showing only the hulk of its stone shoulders to the world. Everyone knows the Tower is the place traitors are housed, deep in its dungeons, where unspeakable things occur.

But Whitehall is different. Its turrets can be seen for miles, rising up from the higgledy-piggledy streets of Westminster, white and new and gleaming in the sun, banners rippling in the breeze. There are no arrow slits, no moat, nothing to make you think of your enemies. Even the yeoman guards standing at the gates seem put there for decoration in their red and gold liveries. To Dot it is nothing less than the Camelot of her imagination.

The place is vast. A hundred Snape Castles could fit within its walls. It is like an entire city and busy as the market at Smithfield, with people rushing to and fro doing whatever it is they do. In the main courtyard are the wide stone steps leading to the Great Hall and the chapel. Beyond the chapel, somewhere, lie the King's rooms. Those places are forbidden to Dot.

Through an arch lie the stables, past which sit the outhouses: the laundry, and the field behind, where the linens are pegged out to bleach in the sun; the barns; the stores; the slaughterhouse; the kennels, where the hounds howl, competing with the racket rising from the cockpit each evening and the tennis court, when a lively game is being played. It goes on for ever, only stopped by the river and the jakes, where on a day without much breeze there hangs the most hellish stench.

In the other direction towards Scotland Yard and the courtiers' dwellings, which is where Lady Latymer's lodgings are to be found, there is the tiltyard and the bowling lawn. The gardens lie beyond, set out in squares with high yew hedges, each one its own room. Behind their green walls are found ornamental ponds and aviaries and all manner of blooms. The knot garden leads to an aromatic lavender garden abuzz with bees, and a maze, which Dot has not dared enter for fear of getting lost. It is not for the servants, anyway.

Acres of kitchen gardens are busy with women weeding and planting and uprooting vegetables. If you walk through, past the rows of lettuces like courtiers' caps and the wispy fronds of fennel and the peas and beans coiling themselves upward, all you can hear is the chink of trowels tapping at the earth. Sometimes when she is not being watched, Dot picks a pea pod, sliding her finger along its opening to pluck the peas out from where they nestle in their damp white velvet pockets, popping them in her mouth to savor the sweet crunch.

The kitchens make a whole world in themselves. Here everyone is in a rush: heaving logs, rolling kegs, sparking up tinder, strewing floors, turning roasts, plucking fowl, baking bread, chopping and slicing and mixing and kneading and scrubbing. Meals for seven hundred appear in the Great Hall, delivered by an army of invisible staff as if there has been no effort whatsoever in the making of them. The whole palace seems, on the surface, to run by itself: fresh linen finds itself to beds in the blink of an eye; mud from the floor seems to brush itself away; clothes mend themselves; piss pots gleam; dust disappears.

Dot goes about in a bewildered stupor, hardly knowing where to put herself in all this. Strictly speaking she shouldn't be here at all. Apart from the palace workers only noble servants are allowed. Even they are apparently frowned upon by the Lord Chamberlain as, despite the size of the place, there is not the space to lodge everyone.

But Lady Latymer had insisted on bringing her. "You are as close as family and I have no intention of leaving you behind," she had said.

Dot was relieved. She'd been worried sick at the idea of going back to Stanstead Abbotts and squeezing herself back into her old life.

Their lodgings are among such a tangle of buildings that for the first three days Dot became lost every time she went out. The room is surprisingly modest. She'd imagined a chamber with tall glass windows and a great bed like the famous one at Ware that can sleep ten men and none of them touching. Lady Latymer had explained that it is only the dukes and favorites who have the grand chambers in the palace itself, and even some of the earls and countesses are crammed into a room as small as theirs.

They are lucky to have this room at all, it seems, for many have to find rented rooms beyond the palace gates. In fact, Lady Latymer appears quite happy with this arrangement. Dot has heard her say to Meg, "If the King had designs on me, I would doubtless be lodged in the palace," she'd said. "His head must have turned elsewhere."

But Dot is sure the main reason Lady Latymer likes being tucked out of the way is because she can snatch the odd secret tryst with Thomas Seymour. Now there is true passion. Dot cannot erase the memory of seeing the two of them together in the physic garden at Charterhouse. Thinking of it makes her wonder what it must be like to have a man on you like that. She can't imagine for the life of her a boy like Harry Dent or Jethro going at it like a dog on a bitch in the way Thomas Seymour did with Lady Latymer.

At night she allows the scene to run through her mind and touches herself until her belly clenches. Then comes the hot liquid flood to her head. She doesn't care that it is a sin. Why would God make it feel so good, if it is so bad? Meg has never said a word of what they saw in the physic garden and Dot hasn't dared bring it up for fear of upsetting her. At least there has been no more talk of a marriage for the girl.

Meg is supposed to sleep in the maids' chamber in Lady Mary's apartments but mostly she sneaks down to her stepmother's bed. Dot cannot imagine her in a dormitory with a crowd of other girls who must talk into the night about boys: which ones they fancy, who they have kissed, and all that. Meg is most often at prayer these days, or biting her nails, or sitting at dinner pretending to eat.

Dot has a pallet in an alcove, which is quite comfortable enough, and has a little curtain she can pull across for privacy. They are very well like this, the three of them, though it is lonely during the long days when Lady Latymer and Meg are doing whatever it is they do with Lady Mary—strolling in the gardens and a good deal of embroidery and a lot of going to Mass, as far as she can tell.

She misses the jolly atmosphere of the kitchens at Charterhouse where she would sit by the hearth and lark about with the others once her chores were finished. There is not much to do here, save for tidy their small lodgings, give things a good clean and see to the delicate laundry. The rest goes to the laundresses, who sit in a steam-fugged room stirring great vats of linens and then hang it all out to dry on the hedges in the yard, like white flags. Dot has to see to the mending too, stitching on hooks and eyes that have come loose or darning any rents.

It doesn't take her very long, so she has been exploring. Occasionally, when everyone is at Mass and the place is empty, she takes off her shoes and slides down the long polished corridors, pretending to skate on ice.

The lad who delivers the firewood each morning, Braydon, a scullion, has been friendly enough and has shown her the ropes: where to find kindling, where to empty the chamber pots, where to find herbs for strewing, where she is to take her meals, and such like.

He has even shown her a litter of kittens curled in a bundle at the back of the wood store, which was nice, and then he tried to kiss her, which was not. Kind though he may be, Braydon is pimply and pink-faced and only after one thing. He has sulked since then, ignoring her, and he must have said something to the kitchen lads, for they give her funny looks and whisper when she passes.

Occasionally Meg is able to sneak away unseen or feign a headache and they go and lie in the long grass in the orchard, where the meadow flowers are blooming. If they lie completely flat they can't be seen from a distance and can pretend they are all alone in the world.

Meg tells of how it is in Lady Mary's chambers, how unkind the girls can be to each other and how no one says what they really mean.

"They all twist their words," she says. She doesn't like it. But then Meg is not one to slide easily into another life.

"And Lady Elizabeth, what is she like?" Dot had asked once.

"I've never seen her. She lives somewhere else and she is absolutely never talked about."

"But why?" Dot couldn't understand why the King's youngest daughter would not be there.

"The King doesn't want to be reminded of her mother. Or that's what they say." Meg made a chopping motion at her neck.

"Nan Bullen," said Dot under her breath, as if just saying it out loud might turn her to stone.

"Yes, Anne Boleyn." Meg half covered her mouth with her hand.

"And Prince Edward. Tell me about him."

"I have not seen him either. He is kept away from London for fear of disease. But he is talked about all the time. Every snippet of information is passed around, what he has eaten, what he wears, the color of his stools, the smell of his farts . . ."

"Margaret Neville!" gasped Dot. "What are they teaching you up there?"

"They are quite foul-mouthed, those noble girls."

Dot was secretly pleased that she was showing a little spirit.

In the evenings after she has supped, Dot sits on a low wall from where she can watch the palace windows glowing yellow and can see the silhouettes of people dancing and carousing upstairs, where she has never been, and can listen to the music that trickles out into the gardens. She tries to imagine what the King might look like, wondering if he has a halo like in a church painting.

Not even a month after they have settled in, Dot learns that the court is to move—all of it—for the summer. If she thought everyone was busy before, then she couldn't have imagined how much more so they would be now. Everything must be prepared for the move: hangings are being taken down to the yards and beaten before they are folded into linen bags and packed into chests; dresses are carefully layered in sheets of muslin with camphor to ward off the moths; the plate is stacked into boxes packed with straw and furniture is dismantled. Almost everything movable is to be taken.

They will go by barge, says Lady Latymer, to a palace even greater than this, called Hampton Court. Dot is to leave this afternoon, in a cart with the luggage and Rig the dog. They will be in the train with the Lord Steward's men and their cartloads of equipment, and the yeomen, and the Grooms of the Wardrobe with all the King's vestments and hangings and cushions and carpets, and the Master of the Horse and the stable lads, who will bring the favorite hunters.

It is said the hunting is good at Hampton Court and that they will eat venison almost every day they are there. The harbingers left this morning, so things will be prepared and the kitchens set up. When the King and his household arrive tomorrow there will be a feast prepared. Lady Latymer and Meg will travel with Lady Mary in one of the royal barges alongside the King. They will arrive gliding on the water, as if there has been no effort at all to get them there. Everything must seem to happen as if by magic.

Meg is tetchy and tense about the move. "More change, Dot," she says. "It is too much."

Dot takes her to the orchard, where they hide from the world for a few precious minutes.

"I miss you," Meg says. "They never talk of anything but marriage up there."

Dot takes her wrist, noticing that she is thinner than she was a month ago. With all the talk of marriage, no one could get a child on Meg like this anyway, she wouldn't be capable, she doesn't even bleed any more. "There are some things in life that cannot be changed."

Meg snuggles in so close to her that Dot can feel the whisper of breath on her cheek. "I wish we could share a bed, as we used to."

11

Katherine watches from one of the window alcoves in the western corridor, as Lady Mary's wardrobe—a dozen trunks, which she had overseen the careful packing of herself—are loaded onto a cart below.

The day is fine and she is looking forward to leaving the heave and press of Whitehall. A rotten stench is emanating from the jakes, the vegetable gardens are all but empty and the rumor of plague hangs in the air—it is time to move on.

She should be at Mass but she wanted a moment alone and hopes Lady Mary won't be upset by her absence in chapel. Though Lady Mary will doubtless be so intent on her worship she won't notice who is or isn't there. Someone is bound to tell her—hawk-eyed Susan Clarencieux or vindictive Nan Stanhope probably—but she can always say she wanted to make sure the trunks were all correctly loaded.

Despite her misgivings Katherine has enjoyed being at court, where something is always going on, a round of feasts and masques, and she can forget the past a little. Even the gossip and intrigue has its own fascination. And there is the pleasure of both being reunited with old friends and under the same roof as her sister.

Cat Brandon, another with whom Katherine shared the royal schoolroom long ago, has been about often with her rapier-sharp wit. Cat, unlike Nan Stanhope, carries no airs and graces, despite being the Duchess of Suffolk. Katherine and she share an interest in the reformed faith, discreetly sharing books of new ideas. They talk of the shifting sands of belief, how the wind seems to be changing again. Reformers are fined for eating meat on fast days and the English Bible has been banned for all but the nobility.

Bishop Gardiner is at the bottom of it. He would have England back in the Pope's pocket if he had his way. But the King, however much he cleaves to the old ways as he advances in age, would never sanction the loss of his position as Head of the Church. Gardiner's presence sits heavily over the palace, his eyes everywhere. Even so, there is little he can do to stem the whispers of reform, for some of those closest to the King, and with the greatest influence, champion the new religion—Thomas's brother, the Earl of Hertford, for one. So, the books are quietly passed around and a blind eye is turned, but you can never for a minute think that people don't know your business in this place.

In spite of that, court has been a welcome respite from the gloom of Charterhouse and sitting alone with her guilt. Katherine, for all their differences of faith, likes Lady Mary. They pass their time in the privy chamber, reading to each other, or embroidering, chatting easily about all manner of things.

Poor Mary has often been laid low with agonizing headaches so Katherine concocted a tincture for her, a mix of feverfew and butterbur, and administered cabbage compresses to her forehead. Mary has been a little less crumpled and fragile as a result and the King seems to like her the more for it. He is a man who has no patience for the ailments of others, though likes a fuss made of his own ills, she has noticed.

But the greatest attraction the court has to offer Katherine is Thomas. They have managed only the odd moment alone together. They have indulged in the occasional brief kiss, snatched in the alley beside her lodgings, and once in the gardens after dark they had lingered by the river, watching it glisten silently, not daring to touch for fear that they might be seen from one of the palace windows. A hungry grapple behind the stables had left her mouth bruised and her head spinning.

They see one another in public countless times a day, pretending they are no more than acquaintances. She is not naive enough, though, to think that nobody notices the looks that pass between them, however well concealed. You can't scratch an itch around here without everybody knowing about it one way or another.

Nan Stanhope's bulbous eyes watch everybody constantly so she can feed her husband, Hertford, little snippets of information: who is allied to who, or who has argued with who, which ladies are sporting new jewels and what they are reading. Knowledge is power in this place and the Earl of Hertford is at the top of the pile.

The King has visited Lady Mary's chambers daily, sometimes twice a day. To Katherine's relief, he has not appeared to show her any kind of special favor. She has received the same courtly compliments that he dishes out to all the women and he has certainly not favored her with her lodgings.

He does favor her for a game of chess, saying that she is the only one who gives him a proper challenge. "The rest are too scared of me to play well," he whispered once, which made her wonder about what it must be like to have nothing but insincerity all around you constantly. It must have been ever thus for him, or perhaps not when he was small, for he wasn't raised to be King. If his brother Prince Arthur hadn't died, the world would have been entirely different. England would surely still be allied to Rome.

Katherine treads carefully, measuring her behavior, doing nothing to lead him on. He gave Anne Bassett a fine little pony recently, which makes her family think she's in with a chance. Their smugness sits on them like a layer of polish. They still have the impression that Katherine is an adversary, unaware that she would give her eye teeth for them to win this race. Katherine has stuck resolutely to her black mourning garb and little jewelry save for her mother's cross—her only embellishment.

Seymour, though, has told her that the black only serves to make her skin seem all the more lustrous. "Why would you gild a lily?" he'd said.

She made it clear that she is not the type to be moved by those kind of words. "Empty words," she'd called them. But she *is* moved. She can't help it. He only has to direct a glance her way and she feels herself burn. The flatteries don't seem empty on his lips where they would on others'.

She hears the click of footsteps approaching in the corridor, feels a hand on her shoulder, picks up a waft of cedar and musk, his scent.

"Thomas, not here," she breathes.

"We are safe; there is no one about. Everyone is at Mass, listen."

The rhythmic incantation of the Eucharist emanates from the

chapel below. Out of the window the sun is setting, coloring the sky with a thousand shades of pink as if the heavens are revealing themselves. He turns her to face him. His face is blighted, shot through with something—anger, concern, fear, she is not sure which—and she seeks sign of his fondness but cannot find it.

"My brother tells me the worst." His eyes skit about like flies.

She tucks a hand around his warm neck, drawing him in for a kiss, but he pulls away with a strangled "No."

"What is it?"

"The King wishes to take you for a wife." His voice cracks slightly on the final word but his face reveals little. He is not a man to wear his weakness for all to see, but she notices the shrink in his demeanor as she finally, momentarily, meets his eyes. "I feared this."

"It's nothing. The King has barely given me a second glance this last month. It's nothing but gossip."

She laughs, but his face is grave.

"Gossip?" He looks forlorn now.

"The King has said nothing to me. He would have said something. You have no need to worry." She is babbling now.

"No, Kit." He is firm. "It's not rumor. He has sent me away." He still won't look at her.

She cannot bear it, longs to grab his arms, wrap herself about him, sucker herself to him like a limpet. "Look at me, Thomas . . ." But he cannot tear his eyes away from the windowsill. "Sweetheart."

"I am to go to the Low Countries—indefinitely."

"The Low Countries, what? As ambassador?"

He nods.

She takes his hand to plant a dry-lipped kiss on it. "I don't understand. Is it not an honor to represent the King overseas?"

He grabs her own hand in both of his, squeezing it, his ring digging into her so hard she imagines the Seymour arms being forever indented on her palm. His hands are warm, hers cool. "Away from the court. Out of sight, out of mind. He's getting rid of me."

"No." She is confused, can't quite get her thoughts straight. "It is an honor?"

"You don't understand." His voice is raised and angry now. "Away from court I will have no influence. I will be nothing. And ..." He stumbles over his words, spitting them out like rotten teeth. "And *he* will have you."

"He will not have me. You are imagining it, Thomas."

"You don't know him as well as I do."

"You will go and do your duty for the King and in a few months you will return covered in glory and we shall . . ."

She waits for him to say it—*we shall be wed*—but he doesn't.

"I know men." His jaw is clenched. "I know what a man like him will do to get what he wants."

"You have no proof. It's nothing but rumor." But a splinter of doubt is burrowing under her skin.

"He *will* have you."

His words finally hit her like a clean blow to the gut. How is he so sure? She feels herself begin to crumble. His words are eroding the story she has been telling herself. If she could only run and keep on running, escape from this place.

"Come away with me," he whispers, as if he can read her thoughts. His breath is hot in her ear. His beard tickles her neck.

"We will go abroad to some remote place ..."

But they both know that this is as impossible as traveling to the stars.

She presses a finger to his mouth, feeling her core freeze over.

She had woven images in her mind of the two of them, designing great tapestries depicting their life together away from the prying and wheedling of the court, but these are unstitched in an instant.

She knows as much as he that the King's wrath would seep into even these secret imaginings and blacken them. And to imagine her dear Thomas's severed head stuck on Tower Bridge for all to see. She shivers. And Seymour is an ambitious man. He could never be satisfied hidden away from all this, even if it were possible. She knows him well enough. Another piece of her story unweaves.

"This is God's will," she says.

"The King's will." A vein throbs in his temple.

She puts her thumb on it, feeling his pulse, feeling the life in him, releasing a long sigh and murmuring a defeated "Yes."

He turns sharply away from her without even a kiss or a tender look, his cloak making an extravagant flourish in his wake.

"It is the same thing," she says, but he is out of earshot.

She cannot gather up the scattered pieces of herself, parts are missing, crumbled to dust. He rounds the corner out of sight, leaving her with a gaping void, out of which comes the treasonous thought that perhaps God will claim King Henry for himself before too long. She leans into the window, clutching the sill, as if she can hold the fragments of herself together. She hears the bustle of people leaving chapel, mounting the stairs, passing her as if nothing has changed. They don't notice her, pale as bone, framed in the casement.

"If it is not the Dowager Lady Latymer. And where were you at Mass?" Nan Stanhope is wafting a nosegay in front of her face as if the stench of the minor aristocracy is more than she can bear. "I hear you have been seeking a husband among the dregs of my family."

Katherine says nothing but maintains a steady gaze on the woman.

"I'd have thought you could do better than a younger brother, *my* brother-in-law no less." Her eyes swivel like a reptile's.

"I think you are mistaken," Katherine says. "There is a good deal of gossip in this place and little of it true."

"Everybody knows." Nan's eyes gleam. "The King knows. That is why Thomas is being sent away."

"Is he?" She pretends it is nothing more than a snippet of gossip, willing herself to remain calm. So it *is* true. Nan Stanhope would know, with her husband in the King's pocket as he is.

"The King doesn't like that kind of carry-on."

"I don't know what you mean." Katherine tries to read her for signs that she might know more, something of the King's own intentions.

But Nan is giving nothing away. Surely, Katherine reasons, the woman would be making some attempt at ingratiation if she'd got a sniff of anything about the King wanting her for a mistress. Nan Stanhope, of all people, knows how to play the court game, how to curry favor in the right places.

"Clever Katherine Parr playing dumb." Nan wears a sideways smirk. "Not like you."

Katherine can feel the anger rising in her. She redraws the benign smile onto her face. "Will you be traveling in Lady Mary's barge tomorrow?"

She knows full well that Nan will not be, for she herself had helped compile the list of those traveling with Lady Mary. She hates herself a little for stooping to Nan's level but knowing what a stickler her adversary is for pecking order, she can't resist it.

"Perhaps." Nan's eyes flash.

"I shall see you then." Katherine continues to smile.

"But . . . I may travel a day later . . . business."

Katherine nods her head, saying, "Countess," before walking away sedately, resisting the overwhelming urge to run.

One foot in front of the other, she passes through the gallery, one step at a time, down the stairs, across the courtyard, eventually arriving at her rooms, which are thankfully empty.

She flings herself to the bed, allowing at last the tears to come, in great gulping sobs. The thought of Thomas's absence has run itself through her, as if a poison has got into her blood, and she wonders if she will ever be the same again.

I2

Hampton Court Palace, June 1543

Dot follows the Lord Steward's man up the steps, through the Great Hall and the watching chamber, along the gallery, round a corner, past the King's chapel and into a set of rooms that are so magnificent she can't help but gape in awe.

The paneling is carved so delicately into folds that she yearns to touch it just to make sure it is really wood and not linen, and the intricate plasterwork on the ceiling is painted a blue so bright, the kind of blue you'd imagine was the color of the sky in Heaven, and it is all picked out in gold and dotted with red and white Tudor roses—in case you forget whose palace it is.

The hearth is like an enormous marble doorway, high enough for a man to stand inside, with firedogs so beautifully wrought they look like the earrings of a giantess. There are more windows than Dot has ever seen in one place all together, flooding the rooms with sunlight. She assumes they must be Lady Mary's chambers and that their rooms will be in the warren of corridors she imagines lie beyond.

But the Lord Steward's man says, "Here we are," and the small army of men who have lumbered up behind them with all of Lady Latymer's belongings begin to dump them in a great stack on the floor.

"These are Lady Latymer's things," Dot says.

"Correct." The Lord Steward's man looks at her as if she is an idiot. "These are the rooms assigned to Lady Latymer."

"That can't be right."

"Are you contradicting me?" He waves a piece of paper under her nose. "Lady Latymer—Four rooms on the East Wing off the gallery: watching chamber, privy chamber, bedchamber, wardrobe. In black and white." He points to a line of writing.

Dot, not being able to read, is none the wiser.

The Lord Steward's man leaves her alone with the porters—two are hooking up a set of wall-hangings, while another pair are constructing a large canopied bed next door. Dot wanders from room to room waiting for the Lord Steward's man to return and say that there has been a mistake, that these are not Lady Latymer's rooms after all and lead them off to a cramped little garret somewhere. He doesn't return.

If Dot had been impressed by Whitehall Palace, she is awestruck by the magnificence of Hampton Court. They had approached on the London Road, a great train of them, she near the back, perched on a bone-rattling old cart, holding on for dear life, with Rig tucked under her arm. Someone had shouted out that the palace was in view and she had stood, finding a foothold on the stack of luggage to get a view.

There it was, in tantalizing glimpses between the trees, the brickwork chimneys and crenellated towers soaring up to the sky. She couldn't peel her eyes away as they trundled into Base Court, the windows winking in the sun, the pink brick casting a rosy glow over the cobbles and the fountain, an explosion of diamonds, at its heart. Dot wondered if she hadn't been caught in a dream, somehow found herself inside the marchpane castle that she had seen being made in the Whitehall kitchens as a centerpiece for one of the King's banquets.

She'd followed the Lord Steward's man in a daze, past statues and murals and tapestries stitched with golden thread that gleamed as if they were images of Heaven itself. She wanted to stop, take time to admire it all, to look up at the carved ceilings and out of the windows at the gardens and fishponds that she saw only in flashes as they passed. But the Lord Steward's man strode ahead as if he was late for something and she tripped along behind him, doing her best to keep up. For all the splendor of the place, it is Lady Latymer's rooms that are the best of it because Dot will be bedding down there too, or so she has been told.

She is shown the kitchens, which are got to by a set of steps beyond the great watching chamber. She can barely count the number of cooks and scullions and squillery lads and other people, rushing to and fro, heaving animal carcasses or stirring vats of sweet-smelling liquid or kneading huge balls of dough, preparing for the King's arrival tomorrow. It is as hot as Hell must be, with the fires burning and the spits turning and bubbling pans giving off steam.

As she is taking it all in, feeling rather lost if truth be told, a girl approaches her. This is unusual. As far as she has seen there are not many girls about, apart from in the laundry. She has a round face with apple cheeks and has a hefty weight to her.

"I am Betty." Her smile is full of mischief. "Betty Melcher. There are few enough lasses around here so we need to stick together. What's your name?"

"Dorothy Fownten, but those who know me call me Dot."

"Then *I* shall call you Dot, if you don't mind. Whom do you serve?"

When Dot says she serves Lady Latymer, Betty gasps. "She's the one they are all talking about, isn't she?"

Dot is not sure what she means by this so gives Betty a nod, asking her who she serves. Whereupon Betty launches into a speech about how she serves "every blasted soul in the kitchens."

At the end of it Dot gathers that she works in the squillery scrubbing pots and dishes, which explains her red, raw hands.

When Betty has finished listing her chores and complaints, Dot asks if she could show her around the kitchens. "I am quite lost in this place, you see."

Betty takes her to the grain store, and the boiling house, and the fish court, and the wine cellars, and the buttery, and the smoke house, and the still room, and the meat store, and the place where water can be got for washing. Finally Betty shows her the common jakes that drop down into the moat below, where there is room for twenty-eight to ease themselves at once. "In a week or so it'll stink like hell," Betty says, pinching her nose with a grimace.

They return by way of the squillery, where there are a couple of kitchen clerks sitting at desks poring over papers. One in particular catches Dot's eye. He has ink-smudged fingers and dark-green hooded eyes that give her the feeling of looking down a well when you can just about see the shine of water at the bottom. His hair is a conker-colored crop, and there is a little indentation in his chin that she'd like to put her finger in to see if it fits. He looks up, straight at her, but doesn't seem to see she is there. Rather, he looks right through her, seeming to think very hard about something, then begins to count on his inky fingers before dipping his pen and writing something down. Dot's heart pops, her belly pitching.

Once out of earshot, she asks Betty who he is.

"What, that clerk? I don't know his name. They don't really talk to us. Too lowly." She laughs, a throaty cackle. "Why?"

"I don't know, just wondered."

"You've taken a fancy, Dorothy Fownten, I can tell a mile off." Betty nudges her new friend. "I don't know why you'd choose one of them snotty clerks when there's near on a hundred comely fellows about the place. There was one . . ." She tells Dot about all the goings-on in the kitchens after dark, where they all sleep on pallets laid out before the hearth. "Not the clerks, though, of course. They have proper lodgings elsewhere."

As she finds her way back up to the rooms she has the feeling she will like Hampton Court, not least because of her new friend. She flops onto the enormous bed, exhausted from the journey and all the unpacking and making everything ready for Lady Latymer's arrival tomorrow. Lying alone, she spreads her arms and legs out as far as she can reach like a star, thinking of her nameless clerk with his ink-splodged fingers and bottom-of-a-well eyes. She floats off to sleep with the thought that he is a man who can read, ignoring the truth that he is so far up above her in the scale of things, he would likely not notice her if she walked right past him in nothing but her birthday suit.

13

On seeing the rooms she has been allocated, Katherine feels a creeping sense of unease. She is aware that these have been the Queen's rooms since Jane Seymour's time and knows what this must mean.

She cannot keep herself from wondering about Thomas and wishing his discontent had not clouded their parting. His clenched jaw, the scowl, the anger in his eye, is the image she has been left with. It feels like an impossibility to go about as if everything is the same, as if her world has not been tipped off its axis.

A rap at the door jolts her from her thoughts. She gathers herself.

Her brother strides in. "Look at this." He sweeps an arm to indicate the rooms, taking it all in—pricing it all up, probably.

"What are you doing here?" She paints on a smile. "I thought you were keeping the Scots at bay."

"I had some business to attend to down here and thought to visit my sister, who seems to be going up in the world. The Queen's rooms—"

"I wonder what they will cost me."

"Don't be like that, Kit. We Parrs are on the rise thanks to you. And *I* have good news."

"Spit it out, then. Clearly you are bursting to tell me." She can't eradicate the ill humor from her tone.

"I am to be made Earl of Essex. I have not been told officially but I have it from a good source."

"Oh Will." She makes herself sound pleased. "This has been a long time coming. I am glad for you."

She wants to be *truly* glad for him, but she lost Thomas for this. The thought of it is like a nail hammered into her. But it is not Will's

93

fault the King has taken a shine to her. Neither is it his fault that he wants the Parrs to go up in the world. He was bred for that, they all were. Every last noble swaggering about this court is gazing at the stars.

"And your divorce?"

They both know that if he doesn't get his divorce he won't produce a legitimate heir to inherit his long-awaited earldom.

"I thought I should wait before broaching that again."

Wait for what? she thinks. Wait for me to get into the King's bed and sweeten him up? She has a secret admiration for Will's beleaguered wife, who had the spirit to run off with her lover and bite her thumb at the court.

"Surely the King will find some sympathy for your cause. He is no stranger to divorce, after all."

"So you might think, Kit, but as that blasted Bishop constantly likes to point out—*the King's marriages were annulled. He was never divorced.*" He mimics Gardiner's drone. "He's such a *Catholic* he can barely say the word 'divorce' without choking on it. He's got it in for me, I'm sure."

"I doubt it, Will." Katherine knows her brother is given to exaggeration.

"He doesn't like any of us Parrs. We are too reform-minded for him."

"I'm sure Gardiner has other things on his mind than us and what we believe."

"Like wiping the King's arse . . . *and* dragging us all back to the old faith."

"Enough of that now. Come and see the view from this window." She leads him to the casement that has a view over Fountain Court. "See how pretty it is. I shall be able to spy on the lovers stealing kisses in the cloisters." She laughs but she has ignited new thoughts of Thomas. Another nail is driven into her. She wishes her sister were here. She could confide in her. But Anne has had to go to the Herbert estates to interview a new tutor for her son. The thought of her sister's fertility, her children, drives yet another nail in. Even thoughts that seem innocent are treacherous.

"So," says Will. "What of the King?"

"What do you mean?" She feigns ignorance.

"Has he declared himself?"

"He has said nothing. Indeed, until I found myself housed here," she opens both arms out, indicating the sumptuous rooms, "I had not a clue of his intentions."

"He will say something soon, I'm sure of it." Will's eyes are glistening.

"He'll take me for his mistress and I shall pretend it is the thing I want most in the world. We will get some lands and titles bestowed on us—look, you are already to be made Earl of Essex—and then he will tire of me. That is how it will play."

"You're wrong." Will has a strange expression. "You must be able to see, he wants a *wife*, not a mistress."

"No." She covers her face with her hands. "No."

"Since Cromwell went to the block the King has lost the fire in his belly for reform." He lowers his voice, his tone becoming conspiratorial. "Think of it. You—the Queen of England. Think of your influence. You could persuade him to return to the new faith. Our faith. He is slipping back—back to the old ways." Will is simmering with fervor. "*You* could bring him back."

Katherine meets his mismatched eyes. "You think me so persuasive? And what makes you assume he would take me for a wife? You're letting your imagination run away with you."

"Hertford has said it."

"Hertford." Her voice cracks. This is not idle gossip then. Thomas was right. Thoughts of her lover crowd back into her head. "And Thomas? Have you seen him, Will?"

"Thomas has gone. You must forget him—as if he is dead."

This ruthless streak in her brother is new to her. Ambition has got to him. He is no longer the sulky puppy of their youth. Of course not, she berates her own stupidity, twenty years have passed since then.

"But did you see him before he left?"

"I have only just arrived from the Borders. You know that."

There is not a shred of tenderness in him. His fists are gripped tight. He is locked on to his prize and will not be turned. It only begins to fully dawn on her now that these men—the King, her brother, Hertford—have sealed her fate. The King will take her for a wife and she will not have any choice in the matter. She is no more free than she was as a girl.

Will grips her firmly by the shoulders. "It is the King we talk of. You will be *Queen*. You could not rise higher."

"Nor fall further." She feels faint.

There is no escaping her fate. But then, she reasons, if she can't be Seymour's wife, is it such a very poor consolation to be Queen of England and raise the Parrs higher than they'd ever hoped? But then she is assaulted by the sensation of those great paws prodding at her, and his stench, and the terror he ignites, and being tied to him for ever by marriage—the desperate duty of producing an heir at her age, each month hoping, praying she will not bleed.

It is a whore's job, this business of being a woman.

She unclasps her mother's cross, folding it into a handkerchief, stashing it in her box of keepsakes. She can no longer bear to feel it against her skin. It reminds her too much of what she has given up.

Those dead Queens cluster about her, her thoughts running untrammeled. How will she survive this? God is punishing her—he has seen her sins. Was her part in Latymer's death the Devil's work? Murder or mercy or both?

Her soul feels as brittle and insubstantial as a dead flower.

14

Huicke is seated at the far reaches of the Great Hall. The ravaged remains of the banquet clutter the boards. A carved-up hog lies splayed over the table reminding him of the dissections he attended as a student. A large platter of larks has barely been touched, the little carcasses congealing, and a pot of jellied eels has tipped over, casting its contents floorwards.

Beneath the lip of a plate, hidden in the shadows, crouches a small quivering frog. A pie was served at the top table earlier, which the King had sliced with his sword. Nan Stanhope, seated beside the King, let out a blood-curdling scream, followed by a squeal from Lady Mary that then became a cacophony of female screeching.

Huicke, being seated so far down the table, only realized that the pie was full of live frogs when the poor creatures had started to leap desperately about the room to escape the pages who were trying to gather them up. There must have been some kind of reward promised to the one who caught the most, for they jostled and jumped over each other ruthlessly to get at the things. It was chaos and the King looked on with a satisfied smirk, occasionally hollering out encouragement to one or other of the pages.

The purpose of the frog pie would have been the terrified screams of the ladies.

Huicke knows the King well enough. A physician sees things others don't. He has seen him toy viciously with people, even those closest to him, like a boy who kicks an old dog just to hear it yelp. He has also seen him reduced to anguished tears when the pain in his leg becomes too much to bear, witnessed him pacing the room in shallow-breathed panic on hearing news of an outbreak of plague nearby. Yet, most see him as fearless, impervious, brimming with courage.

Huicke had watched the King fawn like a puppy over that little featherhead Catherine Howard. She brought him to his knees, but then he watched him sign the paper that sent the girl to the scaffold, barely looking up from his card game as if he might have been agreeing to his supper menu.

He has seen the King explode at one of his pages who made some petty mistake, shouting purple-faced until the poor boy pissed his hose. But he's seen King Henry comfort a man too, no one of any consequence, just a bereft man who had lost his son. The King took him in his arms and cradled him as a mother might an infant.

The frog quakes in its hiding place and Huicke wonders what will become of it.

The room is too noisy and his stomach hurts with overeating. Udall, who had been seated somewhere near the middle of the room, stands to leave. He must make preparations for the masque he has devised for midsummer night, which will be performed later, if anyone can stay awake after all this food. Five or six of his performers rise too, young girls, who will be draped in the diaphanous costumes that have been designed to cover, and yet reveal, their breasts.

Huicke had been at the fitting. Breasts do little for him, but a glance from Udall can send him into a state of bedazzled arousal. So, as his lover passes to leave the room, he keeps his eyes firmly glued to the table and that plate of massacred larks. Udall runs a scalding finger by-mistake-on-purpose across his back and Huicke can barely contain himself.

The woman sitting opposite him blathers on—something about the Scottish Queen Mary, whether she will be betrothed to Prince Edward, the King's "rough wooing." She tilts a look meaningfully at him for a response. But he can't hear her properly over the hubbub, so he smiles and nods and she seems satisfied. He can't help thinking that the infant Queen Mary will be shoved about like a chess piece in the name of Scotland.

Katherine sits far up the room, just visible if he leans back. She wears her serene smile, the one that fools everyone but him. He knows of the turmoil that roils behind that facade. She talks animatedly with her brother's mistress, who though considered a beauty doesn't manage to eclipse Katherine. Her flashing hazel gaze and ebullient laugh could draw down the moon.

Her brother Will, sitting close to them, has something of his sister about him—the oddly female upturned nose, the shock of copper hair, almost exactly the shade of hers, but where Katherine has a softness about her, Will Parr is all sharp edges. He is making a point, stabbing at the air with his hands in staccato movements. Katherine throws him a stern look and his arms drop. Huicke has seen Katherine put her arrogant brother in his place more than once. There is no doubt who holds sway in the Parr family.

He had watched her when the confusion broke out over the frogs, the women squealing like pigs and leaping on benches. Katherine had appeared entirely unperturbed and when one had landed right beside her she picked it up as if to kiss it, causing a great gust of laughter from the King, before summoning one of the pages, handing over the amphibian and saying something Huicke couldn't hear.

"What did she say?" the woman opposite him called up the table.

"She asked that it be repatriated to the pond in the knot garden," someone called back.

On seeing the King's smug satisfaction as he watched that little event unfold, it dawned on Huicke that just by being herself, her sanguine, light-hearted self, Katherine was playing right into the King's hands. Had she screeched and fussed like all the others, his attentions may have drifted elsewhere. That test was for her and she had passed it with aplomb.

Huicke feels a little knot of fear tighten in his belly on behalf of his friend.

Katherine had called for him that afternoon, had sent her stepdaughter to seek him out. It was the first time, since their conversation in the still room at Charterhouse, that she had asked to see him alone. At Whitehall their paths had crossed often, but the easy intimacy that had previously characterized their friendship was absent. She wasn't unfriendly, perhaps just a little cool with him and a little too polite.

He had had to face the fact that her trust was lost, and he felt it deeply. Even Udall's unstinting amorous attentions didn't entirely assuage his regret.

He arrived in her rooms to find her surrounded by papers. She was talking to her steward about a boundary dispute, scrawling out a letter and saying to him, "Stand firm, Cousins. We will not be walked over. That land was given me by my husband and I have the documents to prove it."

She folded the paper, running her finger and thumb along the fold, dropped a glob of red wax onto the join, thumping her stamp into it. "They are here somewhere." She shuffled through the papers, eventually pulling a document from the pile. "Look, Cousins, there it is, clear as day. The Hammerton boundary runs to the west of the woods, not the east. Those woods are mine, are they not?"

"They are indeed, my lady," he said.

"Take this to the notary, and while you are there have him release some funds for Nun Monkton. They need a new barn. And the man who died, his widow will need something. A few pounds, I should think—for the meantime she must have something to live on—and find her a position in the house, or the laundry, or the pastry kitchen if she can cook. I'll leave it to you, Cousins."

Huicke watched, impressed by her efficient tone, her sense of calm authority.

Once Cousins had taken his leave, they sat together and she took his hand to tell him she had missed his friendship. No words could have made him happier and he felt the closeness surge back, wrap itself around them once more.

"This poor man," she'd said, "he was crushed when a wall collapsed on my land. It pains me, Huicke, that I have to be here and cannot offer comfort to his widow. I should be there but I am compelled to stay at court. Think, Huicke, I could be pickling and bottling in my own kitchens, preserving summer fruits, drying herbs, making remedies, riding out to visit my tenants, looking after things, but I am here surrounded by all this." She spread her arms out with a pained look. "The Queen's rooms, Huicke."

"Kit." He had used her pet name tentatively, unsure if he still had the right to it, given the rupture in their friendship. But she gave his hand a squeeze and smiled. "If there is anything I can do to—"

"There is, Huicke." He realized he'd been summoned for a purpose. "You must tell me of the King's intentions. My brother says he wants this marriage. I don't want to believe it, but look where I have been lodged . . . and apparently Will is to get his earldom. I have a terrible feeling about this." Her hand kept flicking up to her throat as if to touch something that wasn't there. "Be honest with me."

"I *have* heard him talk of it," Huicke had said. "And Anne Bassett has been sent back to Calais."

Katherine's face became gray and strained. "One more thing."

He nodded for her to continue.

She dropped her voice. "Did you see Thomas Seymour before he left? Did he say anything, send a message?"

"I wish I could say he did, but no."

Her face fell at this.

"But he wouldn't have said anything. Not to me, not to anyone. It would have been too risky." He'd added that to make her feel better—and it is probably true. Huicke couldn't bring himself to tell her what he really thinks about Thomas Seymour, that he is thankful the man's gone—it would have been cruel.

The servers have begun to bring in the sweets—jellies and syllabubs and sweetmeats—parading them down the hall. Finally they produce a vast platter, carried like a coffin, four men to each side. On it sits a life-size hart, pure white, made of marchpane, so real-seeming it might have been sculpted by Michelangelo himself, its antlers crafted from sugar crystals, its breast pierced with an arrow.

The room falls silent save for the odd gasp of wonder. The servers stop at the top of the table. Everyone waits to see how they will manage to heave the great thing up onto the dais. But they stay where they are. People rise from their seats to better see who has been presented with this creature. Huicke leaves his seat and walks forward, hoping it is not whom he thinks.

But it is—of course it is. A lump forms in his throat.

The hart signifies love and the arrow needs no explaining—the King is declaring himself. Katherine stands, her face beaming with pretend delight. She glances briefly toward the King, who nods, with a triumphant smile, and blows her a kiss.

Nan Stanhope is unable to hide her sour look and Huicke cannot help but feel a little thrill of satisfaction to see the woman's nose put out of joint. Katherine manages to maintain her feigned delight but Huicke knows what she is thinking—those great fat hands grabbing at her flesh.

"Pull the arrow," commands the King.

As she does it blood, or some substance that looks like it—spiced red wine, perhaps—spills from the white animal, staining its breast scarlet. A cup is placed beneath, gathering the red liquid, before it is served to the King.

He lifts the cup towards Katherine—"To love!"—and swigs it back. He throws the cup away and the room is silent save for the clatter of it as it lands.

Then the hall erupts with applause.

In that single gesture Katherine's fate is publicly sealed.

PART TWO

Be swift to hear and slow in giving answer.
Katherine Parr

15

Hampton Court Palace, June 1543

It is Hertford who comes to fetch Katherine. She follows him down the long gallery. From behind, the set of his shoulders, his swinging gait, are so much like his brother's that it sends a pang of despair through her.

The King is waiting in his privy chamber, standing, thick white-stockinged legs apart, hands on hips, in a parody of the great Holbein that hangs at Whitehall—the image of the King. But it is a grotesque parody before her. You'd not think him the same man except for the jewels and the elaborate attire.

The sheer mountainous height and girth of him in the small room make her feel like a doll, in a doll's house, where some careless child has tossed a great puppet far too big for the place. He looks at her with a jowly smile, taking her chin between his thumb and forefinger and turning her face up to his.

Hertford backs out of the room and closes the door. Though she doesn't much like the man, she wants to shout at him to stay, not to leave her alone with the King. She has never been alone with him before and feels a rising panic, for she knows what is coming and grasps mentally for some way to stop it.

His voice, when he eventually drags his eyes away from his appraisal of her, surprises her with its softness. He asks her to sit with him so he can show her a book of hours that had belonged to his father. It is a wonder, so fine, its colors so vivid, the gilt work so intricate. She quite forgets that this tender old man beside her, carefully turning the old vellum pages, pointing out the details in the text and showing her where someone had once pressed a flower between the pages, is King Henry himself. He places the flower ghost on her palm, a weightless fragment.

"It was my mother pressed that flower, when I was a boy." Suddenly the thing feels like a great weight in her hand, as if the whole of history is pulling her down.

"Please take it, I am afraid to break it," she whispers, nervous that the slightest breath will blow this fragment of Tudor heritage away.

He compares *her* to a flower, a rose, just an empty flattery. He shows her, too, the place where his father had written in the margin beside an image of Christ crucified, deciphering for her the spider's web words: *Arthur, rest in peace*, translating the Latin. Though her Latin is at least as good as his, she finds herself feigning ignorance.

"That was my brother."

She touches a finger lightly to the dry words. "Prince Arthur."

"I know what loss is," he says. "Your husband suffered greatly but now he is with God, and *you* must live."

She wonders whether Latymer is indeed with God, or in that other place, thinking again about the circumstances of his death, her part in it. The thought silts her up, makes her speechless.

The King seems to think she is dumb with awe of him and perhaps she is. She finds it is impossible to know exactly *what* she thinks here and now, with history bearing down on her and she expected to take her part in it.

"I have chosen you to be my Queen."

It is not a question in the normal manner of a proposal, where she might at least feel allowed the pretense of a refusal. She wonders if the King was ever refused anything, then remembers Anne Boleyn, who, it is said, refused him for years and drove him quite mad with desire— mad enough to send her to the block at the end of it.

She sits very still. Pieces of Seymour hover in her mind: his long fingers, the scent of him, his bright laugh. The thought of what she will have to do with the King, as his wife, repulses her. She doesn't have to answer him. It is not a question, after all. It is already decided.

"We shall be wed here at Hampton Court." He squeezes her waist.

"In July." And he goes on listing the details of it, what they will feast on, what psalms will be sung, who will attend.

She hears none of it. Her time has run out. July is almost upon them. She has to employ all her resistance not to cringe away from his hand on her waist, assailed by the thought of where that hand will go once they are wed. She forces her thoughts onto the other things: the jewels, the lands, the honors, the Parrs soaring. But none of that can erase her revulsion.

"You shall call me Harry," he is saying, "when we are alone. Now we are betrothed we will have time to know each other."

She manages something like a smile.

The King laughs, his doughy cheeks quivering. "Let's drink to it."

Hertford appears as if by magic, with a jug of wine, pouring it into glass goblets. She realizes a time had been pre-arranged for his return. After all, everything else has been pre-arranged, staged like one of Udall's masques. Watching Hertford pour the wine she thinks of his poisonous wife, managing to find a little spirit at the idea of Nan Stanhope having to stoop and grovel before her when she is Queen. She admonishes herself for entertaining such pettiness, but knows she is clutching to find reasons to celebrate.

The glasses are Venetian and delicately etched with a pattern of vines. She has never drunk from glass before. It is a good feeling, the cool of it on her lips, but the wine, which she supposes must be a fine one, tastes sharp. The King swallows his down and throws his glass into the grate where it shatters, making her jump.

"You too, Katherine." He takes her arm, flinging it. The glass flies from her fingers, breaking against the stone chimney piece. "Come, Ned, drink with us." Hertford is grinning. "And Katherine." The King's raisin eyes glitter. "You can be the first to tell your brother he will get his title."

She wishes that she could muster the guts to ask for Will's divorce too, to milk this for all she can get. Isn't that what it is all about? But she remains silent.

She couldn't speak if she wanted to.

16

Dot is in the squillery, pretending to scour the big copper wash-basin, which is already as clean as it is possible to be. It was never really dirty in the first place but the swilling and scrubbing means she can watch William Savage from the corner of her eye. That is the name of the kitchen clerk who has got inside her head and will not be budged.

Betty had only gone and asked his name, straight out just like that. Dot would never have dared, though she might have if the very sight of him didn't make her belly feel full of eels.

She feigns scrubbing to stay a little longer in his presence, watching askance as he marks things down in his ledger, though he seems not to notice her at all. His hair keeps falling forward and he has a way of pushing it back with his arm. Dot supposes that's so he doesn't rub the ink from his fingers onto his forehead.

She imagines running her own fingers through that hair. It would feel smooth and soft like Lady Latymer's silk shifts. He would wrap an arm around her, pulling her towards him close and say . . . What would he say? She cannot imagine that he would have anything to say to *her*. It is a silly dream, and besides, her hands are quite raw with rubbing at a clean basin. She gives up and goes into the yard to find Betty, who is skiving in the hayloft above the stables.

"Been loitering around William Savage again?" Betty shifts over to make space for Dot. "I don't know why you don't just offer him a squeeze. That's what you want, isn't it?"

"I couldn't." Dot wishes things in her world could be as straightforward as they seem to be in Betty's, who offers her "squeezes" about quite generously as far as Dot has gathered.

"You could trip over in front of his desk and accidentally let one of your titties fall out." Betty emits a raucous peal of laughter.

"Begging your pardon, good sir." Dot is laughing too. "I slipped on a pat of butter."

"Let me help you put that titty back in your dress." Betty drops her voice an octave, causing them both to laugh until they're completely out of breath.

"Why would an educated man be interested in a nobody like me?" Dot says, suddenly serious.

"But you serve the lady who will be Queen. You could have any clenchpoop in these kitchens if you wanted. All you want's a fumble, it's not like you want him to *marry* you."

"True." But that *is* what she wants, however far-fetched, and though William Savage hasn't even uttered a single word to her she can't help thinking of it. She knows well enough that people stick to their own kind.

"You could even have that one." Betty points out of the loft hatch towards the weasel in charge of the wine cellars, who is known for slinking about, spying on the young girls in the closet.

"Urgh!" Dot cries. "And *you* can have Big Barney."

That starts them off laughing again, for Big Barney is the halfwit who cleans the jakes.

"I wish *I* could serve a great lady instead of scraping blasted pans day and night." Betty makes a mock scowl.

But they both know that Betty wouldn't make a good upstairs maid for she has a filthy mouth and can't keep it shut for a minute. Secretly, though, Dot is a little jealous of Betty, who's happy to sleep before the squillery hearth and has nightly cuddles with the kitchen lads.

She'd like to try it, just the once, to see what it is like, properly, not like the fumbles she had with Jethro or the chaste kisses Harry Dent used to give her. Dot must be content with her thoughts of William Savage. It is not so far-fetched to imagine that he might, one day, look up from his papers and smile at her, and she will smile back. The very thought of it makes her go soft inside.

"Lady Latymer will be wondering where I've got to." She gets to her feet, brushing the hay off her dress.

She climbs down the ladder and gives herself a final brush-down before collecting the copper basin to take back to Katherine's rooms.

Meg is in the outer chamber, sorting embroidery silks. "There you are, Dot. Where have you been? Mother wants the hearth laying."

"A fire in July?"

"The King has asked for it."

"The King?"

"He is in there with her."

"In there?" Dot points to the door, open-mouthed. "I couldn't . . ." There isn't much Dot is afraid of but the idea of encountering the King is making her queasy.

Meg spools a skein of green thread around her fingers, tying it neatly in the middle and placing it in the sewing basket. Dot picks up a piece of fabric from the pile beside her. It is ready for stitching, stretched into a wooden round with a pattern picked out in ink. Even without being able to read she can see that it is the intertwined initials H and K.

Meg makes a little sigh. "I wish we could turn back the clock." A shadow passes over her features.

Dot wonders if she might be thinking of how far she would have to turn that clock back to get to a time when things were truly easy.

"This is not so bad. All this luxury and your mother to become Queen." But she is thinking about the two other Queens, wondering about all the initials embroidered for them and what became of them.

"It is not a good thing." Meg is looking at her hands.

Dot remembers Katherine telling her that Meg is one of the world's pessimists. She'd had to ask what the word meant. It is a curse, she thinks, to be a pessimist. She wishes that Meg could simply discard her worries. But if the world, or God, conspires to do what has been done to Meg, then you would surely become a pessimist whether you chose it or not.

"You'd better get on with the hearth." Meg reaches out to pluck a strand of hay from Dot's apron with a raised eyebrow.

"It's not what you think."

"Not my business," Meg says. "There's a scuttle of coal over there." She points to a bucket in the corner.

"Coal?"

"The King prefers it. The heat is good for his leg, apparently." Dot's nervousness must show on her face, for Meg says, "Don't worry. Just curtsy, right down low, and say nothing. He'll likely ignore you completely."

Dot cannot imagine what the King is like, has not even seen him at a distance despite the time she has spent at the palace. There is a picture in her head—it is the one you see on the woodcuts where he is quite magnificent, standing square, staring out as if nothing could touch him. Dot picks up the bucket and the tinderbox, tucking the hearth brush under her arm.

"You'd better get used to it, Dot. She will be his wife in a few days."

Dot takes a deep breath to calm her nerves before knocking on the door to the inner chamber.

"Enter." It is Katherine's soft voice.

Dot lifts the latch and pushes the heavy door with her shoulder, clanking the bucket against it, mumbling an apology as she steps red-faced into the chamber, dropping down into a deep curtsy.

They are sitting by the window, Katherine on a stool and the King on a wooden chair with his leg propped up on her lap. To Dot's relief he doesn't look at her or even stop talking. It is as if she doesn't exist.

Katherine nods at her silently with a smile.

Dot can't help but keep glancing at the two of them as she starts to build the fire. He has his ham of a hand on her leg, and he looks nothing like the King. He is a bulging, lardy old man, not even one little bit magnificent, and Katherine looks like she might be his daughter or a niece.

Dot has never laid a coal fire before and wishes there was someone to ask. But she puts in plenty of kindling and hopes for the best. She wipes her hands on her apron, leaving smears of black, hoping none of it has got onto her face, then sets to lighting the tinder.

The King is talking quietly in a low growl. "Sometimes I wonder what an ordinary life would be . . ."

Dot glances over to see Katherine stroke her fingers over his beard. A spark lights the tinder. Dot blows it gently, watching the little blaze gather, tipping it into the hearth, all the while listening to the King's rumbling voice.

"... a life where people do not simply tell me what they think I want to hear."

"Harry ..."

Dot has never imagined that anyone might call him Harry. It is such a commonplace name for the King.

"... perhaps people humor you because they are afraid."

He shifts, his chair creaking loudly under his weight. "That Florentine, can't remember his name ... names seem to drop out of my head these days, Kit. He said it was better that princes were feared than loved. It takes such a great effort to be constantly feared. It has made me do things ..." He doesn't finish.

"Niccolò Machiavelli?"

Dot cannot make much sense of what they are saying.

"We all do things, Harry, that prick the conscience."

"*You* do not humor me. You are the only one with the courage to speak the truth. I noticed you first for that."

Dot blows into the fire until the coals glow brightly.

"I strive to be honest. It is what God asks of us, is it not?"

The King lifts his hand to the back of his neck, rubbing as if in some discomfort. "Do you feel a draft, Kit?"

"No, but the window is open a crack. It must be that."

He is on his feet at the window, pulling it shut. It sticks and he tugs at it so hard that one of the panes breaks and the latch comes away in his hand. "This cursed thing," he shouts, rapping it hard against the sill over and over, gouging holes in the wood—thud, thud, thud, splinters flying.

Dot shrinks into the corner, not looking, hoping not to be noticed. It is the sound of a butcher's cleaver.

Katherine is rubbing his shoulders. Dot can't imagine how she dares approach him. His face is purple like a bruise and beads of sweat have broken out on his forehead.

He is utterly at the mercy of his frustration—like a vast infant.

"Let me take that." Katherine tries to gently prize the broken latch from his grip.

But without warning he throws it with force towards the hearth where Dot is crouched.

She ducks her head. It flies past her, landing with a great clash against the scuttle. Dot's heart is going like a forge hammer and her hands are shaking so much she can barely keep hold of the hearth brush. She doesn't dare get up to leave for fear of drawing attention. The King sits back down with his head in his hands, breathing heavily while Katherine makes soothing noises and continues to rub his shoulders.

She looks briefly over at Dot, lifting her eyebrows as if to ask, "All right?"

Dot nods and Katherine brings a finger up to her lips in a silent shush. The King says nothing, doesn't even glance in her direction to see if her head is still attached to her shoulders.

When he does lift his face he mumbles, "I am afraid of myself sometimes." He looks collapsed and forlorn. "These rages come upon me. It is as if I am someone else. As if I am possessed."

Katherine strokes his sleeve, murmuring something.

"I fear I might lose my mind. The weight of England bears down on me." He is silent for some time, picking at a jewel on his doublet. When he speaks again it is barely more than a whisper. "I wonder what I have done to my country by breaking with Rome. I feel ... England is fractured at the heart."

Dot has never thought that the King might have doubts like any other man. Is he not told what to do by God?

"The past must be accepted ..."

Dot has heard Katherine say this often, to Meg in particular.

"... it takes mettle, Harry, to change things as you have done."

As she says this, the King seems to grow larger, shinier, his eyes brighter.

"And it is my firm belief that you have God on your side."

"He gave me a son," says the King. "That is surely an indication of his pleasure."

"And a fine one too."

"Will you give me a son?" He is like a small boy asking for a sweetmeat.

"If God wills it." Katherine smiles but Dot knows she isn't smiling inside. Dot remembers the dead baby and how it sent her nearly mad with grief.

17

"We have been granted the Abbey at Wilton." Anne sits beside Katherine on the window seat in her watching chamber. A gown is draped over their laps and they are inspecting the seed pearls stitched onto it. It is to be Katherine's wedding gown.

"Will you live there?" Katherine cannot bear the thought of her sister far away in the Wiltshire countryside.

"I don't like the idea of it." Anne wraps and unwraps a thread round her finger. "Sacred land."

"Wilton saw no violence," says Katherine. "The abbess handed it over quite willingly, I believe, and was pensioned off."

Katherine cannot help but think of all the other great abbeys, reduced to little more than rubble, the monks tortured and terrorized, the utter devastation—Cromwell's doing. In the name of the King, she reminds herself. She remembers Latymer telling her of the holy men he saw—a score at the very least, he had said—strung up from the trees, their guts spilt, near the Abbey at Fountains.

"That's a blessing. But even so, I shall stay at court. My husband likes to keep me close. And besides, I want to stay near you."

"Heaven knows I shall need you." Katherine looks around the room where pockets of ladies are scattered about, women she barely knows.

She has no inkling of their allegiance. They listlessly waft fans in an attempt to stir the July heat. A trio of fat black flies circles—occasionally someone swats at one of them with a fan. Katherine reaches up, unlatching the window to let in a whisper of breeze.

People have been arriving all day—for the wedding. She wonders if it will be a blessing or a curse, this marriage of hers. She remembers her brother's fervid excitement: *You could persuade the King to return to the new faith. Our faith. He is slipping . . . You could bring him back.*

Danger whispers in her ear. Her sins make her weak. She is afraid. Afraid of what, she isn't sure. It is a nebulous fear that poisons the very air.

"I could command you to stay," Katherine quips. If she pretends to be unafraid then perhaps she will convince even herself.

"You will be Queen!" Anne's exclamation is filled with surprise, as if this is the first time she has really considered what is happening.

For the last weeks Katherine has been appointing her household, shoring herself up against the court vipers with a few she trusts, like her childhood playmate Lizzie Tyrwhitt and her mother's friend old Mary Wootten, who was at court long before any of them can remember and knows everything worth knowing.

She keeps Huicke close too, has appointed him as her physician. The King is pleased with this—feels it is his doing. Perhaps he thinks Huicke will continue his espionage. But Huicke is *her* man. She knows it in her bones that he won't betray her again. And anyway, there is nothing to betray yet, though that doesn't necessarily mean anything in this place.

She is becoming used to it all: the court flatterers who want something from her; the endless string of mothers seeking to place their daughters in her household; the artists and craftsmen; the bookbinders; vintners; preachers; mercers; the grand ladies and countesses who had barely given her a thought until now.

Lady Mary is announced, swaying in slowly, half choked by an elaborate array of jewels. Susan Clarencieux is on one arm and her sister Lady Elizabeth on the other. Elizabeth cannot even be ten, yet she is tall, almost as tall as Mary, and seems, with her self-possession, far older than her years. Her plain gown only serves to accentuate her striking looks: an intense, intelligent gaze and flame-red hair, hanging loose to her waist.

She clutches a book to her breast. Hers is the bearing of a Princess—head high, half smile, inscrutable—and whereas Mary crouches slightly, weighed down by suspicion and disappointment, Elizabeth seems completely untouched by her father's rejection.

Katherine is reminded immediately of the King as a young man. She resembles him greatly and Katherine wonders if this will be the girl's saving grace.

The three of them stop before her, to offer their congratulations.

"You shall be my stepmother tomorrow." A wry smirk passes over Lady Mary's mouth, as if the idea amuses her. "My previous stepmother was a decade younger than me. At least you are older, if only by four years . . ." She pauses, a shadow darkening her features. Mary should have been a bride years ago, and must be feeling left on the shelf. "And we are friends."

"We *are* friends." Katherine takes Mary's hand. "And I shall do all I can to . . ." She seeks for the tactful way to tell Mary that she hopes to have the blot of illegitimacy lifted from her. ". . . to forward your case."

A rare natural smile breaks over Mary's face.

Elizabeth steps forward. "I shall be proud to call you Mother." She recites a poem in faultless Latin, the words tripping easily off her tongue.

The gathered ladies are clearly impressed, fascinated by this royal girl who has been so long away from court. Mary, though, cannot hide the brittle sneer that has fixed itself around her mouth. Katherine is reminded that it was Elizabeth's mother who caused the downfall of Mary's and makes a silent pledge to achieve a rapprochement not only between the girls and their father, but also between the two sisters.

More ladies arrive, two are the King's nieces. Margaret Douglas, the daughter of the King's elder sister, carries a small dog in her sleeve and has an impish flash in her eye, which lends some credence to her reputation for waywardness. Her cousin, Frances Brandon, who is great with child, insists on speaking in French lest anyone forget that her mother, the King's younger sister Mary, was once the Queen of France.

Katherine has a moment of inward amusement at the idea of these grand ladies, the greatest in the land, paying court to her, plain old Katherine Parr, who should barely have the right to look these women in the eye. Cat Brandon arrives, late and breathless. She doesn't care a mote that she is Duchess of Suffolk or about her place in the order of things. Nan Stanhope smiles stiffly from afar. Who fits where and who follows whom is a fixation for her. Even in the schoolroom she used to pull rank on Katherine, so there is some satisfaction watching her fight to keep that smile fixed to her face.

Meg hovers, drooping in the July heat, with wisps of damp brown hair stuck to her forehead and an anxious air. Cat takes her by the hand to draw her to Katherine's side.

"What is it, dear?" Katherine knows she'd far rather be in the anteroom with Dot than here. There will be precious little privacy for any of them now.

"When you are Queen, what shall I call you? Will it be Your Majesty?" She speaks very quietly, as if in fear of ridicule.

"Majesty is only for the King. It is madam, or Highness, I think. We shall ask my sister. Anne is a fount of knowledge on protocol—"

"It is madam usually, and Highness formally," interrupts Nan Stanhope, who must have been listening from across the room. "Though there was one Queen who preferred Highness all the time." They all know she means Elizabeth's mother, who is not ever to be mentioned by name in public.

"Anyway, Meg," says Katherine quietly, "in private we shall be just as we have always been and I shall still be *Mother* to you."

A wan smile washes over her stepdaughter's face.

"And," Katherine continues with a wink, "you may yet marry a marquis and *we* shall all have to call *you* lady."

Meg's smile is swallowed up, and Katherine realizes her mistake.

"I shall never marry." The poor girl seems on the brink of tears. "I plan to stay with you always."

"One day a man will steal your heart," says Cat Brandon.

Katherine cannot help but think, with a painful squeeze in her breast, of Thomas in some foreign court, dazzling the ladies, with the broken shards of her heart in his pocket.

"I only meant it lightly, dear," says Cat on seeing Meg's distraught expression. "Come, remember the reading." She hands a book to Meg, whispering something in her ear and indicating for the women to gather round.

"What is all this?" Katherine can see they are up to something.

Meg has managed to pull herself together and seems enthralled by Elizabeth, unable to tear her eyes away. "It's a passage my Lady Suffolk would have me read to you"—a blush spreads over her breast and up to her throat—"in celebration of your marriage."

Meg holds the paper high to hide her face. Katherine notices her nails, so viciously bitten down a few weeks before, have begun to grow again, hoping it is a sign that the girl may finally be escaping her past. Katherine cannot help but think of her own past, from which there is no escaping.

Meg takes a deep breath. Cat is unable to contain a burst of laughter, and a tittering breaks out among the ranks of women.

"*Arrêtez*," barks Frances Brandon.

The giggling subsides and Meg clears her throat. "'The Prologue of the Tale of the Wife of Bath.'"

"Cat!" Katherine feigns shock. "You vixen."

"It was Udall who put me up to it," Cat says. "We thought it appropriate given the Mistress of Bath was four times widowed and five times married."

A gust of laughter runs round the room.

"Udall. He's a sly one." Huicke had introduced his lover to Katherine a few days ago. She had liked him, with his irreverent humor and acute intelligence. "Where did you get hold of a copy, Cat?"

"I *borrowed* it from my husband's library."

"Well, mind he doesn't find out, or he may think you corrupted and try to divorce you. And anyway," Katherine continues with mock hauteur, "you know well enough that, unlike your Wife of Bath, I have only buried two husbands and am merely on my third."

They all explode into laughter at this.

A commotion and shouting from the courtyard below silences them.

"My Lady Latymer," comes the cry, then once more, louder, "My Lady Latymer!"

They hear the clatter and rattle of liveried horses and the unmistakable chink of arms. The smile drops momentarily from Katherine's face. She cannot hear that sound without thinking of Snape. Meg, beside her, pales visibly, gnawing at the nail of her thumb.

"It is the King!" Even Margaret Douglas seems excited, rushing to the window, though the King is her uncle.

Katherine paints on a perfect demeanor, agreeable, docile, joyful, as if she is playing Queen in one of Udall's masques, but she feels far from any of these things.

"Your Majesty." She leans from the casement, waving. "To what do I owe this honor?"

The King sits astride a great foaming roan mare whose girth matches his own. He is draped in acres of gilded mud-spattered cloth and surrounded by at least a dozen men, most of them husbands of the women around her.

Six black greyhounds have dropped to the ground, their puce tongues lolling in the heat. A rabbit skitters across the verge nearby and only a single hound bothers to rise and lope after it half-heartedly. It gives up when the rabbit hops into the undergrowth, rolling onto its back in the long cool grass, writhing about comically.

"We are come from the hunt," calls the King, "and wanted a sight of our wife on the eve of her wedding."

Katherine waves again, wondering if the royal "we" means himself and God, or him and his other self—for he is known, after all, for having two sides. Will he use it even in the bedchamber?

The idea of the bedchamber shoots her with panic. She looks down, dizziness gripping her as she imagines falling to the cobbles below. She has confided her fear of her wedding night to Huicke, who suggested she keep her eyes firmly shut and think of someone else. They had laughed about this but it becomes less of a laughing matter as the time draws near.

It is my duty, she reminds herself inwardly, repeating it over and over, like an incantation. "I am honored, Your Majesty."

Two men stride into the yard, bearing between them a small freckled deer strung onto a pole, its head drooping pathetically. "Have her brought to the Queen's privy kitchens," shouts the King. "She is a gift for our wife to be."

Katherine, not usually squeamish, can't bear to look at the creature, for its very deadness.

18

Dot helps Katherine into her robe. The two women don't speak. They don't need to. They have performed this ritual, almost daily, for some time, and though there are now four new maids of the chamber to help her dress, Katherine prefers Dot.

Dot knows every crevice of her mistress. She has plucked the wayward tendrils from her hairline; cut her nails and scraped away the dirt from under them; trimmed her coarse nether hair, surprising as a winter orange; washed the bloody cloths from her courses; rubbed the hard skin off her feet with a rough stone; slathered her skin in unguents; brushed her hair, a hundred strokes morning and night, combed the lice from it, oiled it with lavender, plaited it, pinned it; cleaned the sleep from her eyes; applied a compress to her blisters; bathed her feet in cool water to combat the summer heat; and tied her into her kirtles and hoods, laced the ribbons on her slippers and nightgowns. She knows Katherine's body as well as she knows her own.

Today she rouges her cheeks, making her eyes seem brighter. They make Dot think of the river at sunset when the sun seems to get into its very depths. Dot likes to sometimes sneak off and sit alone beside the Thames, watching the boats, wondering where they are going. She knows the river meets the sea somewhere far off, and that the big ships can travel for weeks without seeing land at all—it is quite a thought.

A painting hangs in the long gallery, of galleons tall as cathedrals, tossed about in a boiling ocean. Given the lowly place Dot came from and the fact that she is here at Hampton Court Palace and serving the next Queen of England, she thinks she might have a chance of one day seeing the sea. She has to give herself a pinch every day to believe she's not dreaming it all up. Anything seems possible. Anything, that is, except a smile from William Savage, who has still not acknowledged her, despite her frequent visits to the squillery on one or other trumped-up errand.

Katherine kneels at the wooden altar at the far end of the chamber. She silently mouths a prayer and Dot wonders what she prays for—not to lose her head like the other Queens, perhaps. Her imagination plays a trick on her, making her see, rather than the prayer stand, the block. The thought makes her panicky, her heart clapping out of control.

Pull yourself together, daft girl, she tells herself, bringing her imagination into check.

She dusts the dresser, lifting the objects, the ivory comb, the silver-backed brush, the pot of scented oil that smells of strange spices, the heavy necklace that had rubbed a tender welt on Katherine's neck. It is set with stones the size of her thumbnails and the color of raw kidneys. She replaces it in the box, where there are velvet indentations that fit its shape exactly, in the way broad beans nestle in their pod.

She knocks over a bottle of rose water with a wayward elbow, spitting out an apology as the bottle hits the floor with a clash. It doesn't break but its stopper flies off and the water spills, leaking down between the boards. The smell of roses spreads out through the room. She picks it up, noticing that her stockings don't match, wondering momentarily how she manages to do everything she is supposed to when she cannot manage to turn herself out properly.

"What is it?" Katherine looks up from her prayers.

"I'm so sorry, my lady, it is the rose water."

"It doesn't matter, Dot. We will have rivers of rose water. Enough to bathe in."

They both laugh at this. Dot has the impression that Katherine has only just realized what it means to be Queen, that everything will be at her fingertips, no matter the cost.

The gown, her wedding gown, is spread out on the bed. It is a wonder, red and gold, encrusted with pearls and jewels, and is so heavy that it took two of them to carry it from the wardrobe yesterday.

Katherine lets her robe slide to the floor. "Help me into my kirtle first, and then we will call in Anne and Meg for the rest."

Dot holds the kirtle while her mistress steps into it, then laces it tight at the back. Its acres of taffeta smell of the pressing iron. Next she attaches a pair of embroidered sleeves, tying them carefully at the shoulders, taking extra care that the bows are neat though they will not even show once the gown is on.

"Did you know, Dot, what an astrologer said of me when I was an infant?"

Dot tries to mumble in response, but her mouth is full of pins.

"That one day I would be Queen. Said it was written in the stars. It became a bit of a joke in our family and they all used to tease me and call me Majesty when I got above myself. We laughed about it because it was the most unlikely thing imaginable."

She stops, seems to be thinking hard about something. Perhaps she is thinking of that handsome Thomas Seymour, who has disappeared without a word.

"Things have a strange way of turning out the way you least expect in life. Sometimes I wonder if God has a sense of humor."

Dot doesn't understand what she means, for it is no laughing matter getting married to a king—especially this one.

She fetches Anne and Meg, and between the three of them they heave the gown onto Katherine. She stands straight as if it is light as a feather, not woven through with gold thread and stitched with as many brilliants and pearls as there are stars in the sky. Katherine allows in a few of the younger girls who have been poking their heads around the door, twittering with excitement. They pretend Dot isn't there. They don't know how to place her, don't know how to address a girl who is nothing more than a skivvy but is as close as a daughter to the woman who will be Queen in a few hours.

Dot doesn't care. She's used to it and knows her place. But she knows, too, that there are people who get a foot in the door of the court and end up climbing higher and higher. Cromwell was the son of a brewer or a smithy, or something like that, and Wolsey, who Dot has only vaguely heard of but knows was a cardinal, which is the most important thing you can be in the Church—except for Pope, of course—well, his pa was a butcher. She has an idea that both Wolsey and Cromwell came to a sticky end but she tries not to think about that part of it.

The dress and gown are on. Dot can't imagine how Katherine can look so cool and collected in the summer heat, made worse by the privy kitchens underneath her rooms. The stink of boiled cabbage wafts up through the boards, erasing the remains of the rose scent.

Dot undoes a sheaf of lavender, strewing it about the room. Meg plaits Katherine's hair and coils it up on the back of her head, fastening it with ribbons, and Anne lifts her wedding hood from its box. The young girls cluster round. Dot hangs back, leaves them to it. She has seen the hood close up already, with its diamonds and golden fringing, has even tried it on when no one was in the room, felt its dead weight pressing at her temples.

Katherine smiles but her left hand is clenched so tight her knuckles look like shelled almonds. "I am ready," she says, picking up her prayer book.

Meg looks as if she's drowning.

"Thank you, ladies."

She sails out of the room in her prison of a dress, her hand still a fist, with Meg and Anne just behind. None of the maids will go to the service, which is in the Queen's closet. Only about thirty will attend, not like you'd think a royal wedding would be, with crowds and a procession through the streets afterwards. Dot supposes that is because it is the King's sixth wedding.

Katherine is going to have to share a bed with him. The King may be the King but Dot knows he is nothing more than a man got up in glitter—and a fat old one at that, with a rotten stink about him and a vicious temper. It makes her skin crawl.

19

The Queen's closet is airless. Bishop Gardiner drones through the service. He wears a benign smile, but his eyes have a cruel look that belies it, and Katherine can't help but remember that choirboy with the broken finger.

"*In nomine Patris et Filii et Spiritus Sancti.*"

"*Amen.*"

A cramped row of white-clad choristers stands to her left, just visible if she swivels her eyes. There is barely space for the guests as it is, and she can feel the press of people at her back.

Her thoughts wander. She cannot focus her mind on the service. She is pinned down by the weight of her dress, like one of Dante's hypocrites in a lead-lined cape. Is it not hypocrisy to marry one when her heart is given to another? She would not be the first who has done that. She dares not turn and look at the King beside her. His breath whistles and wheezes, and his pungent perfume competes with the fog of incense that billows from the thurible, further congesting the stuffy room.

"*Hoc est autem verbum Domini.*"

"*Deo gratias.*"

She thinks of the vows she is about to make, thinks of God up there inspecting her sin-blotched soul and wonders—not for the first time—if this is her punishment wrapped in gold.

Her stomacher is tied too tight, making her breath shallow, and her knees complain despite the velvet cushion beneath them. Lightheaded, she fears coming to stand and passing out, ruining this fragment of history which will be written about, remembered, for ever.

Her thoughts drift inevitably to Thomas, of how he might have been here beside her, if fate had dictated a different path. The notion burrows under her skin. The part of her that harbors him is numb, has become so accustomed to the constant wrench and hurt that it feels nothing.

She had hoped, in the weeks after he left, for a letter, something, anything, to indicate that she was not forgotten, but nothing came. She wants to assume he is afraid of the King's wrath but a doubtful part of her fears worse. She has no right to hold his heart. She imagines him clustered by ladies, beauties all, offering himself up to them.

She stops the thought before it takes hold, thinking instead of the other times she has knelt before God and spoken vows of marriage. She was younger than Meg when she traveled from Rye House to Lincolnshire to marry Edward Borough. She didn't question it. Her whole life had been a preparation for marriage, and as she traveled north she had no misgivings, no fears of wedding a stranger. Edward was a pretty boy, thin as a whip and sweet as a puppy. She had met him only the once, briefly and formally, but he had sent a drawing, which she'd kept under her pillow.

. . . hoc est autem verbum Domini—Deo gratias.

She thinks how innocent she was and how lacking in ambition. Circumstance has foisted ambition on her now. She had made those first vows without a second thought. But Edward Borough was buried within two years, her mother too. To lose a mother and a husband within months of each other, cut loose in the world at nineteen—she had thought then that life couldn't possibly be harder than that.

How wrong she was. Latymer came next. He seemed so safe, so easy to love. She loved him as one would a father. It was *his* love for her that drove their union. When he made his vows in the chapel at Snape, his eyes welled with tears. She had never seen a man cry before, had thought them incapable of it. How little she knew back then, how little of men, how little of the world.

Her thoughts circle, crows about a tree.

Gardiner stops his drone and a boy begins to sing. His voice is clear as diamonds and reverberates in the small space, lifting her up, away from her cares. The King's hand reaches for hers and she opens her eyes to look at him, seeing that he, too, is transported by the music. A small smile moves over his mouth and for a moment he is not the King, just an ill-judged old man.

Could she love him as a father? At times she feels she could. But what of those moments when he is like an overgrown infant, in a tantrum? What of the other side of him: the blustery, vain pig-headed man with a vicious streak? She cannot reconcile all the different parts of him into one person. Is he thinking of the marriage vows he has made five times before?

The white cloth is flung over the altar and the paten of bread placed on it, then the chalice. A knot of panic tightens in her and she becomes aware of a small voice buried deep within shouting out, like a voice in a dream that makes no sound.

The host is raised.

Her eyes follow it.

The bell chimes, a thin high ring, the blessing murmured.

. . . *corpore Christi.*

A chink and trickle as the chalice is filled—the bell again.

Eyes up.

. . . *sanguine Christi.*

Does the King truly believe that in this moment the wine has *become* the blood of Christ? She cannot accept that a man of such acute intelligence could believe it so.

Of all the things they have talked about, they have never fully discussed their faith. It is assumed that she believes as he does. But how *does* he believe? Mass that was recently in English is now in Latin as before. You could not tell from this service that there had been ten years of change and struggle.

The King is becoming conservative in his old age. The thurible swings, chattering faintly on its chain, drenching the room in a new cloud of incense. Perhaps he is afraid to meet his maker knowing the atrocities that have been committed in the name of the English Church—his Church, his name.

How great a weight it must be for him to bear, so much greater than her hypocrite's cloak.

He is slipping back—back to the old ways. You could bring him back.

She opens her lips and Gardiner presses the host onto her tongue. It sticks to the arid roof of her mouth, tastes yeasty. She longs for something to quench her thirst, imagines snatching the chalice from the bishop's hands and swigging it back—but then the idea that it is blood fixes itself in her head.

She slaps her imagination down—it is just wine, sanctified perhaps, but wine nonetheless.

They stand. Katherine's head spins, everything is momentarily black. She grabs hold of the prie-dieu to stop herself falling and can hear the King make his vows, distantly, as if from the other end of a tunnel.

Before she knows it she is repeating Gardiner's words like a parakeet . . . *ego tibi fidem* . . . the ring is pushed onto her finger and the King presses his damp mouth to hers.

She shuts her eyes tight.

It is done.

She is Queen.

She turns to face the guests all smiling. She wonders what they are thinking behind those smiles, whether they are thinking of little Catherine Howard screaming down the long gallery not forty feet from where they now stand, or the Cleves wedding and how Henry could barely spit out his vows, or Anne Boleyn waiting for the swordsman to arrive from France to decapitate her.

Meg isn't smiling, she's not even looking. She is listening intently to something that Elizabeth whispers in her ear. The two of them sit hand in hand seeming quite enchanted with each other, in the way girls can be. You wouldn't think there was such a difference in age between them, for Meg is a slight little thing and seems barely a day over fourteen whereas everything about Elizabeth belies her tender years. It is a warming sight for Katherine. After all, they are sisters of sorts now and Meg needs a companion to drag her away from her misery.

The women cluster around her, simmering with excitement.

Henry takes her elbow. "They will all want your favor, now you are Queen."

It feels like a warning.

20

The wedding banquet is a whirl of color and sound. Acrobats fly through the air, a fire-eater swallows a ball of flame, a juggler flips onto his hands. He is juggling with his feet, and musicians play with unceasing jollity. The King claps along beside Katherine, feeding her occasional titbits with his fingers, as if she is his favorite hound.

Surrey strides up to the dais, standing before them to recite:

> The golden gift that Nature did thee give
> To fasten friends and feed them at thy will
> With form and favor, taught me to believe
> How thou art made to show her greatest skill . . .

He catches Katherine's eye. Seeing Surrey reminds her of the absence of her brother, who is back at the Borders. Such irony that he isn't here to witness the greatest triumph of the Parrs. He is the only one of them who would truly appreciate it, but she is partly glad he is not gloating beside her.

> . . . Whose hidden virtues are not so unknown
> But lively dooms might gather at the first:
> Where beauty so her perfect seed hath sown
> Of other graces follow needs there must . . .

She notices a look on Hertford's face as he watches Surrey. It betrays something deeper than dislike. It is easy to forget how much hatred circulates in this place where everyone takes such pains to appear polite. The Howards and the Seymours sowed their hatred over the fall of Surrey's first cousin Anne Boleyn and the rise of her successor Jane Seymour.

They have vied for position for a decade and Hertford holds the trump in his nephew Prince Edward. But the Howard veins course with royal blood and Surrey will one day be the head of the family: Duke of Norfolk. It is a fight that cannot be lost or won.

> ... Now certes, lady, since all this is true,
> That from above thy gifts are thus elect,
> Do not deface them then with fancies new,
> Nor change of minds let not thy mind infect,
> But mercy him, thy friend, that doth thee serve,
> Who seeks alway thine honor to preserve.

Henry claps heartily at this. "Bravo, Surrey!" and turning to Hertford asks, "Do you not have a ditty in praise of your new Queen, Ned?"

Hertford flushes and forces a smile onto his face before offering a convoluted excuse, but the King isn't listening.

Dish after dish is placed before them, each one more elaborate and richer than the last. Katherine picks at her food, trying not to think about what comes next. She sluices back another gulp of wine. She is giddy with it already.

Prince Edward is paraded in, followed by a small entourage. Everyone stands, necks craned, to get a rare glimpse of this small boy kitted out in a jeweled doublet like his father, whom he will replace one day. The King puffs up with pride as his son recites a passage from Livy recounting the Sabine wedding. Katherine wonders whose idea that was and whether anything is meant by it: whichever way you look at it, the Sabines did not have a smooth path to matrimony.

When he is finished, the King praises his son. "Only six and fluent in Livy. You are a wonder, my boy."

Hertford gives Surrey a derisive stare, as if to say, for all Surrey's blue blood and poetry, it is he who holds the trump in this boy, his nephew, the heir.

"Come and congratulate your new mother," the King commands.

Edward steps forward and bows. He is a stiff little thing with a mouth so pinched it seems incapable of a smile.

Katherine stoops down to his level, taking both his hands. "I am glad to be your mother, Edward. I hope to see you more at court if your father permits it."

"I will do as I am bid," he replies, in a clipped little voice.

A cheer goes up as a sugar galleon floating on a sea of mercury is brought in. Edward's eyes widen but that is his only sign of anything resembling joy. A taper is lit and its confectionery cannons are fired with a series of almighty cracks.

Meg jumps at each, blanching in fear. Katherine overhears Elizabeth tell her she will have to learn to hide her fears if she is to survive in this place—only nine, and already so perceptive. Edward is clearly not the only bright Tudor child. The Prince is led away.

The boards are moved back and Lady Mary starts the dancing, partnered by Hertford. They move cautiously about the floor in a polite pavane. Nan Stanhope is partnered by Wriothesley and cannot hide her disdain for him. Anne, who has carried a worried look about with her all day, at last drops her cares to dance with her husband. They coo at each other like newlyweds. Katherine suppresses her envy.

There will be no dancing, no ordinary pleasures, for the new Queen.

The tempo lifts. Elizabeth pulls Meg away from the table and into the row of dancers, Elizabeth lined up with the men, Meg opposite, seeming not to care that all eyes are on them. The keenest mothers hustle their sons forward to dance with either one of them, causing slant-eyed looks from some of the other maids.

Elizabeth trips coquettishly through the steps while Meg looks a little bewildered and entirely captivated by her new stepsister, unable to drag her eyes away from the girl as she is spun from one boy to the next, then back to Elizabeth, who each time whispers something in her ear before being twirled away again. It occurs to Katherine that Meg could join Elizabeth in the country at Ashridge. It would get her away from court.

Elizabeth's maid arrives and hustles her up to the dais to bid goodnight to her father. The King barely looks at her but Katherine leans across the table and kisses the girl's cheek, saying, "Your father wants you to return to Ashridge tomorrow."

Elizabeth can't quite hide the look of disappointment that flickers over her face.

"He worries for your health here at court."

This is a lie. He worries only for Prince Edward's health. Elizabeth is barely ever mentioned.

"I will send Meg to join you there soon. Would that please you?"

Elizabeth nods with a smile.

If nothing else, Katherine thinks, she will try to be a mother to these lost children.

Katherine nods to the cup-bearer, who refills her goblet. It is gold, heavy as the holy chalice. She feels the future bear down on her. In a minute the King will stand and take his leave and she will be carried off by her ladies, to be made ready for her marriage bed.

A server offers a plate of fancies. She takes one, biting into it. The sugary taste pervades her mouth, unpleasantly sweet. She would like to spit it discreetly into her napkin, but she is the Queen and too many eyes are on her. She will have to get used to that; nothing she does will go unnoticed on from now on.

She takes another gulp of wine.

The King stands to leave.

21

The door to the Queen's rooms bursts open and a crowd of excited ladies spills in, chattering and colorful as the birds they have in the aviary at Whitehall. They flutter around, falling over each other to curry favor with the new Queen.

Even that sourpuss Nan Stanhope sports a smile as she pours wine into Katherine's cup. Dot wouldn't trust her as far as she could throw her. Earlier she overheard her say, in a voice bitter as ragwort, that Katherine was nothing but a jumped-up country housewife.

Katherine bids them all leave, so that just Meg and Anne and Dot remain. She lifts her own hood off, catching a strand of hair in one of the jewels, wincing. Anne has to cut it away with the embroidery scissors. Dot takes the hood, heavy as a bag of potatoes. There are new raw welts above Katherine's ears where the wires have pinched. She stands, arms out, while the three of them dismantle the dress, layer by layer: overgown, sleeves, bodice, kirtle.

She chats, commenting on the feast. "I wish you could have seen the sugar galleon, Dot, it was truly magnificent." She doesn't complain, not about the heat, nor the welts, nor the blisters where her shoes have rubbed, nor the places where the dress has cut into her skin. All she asks is to be sponged down with cool water.

She has a high color in her cheeks and seems tipsy from the wine, as she is laughing and spirited, ribbing them all. It should be them teasing her, given she is going to her marriage bed, but they can barely muster a laugh between them.

"What are all these long faces?" She pats her sister on the back.

Anne mumbles a reply with a fleeting smile.

"To think, I could soon be carrying a royal Prince in my belly."

It isn't the thought of the baby in her belly—which is a good thought, Dot supposes—but the way it would get there. Dot may not know much about it but she knows enough to imagine that huge stinking man, huffing and puffing on top of her.

And what if there is no Prince? After two marriages, producing not a single living infant and Katherine thirty-one already . . . Dot packs away that thought. She is sure that it is on Anne's mind too, judging by her grim expression.

"You seem to like your new stepsister," Katherine says to Meg.

The girl bursts into a blush, trying to hide her face in the lappets of her hood.

"I'm glad. She is a sweet girl, but her father doesn't favor her. She is to be packed off back to the country tomorrow."

Meg seems to fold in on herself, hearing this.

"I plan to work on him, though. It would be good for her to be at court with her family. Or perhaps you could pay her a visit."

"I should like that." Meg stifles a yawn and Dot notices her surreptitiously pass some food, that is hidden in her sleeve, to Rig, who scurries to the corner with it.

It seems improbable to Dot that Meg would really like to leave and go to some girl she hardly knows.

"Tired?" Anne asks her.

She nods. "Where am I to sleep tonight?"

"The maids' room with the rest of the girls, I suppose," Anne says.

"Let her stay here. I shall not be using this bed, after all." Katherine forces out a little laugh.

"And what of me?" Dot feels all of a sudden out on a limb. "Where am I to sleep?"

"You will sleep in the anteroom of the marital bedchamber," replies Anne. "It is rather drafty but there is a hearth and logs. That way you can hear the Queen if she rings. I will leave this." She picks up a small silver bell, ringing it.

It sounds like the bell they ring in chapel when the bread is supposed to turn itself into Christ's flesh. Katherine has picked up Rig and is cradling him and cooing at him as if he's a baby. They drape a black satin robe over her fine silk nightdress and her sister hands her a pomander of lavender and orange oil.

Katherine brings it to her face, inhaling it with a sigh. "I am ready."

She makes for the door, but abruptly she returns, to grab her cup, swigging back the dregs of her wine and flinging it away. It lands with a loud clatter against the paneling. Then she marches from the room with Anne and Meg following, looking miserable as mourners at a funeral, to deliver Katherine to her marriage bed. Dot herself had changed the linens on the vast bed, sprinkled them with fragrant water and layered it up with silk covers and cushions all newly embroidered with the entwined initials of the new King and Queen.

She shivers and starts to tidy the chamber, picking up the cup from the corner where it was thrown. There is a streak of red wine on the wall hangings. The cup is badly dented and one of the jewels in it has shattered.

She collects the washing into a basket, stacks the dirty cups and plates, and snuffs out the candles, breathing in the churchy smell of the beeswax, so much nicer than the tallow they use downstairs that sputters and smokes and stinks as it burns.

Picking up the ewer of dirty water, she balances the dishes in her other arm, and leaves the room, kicking the door shut behind her with a foot. One of the King's pages is passing in the corridor.

"Begging your pardon," she mumbles, adding, "sir," because, though he is a good five years younger than her, he must be the son of a knight at the very least, if he serves the King.

"What is it?" He doesn't try to hide his impatience and looks at her as if she's something dirty on the sole of his shoe.

"I don't know what to do with this." She holds out the dented goblet.

"Did you do this?" He snatches it, inspecting it.

"No, sir, it was an accident. The Queen . . ."

"So you wish for the Queen to take the blame for your clumsiness." His voice is blunt and he looks beyond her as if he might catch something nasty just by meeting her eye.

"No, I didn't mean—"

"I've heard she'll protect *you* no matter what. I wonder why."

He caresses the cup's sharp rim with the pad of his thumb. "I shall have to take it to the chamberlain and he won't be happy." At this he walks off, saying over his shoulder, "I've got my eye on you, Dorothy Fownten."

She wonders how he knows her name, making a mental note to avoid him in future. She can look after herself—as tough as old boots her father used to say—but people at court don't behave in the normal way and she knows that here you can have enemies and not even know it.

The privy kitchen is dark, the smell and the heat of it intense, roasted meat battling with the rotten stink of the pig bucket and the smell of the pottage that always makes her stomach turn.

The remains of the sugar galleon sit like a skeleton on the table, with a couple of the kitchen lads picking at it. Some of the servants have gathered for a drink and are feasting on a platter of leftovers, laughing and joking. Betty is among them but Dot slides by, hoping not to be seen. She doesn't feel quite right for, though she is a servant as they are, she is not treated as one of them—except by Betty. But Betty likes anyone who's prepared to listen to her rantings. Besides, she can't linger in case she is needed upstairs.

She stacks the plates on the dirties' table and empties the ewer in the drain, noticing William Savage, still at his desk, scratching away with his pen in a pool of candlelight.

Her heart makes a somersault.

"You," he calls out.

She turns round, to see who's behind her, but there's no one there. "Me?"

"Yes, you." He is grinning.

She thinks he might be laughing at her for some reason and imagines with a sinking feeling that she has soot on her face, or worse. She notices a single dimple has formed on one cheek, giving him a sweet lopsided look. She wants to gaze at him, drink him in with her eyes, but dares not and looks instead at her hands, wishing they were small and fine like a lady's and not the great big ugly things they are.

"What is your name?"

"Dorothy Fownten." Her voice croaks.

"Come closer, I can't hear you."

She takes a step towards him and says her name again, a little louder.

"That is a pretty name. Like the maidens in stories. The Lády Dorothy awaits her knight."

She thinks he's teasing her but his grin is gone and is replaced with a look that digs right into her.

"But I am never called anything but Dot."

He gives a little laugh, which makes her feel small and silly. "Like a full stop."

Dot doesn't know what he means by that, so says nothing and keeps looking down at her hands.

"I am William Savage."

"William Savage," she echoes, as if it is the first time she has heard it.

"You serve the Queen, do you not?"

"I do." She risks a brief glance at him before returning to the minute inspection of her fingernails.

"And I suppose you are about to tell me you must return to her chambers?"

Dot nods.

"Off you go then, or she will miss you." He turns back to his papers.

She can hear the scratch of his quill as she walks away, floating up the stairs, a throb in her chest as if Cook has got in there with an egg-beater.

She fetches her things, taking them into the anteroom, not more than a corridor really, unrolling her pallet and setting it down where it is warmest by the embers of the fire. She curls up, wrapping her arms about herself, unable to even imagine how it would be to have his arms around her.

She creates pictures in her head of him, that single dimple, the cleft in his chin, his inky fingers ... *Like a full stop*. She wonders what he meant by that. Rig whines. He is crouched outside the door to the great bedchamber, his nose pressed tight to the crack at the bottom of it.

She can hear muffled grunts and moans beyond, animal noises. The King is a man as well as a king, she reminds herself. As if she could forget. The sounds become louder, more urgent, and there is a crash. She wonders if she should go in, if something is wrong. Katherine would surely ring the bell. Then there is a burst of laughter and more groaning. She cups her ears with her palms but the noise won't stop. Rig begins to whine.

She shushes him, and seeing his sad cocked head, she pats her bed.

He scampers over and creeps under the blanket, tucking himself into her for comfort.

"William Savage," she whispers into the dog's warm fur. "Will Savage. Bill Savage. Mistress Savage, Dorothy Savage."

22

The bell rings early, a silvery sound that creeps into Dot's sleep. She gets herself up but hesitates before the chamber door, anxious, remembering those sounds from the night before. She cannot shake off her fear of the King.

She was never a scaredy-cat; as a little girl she was always the first to mount the unbroken pony or catch the angry dog, even when the boys wouldn't, but she *is* afraid of the King. You never know when he's going to burst out in anger, and everyone creeps and grovels around him. She's glad to be a nobody, too small to even be seen.

She hears Katherine's voice respond to her soft knock, and creeps in, relieved to find her alone. She spots another door on the far side and supposes it must lead to the King's rooms. Katherine is out of the bed and standing wrapped in a coverlet, by the window, looking out at the palace gardens below. It is early and the sun is still low, shining behind her, making it seem as if she wears a halo like the Virgin.

"Good morning, Dot. It is a fine morning, is it not?"

Dot still can't see her face properly for the brightness of the sun, but her voice is calm and has the sound of a smile in it.

"It is . . . madam." She stumbles over the new address.

"It will take time for you to become accustomed to all this." She sweeps her arm in an arc towards the bed. "I can see your concern. Don't worry. He is just a man beneath all the gilding . . . and I have had two husbands before—I know what men are like."

Dot can't help but think of Murgatroyd.

She wonders what Katherine is thinking but it is impossible to know.

138

"I need something to wear." Katherine hands over a crumpled pile of fabric, her nightclothes, which Dot hasn't noticed until then. She unravels them, holding them up, seeing that the fine chemise is ripped from top to bottom, torn right through the beautiful embroidered flowers Meg took weeks to craft.

Dot cannot imagine how something like that could happen between a husband and wife. To her it is as if the Queen herself has been torn, and not just her shift, as if the fine fabric is her very skin. But Katherine seems to think nothing of it.

Dot recalls how carefully Meg had drawn the design and the trouble she'd had finding thread of the perfect green—Tudor green for the King. It would be impossible to mend, the ivory silk is so precious. She herself had cut the cloth—it had been thick and creamy, resisting the scissor blades—and she had stitched its edges together, imagining stupidly that it would be a nightgown for a perfect romantic union. She fingers the fabric, noticing a drop of blood on the pale silk.

"The King is a passionate man." Katherine speaks plainly, as if she can see into Dot's thoughts. There is a tiny sneer to her mouth. "Make sure no one hears of this. The gossips would make quite a meal of it."

There are too many secrets in this place, Dot is thinking as she leaves with her pile of evidence. People whisper in corners, swapping information. But no one notices Dot, who moves around as if she's invisible. Even that page from the previous night who said he had his eye on her wouldn't be able to pick her out in a line of common maids. If she cared to listen she could find out more about the court intrigues than she would ever know what to do with.

She returns to her mistress with a clean silk chemise and another black robe. She understands that things must appear to be seamless, for there are eyes and ears everywhere and even Queens can be easily got rid of.

"What I would really love is a scalding bath to soak in."

"Shall I prepare one, madam?"

"I don't think there's time. I have people." She sighs. "Endless people . . . It is quite relentless, Dot."

Dot wonders how it is that even the Queen can't have a bath if she wishes it.

Katherine holds out her hand for Dot to pass the clean shift and robe. There is a purple bruise on her upper arm.

"You don't want me to—"

"No, I can manage. That will be all."

Dot turns to leave.

Katherine adds, "Keep an eye on Meg for me, won't you?"

"Yes, madam. I always do. Meg is like a—" She stops herself, feeling uncomfortable saying out loud that Meg is like a sister. Now Lady Latymer is the Queen it seems wrong somehow to say such a thing.

"I know you do. You have always been so kind to her . . ." She looks for a moment out of the window where a couple of gardeners are trying to shoo a deer out of the vegetable garden. "I sometimes ask myself what it is that ails her so. I know there have been things . . ." She lets her words drift unsaid. "I would have thought she'd be . . . well . . . better by now."

Dot feels her secret weighing down on her; she wants to tell Katherine what really happened at Snape, but what good would that do? Anyway, she promised Meg and so she will keep her mouth shut—as she has these last six years. She will keep her mouth shut about everything. She knows how to keep a secret. And around here that's more important than ever because anything can be turned into trouble.

23

Ampthill Castle, Bedfordshire, October 1543

Daylight struggles to reach into the chamber, where courtiers are scattered in clusters. Old Mary Wootten reads aloud to a pair of women. The three of them, wrapped up in their outdoor clothes, sit beside the drafty window to make the most of the light.

Nearby a gaggle of girls puffs through a series of dance steps with Will Sommers mimicking their moves, making it hard for them to concentrate without giggling. Meg hovers with her back to the wall, too shy to fully join them.

Katherine and her sister sit beside the hearth. It doesn't draw properly, but despite the smoke making their eyes smart, the idea of opening the window and allowing in more cold air is anathema.

"This place is horribly damp." Anne signals to one of the pages to stoke the fire. "My gown still feels like wet clay. Have you looked behind the hangings? The walls are moldering away."

"Wasn't the Queen sent here when she was first ousted?" Katherine absently strokes Rig, who is snuggled on her lap. Between themselves the sisters often still refer to Henry's first wife thus, through force of habit—she was Queen for twenty-four years, after all.

"I believe so, poor woman. The place she was sent next was far worse."

Katherine looks around to see if anyone has overheard them. "I don't suppose we should really talk about her."

They sit in silence, surrounded by the bustle and clamor of the room.

"I long for a little privacy." Katherine speaks quietly. "Not to have to constantly watch what I say."

A clerk approaches with some papers for her to sign. She scans them. The clerk hovers, swaying from foot to foot.

"I can assure you, madam, that all is correct." He dips a quill, proffering it for her, unable to quite hide his impatience as she reads on.

"That's as may be, but I'd be a fool to sign anything I hadn't read"—she glances up at him—"don't you think?"

He dithers, seeming not to know whether to withdraw the quill. A drip falls from the nib, leaving a glossy black spot on the floor.

Eventually Katherine takes the pen, making her mark, and returns the papers to the clerk with a smile of thanks.

One of the King's ushers has arrived and is waiting his turn, stepping forward as the clerk departs.

"I am come to convey the King's apologies to you, madam. He is indisposed and will be supping alone tonight."

"Please convey my best wishes to His Majesty. Tell him I will pray to the Lord for his swift recovery." A feeling of lightness comes over her.

Henry has been incapacitated by his ulcerating leg for several days now. That is why they are all still at this godforsaken place, when they should have moved on a week ago.

When the usher has gone she winks at her sister. "We can sup in my rooms."

As long as Henry ails she may have to negotiate his foul temper but in return she has a welcome respite from the marriage bed. When she is obliged to share his bed, she shuts her eyes and imagines he is Thomas—Thomas's hands gripping at her flesh, Thomas's muscled body on her, Thomas's groans. She lives in terror of crying out his name, yet is unable to banish him from her thoughts. When tears well in her eyes, Henry mistakes them for tears of desire. His delight sickens her.

"That clerk looked as if he'd wet himself, he wriggled so." Anne rubs her hands over the fire. "He must have been late sending those papers out."

"None of them can bear that I insist on reading everything I put my mark to."

"You are so like Mother. I remember her saying: *Never sign anything unless you . . .*"

Katherine joins in, ". . . *know exactly what it is and have read it twice through.*"

"I wish Mother had lived to see you now." Anne looks wistful.

Two servants are lighting candles, filling the space with a shimmering glow.

"I'm sure she's looking down on us." Katherine flicks her eyes upward. "But I do sometimes miss an ordinary kind of life, Anne. The hours in the still room, making up remedies. Afternoons in the kitchens, overseeing the salting of fish, the bottling of fruits—managing the estates. There is someone to do everything for me wherever I am now: a chancellor, an apothecary, stewards, ushers, clerks, scribes, cup-bearers, chamberers, physicians." She counts them off on her fingers. "All strangers."

They hear the crunch of hooves on the gravel outside. "It's Udall. Huicke *will* be pleased." From the window Katherine can make out the visitor dismounting in a spill of torchlight, throwing his distinctive laugh into the evening, Huicke already rushing down the steps to greet him.

"Good," says Anne. "Things always liven up when he's at court."

Katherine calls over one of the pages, instructing him to invite Huicke and Udall to join her in her rooms for the evening.

As she stands to leave the entire room sinks to its knees. She wishes she could tell them to stay upright, to pretend for once that she is not the Queen.

Udall entertains them at supper with his mimicry, playing both parts of a conversation between Gardiner and Wriothesley that has them creased with laughter. They are a small group: Katherine and her sister, Cat Brandon and Meg, with the two men—a trusted few.

Once the meal is cleared, they move to the fireplace, spreading out on cushions, the women loosening their stays and removing their cumbersome hoods. Udall sits with his back resting against the wall, Huicke leaning against him, his hand resting on his lover's thigh. In this company they are safe, but they could both hang for the peculiarities of their desire if the wind were to blow in the wrong direction.

Udall refills their cups, raising his: "To change."

"To the future," says Cat.

Huicke clanks his cup to Katherine's. She swigs back the warm sweet wine and listens to Udall tell of a recent solar eclipse in the Low Countries.

He describes the arrival of evening at midday, how the birds fell silent as the light eked away: the blood-red sky, the black disc of sun haloed in flame, the flash of light at its lip heralding the glorious new dawn.

"What can it be if it is not a sign that the great changes are crystallizing?" Udall waves his hands animatedly. "Why else would God extinguish the day with such drama, if not to show he is casting a new light on humanity?"

Huicke throws a log on the fire. Without speaking, they watch how the flames lick around it, crackling, catching the bark, spitting sparks upwards.

"And listen to this," continues Udall to his enthralled audience. "I know of an astronomer from Poland—Copernicus—who says the Sun is the still point around which the universe turns."

Katherine cannot make sense of such a statement. "Why are we all not giddy with turning if the Earth spins round the Sun?" Her question provokes laughter but they all have the same question on their lips.

"Surely we would all fall off," says Cat.

"This Copernicus fellow, is he fond of wine?" says Anne, smirking. It is she who is drunk and slurring. Katherine, too, feels lightheaded as they all dissolve into laughter.

All except Udall: "Don't you see what this means?" He has become serious. "You may well think it all a joke but I see it as a symbol of our quiet revolution. We have been wrong about the very essence of the universe for centuries and now is the time for change. The heavens are newly mapped for our Reformation."

Katherine's mirth is staunched by the profound sense of a whole new world coming into being.

"But it will not be straightforward. English Bibles are being removed from our churches. You don't see it here at court"—his eyes flash, reflecting the flames—"but out in the real world there is a return to prayers for the dead and relics, holy water, all the old superstitions and the Mass fed to the congregation in Latin that nobody understands."

"Luther is still tolerated but Calvin is now forbidden, even at court," says Huicke.

"Then we must work to keep the gospel in English," says Katherine. This belief runs deep. For her the old religion is dark and corrupt, championed by brutes like Murgatroyd and the dissembling Gardiner. "I can bring it up with my husband." She knows she must negotiate the fragile balance of Henry's volatile moods and whims as deftly as a tightrope walker. A slip in the wrong direction might easily lead to a fall.

"That's something, but there's more to it." Udall is firm.

"How so?" Anne looks confused.

Cat articulates what they are all thinking: "Isn't the desire for all to read and understand the gospel for themselves at the heart of what we all hold dear?"

Udall leans forward. "We must rediscover the word of God, just as Copernicus has seen the universe anew, we must look more deeply at the interpretations."

"I don't understand," says Anne.

"Rome has muddied the water for centuries for its own ends. Think of this: *hoc est corpus meum*—this is my body—more familiar to you than your own names. We accept it is symbolic. But have you considered the finer points of translation?"

Katherine looks toward Meg, in the grip of Udall's words, the light from the fire playing on her pale face.

"Calvin interprets *est* as 'signifies' whereas Luther translates it as 'is.' This *signifies* my body is not the same as this *is* my body." He slaps his hand to his knee. "*That* is why Calvin's works are forbidden, because they offer a new truth. The Catholics don't want freedom of interpretation. What they want is to keep people ignorant so they can be controlled."

Katherine realizes in that moment that she has never fully understood what it means to reform religion, to forge new beliefs. The break with Rome and all its corruption, the gospel in English, this is just a small part, just one color of thread in a whole tapestry that tells the story of mankind.

Udall is suggesting more subtle ideas, which force her to question things she had never thought to doubt. She can see now, the responsibility that lies behind a desire to read and think for oneself and not be spoon-fed dogma in a dying language. Her head throbs with new ideas—a vision of a pristine world.

"Everything must be questioned, then?"

"Yes." Udall points to her. "It is our mission."

They all sink into their own musings until Huicke stands, shaking his head like a wet dog. "It's a cloudless night. Let's go up to the roof and look at the stars."

They follow the two men up a winding staircase. It is so narrow Katherine's skirts brush against the damp walls and she wonders how Huicke and Udall know the secret passages of this remote place. A low door opens. They duck down through it onto a wooden gantry that leads to a crenellated turret. The air is sharp and cold, the sky awash with stars and a fat moon watches them, six miniature figures, below. They gaze upward, whirring with their own private thoughts, silenced by the sheer extent of the heavens.

"Did you see it?" cries Anne. "A shooting star."

"I did!" Meg's face is the image of wonder.

Anne strokes the girl's hair. "It is a sign that good things are coming to you."

Katherine wishes she shared her sister's indefatigable optimism.

She wanders away to the other side of the turret, pressing her back against the cold wall and closing her eyes, imagining the Earth revolving around the invisible Sun, until she feels its spin.

Udall has lit a fire in her that is sparking ideas in her head. *In exordium eram Vox . . . quod Vox eram Deus*: In the beginning was the Word . . . and the Word was God.

She understands. Language and meaning are everything. God resides in interpretation. She thanks her mother for insisting she was properly educated. The relentless plowing through Lily's Latin Grammar now has an application.

Her thoughts are full of it all, but Thomas sits like a ghost at the edge of her mind. She imagines him grappling with the same ideas of reform in his faraway court, but this is fancy, for he is far more likely to be spending his evenings chasing foreign beauties than pondering ideas of religion. She is clutched with shame at her own petty jealousy but the thought of him loving another tears her apart. Forcing her mind back to her theological contortions, she resolves to commit him to the past, finding peace in that.

"Penny for your thoughts." It is Udall who has left the others to join her.

"My head is teeming. I couldn't begin to say."

"There are books that would interest you. I can have them sent."

"Books?" She feels a whisper of fear at the idea of such ideas on paper. Talk creates only hearsay, but words in ink . . . well, that is proof. But the tug of the new is irresistible. "Do you not think it too great a risk?"

"You'd be surprised. Banned books can be found in all corners of the court. The court is not the wider world. Blind eyes are turned—it is nothing unusual."

"No one must know."

"Trust me." He smiles.

Udall may be wild and always brushing up against some scandal or other, but Katherine does trust him. He treats her as a woman rather than the Queen—there is honesty in that.

The very idea of the books he talks of fixes itself in her mind. She has an urgent compulsion to see them, feel their paper beneath her fingers, smell their ink, read them for herself.

There is that hidden part of her, so much at odds with the sensible Katherine she shows to the world—a recklessness that will not be quelled. It is the woman who might have thumbed her nose at the court and eloped with Thomas Seymour—though didn't, all that emotion quashed.

Besides, she is protected by the King's love. And doesn't he love to hear her talk? Isn't he fascinated by it all, too, when he says, "I love this mind of yours, Kit. Tell me more of what you think"?

They have often talked deep into the night, discussing the Six Articles of Faith, the doctrine that is undoing all the changes, that insists on transubstantiation, that would burn those who refute it. She never mentions Calvin but they talk freely of Luther. Henry, equally curious, mines his knowledge of Greek and Hebrew, applying it to Luther's theories.

She has sensed his beliefs wavering.

"True meaning lies in the heart," he has said.

She imagines herself as the catalyst that will crystallize the King's beliefs, the beacon leading him to fully embrace the new faith. She thinks of it as her mission, her penance, the act that will absolve her sins.

He is slipping back—back to the old ways. You could bring him back.

When she is next alone with Henry she tells of Copernicus and the new map of the universe, the world spinning about the Sun.

"I have heard of this new-fangled nonsense." He guffaws, sending out pungent clouds of foul breath, making her blench.

She must sit and smile and play the fool.

"You remind me of . . ." An unexpected cruel look scuds over his face. He doesn't say who she reminds him of.

Her sister once told her that Henry used to talk of theology deep into the night with Anne Boleyn.

I am different, she says to herself, I do not cast spells or whore myself as Anne Boleyn did.

Did Anne Boleyn really do all she was accused of? She died for it, but Katherine knows well enough that does not mean the accusations were true.

Despite her husband's public adoration, his gifts, his fondness, his apparent fascination with this mind of hers, Katherine's thoughts hide in the dark and tendrils of fear wrap invisibly round her.

Was he not also fascinated by Anne Boleyn and her ideas?

There is no escape from his dead Queens.

24

Tomorrow they leave for somewhere. All Dot knows is that it will be a day's ride. Meg is not to come with them, as she is to join Lady Elizabeth at Ashridge. Dot will miss her but it will get her away from the court, at least.

She makes a mental note of everything that has to be done: two riding habits to be brushed of mud; four shifts to be got from the laundry, if they are dry; something to be done with Katherine's purple gown, which is smeared with thick white dust that will not be budged with brushing. She must clean Meg's outdoor shoes and find the missing silk slipper that has probably been chewed and hidden by Rig; stitch the hole in the Queen's new kirtle . . .

She tidies and sorts, putting things into piles. She is getting used to all this moving about—the packing and the unpacking, getting the gist of a new house every few days.

William Savage travels with them. He is part of the Queen's retinue now, as is she. It doesn't mean he talks to her, though, but he is usually to be found somewhere near the kitchens, counting on his inky fingers and writing in his ledger.

Once she found him late at night in a music room in some house or other—there have been so many, she forgets—playing on the virginals. She tucked herself behind the door, unseen, to listen. Of all the music she had heard at court, and that is a good deal, from the best musicians too, she had never heard anything like this. She closed her eyes and imagined she was in Heaven itself and surrounded by angels.

She has not heard him play since, though she sometimes searches late at night for another music room—saying, if she is stopped by an usher or one of the guards, that she is lost.

Dot picks up the big basin that the Queen uses for washing, straining under its weight, heaving it down the stairs to empty it in the squillery, hoping to find William there. It is mid-morning and that is the time he does the accounts. She sees him bent over his desk and her breath is caught a moment.

"Dot," she hears, as she passes him, thinking she is imagining it, for he never says anything to her, not ever. Not since the day the Queen was married when he asked her name.

She turns.

He rises, his chair scraping on the flags, and beckons her to follow him, pressing a finger to his lips.

Placing the basin down on the floor, she walks behind him into the grain store, without a word.

This is her moment.

Her heart taps fast, like a woodpecker.

She is not quite sure what to expect, a kiss, a proposition, a cuddle—anything will do.

The grain store is dark and it smells dry and yeasty and summery, taking her back to the smell of her pa after a hard day's thatching. When her eyes become accustomed to the dim light she can see the grain sacks, like a row of kneeling monks in the far corner where William is crouched, reaching behind one of them for something she can't see.

He stands and takes her by the arm, pulling her close. Breath held, she readies herself for the kisses she has imagined for ever.

"I have something for you to give to the Queen." His mouth is so close to her ear that she can feel the tickle of his whisper. "You must not breathe a word of this to anyone." He presses a package into her hand. "No one must see it. Hide it beneath your skirts."

"But what is it?"

"It is a book."

"But what—?"

"You want to be of service to the Queen, don't you?"

She nods.

He hesitates. "You do know this could be dangerous, Dorothy Fownten? Will you still do it?"

"I will do anything for the Queen," she says, thinking, I will do anything for you too, William Savage.

"I suspected as much." He watches as she lifts her skirts and tucks the book under her kirtle. "You are a good girl, Dot."

And that is it.

They are out in the corridor again, he back at his desk and she heaving the heavy basin off the floor. There has been no kiss, no fond word. But as she passes by again, having emptied the basin, he gives her a look. It is no ordinary look. It is a look that comes with having a shared secret.

That is the first book. When they finally arrive back at Whitehall some weeks later, there are more, several packages, and always the same subterfuge. But still there are no kisses. Somehow, though, the very stealth of it seems more, much more, intimate and draws an invisible circle around her and her ink-stained William Savage.

She wonders why it is that these books need be so secret. Sometimes at night when the Queen is asleep she lights the nub of a candle and opens one of them.

They are beautiful things with richly decorated covers, embossed in gold, but it is the words that fascinate her, black, dense and mysterious. She turns the stiff pages silently, feeling the dryness of them under the tips of her fingers, holding them to her face to breathe in the scent of them, dust and wood and the leathery smell of the tack room.

It is William's smell—a book smell. She finds the letters of her name, the letters she knows, a little crouched "d" here, a surprised "o" there, a tall "t" elsewhere, trying to fit them together, to make sense of them.

25

The clergy is out in full for Margaret Douglas's wedding—a big dynastic affair, everyone in their state regalia. St. James's Palace is buzzing with impressed ambassadors who will all be writing to their respective potentates of the marvelous marriage that will unite Scotland and England.

It is not the betrothal between Prince Edward and the infant Scottish Queen Mary that Henry had so desired, but it is the next best thing. The King's niece is marrying Matthew Stuart, the Earl of Lennox, who has only the baby Mary and the vacillating regent Arran between him and the throne of Scotland.

There will be some Scottish noses put out of joint by this, no doubt, particularly since Hertford sacked Edinburgh, burned it to the ground barely a month ago. Little else has been talked of in England—Arran on the run—and this wedding is the cherry on Henry's cake.

The floor clears as the bride and groom stand to dance and the Bassano brothers gather around to play for them. It was Will who introduced the Bassanos to court—they've done all right for themselves. Everyone around the Parr family has gone up in the world since Katherine's marriage, as if they have been filled with yeast and left on a warm shelf to rise.

Margaret's smile flashes. She is clearly bedazzled by her new husband.

"Look at them," says Anne, who is seated beside her with Elizabeth and Meg. "If ever I saw a love match."

Katherine sees how Margaret's hands can barely restrain themselves, taking any opportunity to touch her new husband, stroking his beardless face, squeezing his thigh, grabbing his wrist. Margaret is a flighty creature, too fond of romance, but Katherine has become close to her despite her headstrong ways and is glad to see her married.

She had seen the inside of the Tower for her unsanctioned liaison with one of the Howards. A girl so close to the throne must mind who she falls for. But this marriage is a happy match, that is clear, and Katherine is glad her friend is not being hitched to some rotten frog prince to gain back some lost amity with King François.

There is something about Lennox—the self-assurance, the swagger, the way he consumes his bride with his eyes, the way he grips her waist—that reminds her of someone else. Though she tries to staunch all thoughts of that person, she cannot help but put herself in Margaret's place, feeling those hands clasping her about the middle. It is a year since she last saw Thomas. She looks at her own hands—which, like the King's, are heavy with rings—and absently pushes the wedding ring half off and back on again. It scrapes her knuckle painfully.

She watches her husband sitting, relaxed, leaning to one side in his throne, ankle resting on his opposite knee, barely able to hide the smug satisfaction in his demeanor. He waves his hand about as he talks to one of the ambassadors, his own rings winking as they catch the light.

He is in rude health once more and no longer needs the wheeled contraption that was contrived to get him about his palaces when he was in too much pain to walk. He had been suffering greatly. She and Huicke had concocted a poultice for the ulcer on his leg and she had tenderly applied it daily, wrapping it in clean bandages, gagging at the reek of it.

Now he's better, Katherine is once more subjected to the nightly assaults. Still no seed germinates in her, despite all that. Henry continues to dote on her, has barely uttered a sharp word to her in their year of marriage, except in the bedchamber. But what goes on in there is not bound by ordinary convention.

The reluctance of his elderly body drives him into desperate rages for which he is pitifully sorry come the morning. Katherine's resilience prevails—Henry is not the first vicious man she has had in her bed. She rarely thinks of Murgatroyd these days, doesn't allow herself to remember how there were dangerous things about him that shamefully ignited her desire.

Henry wants another son. That is the source of his rage. When he fixes his pebble gaze on her, to ask, "So, wife, what news?" all she can do is lower her eyes and shake her head, a band of dread clamping itself around her empty belly.

The King is sharing a joke with Suffolk, who squats uncomfortably beside him. They watch the ladies dancing, pointing out little Mary Dudley who is thirteen and new at court. She is light as air on her feet, and slinks through the dull steps of the pavane, charming and knowing as a cat. Suffolk whispers something. They laugh and Suffolk makes a lewd pumping gesture with his right hand, which seems all the more grotesque in a man as old as he.

Katherine notices her sister is staring at her wrists, about to comment. She pulls her sleeves down to cover the purple bruises flowering there. Henry held her down last night, one fat hand over her mouth, spitting "whore, bitch" as he tried to find some life in his flaccid cock. She had shut her eyes tightly and begged the Lord for a son this time. When he was done, he had rolled off her and softly kissed each bruise, whispering, "Katherine, you are my own love."

They lit a candle afterwards and talked of faith, comparing Augustine's doctrines with Luther's, dissecting ideas. As ever, she carefully avoided any mention of Calvin and his notion of self-knowledge and knowledge of God being inseparable—something that has been on her mind much of late.

When they talk in this way she can feel Henry's fascination on her—it is something to have all the attention of such a man. It is a blessing and a curse, this marriage of hers. She occasionally senses a readiness in him to turn away from the old faith, back to the new. But she must be canny as a magician, and last night she had misjudged it.

"Might you be of the mind to consider relaxing the laws on English Bibles?" she had suggested, her tone light, while he stroked her hair. "Your subjects would surely benefit from reading the scriptures in their own tongue . . ."

He retracted his hand abruptly, a ring catching painfully on a strand of hair, his fascination gone in an instant. She knew immediately she had gone too far, silently admonishing herself for her lack of caution.

"And risk my people falling to heresy? You get above yourself, Katherine." All the tenderness had dissipated from him. "You are a *woman*. You could not possibly understand these things. What do you know of my subjects or their need for spiritual guidance?"

She understands these things as well as he, though she wouldn't dare contradict him. She understands his fear too—fear of following his heart with reform. She understands that the Emperor and the French King have been biting at his heels since he broke with Rome. Henry cannot bring himself to return to the Pope, to hand over his absolute power, but neither can he embrace the new faith fully. So England sits on the fence and people hustle in dark corners to push things one way or another, while Katherine must hold her tongue.

And now Henry has joined forces with the Emperor to fight the French. They are planning a twofold invasion: England from the north, the Emperor from the south.

He has wanted a war for some time, dreams of martial glory before decrepitude overcomes his vanity. She wonders what will happen to her when he has gone to fight his war—when the cat's away—will Gardiner and his Catholics make their move?

She catches Bishop Gardiner, deep in conversation with Wriothesley, snatch a glance at her. He looks swiftly askance making her feel, for an uncomfortable moment, that those black eyes have seen into her thoughts.

Cat Brandon approaches, a puppy in her arms, to take a seat beside Katherine. "I see he's got his eye on you." She means the Bishop. "Goodness only knows what those two are plotting."

Katherine raises her brow, saying nothing, and strokes the little dog. All of a sudden the animal jumps to the floor, scampering across the room.

Cat stands calling, "Gardiner, behave!"

The Bishop turns a furious glare towards her. "What is this?"

"I'm admonishing my puppy." Cat gives him a look of innocence, head tipped, eyes wide. "I named him after you."

Anne disguises a snort of laughter with a cough, mustering Elizabeth and Meg to catch the dog.

Gardiner makes a taut smile. "Most amusing."

"I was waiting for that," whispers Cat, returning to her seat. "Did you see his face?"

"You have some gall." Katherine stifles a smirk.

"He needed pulling down a peg or two." Cat smooths down her skirts. "We must all fight for our beliefs in whatever way we can. Let me tell you what I did to Wriothesley the other day. I approached him with a copy of *Psychopannychia*, asking if he would translate a passage for me."

"Calvin—you asked him to translate Calvin?" Katherine can't hide her shock.

"Yes, Calvin! I pressed the book into his hands. He held it as if its pages were infused with poison." Cat is enjoying herself. "'Where did you get this?' His voice went up an octave and his face turned from red to purple to gray. I told him I found it in a window alcove and that my Latin was so lacking I couldn't read it."

"How did he respond to that? He must know you read Latin."

"Apparently not. He fumbled and stuttered." She mimics Wriothesley: "'This book is . . . it is a wicked thing . . . it will infect your mind like the pox . . . I must take it . . . it is only good for burning.'"

Katherine admires Cat's fearlessness but Cat is not the Queen and doesn't have so far to fall. She knows well enough that until she gives Henry the son he desires, her position will always be precarious. Queens have been ousted before. She has carefully cultivated a veneer of ambiguity about her personal beliefs. As far as the wider court is concerned, she submits to her husband's views, as do all good wives, but in private she relishes Calvin and all the other forbidden books.

Udall had set up the deliveries, as he'd promised. His friend William Savage, who oversees the kitchen accounts, receives them in the squillery, hidden in among the groceries. Savage passes them on to Dot and so to Katherine and her women. She feels the constant forensic gaze of Gardiner and his crowd. They wouldn't dare touch her or her household while she basks in her husband's favor.

The girls are still chasing the puppy. Elizabeth beguiles a handsome young usher with a dazzling smile, enlisting him to help catch the animal. She and Meg whisper, heads together, watching him scramble about after the creature, who is taking it for a game.

When he finally returns, Elizabeth shakes her head at him, indicating that he should hand the dog to Meg. Meg now offers the boy a dazzling smile of her own. He blushes and moves to say something, but she cuts him off, turning her back, hooking an arm through Elizabeth's to walk away. The poor usher is left in confusion.

"You'd better start thinking of matches for Meg," says Anne, who has also been watching. "Before things get out of hand."

"Elizabeth's brought her out of her shell." She has been glad to see her stepdaughter revived by Elizabeth's spirited influence, but she can't let it go too far. "Henry's sending her back to Ashridge in a day or so. I'll keep Meg with us for a while."

"Probably for the best."

Katherine has been fostering her relationship as stepmother with Henry's two girls. Elizabeth has been writing to her. She had sent her a poem in both French and English, beautifully inscribed in a flawless hand, a formidable thing for a girl of ten.

Katherine has grown fond of Elizabeth and doesn't approve of the way her father keeps her at a distance. She'd sent Levina Teerlinc, a painter new to her household, to make a likeness of her. Now when Henry visits the Queen's rooms, he sees his younger daughter on the wall of the presence chamber, her delicate hands clutching a book, looking for all the world unmistakably a Tudor. Just her mother's dark hooded eyes betray her Boleyn blood.

Katherine's brother approaches. He has been dancing, is pink-cheeked and breathless, his shirt untied at the throat. He sits between his sisters and Katherine leans forward to tie it for him, telling him to sit still as if he is a child.

"What do you want, Will?" She knows him well enough to know he is about to ask a favor.

"It's about my divorce petition."

"Not this again. I have talked to him. He will not budge."

"It's one law for him and another for the rest of us." Will is angry and a little drunk.

"You've had your fair share of favors," says Anne. "You've been made a garter knight. There is no higher honor. And you are Earl of Essex. Kit does her best for us."

He stomps off to join Surrey across the room.

The King beckons Katherine and, trying to decipher his expression, she approaches, weaving her way through the dancers. Gardiner is bent over him, almost but not quite touching his sleeve, saying something. She wonders, with a pang of apprehension, if the Bishop is pouring poison in her husband's ear.

Her worries dissipate as Henry greets her with a warm, jowly grin, batting Gardiner away with a swipe of an arm, as he would a fly. She lowers herself onto the stool at his knee. Gardiner glares at her, turning away, his fox fur flicking like a devil's tail.

"We have something of importance to tell our wife." Henry's congenial tone suggests he is in an indulgent mood.

She meets his eyes, glass beads half swallowed by flesh. They are creased at the corners, no sign of the menace she has become familiar with. This is a good mood indeed.

"I have decided that you"—he speaks very quietly so as not to be overheard—"will take my place as Regent when we go to fight the French, Kit."

"This is a great honor, Your Majesty." Katherine keeps the thrill of triumph that surges through her in check, as she takes in what this means. She will be at the helm of England. Not since Catherine of Aragon has he handed over so much power. "It is too great an honor."

"I trust you. You are my wife."

Gardiner is hovering, attempting to listen.

"What is it?" Henry snarls at the Bishop, who attempts an ingratiating smile, more of a grimace than anything.

"Your Majesty, if I may be so bold . . ." He stumbles for words. "There are some matters of state—"

"Not now," barks the King. "Can't you see we are talking with our wife?"

Gardiner begins to stammer something—an apology, perhaps.

The King cuts him off. "We are discussing her regency." Gardiner blanches, the color of tallow. "Queen Katherine is to be Regent when we are in France. What think you to that, Bishop?"

Gardiner is so quick to drop onto one knee that he knocks his elbow on the arm of the throne, letting out a yelp of pain. Katherine understands now that Gardiner had been hoping for the appointment himself. And if the residue of a smirk playing on Henry's lips is anything to go by, her husband is taking great pleasure in the Bishop's disappointment.

When he has collected himself he manages to purr, "It will be my honor, Highness, to serve you." He takes Katherine's hand in both of his. They are loose and waxy, like uncooked pork fat. He kisses her wedding ring. An oily drift of white flakes is spread over his velvet shoulders.

"We are most grateful to Your Grace," she says.

"Now go," snaps the King.

Gardiner creaks to his feet, backing away with the look of a baited bear.

"My council must pass it. Some of them will not like the idea." That glint of mischief lingers on Henry's face. "But that is a formality. We will set up a council for you, my dear. And we intend to draw up a new will, should anything happen while . . ."

She takes his hand. "Nothing will happen. The Lord will keep you safe."

They sit in silence for some time, watching the dancers. Katherine's thoughts are soaring. *She* as Regent of England—she had never thought to imagine such a thing.

Power prickles beneath her skin, shoots growing out from her belly, pushing down beneath the palace, strengthening like the roots of a great oak, reaching, rooting her deep into the earth.

The King's face is spread with satisfaction and Katherine notices his eyes following Elizabeth as she dances with one of the Dudley boys. "Elizabeth is becoming quite a beauty."

"She looks like her father."

"You are right, Katherine, she is a Tudor through and through." He seems excited, his glass eyes dancing, like a child with a new toy.

Henry has reinstated his daughters to the line of succession. She had worked on him for months for this, appealing to his pride, pointing out that they have his sharpness of wit, his splendid charisma, reminding him of the Tudor blood running in their veins, his own Tudor blood. This is Katherine's triumph—the achievement of her quiet persuasion.

And now she has a new victory.

She can see Gardiner, seething, in a huddle with Wriothesley and another of his conservative cronies, Richard Rich. They can only be discussing her regency.

Whether she gives the King a son or not, they cannot touch her now.

"I was wondering if the Lady Elizabeth might come to court when you are campaigning in France. I would like to have our family about me."

"If you did not wish it, my dear, we would command it."

The whispering trio break away from one another and Wriothesley catches her look with his ferret eyes. It is nothing more than a glance, but one brimming with such contempt it sends a shiver through her as if someone has walked on her grave.

26

Dot is cleaning the windowpanes with vinegar, her cloth squeaking against the glass. The fumes make her eyes smart.

It is the Queen's birthday and all the royal children are gathered in the privy chamber to hear Katherine read a letter from the King, who is at war in France.

Things are certainly different with him away. There is a carefree feeling about the palace and Katherine is in good humor. Prince Edward sits on Lady Mary's lap. She sings to him, seeming less miserable than usual, and Dot thinks it a shame she hasn't any children of her own. The Prince is a stony little thing but she manages to tease a laugh out of him. Meg has been in seventh heaven since the return of Lady Elizabeth. They are pressed together, sharing secrets, whispering. They are like bread and butter, those two—never apart. Dot rubs harder at the glass, so hard she fears she might break it.

Elizabeth is like one of the knife sharpener's magnets, drawing everyone in. Even Rig sits at her feet gazing up at her as if she were the Virgin Mary herself. Meg holds her hand. But Dot is not drawn in by her. Dot imagines she is rubbing Elizabeth away with her vinegar cloth like a smear on the window.

Meg is rising up and up, out of her reach. Now she is the friend of the King's daughter and they huddle over books together, taking it in turns to read out loud in tongues that Dot doesn't understand. They have lessons with the new tutor, Mister Grindal, quietly scratching words onto pages while Dot brushes out the hearth and sweeps the floor and heaves the cushions down to the yard to beat the dust from them—getting shushed if she makes too much noise.

Meg is thinner than ever and pallid as a slab of goat's cheese, but she wears a bright smile so no one notices. And Katherine has so much else to do, rushing from place to place, council meetings, hearing petitions, dictating letters.

"See how the Queen is," Dot had overheard Elizabeth say to Meg. "Who says women cannot rule? Who says they must be married and governed by men?"

Meg had laughed, as if Elizabeth were joking.

"If I am ever Queen I shall not be ruled by a man."

Everyone knows she will never be Queen. Her brother will be King and his children after him and she will doubtless be hitched up to some foreign prince—and good riddance.

Dot secretly wishes the King would never return from France. She knows it is a sin to wish harm on anyone, let alone the King, but she can't help herself, because though Katherine is busy she is more brimming with life than Dot can ever remember. The strain has gone from her brow and the painted smile is no more. There is a fire lit in her. She has written a prayer for the soldiers going to fight. It has been printed and passed around, all the ladies nodding their approval—even bitter Nan Stanhope seems begrudgingly impressed.

Dot dumps the rag in her bucket and pulls her duster from her apron, running it over the paneling and the prayer stand. There is a copy of Katherine's prayer there. It is nothing to Dot but a pattern of lines and swirls like rows of stitching on a white shirt. She hates herself for not being able to unpick it.

Once she would have asked Meg to read it to her, but not now—not now Meg has her new little friend. She can't ask Katherine, for she is busy dealing with all of England. She can't ask Betty—Betty is worse than her when it comes to reading and can't even sign her own name.

Dot would be laughed at if she asked any of the cooks, for they already think she has ideas above her station. She knows that Betty has been loose-tongued with them about her secrets and they laugh behind her back, calling her Duchess Dotty. Sometimes when she passes through the kitchens a sudden, thick silence falls. She is not trusted. They don't know where she belongs.

But there is William Savage. And for all the packages she has hidden about her person and secretly delivered to the Queen for him, he owes her a favor. She resolves to ask him when she next goes to the kitchens, though he is to be found there less and less often.

A new clerk called Wilfred sits at the desk. Wilfred has spots and looks at Dot as if she's got the plague. These days William can be found most evenings in the Queen's chambers playing the virginals. He has been the object of her dreams a whole year now. But she can feel him slipping away with his music, out of the kitchens and into the fine world she only inhabits invisibly, like a ghost—a ghost with a duster. She sometimes watches his fingers dance over the keys as she passes to light the fire or bring something to the Queen. It is truly a beautiful sound he makes. She wonders if it is the sound of Heaven.

If she thinks about it, she doesn't know where she belongs either.

Elizabeth has written a poem for the Queen's birthday. Katherine seems more delighted with it even than with her gift from the King. A brooch had arrived from one of the London goldsmiths this morning. It is heavy as a horseshoe and encrusted with precious stones.

She had passed it to Dot without even trying it on.

Alone in the wardrobe, Dot had pinned it onto her own bodice and held up the glass to admire herself. It looked wrong, though, like a lily in a field of dandelions. Her face was wrong too, eyes too deeply set, mouth too wide. When she unpinned the brooch, it pricked her finger and she got blood on her coif. It is impossible to get blood out of white linen.

The Queen is reading Elizabeth's poem out loud, sighing as if it is a letter from a lover. She has to admit that Elizabeth's gift is a beautiful thing. Dot had seen it the day before when it had been left in the schoolroom. She may not be able to read but she can tell that the writing is perfectly even.

Part of Dot wants to feel sorry for Elizabeth, the poor girl whose father has called her a bastard and whose mother, Nan Bullen, was thought to be a witch with six toes and was killed for all sorts of unspeakable things. She *had* felt sorry for her buried in the country at

Ashridge, miles from anywhere, when she should be living in a palace surrounded by courtiers with her father.

Dot secretly also thought that if *she* had a father as terrifying as the King, she would rather be anywhere, even in some gloomy gray place in the middle of nowhere like Ashridge, than under his gaze, which made even great people small with fear—except Elizabeth. Elizabeth wasn't afraid of anything.

When Meg came back from her visit she had described Ashridge, painting a picture of sodden, wind-swept gardens, huge dank rooms where they huddled around smoggy hearths until their clothes stank of woodsmoke. The corridors were so drafty they whistled and the high stone arches were infested with bats that would swoop and squeal at night.

Meg talked about her all the time—Elizabeth this and Elizabeth that. Dot hadn't minded. It was so good to see Meg throwing off the past, finding a little spirit. But since Elizabeth returned to court everything is changed.

On the day of her arrival she had waved a hand in Dot's direction, asking, "Who is *that*?" She hadn't even bothered to lower her voice.

Meg had explained that Dot was the Queen's loyal servant, that she had been Meg's own nurserymaid, and that they had all come together from Snape.

Then Elizabeth had said, "How could *the Queen* possibly want to be served by a rough girl like that. Have you seen the size of her hands?"

But that is not the worst of it, for Dot knows her place. And why would a Princess—for that is what she is, even if no one is allowed to say it—why would a Princess think anything of *her*? No, the worst of it is that this Lady Elizabeth, with her learning and her lineage, has woven a web around Meg. They share their books and their lessons and their bed and they walk side by side in the palace gardens and ride out together in the park. Lady Elizabeth is trouble—it is written all over her. Dot can read *that* clearly enough.

Elizabeth thinks of no one but herself—and the Queen. She is attached to the Queen. Dot has seen her give Rig a furtive kick when the

Queen is turned away, so jealous is she of her stepmother's affection, even for a dog.

The girl is in need of a mother, Dot supposes, though she has her nurse, Mistress Astley, who is worse even than Elizabeth for looking down her nose at Dot. And so it is that Dot's sympathy for Elizabeth has all been used up, and she refuses to marvel over the poem like the others. She hates that this child is writing poems for everyone to coo over, and *she* can't even read.

The two girls come to sit on the window seat near to where Dot is now on her knees, rubbing a wet rag over the skirtings.

"Which would you rather," says Elizabeth, "to be able to fly or to be invisible?"

Dot can barely stop herself shouting out, that is *our* game, the game *I* invented.

"To be invisible," says Meg.

"You have made invisibility an art as it is, Meg Neville. I would rather fly. Imagine being able to soar up above the trees, above the clouds. You could look down on everything, like God." She pauses a moment, twirling a strand of red hair round her finger. "I suppose, if you were invisible you could spy on Robert Dudley. He's the one they want you to marry, isn't he?"

"I don't know." Meg's face drops.

Dot has heard nothing of this but she has seen Robert Dudley about the place, with his mother, who is sometimes in the Queen's rooms. He's nothing but a pup, a good few years younger than Meg. A handsome pup maybe, but he is a little too full of himself for Dot's taste.

"I suppose he's not too ugly. But you won't want him." She leans in and whispers something in Meg's ear.

Meg pulls away with a look of disgust. "That is horrible."

27

Katherine takes a deep breath before entering the council chamber. The room falls to a deathly silence. Wriothesley, ever obsequious, jumps off the bench to pull out her chair.

"I shall stand." She has never yet sat at a council meeting.

She needs as much height as she can get, to stop herself feeling like a small girl before a crowd of grown men. Her gown is Tudor green, lest the council forget whose wife she is, but it is made of a heavy brocade quite unsuitable for the airless August day.

Wriothesley is on his knee now and has her hand, planting a desiccated kiss on the back of it. She can't help herself from remembering Cat Brandon's story of him and the copy of *Psychopannychia*.

The councillors are at the table, loosely divided by their allegiances: Gardiner and his conservative cronies are to one side, with Rich among them, Hertford and the Archbishop, with the reformers, to the other. She has the majority by a whisker.

Wriothesley scuttles back to his seat.

She wipes the back of her hand discreetly against the fabric of her gown. "We shall commence with matters pertaining to the plague." She is careful to keep her voice steady, authoritative. "I intend to issue a proclamation. No one shall come to court whose house is infected."

A few, Hertford and the Archbishop among them, nod in agreement, but most hold a sullen silence. Katherine can feel a sheen of sweat gathering on her forehead, hopes it is not visible. They all agree with her proclamation. Their resistance, though, at being told by a woman, stiffens the air.

"Any who dispute this?" She clenches her jaw and avoids Gardiner's hatchet glare—he, of all of them, mustn't see any diffidence in her. "We shall decide the wording after this meeting." She nods towards the Clerk of Council and continues briskly. "His Majesty requires a shipment of lead."

"This is of the utmost urgency," says Wriothesley. "We must see that it leaves Dover immediately."

"Has it not occurred to you, esteemed counciller"—she barely hides her sarcasm—"that our English fishermen apprehended a French ship off the south coast not a week ago? There are sure to be others. If we send the lead now it is unlikely to arrive safely."

Wriothesley sniffs and says nothing, his squirrel face pinched.

"I say the shipment sails. We cannot leave our troops without the means to arm themselves." It is Gardiner now, looking about for support.

She can feel them all watching her for the remotest sign of weakness, a minuscule twitch of the eye, a catch in her breath. "I think not, Gardiner. Unless it is your intention to offer up an entire shipment of lead and the vessel that carries it, men and all, to our enemy."

A few titters spill out. Gardiner opens his mouth to speak.

But Katherine brings her fist down hard on the table, twice. "The shipment shall remain in dock until a safe passage can be assured."

Gardiner lets out an angry snort, bringing a hand up to touch his crucifix. Hertford smirks, swiveling his eyes across the table. Sometimes he is so like his brother, it gives her heart a jolt. But Hertford is rendered slighter, with his features less symmetrically configured, as if God had practiced on the elder brother and found perfection in the younger. She watches him carefully, as she does them all. Hertford is pale as a field of unharvested wheat, his darting eyes hard to read. But Katherine at least knows that, whatever he thinks of her, they share the same beliefs and are unified by shared enemies.

My enemy's enemy is my friend.

She remembers the line, can't remember where it's from. She'd never thought herself the sort to foster enemies, but then she'd never imagined herself holding the reins of England. For now, Hertford is her friend. She wonders, though, what would happen were the King not to return. Would he turn on her, try to grab the regency for himself? He is Prince Edward's oldest uncle, after all. And history is littered with ambitious uncles.

"Any who disagree?" she says.

It is only Gardiner who lifts a half-hearted hand.

"Carried."

The clerk dips his pen and scribbles.

She moves to the next item on the agenda. "His Majesty is in need of troops for the French campaign. Four thousand men. See that they are mustered, Wriothesley, Hertford." She nods firmly at each of them. "We shall decide how to transport them at a later date. You will be traveling to France soon, will you not, Hertford?"

The atmosphere has warmed a little. She has to prove herself fit to rule in each and every meeting—has to stand firm, no chinks in her armor. Not a man at this table believes a woman capable of ruling. She reminds herself of Mary of Hungary, who successfully husbands three territories. Katherine strives to emulate her example. But even the Archbishop, who is her firmest ally on the council, has reservations. She has had private conversations with him these last weeks, talked much of religion. They have read the same books.

She catches his eye. The Archbishop is a known reformer, whom Gardiner had tried to unseat not so long ago—had plotted hard to get him to the scaffold, but the King put a stop to it. Henry is attached to his Lutheran Archbishop. She can see how it works now, the careful balancing act that has been maintained by the King. Never allowing one faction to gain a stronger hold than the other, keeping them all at bay.

"Now the Scottish Borders," she says. "Hertford, what news?"

Hertford details the skirmishes that need to be kept in hand. The councillors argue about how best to resolve the issue with so many troops needed in France.

"The Scots have been on the run since Edinburgh was sacked," Rich reminds them.

"The troops are better used in Boulogne." Wriothesley sniffs. His constant sniffing irritates. "The Scots pose no threat to us."

"Are we forgetting the lessons of history, councillors?" Her hands are trembling. She tucks them away, folding her arms solidly. "Think back to Flodden Field."

Last time Henry was campaigning in France, thirty years ago, the Scots thought to take advantage. Catherine of Aragon was Regent then—the only other of Henry's Queens he had trusted with the role. Katherine remembers hearing of it as a girl—it was talked of for years, had made a lasting impression. The Queen took a hard line, against the odds, and James IV was killed at Flodden Field. She'd sent Henry the Scottish king's bloody coat—a triumph indeed.

"Recruit more troops, mercenaries if necessary." She leaves no room for dissent. "Funds will have to be released."

It is agreed.

Katherine senses the atmosphere in the chamber shift to a reluctant respect.

She can hear someone practicing the virginals in her rooms, a few faltering bars of a repeated melody drifting in through the open window. It is probably Elizabeth.

Elizabeth seems fascinated by Katherine's regency, begs to sit in on council meetings, offers to inscribe letters of state, to help with anything. That is impossible, but Katherine encourages her interest. They talk of women who have ruled, how femininity must be set aside to earn the trust of men. Elizabeth has the makings of a good Queen, though she will never be more than a consort.

The music stops, there is a faint laugh. Meg will not be far—those two have become inseparable. Meg is quite renewed these days, ready for marriage. Katherine thinks of the women gathered in her rooms, heads bowed over their needlework, a hubbub of quiet chat, a game of cards, someone reading. Her chambers are full of books now, many banned, in innocent covers, tucked away in corners, down the sides of things, treated with caution. They all know those books hold the potential for trouble.

She rejects that thought for fear of weakening—no chinks. Besides, she reminds herself, she is Regent. Henry has made her untouchable. A cat slinks past the window, treading carefully on the narrow sill, distracted for a moment by a pigeon, watching it, crouched, waiting silently, absolutely still. The bird takes to the air and the cat moves out of sight.

The discussion turns to problems with the persecution of French residents in London. It becomes quite heated. Several councillors, voices raised, bay for their deportation, some for imprisonment.

"We are at war with France. These people are our enemies." Wriothesley has a look of distaste. He's the sort to be suspicious of French wine for its foreignness.

Shame *he* cannot be sent to fight the French. He sniffs again and Hertford thrusts a handkerchief at him. He looks at it as if he has never seen such a thing before.

"Blow your nose, man." Hertford's patience is threadbare.

Wriothesley snorts into the linen.

"The problem lies not with the émigrés"—Katherine cuts through the noise—"but with those who persecute them. I am not in favor of deportation. I say we come down hard on the rabble who victimize them."

"With all respect," pipes up Hertford, "if we show too much leniency we are likely to have more trouble on our hands."

"Most of these people have been in London for generations. They can't simply be got rid of." The Archbishop takes her side.

Thank God he is with her. Without Hertford, though, Katherine knows she will struggle to hold her position.

"I will write to the King on the matter." She stands firm. "For the present the émigrés stay, and any who trouble them will be punished accordingly."

Hertford will be gone in days. He is needed in France. She will have to sharpen her powers of persuasion with the council.

She wonders again what would happen were the King not to return. She would be alone at the helm of England, protector of a child King. So it is written in Henry's will. How could she continue this careful tightrope walk without her husband at her shoulder? She would have to find a way, would have to forge powerful allegiances. She asks herself whether she would have the stomach to send someone to the scaffold ... an enemy, perhaps ... but a friend? The thought swims sickeningly in her head.

"Any other matters?"

"Various minor land disputes," says the clerk, holding up a sheaf of papers.

They plod through a list of petty issues and eventually she closes the meeting and leaves the council chamber.

She maintains her erect posture as she walks the length of the gallery and enters her privy chamber. As soon as the door is closed behind her, she slumps against it, tugging at the laces of her gown, pulling the great heavy thing off her, untying her hood, throwing it down as she sinks to the floor, her kirtle spread out around her.

28

Udall stands before the company seated in the Queen's watching room. He wears an elaborate doublet of purple brocade, a color he is not entitled to wear. Huicke had discouraged him, said it lacked respect. But then Katherine enjoys the fact that he's not a hem kisser. She can't abide the sycophants.

Even Nan Stanhope purrs around Katherine's ankles these days like a Siamese cat, suggesting passages from Luther that might interest her or proffering little gifts: a pair of brocade sleeves, a fan, a book. It is true they share certain opinions, but it is clear as day to Huicke that Nan Stanhope is feathering her own nest.

Udall bows, lifting his cap, wafting it in a series of figures of eight decreasing in size. Some of the ladies giggle at this overly extravagant gesture. Huicke exchanges a smile with Katherine. He sees her contentment, has watched her flourish in her position these last weeks. And she has done well. She's even impressed the doubters on her council with her fortitude.

But he can see her enemies circling. They thought this new Queen would lie down and roll over for them, help bring the King back firmly to the old faith. They have found her less easy to control than they had hoped.

And now she is made Regent.

"How was the meeting?" he whispers.

"I'm winning the council over."

"If anyone can, you can."

Wriothesley, Gardiner and Rich go about the palace with faces that would sour honey. He has heard bitter mutterings, too, about the new royal will, making Katherine's regency permanent. None of them like the idea of that, but especially not Hertford.

Hertford's meant to be Katherine's ally, but allegiances are fragile in this court where everything is undecided. He has long had his eye on the regency for himself. He must have been wondering how much longer he would have to lick the elderly King's boots before his little nephew was crowned and he holding the boy's strings. But now there is this woman in the way, a woman who seems able to do no wrong in the eyes of the King.

Huicke hasn't had the heart to remind Katherine that this power of hers is only by proxy, that the Gardiners and Wriothesleys and Hertfords of this world do her bidding precisely because the King *will* return. She talks often of Mary of Hungary—her shining example as Queen Regent—a respected ruler in her own right. But Mary of Hungary has the might of her brother, the Emperor, behind her.

Who would stand in Katherine's defense—her own brother, who is barely the Earl of Essex, and as powerless as all the other court preeners? If the King were to go, they'd all turn on her in an instant. She'd be in the Tower before she knew it. But Huicke will not be the one to interrupt her happiness by reminding her of this. Let her enjoy it, while it lasts, he thinks, watching her laugh easily at Udall's ironic posturing.

Since Huicke's transfer to the Queen's household as her chief physician, no less, and with the King's blessing, people have begun to tease him about his friendship with Katherine. Chancer, charmer, toady, arse-licker, they call him. "A jackdaw knows a crow," he counters, but he would never tell them of his genuine fondness for her.

The air is too thin for friendship at court, so this is precious to him. Queen or not, he cares for her, enjoys her contradictions, the drive to be good, tempered by the sheer will to win, even at cards. She's a fierce adversary and, above all, she is kind. He has seen that, seen the way she treats the servants, with respect, always a thoughtful word to the stable lad and even a smile for the girl who takes down the slops.

People at the palace are too busy looking up to see what lies beneath, but not Katherine. And he will never forget that kiss she placed on the back of his disfigured hand in the still room at Charterhouse. It seems an age ago now, though it is barely eighteen months.

She leans over. "The color suits him, don't you think?"

"Purple—fit for a queen!"

Katherine snorts with suppressed laughter at this.

Even Udall wouldn't dare do it if the King were here. No one can count on the King's sense of humor.

Huicke watches his lover with a throb of desire as he laps up all the attention, strutting about before the Queen's ladies, all eyes on him. Theirs is a fierce passion, but an unsteady one. Udall can be cruel and only recently had refused to touch him, saying, "You disgust me with your reptilian skin," and strutting off to find sport elsewhere.

He had returned eventually, drunk and maudlin, begging forgiveness. Those words hurt but, if Huicke is honest, he disgusts himself. Something fascinates him, though, with Udall—how there seems barely a boundary in him between love and hate.

As Udall strides over the floor, Huicke cannot banish the image of him unclothed, the very maleness of him, his rangy musculature, his smooth firm skin, so unlike his own. Naked, he looks like a farmhand but his mind is the finest, sharpest, subtlest Huicke has ever known, and the most irreverent.

As with Katherine, it is the contradictions he enjoys. She talks of becoming both man and woman in order to rule. Huicke should know about that.

"Your excellent Highness, most gracious Queen Katherine." Udall bows to her. "I humbly present to you the first performance of my comedy *Ralph Roister Doister*."

Lady Elizabeth sits beside Katherine, holding hands with little Meg Neville, who is on her other side. It is one of Katherine's triumphs, to have brought all the royal children together. How the King resisted over Elizabeth. She had talked endlessly to Huicke about it, how it pained her to think of the girl alone out at Ashridge.

And here she is. She is still young but is threaded through with her father's bearing, in the way she holds her head, the directness of her gaze, in the determined set of her jaw. Katherine has taken charge of her education, and says she has the kind of cleverness, a curiosity for things, that would never be happy with the usual spoon-fed learning that is dished out to girls. She likes to grapple with the new and, like her brother, she is growing up more or less in the new faith. If Gardiner were aware of the extent to which the younger royal children are immersed in reform, he would seek some filthy scheme to put a stop to it.

Katherine's little dog skitters up to Elizabeth, climbing onto her knee. Without looking, she sweeps him away with her hand. She is clearly not one to be beguiled by a pair of big wet eyes. Katherine pats her own lap and he jumps up, snuggling into her skirts.

The room hushes as Udall begins to recite his prologue. Huicke has heard some of it before, read some of the early drafts, the usual verses about mirth lifting spirits, but he doesn't know the play. Udall has been distinctly secretive about this one.

A player enters, describing Ralph Roister Doister as a man who falls for every woman he meets, giving rise to a snickering among the ladies. Then on comes Roister Doister himself, garbed up in elaborate brocade and sporting an ostrich feather in his cap the size of a horse's tail.

"It's Thomas Seymour," cries Anne, rousing a peal of giggles from the younger girls.

"Look at the size of his feather," shrieks someone.

Huicke glances to Katherine, who has a determined smile scored across her face, but there is an angry flush on her throat and her mouth is clenched.

The player preens and poses, waving his arms about and then, raising a gale of laughter, talks of wooing a rich widow, while pulling out a mirror and admiring himself in it.

Then on comes the object of his affection, Mistress Custance, a pretty boy done up in red: a red wig, a red dress, round red cheeks. It is clearly meant to be Katherine, for red is her color; all her pages are liveried in scarlet.

"He is brazen, that lover of yours," whispers Katherine, raising her eyebrows.

In spite of Katherine seeming to retain her humor, Huicke feels anger rising through him. How could Udall do this? He surely knows the circumstances—but perhaps not. Her affair with Seymour was never common knowledge, only ever gossip and speculation. It is only

Huicke who truly knows the extent of Katherine's feelings for the man; even Anne is in the dark.

They watch as the story unfolds of Roister Doister's inept and unwanted wooing of Mistress Custance, who is already promised to a certain rich merchant, conveniently abroad, named Gawyn Goodlucke.

Huicke glances to Katherine. Her smile is a rictus. Her foot taps the floor nervously. He tries to imagine what it feels like to have your secret life laid bare so the whole court can pick over the bones of it. She must be thinking it is he who has been loose-tongued, he who has revealed her private world to his lover. He cannot bear the idea of losing her trust again.

He squeezes her hand. "I had no idea."

"These things have a way of getting out. The King knew enough to send Thomas away. The rumor mill was grinding."

Udall has turned Katherine's most precious and painful memory into a joke before the whole court, and a dangerous joke at that, for if the King were to hear of it . . . It makes Huicke's gut crunch up in fear. But he has to admire Udall's gall. If Thomas Seymour were here he'd string him up. But he is not here, nor is his brother—he left for France earlier. And, thank God, nor is the King, for if the King *were* here he wouldn't be laughing. This as good as depicts him as a cuckold. Even Udall wouldn't have risked this performance were the King here to see it.

The evening creeps by excruciatingly. Katherine is welded to the spot, as the puffed-up Roister Doister digs out the path of his own humiliation. *I know she loveth me but she cannot speak*, he bellows.

Huicke leans in towards her. "I wish I had known of this, Kit. I would have stopped it."

"He means only to make us laugh." She is still smiling her ambiguous smile. "You're not to blame." Her resilience is remarkable.

"It's Seymour he's ridiculing, not you. He always loathed the man. I never knew why. Some ancient slight, I suppose."

The boy actor stands alone on the floor. He is absurd with his rouged cheeks and scarlet skirts, too long for him, dragging, tripping him up, his gestures overblown—a hand, big and mannish, thrown across his breast, his mouth aghast, eyes wide and white, voice shot through with desperation. He talks directly to the audience, taking them into his confidence, dropping his voice so they have to lean in and stop their laughter to hear him.

How innocent stand I, he lisps, *in this deed of thought? And yet see what mistrust towards me it hath wrought.*

The laughter stops, leaving the room momentarily silent.

There is an uncomfortable truth beneath the humor—even the innocent can fall. Meg sits still as a stone with a hand over her mouth. Anne hides her face behind her fan, but her eyes betray her thoughts. If her sister falls, her family will tumble with her. Even Nan Stanhope, who has whinnied loudest of them all, is shut up, though she loathes her brother-in-law and would gladly see him humiliated.

Only Elizabeth laughs blithely. Is she too young to understand, or is she as callous as some say?

The ridiculous plot continues to unfold. The grave moment is gone and the mirth returns. Katherine smiles on and on as the thing moves towards its happy conclusion.

"Your Udall is a loose cannon," she says. "How did Aristotle put it? 'In comedy the good end happily and the bad unhappily.' I wonder where my destiny lies."

Huicke doesn't know how to respond.

Katherine grips his hand and draws herself closer to his ear. "Can I truly trust him? He knows much about my reading habits. Talk to him, Huicke. Tell him if he is not more careful I will send him away. Make him understand there are limits to my goodwill."

The players are taking their bows to a spirited applause. Udall enters to a cheer and Katherine throws him a purse which he catches deftly, arm aloft. Huicke's anger still simmers, though Katherine seems blithe as anything.

She calls out, "Magnificent, Udall! You had us utterly enthralled."

People leave their seats, milling about, and cups of wine are handed around. Huicke hangs back, allowing Katherine to congratulate the players and talk to her ladies. Her unerring poise astounds him. Nothing of her exterior reveals her inner world. She is smiling, chatting with the Dudley boy and his mother. She takes Meg's hand and pulls her over, introducing her to the boy. She has mentioned a match between those two, now he thinks of it.

Meg dips into a polite curtsy, but instead of a brief look at the boy, as manners dictate, she stares at him rigidly. Then as she rises her cup topples, drenching his yellow hose in crimson wine. He jumps back, looking at his mother, who has a hand over her mouth. They both seem to be wondering if the spill was deliberate. That is certainly the impression Huicke has. Katherine calls over a page who leads the boy away, his flustered mother following. She turns to her step-daughter, but Meg has slunk away and is sitting in a corner with Elizabeth.

They are close enough that Huicke can hear what Elizabeth says to her: "Bravo, Margaret Neville. That is how to deal with unwanted suitors."

There are some things about women Huicke will never fully understand.

29

"What is this?" William Savage holds the paper with the very tips of his fingers, as if it might give him the pox. He sounds impatient, angry even.

Dot wants to snatch back the prayer, return it to the stand in Katherine's chamber, pretend this never happened. But she is here now and finds a kernel of determination. "I hoped you might read it to me."

"You mustn't give me things like this where people can see."

They are on the stone steps leading to the watching chamber, standing on the small landing where the stairs turn. People pass up and down, shouldering past one another, leaving fragments of conversation in their wake. The sun casts diamonds through the window onto the gray flags. Dot can hardly bear to look at him. He holds the paper close to his body and turns towards the light to read it.

"Oh, it is just the Queen's prayer. Why didn't you say?"

"I . . . I." Her tongue is heavy, the wrong shape for the words, and she feels a hot blush rush all the way up to the roots of her hair. "It doesn't matter," she manages to mumble.

"Oh, but it does." Smiling, he takes her hand. "Come, let's find a quiet spot. Are you needed?" The anger has gone from his face and it is him again, the William who strolls through her dreams.

"I have a few minutes."

He leads her down the steps so fast she has to run to keep up. She notices a small hole in his hose at the ankle, where his heel narrows to meet the base of his calf—a small circle of white skin framed in black, a private part of him. She wants to tell him she can stitch it and she wonders if he has a girl like her, to mend for him and wash his linens.

With a jolt, she realizes that for all her dreaming, she knows nothing of this man, save that he reads and writes and that he plays the virginals like an angel. But most of all, she knows that he is out of her reach. How far, she cannot tell, but he is well-born enough and shouldn't really look at a girl like her—or not for anything more than a tumble in the grain store. But here he is, clutching her hand and pulling her along for everyone to see.

He leads her out into Base Court, where the sun's glare bounces off the windows. It takes a moment for her eyes to get used to the brightness.

The court is as busy as Smithfield, with everyone seeming in such a hurry. Groups of men clatter through, robes flapping, swords glinting, and pages rush about doing this and that. She notices Betty scuttle furtively along beneath the arcade—doing something she shouldn't, clearly, as she's meant to be in the kitchens at this hour. A gardener passes, almost hidden by a bundle of cut flowers the color of lemons, intended for one of the great chambers, Dot supposes. A trio of girls trots past, in the shade of the cloister, practicing dance steps, their skirts swinging.

"No, Mary, it is like this," says one, tripping through the movement. "Your arms should be up." She lifts her arms, tiny fingers beautifully arranged at the end of them, looking like some kind of splendid butterfly with her red and gold sleeves spread out like wings and beguiling insect eyes flitting to see who might be watching.

She glances at William to see if he watches them too, but he doesn't. His eyes are on Dot, inspecting her minutely. She feels uncomfortable, hot, with the sun beating down, exposed.

"You know, Dot, you are prettier by far than most of these palace girls that wander about the place with their noses in the air."

She doesn't believe him. In her plain coif and drab dress, hardly prettier than a grain sack, she is invisible next to these gaily clad beauties tripping through the court. She tries desperately to think of some kind of witty reply, any reply, but nothing comes except a barely audible "no." Her own inferiority crushes her: the country lilt in her voice; her skin, not pale enough; the scrubbing-brush calluses on her man-sized hands, which she hides away beneath her apron.

"So, you want me to read this to you?"

She nods.

The girls are still skitting about. One sings a song in French—or Dot supposes it to be French as everyone here, apart from the ordinary servants, seems to speak it. *They* can all read, and she hates them for it, hates them for their luxury, for their delicate airs, their fine limbs and finer skins, their blue blood, the fawning tutors that painstakingly teach them their letters. But mostly she hates them for the way they make her feel—lumpen and awkward and stupid.

"Has no one ever taught you?"

She shakes her head, eyes cast downward following a train of ants making their way over the cobbles.

"But you would like to read?"

She listens carefully for the mocking tone in his voice but doesn't find it.

"I would." She doesn't know how, or what it is about him that she suddenly feels she can trust, but she finds her tongue at last. "I *truly* would."

"It is a crime that clever girls like you are not taught."

He called me clever, she thinks, feeling that she might boil over with it all. "But I come from a simple family and I have found myself in this place. Where I come from no girls could read, nor half the boys. I don't really belong here, Master Savage."

"You belong here as much as the next person." He places an arm around her shoulders, giving her a squeeze that turns her insides to aspic. "Now tell me," he whispers in her ear, "would you like to read the Bible for yourself?"

"I would. When I see all the ladies with their books—"

"Hush." He places a finger over her lips. "You must keep these things to yourself."

His touch, the nearness of him, is making it difficult for Dot to breathe. A couple of riders career into the court, dismounting and chattering. An untidy blare of pigeons squabbles over a crust. The chapel bell sounds out twice.

"I have to go." She starts to get up, but he grabs her hand to pull her back down.

"I will teach you to read." He seems pleased with his idea, his eyes wide and bright and lovely.

"I'm sure I shall never be able—"

"You will. It is not as mysterious as it appears. Come later when the Queen has gone to bed and we will start with the prayer." He pulls her towards him and gives her a kiss, as light as a feather, on her cheek. "I am looking forward to it, Dot."

He walks with her to the door, opening it for her as if she were a countess at the very least.

"You know this must be a secret."

She nods, understanding that there is something grave and powerful about written words and being able to read them.

"Let them think we are summer lovers." He turns her face to his with a touch to her cheek.

She has no choice but to look at him. He seems younger, somehow, than she had thought. She'd never noticed how sparse his beard is, so the cleft in his chin and that dimple are visible, and how his skin is as smooth as a child's. There is a gleam of excitement in his eyes as his gaze dances over her face. She wonders what it could be he sees there.

He presses his lips to her ear. "Go."

Her head is in a spin as she returns to the Queen's chambers. Her giddiness makes her clumsy. She spills a pan of water on the matting and drops a carton of oranges that roll across the room. She has to prize one from Rig's jaws, who thinks it's a game. She forgets Katherine's hood when she brings her dress in and ties her left sleeve on her right arm.

"You are distracted, Dot. More than usual." Katherine is looking keenly at her. "I smell love on you." She laughs lightly. "You enjoy it, my dear, for there is precious little chance for love in this life."

Dot doesn't miss the fleeting look of sadness on her face. She has noticed a change in Katherine recently. She had been so very bright since the King's departure, so much the Queen, but there is something that has got under her skin and given her an edge, though most don't see it. Dot hears the ladies talk of how remarkable she is, how efficient, how well she manages the council.

"Those old goats are eating out of her hand," Cat Brandon had said, and Anne had called her formidable.

And Nan Stanhope's sour face was a sight to behold when even that old Lady Buttes, who doesn't seem to have a good word for anyone, said, "For all her middling birth she has the bearing of a Queen."

It is only Dot who knows the secrets of the Queen's body, and none but Dot witnessed her look when her monthly courses last came, and how hollow her words were when she said, "Next time, Dot. Next time." She had mixed a tonic for the cramps and gone back to her business.

Dot thinks it is a blessing the King is not here. The great bedchamber lies unused and Katherine's pale skin is free from bruises.

30

Eltham Palace, September 1544

Katherine urges Pewter on. She can feel his exhaustion, but as they reach the brow of the hill and the palace comes into sight he picks up his pace—urged on by the thought of a bucket of oats, no doubt.

Eltham's ancient stone is the color of winter skies, but in places it blooms with bright lichens and mosses, seeming to have grown out of the ground as if conceived by nature herself. It is a place that has housed Kings and Queens for hundreds of years and seems to know it, for it has a dignified look sitting like a jewel at the center of its rolling parkland, encircled by a placid green moat. The trees around it are on the turn, crisping at their edges, taking on a new palette, heralding autumn.

She can see Mary and Elizabeth, with little Edward and a group of youngsters, far ahead, almost at the gates. Their horses were fresher and they took the last leg at a gallop. She watches the way Edward controls his skittish pony, quite at home in the saddle.

Katherine has been determined to create a feeling of family for this disparate collection of souls who, for all their privilege, have been so lacking in love. Even Edward, the apple of his father's eye, the answer to everything, has been so wrapped up, so kept away from things, that he has become uncomfortable with affection. She hopes that will change.

In the meantime, she has witnessed a new closeness flourish between the two sisters. They have ridden out together daily since they arrived and Elizabeth has taken to sharing Mary's bedchamber. Katherine had long hoped to achieve this, but her pleasure in it has been tainted, for Meg has been left out in the cold as a consequence.

Meg really should be married by now—but since that business with the wine, the Dudley boy is out of the question. And besides, she seems to be sickening with something. She's barely been outside for weeks and has taken on the pallor of a ghost. She slips into Katherine's bed in the night, wheezing badly and occasionally wracked with terrible fits of coughing. Katherine has called for Huicke from London. He will know what to do.

The palace beckons. Henry spent his childhood at Eltham and she tries to think about him—plump and small, just the second son, not bred for greatness like his brother—skipping through this place. She struggles to imagine him as a child. In her mind he is more like one of those heathen gods from the myths that appeared fully formed from the belly of a great fish or a rent in the earth.

He will return soon, full of bluster from his great victory at Boulogne. Hampton Court had been jubilant on hearing the news that the French were defeated. She is waiting for word that he has landed at Dover and feels her freedom draining away, but for now she will immerse herself in the pleasures of this place.

As Pewter clops through the stone arch and into the cobbled court, a thin rain begins to fall. She dismounts and leads him to the trough for a drink, scratching between his ears, making him press his muzzle up to her shoulder and flare his nostrils.

"Let me take him, madam." The unfamiliar groom doesn't meet her eye, because she is the Queen and he is unsure of himself.

She smiles to put him at his ease, handing over the reins and asking his name.

"It is Gus, madam." He looks at his hands.

"Thank you, Gus. Will you give him some oats and rub him down carefully? He is not as young as he was."

Gus leads Pewter away. Katherine sits for a moment on the edge of the trough, putting her face up to the cold spray of rain, imagining she is not Queen and can do as she pleases. But the rain gets the better of her and she takes herself through the vast wooden doors into the hall. Anne is inside and they sit together by the fire to drink a toddy.

"This hall is full of drafts," says Anne.

"We have been spoiled by the comforts of Hampton Court and Whitehall."

"This place reminds me of Croyland. Do you remember going there, when we were girls?"

Katherine looks up at the high hammer-beamed ceiling and the way the muted light filters through the thick glass, shimmering over flagstones that are shiny and uneven with age.

"It *is* like Croyland."

She remembers that great abbey, the way it dropped a cloak of silence over everything, a hush that made her ears ring with emptiness. She thinks of the solemn hooded monks, their soft shuffling, the haunting harmonies of their plainchant, rising up to the vast arched roof, and the colors, the vividness, the richness, the splendor crushed by Henry's reformation. And though she doesn't believe in what it stood for, she wishes that some of that ancient splendor, that particular quiet, could have been retained.

"It is a shame those places are no more."

In her heart she feels the loss of it all as something desolate. She understands why people are still so aghast at the spoils of the Church being divided up between the nobility.

"Do you ever wonder if it was worth it?"

"I believe it *was*, Kit. Truly I do."

Katherine sometimes envies her sister's certainty about things. "Even the horror?"

"Yes, even that. For without that our new world would not be born. And you? Surely you don't doubt it, after all you suffered at the hands of the Catholic rebels."

"It is not doubt I feel. No, it is more like a . . ." She struggles to find the right word. "A sadness."

There is a shriek of laughter and Elizabeth runs across the minstrels' gallery with Robert Dudley in pursuit.

"That girl is nothing but trouble." Anne frowns. "Have you seen how she winds Robert up like a spindle?"

"She has a wild streak, it is true. But she is good at heart. You are too hard on her, Anne."

"She has you around her finger, too. She's trouble, I tell you."

"She's misunderstood."

"And what about Meg? Elizabeth took that boy from under her nose. He was meant for Meg and now he can't see beyond that little minx."

"Meg didn't like him." Katherine, her annoyance rising, objects to Anne's choice of words. "Besides, Meg is unwell, that is all. She hasn't been able—"

She is interrupted by the entrance of a page who hands Anne a letter.

Anne makes a little noise of excitement as she tears open the seal, scans the words. "Kit, this is news indeed." She screws up the paper, throwing it on the fire and watching it burn, then takes the poker and pushes an escaped fragment back into the flames. Leaning in close, she says, "The astrologer is to visit this very evening."

It needs no explaining. They have been planning it for weeks. Anne Askew, who has abandoned her husband to preach the new gospel, is coming here to Eltham. Just the thought of such a woman sends a thrill through Katherine—a woman of such courage. Anne Askew's name is whispered in reverence among the reformers. She is known for her sermons refuting transubstantiation, and has a distribution network for forbidden books. She is everything a woman shouldn't be, and Katherine so admires her for it, has sent monies, anonymously, to fund her gospeling.

Gardiner mentioned her in a recent council meeting. "That cursed heretic," he called her. "This is the outcome of the education of women. I will have her burned if it is the last thing I do."

But Anne Askew has slipped through his fingers. She has powerful friends, and one of them is Cat Brandon. Cat has organized the visit in the utmost secrecy, taking the greatest risk on her own shoulders, careful to keep all but the basic facts from Katherine.

Anne Askew is to be brought here to Eltham in the guise of an astrologer. No one must know, just Katherine, Cat and Anne. Even Huicke has been kept in the dark, lest it somehow slip out to his loose-mouthed lover. The Queen cannot be seen to be involved with such heresy. Everyone, even the servants, must think she is consulting an astrologer, for the good of the country, to see if more victories will follow for England, or to see if she will conceive a son.

Let them think what they like, as long as it is not the truth.

"Anne," she whispers. "It is really happening."

The secret throbs inside her, the danger of it making her feel alive, closer to God.

Katherine is in the hall with Cat Brandon when she hears her brother's voice outside.

"Make way for the Queen's astrologer."

She had not known that Will was to accompany Anne Askew. Cat had told her next to nothing, said it was better that way. She rushes towards the doors to greet him but Cat grabs her arm, holding her back.

"Someone will notice your excitement. It is written all over you. You need to better accustom yourself to subterfuge." Cat leads her away to her privy chamber.

She is right, Katherine is aflutter with it all.

Cat hustles everyone out. "The Queen will consult her astrologer alone."

The women leave their needlework and their books, wandering out to sit near the fire in the hall.

Will strides in then, with a tall figure beside him, tall as a man, enshrouded in a cloak so even the face is in shadow. When the cloak is thrown off Anne Askew stands before them in man's boots, man's hose, man's doublet, man's cap—and quite a convincing fellow she is. But she drops into a deep woman's curtsy. Her face is open, her wide-set eyes warm.

"I am glad, Highness, to have this opportunity to show my gratitude for your support."

Will steps forward and pulls both his sisters to him in a double embrace, and for an instant she is not Queen any more, just one of Will Parr's sisters.

His eyes are ablaze. "You've told no one?"

"No one," Katherine confirms.

He produces a large astrological chart, unrolling it across the table. "Just in case."

God only knows where he found such a thing.

"I shall guard the door." He places a hand to the hilt of his sword. "That other door, where does it lead?"

"Only to my bedchamber."

"And there is no other entry to your bedchamber?"

Katherine shakes her head, the danger of it all suddenly rubbing up against her excitement. They could all burn for this.

The three of them—Anne, Cat and herself—gather on the hearth cushions to listen.

Anne Askew pulls a Bible out from beneath her doublet and taps it, saying, "This is it. This is the word of God. We need nothing more . . . no unwritten verities to govern the Church."

Katherine is enthralled. She says nothing new but it is the way in which she says it, her fervor, her belief, that crystallizes the message. No one could listen to her and not believe in their heart that she speaks the truth.

She talks of the Mass. "How can man say he makes God? Nowhere in the Bible does it say that man can make God. It is the baker that makes the bread and they would have us believe that that baker makes God? It is a nonsense.

"If that same bread was left a month it would turn to mold. There is the proof that it is nothing more than bread. It is all here." She takes Katherine's hand, touching it to her Bible. "I have been chosen by God to spread this gospel and I am blessed to be here imparting God's word to the Queen."

"It is I who am blessed, Mistress Askew."

The woman shuffles through the pages, seeking a passage, finding it with an "ah." She quotes a line, running her finger beneath it: "'Behold the lamb of God.' If the Catholics do not believe that Christ is indeed a lamb, then why do they insist upon such literal translation of 'this is my body'?" She taps her Bible again, her eyes shining. "This book is the light that will lead us—this alone."

When her whispered sermon is done, Katherine hands her a purse.

"I will send more, if you so need it. Continue your most excellent work, Mistress Askew."

They murmur together: "Scripture alone, faith alone, grace alone, Christ alone, glory to God alone."

And then she is gone, whisked away by Will, shrouded in her cloak.

31

"What said your star-gazer?" Lady Mary has let her curiosity get the better of her. "Are you to bear a son for England?"

"Oh, you know these people," Katherine replies. "They talk in riddles—full of ambiguity. But I hope, Mary, I hope for an heir." She is surprised at the ease with which she finds she can lie, doesn't like it. "And I pray the Lord will favor me with a child."

She is working on Mary, chipping away at her faith, hoping to convert her. Perhaps some of Elizabeth's belief will rub off on her sister. They seem to become closer daily. Mary is intelligent enough but she hasn't the spark of Elizabeth with her formidable mix of the frivolous and the sanguine. In her heart Katherine believes that, of the three, Elizabeth is the one who would make the best monarch, though none would agree with her. Edward is so very stiff, while Mary is overly governed by her emotions, more volatile than her sister, so brittle, and never seems able to shake off her whiff of tragedy.

Katherine does her best to draw Mary into the theological talk that often goes on well into the night but Mary's faith will not be rocked. For her things are as they are and always have been. She has an intractable streak. She seems rooted to the old beliefs in memory of her mother, as if it would be a betrayal to entertain anything else. Her loyalty is blind and Katherine sometimes wonders whether that will end up being her salvation or her downfall.

In the elevated place they inhabit the potential for downfall is always skulking in the shadows.

But Katherine's newfound evangelical tenacity, spurred on by Anne Askew's visit, is a match for Mary's mulish nature and she eventually persuades her to help with a new project. It is a translation into English of Erasmus's *Paraphrases*. Erasmus is not forbidden, after all. But in English . . . Udall had given her the idea.

If Katherine is really honest with herself, it had appealed to her vanity to publish something. It had seemed not enough to be just another childless Queen, not when there have been so many of them, and most barely remembered. She thinks often of Copernicus and the solar eclipse, symbol of the great changes taking place, seeing God's hand at play. She burns with the desire to leave something behind on this earth, a legacy, to be seen by history as one of the torch-bearers for the new religion.

The thought of Anne Askew and her courage drives her on. *She* will be remembered for her gospeling. Katherine, then, will be remembered for bringing the great writings, the new ideas, to ordinary people in their own language. One day she will write other books, her own ideas. But she scarcely even allows herself to think of this, it is so very unwomanly, so very upside down. Instead she tells herself that it is her obligation as Queen and as an educated woman to use her learning for the greater good.

This is what she tells Mary too, appealing to the girl's sense of duty, reminding her of the high and unwavering esteem her father has for Erasmus. And Mary has her vanity too, wants to be seen for her depth.

"Only *you* have the subtlety of mind to take on a work such as this." Katherine watches Mary's fingers worrying at the rosary that hangs from her girdle, which was once her mother's. She has her father's hands and Katherine sees what a curse it is for a girl to be forever held up to her sister when that sister is Elizabeth, who has hands like pretty finches and who has inherited the unassailable magnetism of their father. Mary has to make do with the worst of him—his stubby fingers and volatile temper, and those unsettling eyes.

What Katherine is really saying to her is, I'm choosing *you* and not Elizabeth for this task.

"I will keep the book of John for you. It is the best of them and will suit the intricacies of your mind, Mary."

Mary's head slowly moves from side to side, and all Katherine can hear is the September rain pelting at the window. But then she looks up with her father's eyes—like beads—and says, "I will do it."

Katherine has the feeling at last of gathering the lost soul of her eldest stepdaughter in. She knows that in time Mary will come round, and that this translation will work its way into her, that it will be a release for her from the tortured memories of her mother, from the grip of Rome.

Katherine and the children have made paper boats and are floating them on the Eltham moat to see which one stays up the longest, contriving always that Edward's should be the winner. He is learning from an early age that the world conspires magically to favor him. After all, he will be King one day and that is the way of things for kings.

Meg sits apart on a stone bench, swaddled head to toe, white as a statue, reading. She has shown little sign of shaking off her illness and Huicke has been delayed. Katherine worries but at least today it is dry enough for her to take the air.

After days of relentless rain it is at last one of those bright cold autumn days that seems to make the color of everything all the more intense. They are well protected from the chill, in furs that Katherine has had sent from London. She dispatched her letters to the council early this morning. There has been nothing important to decide since news came of the King's victory. She can feel her grip on things slipping away as Henry's return becomes imminent.

She prepares herself for their reunion. Months away at war will have left him hungry with desire. She tries not to think of it—performing her wifely duties. It makes her feel sick to the stomach. Perhaps the effort of campaigning will have left him exhausted and incapable.

It is Meg who first hears the horses. "A herald approaches." She waves. They all stand to watch the moat bridge, seeing the group of riders with the King's banner flying above them.

So, this is it, thinks Katherine. They are here to announce the King's return.

They pull up hard when they see that the Queen stands there before them, and jump down from their horses, dropping onto their knees. Formalities are exchanged and a letter is put into her hand.

He wants to be reunited at Otford. She is to send the children away and take just Dot to serve her. Otford is not a place she knows, but she thinks it once belonged to Cranmer, and is not, she believes, one of the grand houses. It is a more modest place—more intimate, she suspects—which is an indication of the King's state of mind.

Katherine must gird herself once more and become the dutiful wife, must conjure up some counterfeit desire. Sometimes she feels little better than a Southwark jade with all the acrobatics she must contrive to excite her husband—only *her* actions are sanctioned by God.

And, she thinks bitterly, the rewards are greater.

32

Otford Palace, Kent, October 1544

The still room is not a proper room in this house, more a cupboard with no window and a curtain for a door, separating it from the buttery. To get inside Dot must squeeze herself past the kegs of beer and wine that have been brought up from the cellars for the King's visit.

This house is low-lying and damp. The walls are cold to the touch, like uncooked pastry, and they crumble away if you brush too hard against them, leaving smears on your dress. The better rooms have paneling, but even that is full of worm and like lace in places.

In the last year Dot has trekked around so many houses, having to become quickly accustomed to the quirks and corridors of each one, and the staff too. Mostly they leave her alone but some wheedle themselves around her because they imagine she must have more influence than she does.

As soon as she is more or less settled in one place, it's time to move on. She feels she might go completely mad for all the hefting, the packing up, the unpacking, the always needing to know where to lay her hands on anything anyone might need. She can't count the times she's rolled the Queen's jewels into their pouches, layered her good dresses into the trunks, folded the linens and the stockings and the partlets and the caps and the hoods. Half of it is usually damp from the sodden weather and has to be aired at the other end for fear of mildew, only to be packed and folded again the next day to go to the next manor or palace. And then there is the hunting dress. You wouldn't believe all the bits and pieces. And the mud—the mud is the worst, clumped on the boots, spattered on the riding habits, clinging to the hems of the dresses, dried clods of it all over the floor.

She wouldn't mind any of it, except for the fact that William Savage has not traveled with them to Otford. The Queen sent him to Devon, to look over one of her manors. It must be an honor, because she'd never seen him quite so excited about anything—well, practically never. Dot has only the vaguest idea where Devon is, somewhere far off to the west, in the bit of England that looks like the hind leg of a dog on the map. William had shown her, pointed it out in the map room at Hampton Court.

She holds her memories of him tight: the kisses in the grain store, remembering the heat of his breath, his fingers fumbling and burrowing, and the way he had her panting like a dog, her heart racing so she thought she might drop dead with the excitement of it all. Each time they came together he discovered a new part of her, bits of her own body she barely knew existed, and him grunting with desire at each uncovered mound and furrow. There was the shock of it, too, when he took hold of her hand and put it to his groin and she could feel his thing through his hose. The very hardness of it made her lose her breath when she thought of where it was supposed to end up.

When she untied his laces it burst out, as if it had a mind of its own, and swelled beneath her fingers—too much, she thought. It was surely not possible that this thing could get inside her, as Betty had told her it should. But when he lifted her skirts and directed it to the wet part of her, it fitted like one of the Queen's kid gloves. She could never have believed such pleasure existed. It was the pleasure of sin, she knew that much only too well. She sluiced herself with stinging vinegar after, which Betty swore was the best way not to get a baby.

She sometimes imagines he has gone on a quest or a crusade and that she is his maiden waiting for his return, when he will take her in his arms and tell her of his adventures. But Devon is hardly the Holy Land, and there is not much adventure to be had collecting rents or whatever it is he's doing there.

Anyway, she is too busy with all the moving about, and all the mud, to have much time for thoughts of William. Even at night she beds down so late, once the Queen and all the royal children have had enough of the cards and the chess and the poetry and—most of all—the talking. There is such a lot of talking. Dot wonders how they can think of so much to say. So by the time she unrolls her bed she can barely keep her eyes open, and all thoughts of William are lost in her exhausted sleep.

It had rained, too, bucketing down for a good ten days. She thought she would never get dry. But now the watery autumn sun is back and it is quite warm again. She is glad of that, for Meg's sake, as she can't shake off her illness. Meg left Eltham for some house whose name she's forgotten already, with Elizabeth, whom she's frankly glad to see the back of, and Prince Edward, who's a stuck-up little so-and-so, if truth be told.

Dot is worried about Meg. She had seemed to rally, but it didn't endure, and in the last few days she's developed a terrible wracking cough that makes Dot think she'll bring her guts up. She is permanently exhausted and drops off to sleep barely an hour after she's risen. But, worst of all, she seems hardly to make sense any more, seeing angels and devils all over the place, raving and talking a lot of gobbledygook. Dr. Huicke has been sent for. She prays he will know what to do.

She leaves the still-room curtain open so she can see what she's doing without having to light a candle. She doesn't know where the candles are kept in this house and can't be bothered to go looking for the right person to ask. She places the Queen's physic box on the table and opens it. It is divided into small compartments containing differ- ent herbs, each carefully labeled.

Katherine has asked that she make up a poultice for the King's leg in the way she has shown her, finely crushing one part each of golden- seal, comfrey and slippery elm and adding witch hazel, then scooping the mix into a length of cheesecloth and tying its ends.

Though she knows all the plants by smelling them, Dot looks for the letters: the "g" like a meathook; the "o" like the mouth of a choir- boy; "l" like a sword; "d" like a mallet; "e" like an ear; "n" like a church doorway. She sounds them out in groups, forming the words from them. She never told William how she remembered the shape of the letters for fear of seeming stupid. But she doesn't feel stupid now as she reads out the names of the herbs in the box, for she is a girl who can read and every word is a secret victory.

She takes a scoop of each and works at them with the pestle, crushing them into a fine powder, picking out the tough stems and dribbling in the witch hazel. The smell of it is sharp in her nose, making her eyes water. She re-corks the bottle quickly, as Katherine has shown her, to stop it disappearing into thin air. Laying out a square of muslin and doubling it, she then spoons in the mixture, tying it carefully before putting it in a wooden bowl. She tidies everything up and squeezes back past the kegs, finding her way through the tangle of corridors, counting the doorways so as not to get lost.

Katherine is in the King's chambers. He sits in the window. Dot has never got used to the sheer size of him. He sits with his legs spread wide and a codpiece so big she'd giggle at it if it weren't for the fact of whose it is. Katherine sits on a low stool, looking up at him, making Dot think of the way Rig looks up at her with his big eyes, when she can't find a way to say no to him.

The King has brought Katherine a small monkey as a gift. It has an odd little old man's face with brown glass eyes and pink pointed ears that jut out from either side of its head. Its hands are the strangest things—human, but not—and it hangs by one of them from the curtain pole, making little tutting noises like the call of a stonechat. The Queen has named him François, which, she said, amused the King greatly for that is the name of the defeated King of France.

The King looks older, and bigger than ever, his face all puffed up like a harvest moon. You wouldn't have thought Boulogne had been the great victory everyone is on about, given the slump in his shoulders and the way he's ranting on about the Emperor who, Dot gathers, has betrayed him in one way or another—something to do with King François and a treaty.

Katherine reminds him of his triumph at Boulogne, says it's his Agincourt, which is an ages-ago battle against the French that people still talk about as if it were yesterday. The King seems to sit a little straighter after that. He calls her "my darling," "my sweetheart," "my dearest Kit," "my own true love," but the Queen seems to have shrunk and is not quite right under her poised surface. Next to the King she is small and stiff.

"Would you help me with the King's poultice, Dot? Bring the stool so His Majesty can rest his leg." She begins to unlace his hose.

Dot, embarrassed, looks away, searching for a cushion to make him comfortable. She can't help but think of her own fingers unlacing William's hose. How different this is, how lacking in passion, as the King heaves his weight away from the settle and Katherine deftly pulls the garment from under him. He drops back into the seat with a groan, wrapping his robe about himself for modesty, and lifts his leg onto the stool. He does all this without once looking at Dot. It is as if she isn't there, as usual, and she's glad of that.

"My dear, we can have one of our men deal with this," he says.

"But I am your wife, Harry, and it pleases me to soothe you."

He gives a little grunt of satisfaction in reply and pats her behind as she bends to unwind the bandage, leaving the ulcer bare. The wound seems to writhe and as Dot kneels to clear away the piles of dirty bandages, she sees it is teeming with maggots like a side of rotten meat.

She gags, and the monkey begins to screech, swinging about, then jumps down to inspect the King's leg for himself with more shrieking. One of the pages comes rushing over and makes quite a meal of catching the little fellow, chasing him around the room, diving for him and bashing his head.

This raises a laugh from His Majesty. "Come on, Robin! That monkey's getting the better of you."

Robin becomes red-faced and frustrated but eventually manages to get a hold of the creature by the tail and bundles it into the hands of one of the guards outside the door. Dot's attention returns to the fact of the King's maggot-ridden wound.

"The grubs seem to have cleaned this up beautifully." If Katherine is disgusted, she doesn't show it. "Pass me an empty bowl, Dot."

Dot doesn't respond. She is quite paralyzed with revulsion, but can't tear her eyes away from the writhing, maggoty mass.

"Dot." Katherine leans over her to pick up the bowl for herself. "Would you tear some fresh muslin for bandages?"

The muslin is across the room on a side table and Dot is sure Katherine has given her this job deliberately. She walks away, relieved, but can't help glancing back to where her mistress is wiping the grubs from the wound and into the bowl. Dot wonders how she can be so sanguine, wishing she could be more like that herself.

The King winces and sucks in his breath through his teeth, shifting in his seat.

"Was it Doctor Buttes's idea to use the maggots?" she asks.

"It was."

"A good idea indeed. Look, Harry, at the thorough job they've done. I've never seen them used before, only heard of it."

They both look at his leg as if looking over a piece of French silverware.

"What wonders God has created." She takes the poultice, inspecting it, holding it up to sniff it and gently presses it against the wound. "You have done a good job with this, Dot."

Dot swells warmly with the Queen's approval. The King watches his wife in silence, head tipped to one side, and a tender expression spreads over his face the like of which Dot has never seen on him before.

"Robin, would you kindly remove these dirty things." Katherine nods in the direction of the maggoty bowl and the dirty muslins.

He collects it all together and leaves. Dot knows it should have been her job to clear up, and that her mistress has spared her the grubs.

When the page has left Katherine asks, with that dewy-eyed look that is not hers at all, "Shall I send for the musicians, Harry? I think they would lift your spirits."

"We are too angry with that fiendish Emperor for enjoyment."

"Oh Harry." She strokes his fat face. "The Emperor could never be trusted. His word means nothing."

"But he was my ally. He went behind me, made a treaty with France." He has the sound of a sulking boy. "We were supposed to conquer all France together. I would have been covered in glory. I would have been remembered like the fifth Henry."

"What do you think you can do to put the Emperor in his place?"

"We could join forces elsewhere, I suppose, but who with?"

"Who else is there? Now France is in the Emperor's pocket and the Pope is with them, that leaves . . ." She stops, seeming to wait for him to finish her sentence, but he looks deep in thought and says nothing. "If you looked further east, perhaps?"

"Turkey? That is an infernal idea." He slaps her idea down.

But she will not be blown off her course. "Not so far east as Turkey."

"The German Princes! We could make an agreement with Holstein and Hesse. They have a vast army. And Denmark too. All the Lutheran Princes. The Emperor . . . Ha! I'd like to see his face then."

"Yes." Katherine is like a tutor finally squeezing the right answer out of a student.

"We can throw in one of the girls to boot."

"But Elizabeth is so young." Katherine's fist is furled like a tight new bud that would break if you prized it open. Dot hasn't seen that for months. "And Mary, her faith . . ."

"Nonsense." The King laughs. "Mary needs marrying off before she's an old maid. If she has to marry a Lutheran, so be it." He strokes a hand across Katherine's throat before lifting her face to meet his. "Kit, you are a wonder. Not one of my council came up with such an idea."

"But Harry, the idea was yours."

The King seems to mull this over. "You are right, my sweet."

Dot wonders at the cleverness of Katherine. Though she couldn't make much of what was being said, the politics of it, she understood just what was happening. It makes her laugh inside to think of Katherine putting all her ideas into the King's head, and him not even knowing.

"Harry, I have the mind, with your permission, to write a book."

"A book." He snorts. "What sort of book? Housewifery? Flowers?"

"I intend it to be a collection of prayers or meditations."

"Faith, Kit, that is treacherous territory."

"I would not dream of straying into controversy."

"Mind you don't." He has Katherine by the wrist, is twisting it.

Dot can see her skin puckered beneath his fingers, but no pain registers on her face.

33

Greenwich Palace, March 1545

Meg is on the bed doubled up with coughing. It had got worse and worse over the winter months. Dot had thought that as the weather improved Meg would rally, but the daffodils are all out now, standing like soldiers in the Greenwich gardens, and Meg is withering like an autumn leaf.

Dot loosens Meg's stomacher and rubs salve into her chest. The girl is shivering. Her handkerchief drops to the floor. Dot bends to pick it up.

There is a red flower blooming in its white folds, sewing a seed of dread into her.

"How long has this been happening?" She has the square of linen open in her hand, the red blot on display.

Meg doesn't look at it, just takes the counterpane and wraps it more tightly round her. "Please would you put another log on?"

"Answer me!"

"It is so very cold."

"Meg." Dot climbs on the bed and takes her shoulders, looking right at her. "How long have you been coughing up blood?"

"A month or two." Her voice is small.

"A month or two?" Dot's response comes out louder than she intends. "What does Huicke say?"

"I haven't told him."

"He is your doctor, Meg. That is what he is for."

Dot can feel the prick of tears. She pulls Meg into a bear hug so

her face can't be seen. Everybody knows that when you start coughing up blood your days are numbered.

Releasing Meg, she goes to the fire, heaving a big log out of the
basket, throwing it in, pushing the embers around it with the poker. It
catches fast, long tongues of flame flicking up.

"I shall have to tell the Queen."

Meg is silent. She is reading a book, a religious one. She never
reads the romances any more. The room is unbearably quiet, just the
crackle of the fire and the rasp of Meg's breath.

Dot picks up the handkerchief and slips out of the room.

Katherine is reciting something to a group of her maids in the
watching chamber. Dot must look like she's seen a ghost, or worse,
for when Katherine catches sight of her she excuses herself, beckoning
Dot to follow her into the privy chamber.

"What is it?" Katherine closes the door behind them.

Dot opens her palm, exposing the crumple of stained linen.

"Father have mercy." Katherine brings a hand to her heart. "Meg?"

Dot nods, she can't speak, her voice has disappeared away into her
and cannot be found.

"I feared as much."

They stand motionless for what seems like an age and then Katherine opens her arms. Dot falls into them, allowing, at last, the tears
to gush out of her in great sputtering sobs.

"I feared as much." Katherine keeps repeating it as if she has lost
her words too.

Dot has never been much of a weeper but now she cannot stop,
feels she is crying out all the tears that never came before. Katherine
is stroking her hair. Dot breaks out of the embrace and dries her eyes
on her pinny, leaving black smudges from where she had powdered
her lids with soot from the charcoal burner. (It was Betty who'd first
shown her that, "to pretty her up," as she put it. Betty was always full
of tricks to get the boys' attentions.)

Katherine takes a cloth from the basin, squeezes it out and wipes it
over Dot's face. The cloth smells slightly mildewy, reminding Dot she
should have boiled it this morning.

"She never fully recovered from that time at . . ." Katherine doesn't finish her sentence, doesn't need to name the place. Murgatroyd may have been dead a decade but he is still stitched through their lives and will not be unpicked.

"That cursed man."

They sit on the settle by the window. There are birds twittering outside; they must be nesting under the eaves.

"I have often wondered why Meg was so deeply affected. Was it her tender years, do you think?"

Dot feels the weight of Meg's secret like a mallet that has hammered her down into the ground so far she can hardly breathe. But when she thinks about it, keeping that secret has served for nothing. "There is something . . ."

"Something?"

"Meg swore me to secrecy."

"The time for secrets is over."

It has been so deeply buried in her and for so long she hardly knows how she will find the words to tell it. "That man . . . He brutalized her . . . He ruined her."

Katherine has both hands over her mouth, aghast. Dot has never seen her like this, speechless, distraught.

"I failed . . . failed, Dot . . ." She pauses, twisting her fingers in her lap. "You should have told me."

"I made a promise."

"A promise." She sighs. "Your loyalty is watertight." She goes back to wringing her hands in a thick silence.

When she speaks again Dot can hear the grief in her voice.

"I thought I had protected her. All these years I thought that by giving myself to him she would be safe . . . you both . . ." She stumbles over her words. "You would . . . both be saved."

"I know it is little consolation but he did not touch *me*," Dot says.

"You have your low birth to thank for that. Small mercies, Dot— small mercies." Her voice is bitter as gentian. "If he had not hanged, I would find that man and tear him limb from limb with my very hands."

There is a clatter in the watching chamber, a burst of laughter and the clop and rattle of passing horses in the court below. Life is the same outside this room, but all Dot can think of is Meg coughing her heart up.

"Some people are not meant to be long on this earth. God is calling her. I hope he won't take his time as he did with . . ."

Dot supposes she is thinking of Lord Latymer and his death dragging out for all those months, the terrible pain of it. Without thinking, Dot picks up Katherine's hand, carefully unfolding each stiff finger, opening it out, rubbing the knuckles one at a time.

The Queen's face meets hers with a look of silent acknowledgment. "But Dot, you know you have been such a comfort to Meg, always. You have been her true friend. Stay close to her. Don't leave her side. I shall try to come when I can but you know how it is for me."

By that Dot knows she means she is at the beck and call of the King and that he has to come before Meg.

The King comes before everything—that is simply how things are, like it or not.

Often Dot wakes to find Katherine, looking for all the world like a ghost in her pale nightgown, sitting on the corner of Meg's bed, singing quietly to her, or kneeling beside her whispering a prayer.

Meg is fading, her petals falling one by one, and these last few days she seems as if she is not really here, but in some other place. A better one, Dot hopes. She blathers about angels, never making much sense, and then she seems peaceful until a fit of coughing wracks her, as if her body is trying to turn itself inside out.

And sometimes she grabs Dot's hand and says, "I am afraid, Dot. I am afraid to die."

Dot sits beside her bed, wondering if all the believing and the praying and reading of the Bible will help Meg when it comes to it.

She stays with her constantly, washing her, feeding her, administering her physic, just as Katherine had done for Lord Latymer. Dr. Huicke comes daily. He says there is nothing that will save her, that he can take some of the pain away with tinctures, that is all. But then they knew that, had known it from the moment Dot had found the blot of blood in the white handkerchief.

Elizabeth doesn't come, though Katherine has called for her. She is at Ashridge with her brother. She *has* sent a letter, which Meg reads over and over again. Dot has read it too. It doesn't say much, just a few platitudes. That is a word Dot learned from William Savage. There has been nothing from him since he left months ago and Dot has tried to forget him, but inside she is eaten up with longing. She tells herself not to be so stupid, that William Savage is no Lancelot, he is just a man who got his end away with a silly lass.

But what of the time spent teaching her to read, and the time spent gazing at her and saying, "There is not a maid in the world like you, Dorothy Fownten, and no one I would rather pass my time with"— surely all that was not just to get a tumble from her? He could have got that from Betty just by patting her on the behind and offering her a cup of ale.

If she lets herself think about it she cannot find a good reason why there has not even been so much as a note. For all that teaching her to read, and not one single letter. Perhaps he is afraid that such a thing might get into the wrong hands and cause trouble for her, but she fears she is forgotten.

Katherine mentioned William's name the other day, said she missed his playing, and Dot had wanted to ask where he was, whether he would return to court. But she was afraid of giving her secret away with a blush, or that it might show all over her that she loves him. Besides, he has been gone so long now she struggles to hold the image of him in her mind. He has faded to nothing, like the ghost patterns the dropped autumn leaves make on the flagstones when they are wet. And now her whole self is taken up with poor Meg, and there is no room left for thoughts of love.

Meg also reads, no, devours, the book Elizabeth had sent to the Queen for the New Year just past. It was written in her own hand, a translation of something in both English and Latin, with a binding worked in red and green. It had been passed around the ladies, who had sighed in wonder at it. Dot had sneaked a look, had just had time to read the title, *Mirror of the Sinful Soul*, before being interrupted and having to pretend she was dusting the table it lay on.

Dot had to admit, begrudgingly, that it was a remarkable thing for a girl so young to produce. That Elizabeth has something others don't have. It is not the brilliant mind, nor the fact that she is the King's daughter—for Mary doesn't have it—but it is something that can't be measured or understood, that makes people, both men and women, fall a little in love with her.

Not Dot, though. Dot knows that what she feels for Elizabeth is pure envy and that envy is one of the deadly sins. But it is *she*, not Elizabeth, who is with Meg now, when it matters, she who lies on the bed next to her and sings her softly to sleep, she who wipes her burning head with a cool cloth and holds a cup of broth to her lips when she is too weak to hold it for herself. She sits in silence to keep her company, while Meg reads out passages from Elizabeth's book in a wheezing voice. Dot would burn that book if she had the guts and if she did not think it would break Meg's heart.

"Dot." Meg half wakes. "Is that you?"

"It is I."

"Can you get me something to write with?" She sits herself up, seems more full of life than she has for days.

Dot feels a trickle of hope.

But Meg then says, "I want to write my will. Would you send for the notary?"

Dot wants to shout, *Why would you do that—wills are for dead people*, but she nods, placing the escritoire on the bed. "I will go and mix your tincture and let your mother know you have called for the notary."

As soon as her will is written Meg sinks into a decline.

Katherine now sits with her constantly too, and Dot tries to keep busy, not think about what is happening. Meg struggles to get air into her body and, though she says nothing, it is clear that each breath is horribly painful.

As she fades, the chaplain is called for. He comes, smelling of incense, and mutters the blessing.

They all sit in silence, and it is as if time has stopped.

Then she is gone.

The chaplain collects together his things and leaves quietly.

Dot and Katherine sit with nothing to say and Meg going cold on the bed next to them.

"We shall dress her in her finest gown," says Katherine. "Help me, Dot."

"But the embalmers—"

"People will want to say a prayer for her this evening. I want them to remember her at her best."

They wash her corpse carefully, as if afraid to hurt her. Dot pretends she is made of wood, like a church virgin. That is the only way she can bear it. She picks up the ewer to fill the basin but it slips through her fingers and shatters on the floor with a crash and a gush of water. Dot bursts into tears as if *she* has shattered, too, and all the water is spilling out of her. She drops onto the wet floor, hiccuping up great sobs.

Katherine sits with her, not even noticing that the water is soaking her silk gown and that the colors of the embroidery are running into the yellow fabric. They sit like that in a damp embrace, rocking back and forth, until a page disturbs them, looking embarrassed by their tears.

34

Greenwich Palace, June 1545

Katherine enters her privy chamber with Cat Brandon to find Rig barking manically at François the monkey, who is crouched just out of reach, balanced on the back of a chair and sucking on a plum stone, with his long tail carefully curled up out of danger. In his other hairy little hand he clutches Rig's favorite toy, a wooden mouse.

Katherine hasn't warmed to the monkey. He's a pest, but she hasn't had the heart to get rid of him, despite the fact he has tried to bite her a couple of times. He has poor Dot running around cleaning up the chaos he causes.

Cat's dog scampers in, joining Rig with a high-pitched yapping. The monkey teases the pair of them by waving the mouse about.

"Gardiner, stop that!" Cat admonishes her dog.

The two women turn to each other with a burst of laughter, adding to the noise. It is the first time Katherine has really laughed in weeks. Meg's death has cast a long shadow.

"I still can't believe you called him Gardiner," says Anne, following them into the room. "I'd never have dared."

"The Bishop lost his sense of humor over it." Cat makes a half-hearted attempt to catch her dog but he is too quick for her.

"I wasn't aware he ever had one." Katherine makes light of it but Gardiner is a sinister presence for her.

"He has to force himself to find it when my husband is with me, though it looks more like some kind of convulsion than any kind of amusement." Cat is still laughing.

One of the ushers has Rig by his bejeweled collar and is trying, with his other hand, to catch Gardiner, who's become so excited he's relieved himself on the matting. Dot wipes up the mess and manages to prize the mouse from the monkey's hairy grip. Cat scoops up her dog and the din subsides.

They settle on the cushions, in a pool of sun from the window. In spite of the brightness, the ladies make a somber group now the silliness is over. They are all still dressed in black for Meg. It has been the best part of three months.

Katherine offered Dot a new dress in good black fustian and a hood to go with it, which she is wearing now. She cuts a fine figure in it, though she has already lost the matching partlet and there is a new rip in the skirt where she must have caught it on something.

There is something about Dot's lack of refinement that Katherine finds endearing, especially in this place where everything is run so very seamlessly and people's affectations come to define them. With Meg gone Dot has become all the more precious. Though she would never divulge it, she thinks of the girl as a daughter even more than she does Elizabeth or Mary. The past has attached them one to the other very tightly.

Nan Stanhope arrives, making a kerfuffle about something, shouting at her maid in the corridor. As she enters she throws a backward glare at the poor cowering girl that would sour milk. Katherine swaps a look with Cat, who rolls her eyes. Nan's dress is magnificent, peacock blue, woven through with gold.

"I see you have abandoned your mourning dress." Anne takes the words from Katherine's mouth.

"My best black was filthy."

"Was it indeed," Katherine says. She would love to command her to leave but she must hold her tongue and not make an enemy of her.

Nan Stanhope joins the three ladies on the cushions, all smiles, beginning to tell of a great storm in Derbyshire. "There were hailstones as large as boulders—"

A page enters, interrupting her. "Madam, this is from Bertelet the printer, just arrived." He hands a packet to Katherine with a deep bow.

Katherine feels a thrill as she takes it, ripping the paper wrapping, flinging it to one side. What she holds is the first copy of her very own book—*Prayers or Meditations*. François seizes the discarded wrapping in his monkey hand, beginning to tear it into small pieces.

Katherine holds up the book, turning it over, inspecting it from every angle. It is white calfskin, soft as an infant's skin, embossed in gold. She opens it carefully, turning the pages slowly, not reading—every word of it is written indelibly into her mind—just admiring it.

"Let me see," says Cat.

Katherine hands the book to her.

She turns the pages with a look of wonder on her face. "This is important, Kit."

Anne has taken it now, and begins to read a passage.

> Now I often mourn and complain of the miseries of this life, and with sorrow and great heaviness suffer them. For many things happen daily to me which oftentimes trouble me, making me heavy, and darken mine understanding. They hinder me greatly, and put my mind from thee and so encumber me many ways, that I cannot freely and clearly desire thee.

"Oh Kit," sighs Anne, "this is beautiful."

"You are the first," adds Cat. "The first Queen to publish your own words in English. This makes history."

Katherine's head spins with it: her own words printed there in black ink. As she listens to her sister reading out another passage she, too, feels indelible, as if in some small way she has evaded earthly annihilation. She mourns Meg's loss as deeply as if she had birthed the girl herself, but this book is a salve. When she thinks about it, it is like a birth, though gestated in her mind rather than her belly. It is something that will live beyond her.

She asks the Lord daily why, after two years of marriage, he doesn't bless her with a child, why it is that they all—Nan Stanhope, Anne, that insufferable Jane Wriothesley—all of them, pop children out one after the other, but not her.

Jane Wriothesley had lost a boy not so long ago and was beside herself with grief, wept for weeks, wouldn't eat. Katherine was assaulted with memories of her own dead boy and how her grief had to be buried so deeply it could never be retrieved.

She tried to sympathize with Jane. Jane had others, was almost permanently with child. Katherine had written to her, reminding her that her boy was blessed to be taken by the Lord and that she should try to be grateful that he would not have to suffer an earthly existence. She regretted the letter had gone too far, been too hard-hearted, and Wriothesley had complained to the King.

"God has chosen that child for Heaven, is that not a blessing?" she had defended herself curtly, when the King brought it up.

"You are right, Katherine, always right, but you have upset Wriothesley. He is our Lord Chancellor and we will *not* have him upset. Apologize to the woman."

She had swallowed her words and couldn't quite bring herself to properly apologize, but she had grudgingly invited Jane Wriothesley to sit beside her one evening to watch a masque. Jane had been overflowing with delight about it, fidgeting with excitement to be seated beside the Queen.

But in spite of this favor, Katherine increasingly feels Wriothesley's eyes on her, unpicking her. Now Henry has made him Lord Chancellor, he seems to think himself invincible, seems to forget that Cromwell was Lord Chancellor, Thomas More too—and look what became of them.

Wriothesley's dislike of her, of what she stands for, is palpable, though he tries to hide it. She feels his circle closing in on her, waiting, watching for her to slip up. She has no son—there is one chink in her armor. She has no powerful blood relatives to speak of—another chink.

The King has begun to carry a small silver box tucked in his doublet, containing a few splinters of wood from the cross. But they could as well be from a broken gate. It is a sure sign he is turning back to the old faith—a further chink. It will not be long before they are thrusting some pretty thing under her husband's nose and suggesting he will get a son that way.

But the King is in Portsmouth leading the new campaign against the French, who are pushing at the south coast with their warships. He sends letters telling of his galleons, greater by far than the French ones, he says. She isn't sure if it is better he is away, and can't be tempted by marriageable maids at court, or worse because he's not here standing between her and the Catholic vultures, and at least presenting her with the possibility of conceiving another Prince.

Anne flicks through the pages, looking for another passage to read. Katherine notices that Dot has stopped sweeping the hearth and stands, half turned towards the women as if to better hear what they are saying.

"Would you like to see it?" she asks the girl.

Dot nods and bobs in an embarrassed little curtsy. She wipes her hands on her apron before taking the book, bringing it to her nose to breathe in its scent, holding it carefully as you might a newborn. She opens the first page, running her fingers over its surface.

"Prayers or meditations, wherein the mind is stirred." She is whispering. "By the most virtuous and gracious Princess Katherine Queen of England."

"Dot?" Katherine is astonished at what she has just witnessed. "Since when could you read?"

Dot has an odd look about her and stumbles over her words. "I can't really." She blushes. "I've just picked up a few words here and there, madam."

"You're a clever girl. It's a shame you were not gently born and given a proper education."

It strikes her that Dot must miss Meg at least as much as she does. That she no longer has anyone to read to her.

"What use is reading for a servant maid?" Nan Stanhope is saying just as Huicke bursts into the chamber unannounced.

"My book, it has arrived." Katherine holds out the volume to him but he doesn't take it.

His face is gray and unsmiling.

"What is it, Huicke?"

They are all looking at him now and slowly rise from the cushions like a bunch of black tulips replenished with water. He makes a minuscule gesture with his head towards the usher, Percy, who stands by the door. Katherine returns it with an almost imperceptible nod. François the ape, who has interpreted the new thick atmosphere as one of danger, begins to shriek, providing her with a perfect excuse.

"Percy," she says, "would you please remove that creature. It is giving me a headache."

The usher jumps to it, taking the screaming monkey and leaving the room. Huicke glances towards Dot, who is busy by the hearth.

"We can trust her," says Katherine.

They gather into a circle to hear what it is Huicke has to say.

"Anne Askew has been arrested."

The color drains from each of their faces.

"It is starting," says Anne.

"This is Gardiner and Wriothesley's doing," says Huicke.

"We must get rid of anything that links us to her, any books, letters. The Queen's rooms must be cleared." Cat is ever practical, even in a crisis.

But this is not a crisis yet, thinks Katherine.

Nan Stanhope has her hand over her mouth, eyes wide with trepidation, silent for once.

"Shall I call for Udall to help spirit things away?" suggests Huicke. "He is so very ingenious—"

"No!" Katherine does her best to sound calm. "I think not, Huicke. Let's keep him out of it. Anne, you warn the others." But she sees the flash of panic in her sister's eyes and notices that Cat has seen it too.

"*I* shall warn the others," says Cat. "You go home to Baynard's and make sure you burn anything there, Anne. Can you get word to your husband, discreetly? No one must see that we're perturbed."

Katherine squeezes her sister's hand and turns to Nan, saying, "You should let *your* husband know too. They are bound to have kept it from him." She hasn't moved and is still standing with her hand over her mouth. "Above all, we must behave as if none of this is happening."

They disperse and Katherine beckons Dot.

"Help me pack up the books. I will send for someone to remove them."

Dot nods. She has a smudge of ash on her cheek, which Katherine absently brushes away with her finger.

She drops her voice further. "You must not breathe a word of this." But she knows that, of everyone, Dot can be trusted. Dot is probably closer to her than anyone. "You do understand the seriousness of this. If Anne Askew can be linked to me, we will all burn."

It is only on saying it, and the look of terror on Dot's face, that the words seem to find a foothold in her, and she feels a sensation of heat rising up her body as if the flames are licking at her already.

She is horrified by her own recklessness, as if seeing for the first time that she has brought this danger to her own door willingly. She wants to tell herself that the King adores her, would never let her burn, but she knows only too well that if Wriothesley and Gardiner and that toady Richard Rich can waft a cloud of heresy her way they will all be choked on it. The King will know nothing of it until it is too late.

And the King is not here.

Dot picks up Katherine's book, her new book, the book that, only minutes ago, was the thing that shored her up against obliteration. It seems diminished, just a few leaves of paper bound in hide, and some words—a woman's prayers, no more. She feels like a child standing in the face of things so much bigger than her that she can't make out their shape.

"Not that one, Dot. That has nothing in it that would condemn us."

Part of her wishes her book *did* have something in it to condemn her, that she'd had the courage to fill it with Calvin's ideas, *justification by faith alone*, for that is what she firmly believes.

If she were truly a great Queen she would be prepared to go out in a blaze for that. But she is no Anne Askew, who shouts her faith from the rooftops. *Scripture alone, faith alone, grace alone, Christ alone, glory to God alone.* But then Anne Askew is not Queen, and there is no need to shout when the King's ear lies on the pillow next to you.

She resolves to keep on persuading Henry, gently, towards reform, to bring back the English Bibles for everybody, so people can read God's word for themselves, so they can think for themselves, to rid England of Catholic corruption. In her head she is planning another book already, a better book, one that stands up and loudly announces her faith, the new faith, a book with the power to change things.

A book she will write if she survives.

PART THREE

I cannot bring myself out of this entangled and wayward maze: but the more I seek means and ways to wind myself out, the more I am wrapped and tangled therein.

Katherine Parr—The Lamentation of a Sinner

35

Dot rushes down the long gallery with the infernal François in her arms. This monkey is proving as troublesome as the French King he's named after. He's trying to wriggle from her hold, nipping at her with his sharp yellow fangs. He has already bitten her once and drawn blood.

Her heart stops to see the unmistakable silhouette of William Savage framed in the doorway at the end of the gallery.

She halts, unable to move. All she can think of is the fact that she has a rip in her pinny and her hair is all over the place.

He sees her too.

Her stopped heart starts again, like the clappers. It has been so very long, but there he is, her dearest William.

"If it isn't my Dot. My full stop."

"You're back."

The monkey takes his chance, leaping from her arms, but William grabs him.

"Looks just like you." He chucks the monkey under the chin as you might a baby. She is confused for a moment, doesn't know what he means, until he laughs and his joke eventually sinks in.

He returns the monkey, his hand brushing hers. She smiles, wanting to touch him properly right there, in front of everyone, to push him up against the wall and press her mouth onto his.

But he seems older, bigger, different. His hair is longer and there is no ink on his fingers. She can see the dark dots of stubble on his chin where there used to be a wispy beard, and his clothes are fancy, covered in silver aiglets. He even smells different, of some cloying perfume. He is a stranger, but familiar, and she is made awkward in the face of him.

"Where have you been?" Her voice is no more than a whisper.

"Devon. And I have thought of you every day."

Her heart bloats, making speech seem impossible, but she squeezes out a faint "And I, you."

The monkey leans forward and picks at an aiglet on his doublet, which makes him smile, and the sight of his dimple makes her feel as if the root of her is being wrenched at. She wants to think of something to say but her mind is befuddled by the nearness of him. She wants to bury her nose in the soft part of his throat and find his real smell.

"Who is this then?"

"François. He was a gift to the Queen."

"So are you the Queen's monkey keeper now?"

He's teasing and she can't think of anything bright or funny to say. A silence hangs invisibly between them.

"I have been reading," she blurts out.

"My diligent Dot."

She wants to tell him everything. To tell him about getting rid of all the books and how the whole of the Queen's household had been in a spin of fear, and how Anne Askew was freed for lack of evidence against her—but he must know all this, for he is one of them. (Whether Dot is quite one of them she is not sure, but she thinks that all the carting around of books and knowing so many secrets must mean she is.)

"Things have been—" she begins, but is interrupted.

"I see you have become acquainted with my pet monkey." It is Katherine herself who has glided up silently.

William drops to his knee. "I have indeed, Highness, and a fine specimen he is too."

"As a matter of fact he's rather a nuisance, isn't he, Dot? But he was a gift from you know who, so he's here to stay, I'm afraid. It is good to see you, William Savage. I've missed your playing. So how does your wife? Got any little ones yet?"

Dot feels as if her legs might give way under her. Wife! She had known he must marry one day, but she had assumed that day was years off, and secretly she'd harbored impossible hopes that make her feel, in this moment, that she has been had. Like when one of the fools singles you out for a humiliation so fond, you don't know it till after it's done.

He has a wife *already*? She looks at him for some kind of an explanation but his eyes are firmly directed towards the Queen. And what is there to say, anyway? He is married and she is just plain Dot Fownten—that is that.

She manages to gather herself together and turns to take her leave, but the monkey will not let go of William's doublet. The Queen laughs, making a joke about it. William reddens and tries to loosen the monkey's tightly gripped fingers. Dot, desperate now to remove herself, tugs hard at the animal.

The doublet rips as the monkey's hand breaks free, provoking great guffaws of laughter. A crowd has begun to gather about them and Dot would gladly drop through the floor with the shame of it.

Jane, the Queen's new fool, appears. She has a big round face and a wandering eye and talks as if she has drunk too much ale. It is nonsense mostly, nursery rhymes and drivel, but sometimes there is a strange sense in her madness, as if she is echoing the things people don't dare say. She elbows herself to the front of the gathering and, looking François in the eye, pats her shoulder. The monkey jumps onto it, perching there smugly as if Hell's fire wouldn't burn him.

"The higher an ape climbs," Jane utters, "the more you see of its backside."

This provokes more laughter. Dot is left standing there, desperate to leave, but unable to find the words to excuse herself.

Katherine seems to sense her discomfort. "You go, Dot, I'll see to this."

And she slips away, down the backstairs and out through the courtyard, past the guards at the gate and down towards the river.

The streets are seething with people, carts trundle by, and hawkers shout out, advertising their wares. In her good black dress they think her the kind of person who has the money to buy, and so she is stopped every few steps by someone aiming to part her from the coins she doesn't have. Some of them are quite forceful and she is glad she has nothing, so she can't be fleeced.

The tide is low with great muddy tracts exposed where a few boys, ankle deep in sludge, pick about, looking for scrap metal and other bits and pieces dropped from the boats. A dead stench rises from the black mud.

Two seagulls squawk and fight over the carcass of a fish. Another, larger and with a great hooked beak, swoops down and grabs it from them, flying off to perch on a post with it. The others cark in complaint and continue pecking about among the filth. It is like that, Dot thinks, the strong get the best of things and the rest are left to complain.

She stands on the embankment, watching the slow summer flow of the river and the wherries carrying people back and forth, thinking of the sea somewhere at the end of it where the King is fighting battles against the French—the court is full of it. She imagines throwing herself in, her swollen heart a dead weight in her chest, pulling her under into the depths, being swallowed up and spat out downriver to be picked over by gulls.

Feeling the contour of her penny stitched into her hem, she wonders what her family would think if she disappeared, but they are so very distant and she doubts they would even hear of it for months. It is as if that was another girl, from another world, who lived that life in Stanstead Abbotts, craving after Harry Dent and yabbering with the maids in the village square.

She has a yearning in her for the simplicity of it all and a sense of loss for what she might have had, a string of sprogs and a drunk for a husband and nothing but pottage for weeks in the lean part of the year—all the normal cares.

Dot hasn't wanted for a meal since she can remember and she is now a girl with expectations. Meg left her four pounds a year, more than she has ever imagined, which will come to her soon—or so the notary had said. That may be, but her worries now are so much more difficult to get a grip on, the sense of danger hiding behind the brilliant tapestries, of everything having to be kept secret, and just Katherine standing between her and God alone knows what.

She feels the great burden of all the things she mustn't tell: the books, the reading, Anne Askew, the map of marks and bruises on the Queen's body, the events at Snape. She feels pinned down by all these secrets as if she's nailed to the palace walls through the hands and feet, like Christ.

And then there is William Savage. *My Dot, my full stop*—and what is a full stop but a tiny mark on a page, a nothing, that marks an ending? She will not think of William. He was never hers to begin with. She will pretend he doesn't exist.

Meg's absence is like a hole in her chest. Poor Meg, who disappeared before her eyes. They had been as close as sisters. It had never seemed to matter that Meg was who she was and shouldn't have been sharing confidences with a nothing-special girl like Dot, just a servant, even if she did have a good dress and a well-fed flush in her cheeks.

It was only the months—the Elizabeth months, is how Dot thinks of them—when they lost each other. But that was short-lived. Elizabeth puts a spell on people, that is her way. She takes them if she wants them and gets rid of them when she is bored. Dot has watched her do it. She doesn't blame Meg. Meg who coughed her heart up until it stopped beating. Four pounds a year will never make up for the loss of Meg.

It is only Katherine whom Elizabeth never discards. She has attached herself so close that the Queen cannot see what she is really like. But Dot sees, and she will not let that girl get between her and her mistress, for Katherine is all *she* has left. There are some uses to being so insignificant. To Elizabeth, Dot is nothing more than a dust mouse in the corner of the room and not a threat at all.

She walks back slowly through the evening bustle. It is warm and the square outside the palace gates teems with people who have gathered to pass the time of day and make the most of the last of the sun. Some girls are playing a skipping game, trying to avoid the dogs sniffing about their feet for scraps. A few men lounge against a wall with cups of ale, watching and making comments. Women chat in huddles, babies on hips.

Dot could be one of those women, if her life had not changed course all those years ago. A crier's bell rings out and his call, "Hear ye! Hear ye!" She can see the flash of his scarlet gown through the crowd that has gathered around him and pushes forward to find out what news has drawn such a throng.

"French fleet turned in the Solent. The King's ship *Mary Rose* is sunk. Near on five hundred souls drowned. Vice-Admiral Sir George Carew lost with his ship."

People stop what they are doing, shock on their faces, some fall to their knees in prayer.

Dot tries again to imagine what it must be like, the sea. Like the river—only vast? She thinks of the picture of ships that hangs at the palace, with the sea dark as oxtail soup boiling in a pan.

It strikes her suddenly how it must have been for those men trapped in the bowels of that great ship, sinking down to their watery grave, and how they are all the same when it comes to the end of it. From the Vice-Admiral right down to the lad who scrubs the decks—when you go, you are brought to nothing.

Regardless of how high you have climbed.

36

"He named that ship after his sister," says Katherine.

"Terrible, terrible." Huicke is visibly stricken.

"The horror of it," says Anne.

They are a somber group, sitting for supper in the watching chamber.

"Cranmer will hold a service for the dead."

Katherine picks at some unidentifiable viands on her trencher. They are dry, almost inedible and have been sliced from a monstrous creature: the tail of a peacock, the body of a pig, the head of a swan, the wings of what, she's not quite sure, and in it, various other unidentifiable creatures, stuffed one inside the other.

It is truly macabre when she thinks about it, but this is what they serve to Queens, no matter what. The small group had clapped politely when Cook came up himself, sweating and beetroot-faced from the kitchen, struggling under the weight of the monster he'd created. He'd placed it before her and wiped his hands on his apron.

Katherine smiled and told him he had a unique talent and that she'd never before seen anything quite so . . . she struggled for a word and came up with "wondrous." He seemed satisfied with that.

Susan Clarencieux slips into the room. She has a way of gliding as if there are wheels beneath her dress rather than feet. She is in yellow, as ever, from head to toe, which draws the color from her. Her eyes move over the table, with the look of a bookkeeper counting up how much everything on it has cost, and she sinks into a deep curtsy.

A stickler for correct protocol, she waits, looking down at the floor, until Katherine bids her stand. And though clearly she is here to

convey a message from Lady Mary—why else would she be here?—
she doesn't speak until Katherine asks her to. Katherine hasn't forgotten how off-hand Susan used to be with her before she was Queen.

"Madam"—Susan annunciates clearly in the way an actor
might—"the Lady Mary is indisposed."

Katherine wants to say, for goodness' sake relax. "Is it one of her
headaches?" she says instead.

"It is, madam."

"Oh dear, poor Mary. Will you send her my fond wishes?"

"I will, madam." She seems to be totting up the number of rings on
Katherine's fingers now, assessing their value. "And . . ." She hesitates.

"Yes?"

"My lady asks that you forgive her for not having completed her
translation."

"Please tell her I understand."

Mary has proved reluctant about the translation of St. John. Her
initial enthusiasm had led Katherine to hope that her stepdaughter
was coming round to the idea of the gospel in English. If anything,
it has done the opposite and she has, since the time at Eltham, descended into a routine of headaches, prayer and little else.

Katherine thinks now that she will never be turned, that the memory
of her poor mother is indelibly etched on her. Meanwhile, the reforms
are coming to nothing. The idea of a treaty with the Lutheran Princes
has turned to dust. The Catholics are on the rise, and with the King's
blessing.

Katherine feels the shift of power in the corridors of the court, the
eyes on her, watching—and Mary's snub just adds to it all. But they
couldn't find a way to be rid of Anne Askew. That is a small triumph
and makes Katherine believe in the possibility that she may be forgiven for the sins which have clogged her up for so long.

No one is really eating—aside from Udall, who seems unaffected
by the loss of the *Mary Rose* and all those drowned sailors, even
George Carew, whom he knew quite well. He is quaffing back wine
and refilling his trencher, piling it up, chatting, laughing between
mouthfuls. His callousness appalls her.

She cannot help but think of the five hundred souls lost, and for what? It all seems so futile. French troops pressing at the south coast; the Scots and their border raids to the north; treaties made and broken with seeming ease; nations stitched together as ugly as the monstrous cockatrice on the table, to join forces and kill each other. And for what? To prize another few leagues of blighted land back from someone. And this is civilization.

It is nothing but a struggle over territory, and to what ends? She can't see how, at the core of it, this killing in the name of God has anything to do with faith. It is about power. She sees what her husband has had to become in order to keep the threats at bay, from outside, and worse, from inside. He has had to set his humanity aside. But each death is a tragedy—each lost life leaves a weeping parent, spouse, sisters, brothers, little ones perhaps.

She thinks of Meg, trying to find a way to give her life meaning—nineteen pitiable years, the slow loss of her mind, and a body that turned on her in the end. She can't order it in her head, wonders if there is meaning in anything. The world is only comprehensible when everything is done in obedience to God, but her faith is being chipped away.

But then obedience is a habit deeply woven into the fabric of her, the pattern of it informing everything. If it were taken away, the design of her life would lose all coherence. To be a woman is to know obedience. She sometimes feels she has used up all her wifely sympathy. The King will be back from the coast soon. She lists in her head the things he will be angry about: the loss of his ship; the failure to make a treaty with the Germans; the Emperor who is angry and feels betrayed.

She will be blamed, no doubt, for the loss of his ship, the pain in his leg, the fact that there is no Duke of York in her belly, even the weather. She wonders if she has sufficient patience, though she knows, too, that she has no choice but to find it. And in order to do so, she must draw God closer. The only way she will make sense of things is through Him, through His word. *In the beginning was the Word ... and the Word was God.*

She must focus her mind. Think of Anne Askew—mercifully released. Think of Copernicus's new map of the universe and the eclipse, there is sense in that, heralding the great changes, and she at the vanguard of that. That is her duty. *In the beginning was the Word.*

And when people can read the words for themselves, they will discover that God is no tyrant, but a forgiving and benevolent father. That when he takes lives like that, in their prime, he takes them to a better place. He cuts short their suffering. She must believe this, otherwise—what?

She goes through the motions, her smooth veneer covering the rumble of thoughts in her head. She converses lightly, sips at her ale, makes appreciative noises over the almond jellies and the sweet wine and the crystal glasses, politely listens to Mary Dudley stumble through one of Surrey's beautiful poems, rendering it ugly, watches some acrobats fling themselves about, all with a smile on her face— and when she can, she takes her leave.

She can't stop thinking about something Nan Stanhope said to her the previous day. It niggles at her.

"When you met Anne Askew," she'd said.

They had been talking of the scriptures. Nan is as fervent a reformer as Katherine, Hertford her husband even more so. But Katherine doesn't trust her. How does she know about Anne Askew's visit? It was so very secret. Who could have told? How many others know? Who?

"I have never met the woman." Katherine had looked straight into Nan's reptilian eyes.

Another lie, another rupture to her bedraggled soul. She has become quite accustomed to lying these days.

37

Dot rubs lavender oil into Katherine's scalp, the smell of it spreading into the room, and then begins the lengthy process of dividing her long hair into sections and drawing the fine comb through it.

They do this in silence for some time, with Dot occasionally interrupting her rhythmic strokes to untangle a knot of hair or to pick a stray louse out of the comb. It is a weekly ritual and one both women enjoy for its ordinariness and intimacy.

Occasionally she has envied the simplicity of Dot's life, would have changed places with her gladly, but when she really thinks about it, she can see that hers must be a lonely existence between two worlds. She has never stopped, until now, to wonder whether Dot has someone to comb the lice out of her hair. She owes Dot so much. Sweet disheveled Dot, head in the clouds, always unperturbed, optimistic, but there is something subdued about her today as if she has been dipped in a vat of sadness.

"How is it, Dot," she asks, "are you content, do you have friends at the palace?"

"Not here, madam, but at Hampton Court there is Betty in the kitchens. She is a friend of sorts, though——"

"I have never thought of that," interrupts Katherine. "When we travel we all go together but many of the lower staff do not."

"That is true, madam. But when Meg . . ."

A silence drops into the room like a stone and Dot continues dividing and combing and untangling. Meg's absence hangs over them. But there is something else.

Katherine had noticed a look between Dot and William Savage

earlier, during the nonsense with that damned monkey. It was not a look really, more the opposite of it, the way they had *not* looked at each other, not at all, not even a glance, and she had felt a kind of thickening of the air between the two of them, which made her wonder if there was more to Dot and William Savage than simply the conveying of books to her.

"What do you think, Dot"—Katherine breaks the silence—"of William Savage?"

She cannot see Dot's face and doesn't want to turn for fear the girl will think it an inquisition. But she hears a trembling intake of breath that tells her more than any words could.

"William Savage, madam?"

"Yes, him."

"He is a fine musician. When he plays I find myself . . ." She hesitates, as if seeking the word she wants. ". . . in another place."

"It is true. He has the gifts of an angel."

Again, the intake of breath, like a shiver. And a break in the rhythm of the comb. There is more laughter outside and a soft knock at the door. Anne cranes her neck into the room to bid Katherine goodbye. She will return to Baynard's, she says, for her husband is back.

Dot bobs her a curtsy and continues combing, finding her rhythm again.

"Do you ever think of marriage, Dot?" asks Katherine after some time.

"No, madam, I do not."

"I could find you a good husband. Someone in the professions. You would be comfortable, have a house of your own, children." As she says it she knows it is the right thing for the girl, but she feels suddenly, and intensely, what a loss it would be to her.

Dot tries to imagine a husband doing the things to her that William Savage did. The idea of it makes her feel that the world has turned on its head, dragging the bottom of her upwards sickeningly. She must not think of William. But another man? She thinks of the cooks and the servicemen in the kitchens, reeking of sweat, and their big beefy hands. Or the cloth merchant, whom she went to for fabrics for the Queen yesterday, and the way he laid them out, throwing the rolls over the table, his fingers stroking the cloth as if it were a woman's skin. A shiver of disgust rises up her spine. If not William Savage, she thinks, then nobody.

And if she married, it would mean leaving the Queen. But the Queen needs her. She can't imagine another girl combing out Katherine's hair as she does, dressing her, tweezing her, rubbing witch hazel on her bruises and telling no one.

The Queen needs Dot to hold her secrets. She is the only one to know them all. Even her sister is oblivious to some things. Dot is the only one who can keep them safely.

"I would prefer, if it pleases you, to continue with things as they are."

"Then that is how it will be."

And they settle back into a comfortable hush.

38

Whitehall Palace, June 1546

Will Parr is incandescent with rage. His mismatched eyes flash. He paces back and forth on the oak boards of her privy chamber, unusually disheveled, stockings smeared with dirt, linen shirt unlaced and askew, and he is missing his cap—a faux pas that would, were he not the Queen's brother and so terrifyingly seething with anger, have barred his admittance from her presence.

"Will—for pity's sake, calm down." They are back in the nursery and Katherine is the elder sister dealing with an angry small boy, indignant over some unjust beating or other—but they are not children any more, and this is clearly not about some trivial event. "Stand still."

He stops, feet apart, arms folded over his chest. His forehead beaded with sweat.

Katherine takes his arm. "Come and sit by the window."

She leads him to the bench by the casement and they sit, she with an arm around his shoulders. He is folded up tightly and hunched.

"Tell me what is going on."

"Gardiner!" He takes a deep breath and bangs a fist on his knee.

Katherine grabs his wrist. "Talk to me, Will."

"It is Anne Askew. She is taken again, to the Tower this time. Arraigned for heresy."

A whole year has gone by since Anne Askew was last released and Katherine had felt the threats around her recede. The King, in spite of the box of holy splinters tucked inside his doublet, seems on the fence again, though it is hard to be sure.

She has given up hope of conceiving but has a secret conception of a different kind: her new book *The Lamentation of a Sinner* is almost complete. No one knows of it—it is her private repentance to God, her exploration of justification by faith alone. And though it exists shrouded in secrecy, she has the sense that she will be remembered for this as the Reformation Queen—a Queen who stood up for her beliefs. Her own piece of history to herald the new ways, like the eclipse.

It was written in gratitude for Anne Askew's deliverance.

"She has an instinct for survival, that woman." But Katherine's mind keeps wandering back to the secret visit at Eltham and how Nan Stanhope came to hear about it, wondering who else might know, if it has reached Udall's ears yet.

"It is worse than you think, Kit. I was sent to question her." Will shakes his head. "*Me* of all people. You know what that means? They're rubbing my face in it. They know where I stand on reform. They probably know she is a friend of mine, just don't have the proof."

"I know, I know." Katherine tries to sound soothing. A cold shiver runs through her. "It is me they're after, Will. They want rid of the Reform Queen who hasn't produced a son in three years of marriage. And *you* are that Queen's brother. We will all fall together." The realization uproots her. "What did she say?"

"But Kit . . ." Will grabs his sister's shoulders and twists her torso so he can look directly at her. His eyes are wild like those of an unbroken horse. "They racked her."

Her world seems to slow to a vertiginous feeling, an endless falling. "They *racked* her? A *woman*?" It is unthinkable. "Who? Wriothesley? Rich?"

"Wriothesley *and* Rich were there, but you can be sure Gardiner's behind it . . . Paget too, no doubt." His leg is jigging nervously.

She puts out a hand to steady him. "A gentlewoman on the rack? Surely the Constable—"

"Kingston could do nothing. He left in disgust."

"Will—this is appalling . . ." Katherine grasps for words, unable to arrange her thoughts in any kind of order, a thousand questions grappling for space. "And you, Will—you were there?"

"Wriothesley's twisted mind. He sent me and John Dudley. I don't know what he thought *we'd* get out of her. I suppose he wanted to make it look as if . . . Oh, I don't know, Kit. He's a maniac. He went into a rage and forced us out when we got nothing from her. We listened at the door . . ." He struggles for words. "Her screams." His face is scribbled with horror.

"Poor woman—poor, poor thing." She drops her face into her hands, making a momentary dark place where no one can get at her.

Then, lifting her head again, she asks the question that's like a growth in her mind, "And did she break?" What she really means—and Will well knows this—is, did she implicate me, am *I* next, am *I* to burn too?

She can see Anne Askew's broad face, the wide-set eyes, their fervent intensity. An unbearably vivid image forces itself into her mind, of the woman strapped to the wooden spokes. She can hear the creak and thunk of the machine, iron against oak, can feel the horrible tug in her own hips and knees and shoulders, like the jointing of a chicken, the clunk and suck as the round end of the bone pops out of its cup of gristle.

She can imagine, too, the resolve in the set of Anne Askew's jaw. There is a determination that blazes in that woman, which Katherine has never seen in any man. She has seen it with her own eyes. If anyone is fit for martyrdom, she thinks, it is Anne Askew, and Katherine would give up everything for a pinch of her courage.

"I have never known a woman more brave." Will echoes her thoughts. He has got up and is pacing again. "Whatever they did to her, she stayed tight. Had them running in circles."

It feels like a reprieve, but she is being hounded out now—and if Anne Askew said nothing it doesn't mean others will be so brave. She feels compelled to get herself away from the great stone walls of Whitehall, to find somewhere she can breathe.

"Will, have the groom saddle the horses. Let's ride out and finish this away from here. I'll see if Anne can come. Just family—just us."

Will's face relaxes a little as if he's glad to see his elder sister take control, like she always did when they were children.

"Look merry," she says. "We mustn't let anyone imagine we are perturbed. Just the three Parrs out for a canter, that's all."

"Can't you talk to the King?" Anne is shot through with distress.

They have dismounted at a clearing in the woods at Chelsea. It is a magical place, an almost perfect circle, with soaring trees ruffled slightly by a whisper of breeze, and a carpet of spongy grass dappled with blinking spots of late June sun. The horses graze nearby, the occasional clink of their bridles adding to the chatter of the birds and the hum of insects. It is a little Eden.

"What are you thinking, Anne?" Katherine's voice is strained. "Do you not remember the other Queens? You served them. You know when he changes his mind about . . . He may appear to adore me now. Goodness, all the lavish gifts are testimony to that, but he's . . . he's not—"

"Constant," Anne finishes her sister's sentence.

Is she thinking of Catherine Howard? Anne was there and she has told of the exact tone of the girl's screams, shrill and haunted, like a fox caught in a trap. Katherine has only constructed the scene from hearsay, she never even met the girl, but that doesn't make it less potent. And before her came Anne Boleyn. Will inadvertently brings his hand up to his throat. They are all thinking the same thought.

"I have had three years to produce an heir and have not delivered. Besides, the King is not one of us. Not really."

"But he broke with the Pope himself, dissolved the great monasteries."

"Don't be naive, Anne," snaps her brother. "That had nothing to do with faith."

"No, I suppose not." Anne's ever-abundant optimism begins to unravel.

"But . . ." Katherine unfurls her hand, stretching her fingers out. Her wedding ring is on one of them, the ruby winking at her. The heat has swollen her fingers and the gold bites into her flesh. "I will renew my efforts to convince him. I shall present to him the image of a Reformation King, greater than any he has ever imagined.

"I know him, know what appeals to him and how he enjoys our conversations. The more he gets the taste for reform, and the less he listens to Bishop Gardiner, the better for everyone." Even as she says it, she doubts herself, for hasn't she tried to coax her husband to her way of thinking already? And failed.

"The better for us," says Will. "Kit, had you been a man you would have been greater than us all, than anyone. You will bring the King back to the faith and sod Gardiner and his idolizing Catholics."

"But what of Anne Askew?" Anne is shredding a daisy, its petals scattered over her dress.

A blackbird flits down to the grass, pecking at something with its yellow beak, bright as an egg yolk, and a ladybird crawls up Anne's sleeve, barely visible, red on red. Katherine's sharp eye spots it and thinks of the song . . . *fly away home.* Jane the Fool was singing it earlier.

"We cannot save her now," says Will.

"You mean she will burn? Is there nothing we can do?" Anne the image of horror.

"The machine is rolling and cannot be stopped." Katherine is stabbed with the fact that her book, her thanks to God for Anne Askew's deliverance, was premature—perhaps God is on the fence, like the King. She pushes that thought away. She must not lose her faith, not now.

"But . . ." Anne's words are swallowed up inside her.

"She will not recant. In some ways it is what she wants, to be with God the sooner. I have sent my girl to bring her warm clothes and victuals, to make sure her last days are comfortable."

"Kit, surely that is madness." It is Will's turn to wear the horror mask.

"Be assured Dot knows how to go unseen. She will deliver the package anonymously."

A silence, thick and cold as a slab of wet clay, enfolds them.

Katherine's thoughts are whirring, flitting between the stake—the heat of it, the crackle and spit—and the King. She will formulate her conversation so subtly he will not even realize the thoughts she plants are not his own. She tries to imagine her husband—*I love that mind of yours, Kit*—becoming malleable in her hands, shaped to her vision of the future. A future where they are all safe.

But safety is an uncommon luxury.

"I have sent a bag of saltpeter too."

She had thought of that on remembering an elaborate firework display which had been part of one of Udall's masques and had the whole court jumping out of their skins. He had shown her how the fireworks were made, the scoop of black powder, how it exploded on contact with a flame. He had put a tiny pinch of it on the floor and touched it with a taper. They had watched it fizzle and flare and then explode with a deafening bang. The room had filled with the smell of sulfur. She'd thought of it as the scent of power.

She had gone to the stores this afternoon with Dot, before riding out. They found the powder stash and she tipped a generous quantity of the stuff into a purse that she had hidden among the bundle of blankets and food, explaining to Dot what was to be done with it.

"She can wear it on her girdle. It will curtail the agony at least."

"She will soon be in Heaven." Anne is always seeking to find the happy ending.

But none of them can shake off the image of the fire, the heat of it, the terror.

"I need you to do something for me, Will," Katherine says. "There are some papers that need to be hidden, well hidden."

"What kind of papers?"

"Some of my scribblings, personal ones . . . there are things in them that I fear would—"

"It is done, sister. Tell me where they can be found and I will remove them. Not even you will know where."

She cannot quite bring herself to ask him to burn them.

39

Dot slips out of the palace by the kitchen gates. As she is leaving she passes William Savage, who tries to stop her. Her heart jolts but she ignores it. It has been some months since she's seen him—he was away from court again. He is changed, she notices—hollow-seeming, dark about the eyes.

"My Dot," he calls out to her. "My full stop, my speck. Speak to me . . . Please."

Her heart teeters and her mind reveals old images and sensations— the way his hair curls at his nape, the inky leathery scent of him—but she bats away those thoughts as she has done now for months. *He* is the speck, the spot on her horizon. She walks by him, like he's nothing to her.

She has more important things to do. She is on a secret mission for the Queen. In her hand is a basket covered with a clean square of linen containing blankets and victuals and also a pie. But it is no ordinary pie, for buried beneath the pastry lid is a pouch of gunpowder.

It is Dot's mission to deliver Anne Askew from suffering. This pouch of powder will send her to the next world in an instant. Dot must go incognito, Katherine said, and had to explain the meaning of that word. She must not be herself and, above all, must not be linked in any way to Katherine.

She has thought of the name she will give if she's asked. "I am Nelly Dent," she has said out loud to herself, practicing, trying the name on for size. "And I come out of Christian charity."

Katherine says that there are people who feel sorry for the prisoners and bring them small comforts, that it is quite usual and probably no one will even ask her who she is.

She stops and turns to face him. "William, I am not your full stop. A full stop is a nothing and that is not me, for I may be low born but that doesn't mean I am nobody."

Why is it her heart feels like a guttering candle?

"Dot," he pleads, grabbing for her free hand.

She snatches it back brusquely.

"Let me explain."

"No, William, I have important matters to attend to." She pushes past him towards the gates. His face is so miserable she almost founders, but she finds her resolve and moves beyond him, saying, "Good bye, William," even as she feels the wrench of it.

She scurries down to the river steps and calls to a boatman who is waiting for trade. He holds out his hand to help her into his wherry, which pitches and sways as she steps into it and seats herself on the bench. She smooths out her skirts and places the basket at her feet, still clutching its handle so tightly her knuckles are white.

"Where to?" he asks.

"The Tower."

This provokes a sound from him, an intake of breath through pursed lips, like a back to front whistle. "That's where they've been stretching that poor woman."

She supposes that everyone in the whole of London is whispering about brave Anne Askew who was put to the rack and who will not name names and will never recant. Dot cannot imagine being as brave as that.

"I believe so," she says.

"What do you want, going to a place like that?"

The boatmen are all prone to conversation, even when it is unwanted.

"I am delivering sweetmeats for the Constable's wife."

The Queen had told her to say this.

"And what's your name, if you don't mind me asking?"

"I am Nelly Dent."

She likes the lie, has never told one quite like this before. The odd

omission of the full truth, and perhaps occasionally a little white lie
to make someone feel better about themselves, but a real lie, there is
something exhilarating about it. It is the being someone else that she
likes—the idea that she can put on a new name like a new dress.

"Are you related to the Dents who farm up at Highgate?"

"Distant cousins." She enjoys the ease at which another lie slips out.

It occurs to her, then, that lies breed like rabbits and once one is
out others must follow. These lies, though, are for a cause—for Katherine. Hers is a merciful mission and she wonders if God forgives that
kind of lying.

She dips her hand in the water, letting it trail, enjoying the cool
feeling of it as the sun is hot and there is no shade on the river. Someone has thrown flowers in, marigolds, which bob and float on the
surface, and a few ducks gather round to inspect them.

The boatman doesn't let up with his chat and she nods in agreement without listening, which seems to satisfy him. He witters and
complains about one thing and another, but the tide is going out,
which thankfully makes their journey a swift one, and soon they are
at the water-gates, where he calls out to a guard.

The guard winds a great wooden wheel to let the doors swing
open, allowing their boat to float right up to the steps. The water
sucks and slaps around the boat's belly as she stands to disembark.
Another guard arrives, liveried in scarlet and gold with a halberd and
a ring of keys rattling at his waist.

"What is your business?"

It is only then that her stomach begins to wring in fear, dipping and
rocking like the little boat, but she thinks of Katherine and her mission. And when she looks at him properly, she can see that he is well
past his prime and not really very menacing at all.

"I am to deliver this, sir."

He proffers his hand to help her out of the boat, chirping something about it not being usual to have girls as pretty as her visiting
the Tower.

When the boatman is out of earshot she tells him she has brought
victuals and comforts for Mistress Askew.

The yeoman makes to take the basket.

She holds it tight. "I am instructed, sir, to hand it directly to her maidservant."

"I'll need to see inside. Who knows what you might have in there. Though the state that poor woman's in, she won't be escaping in a hurry."

Dot pulls the cover aside and he makes a cursory shuffle through the contents. Seeming satisfied, he tells her to wait and then ambles over to a small wooden door as if he has all the time in the world. He runs through his keys, inspecting each of them before finding the right one.

Dot's never been to the Tower before. It is not one of the usual palaces, though some of the Queen's dresses are stored here somewhere. She has always thought of it as a great dark place where terrible things happen, but in front of her is a stretch of lawn with little houses about it, more like a village than a prison, and the famous White Tower soars up to the sky with flags ruffling from its turrets, making her think of the castles in the stories.

But beyond are the thick gray walls encircling the place, with their squat towers and long slit windows, and the reek from the moat hangs over the pretty garden. She is only too well aware that behind those walls there are people locked up, awaiting God knows what kind of fate.

She has heard about the torture instruments, the hot pokers, the manacles, the rack. In the kitchens after work the lads talk of these things all the time to put the shivers up each other, making the laundry girls shriek and cuddle up to them closer—when they're not telling ghost stories it is tales of torture. Betty is the worst for the frights, squealing like a piglet so she can get a squeeze out of it.

She sits on a bench in the garden beside the church, which must be very old, for its stones are worn and moss covered. Its windows gleam in the sunlight and it has a bell tower that looks like a dovecote. It is not at all what she had thought the famous St. Peter ad Vincula would be like.

Ad vincula means "in chains" and all sorts of nobles have lost their heads in the shadow of that pretty church. It is William who told her that—William Savage, who knows something about everything and who hammered too hard on her heart until it broke.

She had suffered silently for months after the discovery of his wife. Not saying something is as good as a lie, she thinks, but it has been a whole year and she doesn't want to think of William now. She couldn't bear to go back to that place, that pit, where she did nothing but feel his absence. It was enough to knock all the romance out of her.

She wishes she hadn't seen him earlier, that he would go away and never come back, so she can forget. But it is true, the feeling has faded and there is just the ghost of it now. And when she thinks of the people locked up here, she feels she has no right to her petty sorrows.

Soon a woman appears. She is tall and seems uncomfortable being so big, stooping to hide it. The sleeves of her dress are too short—they show wrists, all sinews, that might look better on a man. Her black skirt is worn and faded to brown at the knees—from praying, Dot supposes—and a linen cap that must have been white once frames a face that is lined with strain.

Dot rises with an unreturned smile. "I have some blankets and foodstuffs for your mistress."

"Thank you kindly," says the woman in a soft wavering voice. The whites of her eyes have a yellow tinge and are bloodshot with it. She doesn't even ask who the victuals are from.

"There is a pouch of saltpeter in the pie," whispers Dot.

But the woman seems puzzled, tilting her head to one side and scrunching her forehead as she takes the basket.

"She must tie it to her girdle when the time comes. It will send her off quickly."

The woman nods and turns, beginning to walk away.

Just then, a quartet of men appears. It seems to be a couple of noblemen, given their splendid clothes and spotless hose, with a pair of pages trotting beside them. Anyone as finely dressed as these could only be from court. Dot has seen their faces before. She can never remember which colors are for which family—it is far too complicated.

They will not let the maid pass, standing in her way like dogs guarding a bone. A page snatches the basket from her, handing it to one of the men. They are from the palace, she is sure now. She drops into a deep curtsy but the maid stays brazenly upright. Instead of admonishing her for it, they look right through her as if she's not there.

"You have brought things for Mistress Askew?" one of them asks.

He wears a collar made from some kind of spotted cat, not really appropriate for the time of year, but Dot has an idea it means he's important. His rusty beard juts from his chin like a river pier. He has the basket, holding it out from his body as if it is full of rats or snakes or something else that bites.

"I have, my lord," she says.

Her voice obeys her and doesn't falter, though inside she is tied in knots. She keeps her eyes from the basket, not wanting them to think anything of it, or that it is important in any way.

"I have brought things to make her more comfortable until . . ."

She does not need to finish, they all know it is until she is dragged out to Smithfield and burned alive. Dot keeps her head down.

"Stand," the man barks.

She jumps to her feet. The other man is hanging back with the pages but she can see his ear is turned towards her. It is a large ear with a long lobe that looks as if someone has stretched it.

She seems to notice everything: the tiny bells stitched to the bearded man's collar; the sliver of leaf-green lining beneath his robe; the little scrap of food that is lodged between his teeth; the way his eyes seem kind but he does not; the russet hairs sticking out from his nose; the way he sniffs and clasps and unclasps the hilt of his sword; the grass smear on the other's white shoes.

"And look up."

She obeys him. He wears a smirk that is half smile, half grimace and she sees a glimmer of recognition in his eyes.

"I have seen you about the palace."

She can see he is trying to work out whom she serves or where he has seen her.

"Who sent you?"

"A friend."

"Do you take me for a fool, you stupid girl? Give me a name."

A shower of saliva lands on her face but she doesn't dare even lift a finger to wipe it away.

"Nelly Dent . . ." She stumbles over the words. "I . . . I am Nelly Dent."

"Did I ask for *your* name?" he snaps. "I am not the slightest bit interested in who *you* are. You are nobody. Tell me who sent you." His last sentence is a shout and he grabs her wrist, giving it a twist that burns her skin.

She will not allow him to see that it hurts, and sets her face, thinking, thinking of something believable to say. She thinks of Katherine. What would *she* say? She would think of something clever, would turn this man's questions right back on him. She would say, "I am the Queen and I do not have to tell you anything," or quote something from the Bible that would flummox him. But Dot *must* answer, and it must be an answer he believes. She *will not* betray Katherine.

"My Lady Hertford," she blurts.

The smirk transforms into a whole satisfied smile. "Ah, you are Nan Stanhope's girl. Now that's better." He gives her throbbing wrist a pat and lets it drop. "Isn't it, Nelly?" He hands the basket back to her, saying, "Now, are you going to be a good girl and show me what's in there?"

She places it on the stone paving and lifts the linen, taking out the contents: the jar of quince jelly, two loaves, a pudding, a bag of salt, a sugar stick, the pie, a good blanket, two linen shifts, a cake of soap and a small pot of cream of arnica for bruising. She lays them all out neatly, taking her time about it. He stands watching, arms crossed. The other man has drifted across and casts his eyes over the display.

He calls one of the pages. "Pass me that." He is pointing towards the pie.

A wave of cold passes through Dot, as if she's been dunked in the Thames and turned inside out, but she continues arranging the blankets, not daring to take more than a glance their way.

The page stoops down to pick up the pie.

But the man yelps, "Not that, you idiot. The sugar."

The boy offers him the stick of sugar. He takes it and bites, crunching through it until the whole thing is eaten. Crystal fragments cling to his lips, and a darting tongue gathers them up.

And then they are gone, off towards the water-gate, and Dot drops to the bench, closing her eyes and releasing a deep sigh, steadying herself before starting to gather the things into the basket. The maid helps, silently, and then disappears, back to wherever it is they are holding Anne Askew, with nothing more than a nod. Perhaps she has forgotten how to smile.

Dot's thoughts are churning. She may not like Nan Stanhope for all the awful things she has said about Katherine and the mean way she treats her maidservant. But two-faced disloyalty and meanness or not, Dot has done her a terrible misdeed by blurting her name out like that.

It was the first name that came to her. And this was a proper lie, a malicious one, not like the other lies she has told, which were merciful lies, if not quite white, then pale and almost innocent.

But this lie is blacker than soot and will leave its marks everywhere. And what shocks her most is that it slipped out so easily. But it is done now, she cannot unsay it.

She wonders what kind of terrible thing she has started by saying that name, can imagine the effect of her lie seeping silently around the palace, and a feeling of dread threads itself through her veins like poison.

40

An oil burner sends out fragrant wafts to mask the reek of rotten flesh.

Huicke packs away his things, corking the jars of tincture and folding his muslin cloths while Katherine pours out a cup of ale for the King and then settles on a cushion at his feet. She picks up a book that is lying open and upside down on the floor, and begins to read from it.

Huicke stops a minute to watch them, recognizing Erasmus. It is the English translation Udall had worked so hard on, the Book of John, the one Lady Mary had had a change of heart about, refused even to have her name attached to. Udall had finished it for her—had changed the whole thing, really—and was distracted for months, pacing the chamber all night, torturing himself over the translation, digging away to find the particular word to convey something specific.

Huicke has never known a greater pedant, though pedantry is Udall's gift, is what makes his translations so much more subtle, so much finer, than others. But the nocturnal pacing and digging, picking away at things, and the endless reading it out loud for an opinion, made him an insufferable companion and Huicke often had to rise in the middle of the night and make his way back down the drafty corridors of the palace to his own lodgings.

The words are so very familiar, he almost knows it by heart. He remembers, too, that when he used to visit Charterhouse daily he often interrupted Katherine reading it to Latymer—in Latin, though. He wonders how it is for her to be always reading to one elderly husband after another.

The depth of her patience inspires his respect, for his own is as thin as watered ale. When she is away from the King she is another person, bright and witty, poking fun, teasing, ebullient, not earnest like this, with her muted laugh and serious smile. She is like one of those African lizards, he forgets the name, that change color depending on where they sit.

Her choice of book—and he is sure it *is* her choice and not his—is an interesting one and gives away the hidden, brazen part of her. It is one of the borderline books, not quite banned, but without a doubt frowned upon by Gardiner and his cronies who would rather everything was in Latin, so that ignorance can reign.

The King rests his big hand across the bare skin just below her neck, stroking gently, running his fingers up and down. She leans over the book to see better in the candlelight and the bones of her spine protrude—a row of stepping stones in a pool of cream. Other women bulge and billow over their clothes, but there is nothing superfluous or fleshy about Katherine.

A stranger seeing her would never imagine she was a woman of thirty-five. She has removed her hood and only her white linen cap remains, which has lost its stiffness and droops, framing her face prettily. Her finger follows the lines of print. He is always surprised by the smallness of her hands. They are like a child's and the way they are weighed down with rings makes them seem smaller still.

She stops to say something, holding the book up to her husband, pointing a word out to him. They talk quietly so Huicke can't quite hear them. The King reaches for his spectacles, lifting them to his eyes and peering through the thick lenses at the page.

They both laugh, prodding Huicke's curiosity as to what they could find so amusing in the Book of John. It is not Katherine's real laugh, though, which is on the edge of abandon, it is a tidy laugh, a chaste flutter.

Huicke is impressed at her apparent levity, for he knows that beneath it she is wrung with grief. Anne Askew burned today—brave

Anne. So many of his friends had, at one time or another, slipped unseen out of the palace to the secret gatherings where she preached.

Earlier, in her chamber, when he had come to tell her it was done, Katherine had flung her needlework to the floor and in doing so had knocked over a jar of French pomade. It shattered, oozing an oily mess across the matting.

"The King offered her a pardon if she would recant. But Kit, she was so sure of her path to the heavens . . . Her faith was unassailable."

"He could have stopped it," she kept repeating. "I can't believe he didn't stop it."

Her face was flushed and she brought her hand down so hard against the table that she bruised it. Huicke had never seen her so incensed, so boiling with rage.

"I am afraid," she whispered to Huicke when her fury had subsided. "For the first time, I am truly afraid. I can feel them about me, watching, waiting, gathering around, hiding in corners, snapping at my heels. I know it has ever been thus, but this has changed everything . . . They are after my blood."

Another woman might have cried over it, but not Katherine. Katherine is made of sterner stuff and tonight's blithe performance with the King is testimony to that.

One of the King's men enters, followed by a page balancing a stack of dishes in his arms. They begin to prepare the table for supper. It is a rigmarole that always makes Huicke snigger inwardly at the absurdity of it, everything being done with the correct hand and nothing being touched that will eventually make contact with the King's mouth, requiring a system of cloths and the deftness of a magician.

Eventually, they are done and the King asks for wine, inviting Huicke to join them, "If the Queen wishes it," which, of course, she does.

And so he, too, participates in the false levity, glad that at least his presence might bring some fortitude for her.

An usher announces the arrival of Wriothesley. Katherine asks Huicke for help with her hood. He picks it up. It is heavy, laden with trinkets and jewels, far too heavy for her slight neck to support.

Though he has often wished himself a woman, Huicke is unfamiliar with women's things and in this moment is suddenly aware of the complication and restriction of their garb and is glad, for once, to be a man. She scrapes her hair away from her face and he helps her into the contraption, as if fitting her into a cage, while the King watches in silence.

"Did we give you that?" the King says.

When she is in it, she turns to him for his approval, dipping her head to one side, making Huicke wonder how she will be able to right it again, given the dead weight of the thing.

"You did, my love, and a fine one it is."

"You see our taste is impeccable. See the way the color of it sets off your eyes."

She smiles in polite agreement, and those eyes dance and glitter as if they are genuinely merry.

Wriothesley enters in a ridiculous ocelot collar, though it is high summer, making a meal out of his bow, bending so deeply from his waist that his beard almost sweeps the floor.

Katherine and Huicke exchange a brief amused look.

Gardiner follows shortly, in his Bishop's togs. He manages to make the plain black and white robes seem quite out of the ordinary— sumptuous swathes of black satin so voluminous they might be bed hangings—and the overgarment is plain lawn cotton but intricately stitched, smocked and ruched to luxurious effect. A starched white ruffle at his throat sits beneath his numerous chins and that down-turned mouth of his. He wears a cross that is so encrusted with rubies and garnets as to make the gold of it barely visible.

The pair of them seem puffed up, exhilarated, smug. It is doubt-less the burning that fuels their elation—though it is not mentioned, not once, during the whole nine courses. But they are reverential to the Queen to the point of absurdity and Huicke wonders about that, senses there is something up, but can't quite put his finger on it.

Surrey arrives, striding in. He looks, with his elongated limbs and black brocade, like a cranefly. Will Parr, with him, is without his usual swagger, wearing a forced smile and exchanging a brief look of con-cern with his sister as they greet each other—an acknowledgment of Anne Askew's death, no doubt. Nobody else notices and the smile is painted back on in an instant.

Surrey has written a poem for the King and fawns a little. He is in and out of favor so often it's hard to stay apace. But as he is top of the Howard pile and heir to the greatest dukedom in England, the King doesn't stay angry with him for long. Anyway, a great fuss is made of the poem, which Huicke judges unremarkable if engaging. But Surrey has charm coming out of his hose and the King is delighted with the interlude.

When the puddings are served, great towering wobbling things in colors that look inedible, the King demands the monkey be brought in and the fools, both of them, if they can be found, for the Fool Jane has a tendency to wander and lose herself.

The monkey, having amused the King by devouring most of a blancmange, struts about the table laying waste to the remains of the meal, then takes its monkey genitals in its monkey hand and begins to pleasure itself to heaving laughter from the King, who makes a deal about covering his wife's eyes.

Surrey and Will Parr laugh heartily, making lewd comments. They are used to producing just the right mood for the King. Wriothesley sniggers politely with him, but Gardiner looks horrified and cannot muster anything approaching a laugh for His Majesty, who prods him saying, "Where's your sense of fun, Bishop? Never seen a stiff member before?"

The Bishop looks as if he'd like to sink into the floor.

The two fools make the most of it by staging a mock wedding, marrying Jane to the hapless monkey, who has desisted its sinful antics. Will Sommers presides—*Do you take this ape?*—draping himself in the tablecloth, in mimicry of Gardiner, ratcheting up the mirth. Gardiner eventually manages a curt half smile but his face looks as if it might break with the effort.

The mayhem dies down at last, the monkey is removed and the conversation turns to more serious matters. They discuss the peace treaty with the French that will be ratified soon, which must be a good thing—for France will be in hock to England for a hundred years— though it puts paid to any hopes of England joining the German Princes in a Protestant league. Huicke doesn't say as much, but he thinks it, and he assumes Katherine has it on her mind too. Anyway, the Emperor is preparing to do battle with the German Princes, so the dream of an evangelical Europe is further away than ever.

"Admiral d'Annebaut will come to ratify the treaty," says the King. "And Essex," he turns to Will Parr, "you will greet him. Demonstrate to him that we English can put on a good show. We will flatter him into submission and have him running back to François with news of our magnificent hospitality."

It's a good sign, thinks Huicke, for it suggests that the King is still favoring the Parrs, but the look Wriothesley exchanges with Gardiner tells another story. A lute player is brought in, to strum in the corner, and Surrey and Will Parr take their leave.

"Your brother continues to petition for his divorce, I see," says Gardiner when Will Parr is barely out of earshot, turning his gaze to Katherine. He knows this is a sore point with the Parrs. "He will never get it, you know."

"What think you of divorce?" asks the King, pointing a fat finger at the Fool Jane, who takes up her skirts and begins to skip back and forth chanting.

"A wise old owl lived in an oak
The more he saw the less he spoke
The less he spoke the more he heard
Why can't we all be like that old bird?"

"Ha," brays the King, "you are wiser than most of my council, Fool."

"What God has joined together may no man put asunder," drones Gardiner.

"Marriage *is* one of the holy sacraments." The King is suddenly serious.

It seems that the two of them have had a conversation in private about Will Parr's divorce already, and this is for Katherine's benefit, a subtle way to put her in her place.

Huicke is thinking about how hard the King laughed at the monkey marriage . . . and all those Queens got rid of. A "sacrament" indeed.

"Erasmus did not think of marriage as a sacrament," says Katherine, who has not spoken for some time.

They all turn to her and then to the King, wondering how he will react to being contradicted in such a way. But the King says nothing, and Katherine seems determined to say her piece, though the atmosphere has turned thick and dark as tar.

She continues, "Erasmus translated the original New Testament Greek *musterion* as 'mystery,' nowhere did he find the word 'sacrament' concerning—"

"You think I don't know Erasmus?" The King gets to his feet, slapping the table hard with a hand that is surely intended for his wife.

Everyone shrinks back.

His Majesty's chair teeters momentarily on two legs then crashes to the floor behind him and a page scurries to pick it up.

His face turns purple, his flint-shard eyes flash cold.

"I corresponded with him weekly when I was a boy, he wrote a book for me, FOR ME, and you presume to suggest that I don't know Erasmus." He is rattling like a pan on the hearth, stabbing a sausage finger towards Katherine.

She sits still as stone, her eyes tipped down, hands folded in her lap.

"I will not be told by a woman. Get out of my sight. GO!"

Katherine slides away from the table. Only Huicke dares stand, tentatively, as she leaves, moving straight-backed towards the door.

The King collapses into his chair with a sigh—deflating visibly. "What is this world coming to?" he murmurs. "To be taught by my wife."

Huicke sees Gardiner exchange another look with Wriothesley, little more than a minutely raised eyebrow and a barely perceptible nod in response, but freighted with meaning. They have seen a way in.

"Huicke," says the King, "go after her, calm her down. See that she is all right."

The irony is not lost on Huicke. The Queen was the least perturbed of them all, or was the best at not showing it at any rate.

As Huicke takes his leave, he hears fragments of Gardiner's hushed words drift over.

". . . harbor a serpent . . ."

He would like to take the man and push his poisonous words back down his throat until he chokes on them.

41

Whitehall Palace, August 1546

Something is up. Dot can feel the heaviness hanging over the Queen's apartments and it has nothing to do with the airless August heat.

The life is sapped out of everything, even the little dogs are flat on the Turkish rug, tongues hanging out, panting for air. Dot opens the windows wide on both sides of the chamber but cannot even raise the slightest draft. Her scalp is soaked beneath her coif and she longs to unpeel her dress and go about in just her kirtle like most of the ladies do when there are no visitors.

And there are no visitors.

Since poor Anne Askew was burned two weeks ago almost no one has come to the Queen's chambers and there have been none of the usual evening entertainments, no musicians or poets, and not even Udall to liven things up—and Huicke, who is almost a piece of the furniture, is nowhere to be seen either.

Old Mary Wootten and Lizzie Tyrwhitt are in a huddle talking under their breath, alert to see who might be listening. No one ever cares if Dot can hear.

"You know what this reminds me of?" says Lizzie Tyrwhitt.

"The concubine," replies Mary Wootten.

Dot knows who that is, for it was the name some people called Nan Bullen when she was Queen. Dot refills their cups from the ewer of small beer.

"This is warm. Is there not a drop of cool ale to be had in the whole palace?"

"No, my lady, not even for His Majesty."

"I fear for her." Lizzie Tyrwhitt looks as if she might cry.

"For us all."

"But she has done nothing wrong. She is a paragon."

"Hmph!" Mary Wootten rolls her eyes up. "That is not the point. If those two get the bit between their teeth . . ." She pauses, pursing her lips. "All hell could be let loose."

Anne leans over with a finger over her mouth. "Keep it down, ladies. I don't want the maids getting the wind put up them." She looks over to the group of girls lounging listlessly across the room.

Dot takes the jug into the privy chamber where Katherine is alone, sitting on a chair, staring out, with a book on her lap.

"Thank you," she murmurs as Dot fills her cup.

"Madam . . ." Dot is unsure of how to say it.

Katherine looks at her, waiting.

"Is there something happening?" she says finally.

"Dot, sometimes it is best to be in the dark."

She is as impenetrable as a block of wood.

"But—"

Katherine puts a hand up to silence her. "If anyone gives you something to bring to me, a book, anything, you must refuse it."

Dot nods. There is a pressure at her temples, as if a band is tightening about her head. Katherine smiles, and where she musters it from is a mystery to Dot, for the atmosphere is so grave.

"Go about your business, Dot. Don't give the appearance of concern. Come, let us see that smile of yours."

She forces her mouth up at the corners and begins to gather a bundle of linens for the laundry.

"That's right, Dot."

The creak of the laundry basket is the only sound in the watching chamber as she walks through, but as she is about to leave the doors are flung open and an usher sweeps in with a bow, asking for Anne.

"Who wants me?" she says.

Dot can hear a quiver in her voice.

"The Lord Chancellor wishes a word with you, my lady."

"Wriothesley," says Anne under her breath.

Dot sees the color disappear from her face and notices, too, that the other ladies have the look of a herd of terrified deer, big eyes watching, as Anne follows the usher silently past Dot and out of the chamber.

Wriothesley is the man, Dot has discovered, whom she encountered at the Tower. She has an image of him crunching at the stick of sugar, all the bits of it stuck in his beard. The lie she told him festers in her gut like a bad shrimp.

"Dot," says Lizzie Tyrwhitt, "what are you doing?"

And Dot realizes her basket has tipped and there are linens scattered all over the floor. She stands like a halfwit, staring at the door.

"Oh, begging your pardon." She starts to shove the fallen things back into the basket.

"Pull yourself together, girl."

Dot, all in a jitter, rushes down to the laundry, dumping the basket and telling the laundress that it is for the Queen but not stopping as usual for a chat. She cannot bear to be away from those awful silent rooms.

Anne returns, white as a corpse, as if she has been terrified out of her life. She is in a nervous dither and will not sit or even stand still. She rushes about looking for things, muttering to herself, "Where did I put my Bible? Where is my psalter? Where is my sister?" and wringing her hands.

When Katherine is fetched to calm her, she clings to her as if she is drowning.

Then Lizzie Tyrwhitt is called out and the room becomes clogged with fear, with them all jumping out of their skins each time the paneling creaks. Katherine sits at the far side of the chamber quietly reading, as if nothing is going on, but beside her Anne is staring ahead and twisting her fingers around and around the tassel of her belt as if she's touched in the head. Dot doesn't know where to put herself and pretends to be busy with darning an invisible hole in a stocking.

Lizzie is not gone long. When she comes back she says, "There is no air in here, I don't know how any of you can breathe," and begins rummaging about among her things, pulling out her fan. "I don't know. I don't know," she keeps saying.

Nan Stanhope is called next. If she is frightened she doesn't show it, walking out behind the usher as if she's going for an afternoon stroll. Dot has to hand it to her that whatever kind of two-faced so-and-so she is, she's not faint-hearted.

Dot pricks her finger on the darning needle. She feels she will suffocate with fear, that her lie will send Nan Stanhope the way of Mistress Askew and it will all be her fault. Her head is whirring with it. She sucks the blood from her finger and tries to rethread her needle, but her hands are trembling too much.

She can't help thinking of that poor Anne Askew burning, wonders if the powder sent her off quickly as it was supposed to. No one has spoken of it, not a whisper. It is as if everything happens somewhere else, and all they can do is sit in these chambers and wonder about it.

Nan Stanhope returns, about half an hour later, looking down that nose of hers, as if nothing is different—and maybe nothing is. She goes straight over to Katherine and whispers something to her.

Every single person in the chamber is watching for Katherine's re-action, but she just nods and continues with her reading. Nan Stanhope, seeming not agitated in the slightest, takes a seat in a window embrasure and begins to play patience. Dot watches her flick the cards out onto the table with her quick fingers; she looks for a trace of anxiety but cannot see one.

Her own fear recedes a little. Surely if there was to be trouble over the lie it would show on Nan Stanhope's face or in her hands. But if Wriothesley was angered with her for sending victuals to the Tower there is no sign of it. In the meantime, another lady is called, and then another and another, each returning looking ruffled and perturbed but Nan Stanhope continues flicking her cards out and barely looks up.

Katherine calls Nan over, saying something to her, and she begins to collect the few books still in the room. She hands them to the ladies who, in a silent commotion, secrete them about their persons, stuffed under kirtles, in hoods, wrapped into linens.

"Even this?" exclaims Lizzie Tyrwhitt, when Nan Stanhope hands her a sheaf of papers. "Wyatt's poetry?"

"Something might have been scribbled in a margin. You never know."

Lizzie nods as she tucks it down her stomacher.

One by one they leave with their secret cargo. Dot is not given a book to smuggle out and she wonders if anyone but Katherine knows of all those books she brought into these rooms.

She feels like a child with no understanding of the adult world.

42

The days go by and there is not a break in the weather. Now the books are gone, the ladies are lost for something to do and they sit about like ghosts. Even the needlework mostly lies untouched. They say little and do nothing, dragging themselves out to the hall for meals and back, but not much else.

Still nobody visits.

Huicke has been sent to Ashridge to tend Elizabeth—she is ailing, they say. Most of the husbands and relatives, who normally drop in from time to time for cards and music, are gone—Hertford to France and the Queen's brother to the Borders. Dot has made it her business to listen to all the whispered conversations. She will not be kept in the dark.

William Savage is still at court. He has new duties so their paths rarely cross—and good riddance to bad rubbish, thinks Dot. She *has* seen glimpses of him in the corridors, and has hidden so as not to be seen by him in turn, but he doesn't come to play the virginals any more. Dot thanks God for that.

No one is in the mood for music, though on most evenings the Bassano brothers can be heard from the King's rooms, their singing and fiddling blaring from the open windows onto the courtyard. Katherine, cool as a cup of chilled wine, is usually commanded to join the King and takes Cat Brandon to accompany her, or Nan Stanhope. They are the ones who are holding themselves together best as they wait—wait to see what will happen next.

The Queen may be cool and calm and going about as if everything is normal, but Dot knows better and sees how she forces her mouth into an uncomfortable smile before admitting anyone to her privy chamber, and how she is at prayer more often than ever.

She has a new bruise glowering beneath her ear and Dot dresses her in high-necked gowns to cover it. Katherine insists on wearing her finest things, the most bejeweled of her dresses, her heaviest hoods, in spite of the cloying heat.

"I must look like the Queen," she says, when Dot asks her if she wouldn't be more comfortable in just her kirtle like the other ladies.

Katherine takes her mother's cross out of the coffer, where it has lain untouched for years, and sits holding it, stroking the pearls between the tip of her index finger and thumb, her lips moving as if she's saying the rosary, before wrapping it in a fold of velvet and tucking it beneath her pillows. It is never worn. Her neck is heavy with the Queen's jewels, monster stones that seem bigger still on her fine frame.

"I would give up all this." She holds up a ruby necklace. "It means nothing." But still she insists on wearing them.

She can be seen each evening, glimpses of her through the open windows across the court, smiling and laughing. Dot wonders how she can manage to muster that merry facade when they all stand on the edge of such a chasm. The King visits most nights and Dot lies on her pallet outside, pressing her hands to her ears so as not to hear them.

Meanwhile, they are preparing the summer move to Hampton Court and everything must be aired while the weather is good. She dismantles the Queen's own bed, unhooking the hangings which hold a year's worth of dust in their folds, to take them to the yard for a beating. She shakes out the pillows and covers, sending the linens to the laundry, separating what will go with them and what will stay here. The coverlets must be aired and the mattress must be turned.

She gets one of the lads to help her, as turning a big featherbed is more difficult even than lifting a fat man's corpse—or so Betty always says, though God only knows how Betty would know what it is like to lift a corpse, fat or not. Dot is looking forward to returning to Hampton Court and having the company of Betty again, for though she is foul-mouthed and talks too much, she is not complicated and she makes Dot laugh. Dot has had enough of this complicated silence.

She and the lad struggle under the weight of the mattress, heaving it up. As it lifts away from the frame Dot feels something beneath her fingers. It is a roll of papers tucked away between the slats. She drops her end with a groan and the lad tuts in annoyance.

"This is too heavy," she says. "Why don't you ask one of the others to come and help us?"

He leaves, shrugging and muttering something under his breath about feeble upstairs maids. When he is gone she pulls the roll out. It is a sheaf of coarse paper, marked and rumpled, furled tightly and tied with a length of frayed red ribbon. She can see that it is written on, for the ink has smudged through in places and she supposes it must be some kind of love letter—why else would it be hidden under the mattress like that—but she wonders how it could be, for if the Queen were harboring a love and exchanging letters Dot would be the first to notice.

She thinks of that other Queen, Catherine Howard, who lost her head for cuckolding the King. They say she haunts the Queen's corridor at Hampton Court. Just thinking of it gives Dot the shivers.

She can hear the lads climbing the stairs, chatting and ribbing each other, and goes to fling the papers on the fire but the grate is dead. There is no need for a fire in this weather and to light one would cause suspicion—and besides, there is no time—so she tucks the roll beneath her skirts. Katherine will know what to do with it. It is probably something innocent, anyway—a letter from her mother, kept for decades and read for remembrance, or a favorite poem or prayer from childhood.

But what she fears is that it is a letter from that Seymour fellow, who has disappeared off the face of the earth.

With the mattress turned, Dot makes her way to the laundry to see if the Queen's linens are dry and ready to be packed. As she is going down the long gallery she is stopped by Jane the Fool.

"Am I to come to Hampton Court tomorrow?" Her wandering eye wheels in her head.

She asked that very same question only an hour ago. Dot wonders why everyone listens to her rantings, when she cannot even remember what she was told so recently. But she was a gift to the Queen from the King, like the monkey, and must be humored.

"Yes, Jane, are you all prepared?"

"Diddle, diddle, dumpling . . ." sings Jane, making Dot regret her question.

A pack of courtiers passes between them, and Dot has to press herself into the wall, so as not to be bumped into.

She can feel the roll of paper under her kirtle. It has slightly dislodged itself. She pushes her belly against it to hold it in place.

The pack strides by, gowns flapping, feathers fluttering. Among them is that man Wriothesley with his pointed weasel face. She dips her head so as not to be seen. They clatter on past and she continues past the pages' room towards the door that leads to the kitchen stairs.

But Wriothesley turns back abruptly, stopping, letting the rest of them get ahead of him, beard thrust in her direction, holding her with his eyes. "You are Lady Hertford's girl, are you not?"

She knows she must curtsy. She can feel the roll of paper slip slightly. But she has no choice. Down she bobs and out it slides, freeing itself from its ribbon and unfurling on the floor at her feet. Praying her skirts cover it, she looks down. That is her error.

"What is that?" he says. "Step aside."

She does as he says, exposing the papers, which sit on the floorboards, written side up. Her head spins. She wants to disappear, grow so small she can't be seen, turn to dust, float away. But she is solid, and here, and speechless with dread.

His face breaks into a smile. "Pick it up then."

She bends and takes the papers from the floor, placing them in his waiting hand, only then becoming aware of how much she is trembling.

"And that," he points at the ribbon which lies in a squiggle by the skirting.

She ducks down for it.

As she goes to stand, he places his foot on her shoulder, pushing her back with the word "Down," as if she's a dog. He holds the ribbon up to the light, inspects it and then throws it back to the floor.

"Scared, are you? Do you have reason to be?"

"No, my lord. It is just—"

"Well, you should be." He has started to flick through the papers, stopping occasionally to read from them. "For this," he taps them with a finger, "is heresy."

Dot notices Jane the Fool still there, one eye roaming the room, the other watching her. She begins to sing in her little-girl voice—"*Ding dong bell, pussy's in the well . . .*"

"Get up," says Wriothesley.

Dot staggers to her feet, pressing herself back against the wall, wishing it would swallow her.

"I forget your name, girl."

"It is Nelly, my lord, Nelly Dent." She gives the Fool a look that she hopes to God will stop her from blurting out the truth.

"Ah yes, Nelly Dent. Lady Hertford's skivvy." He grabs her arm tightly, with a hand that is dry and scaled, pulling her towards him. "*You* will come with me."

His face is so close to hers she can smell the rotten-milk stink on his breath.

"She is the dot on the horizon, the speck in the ocean, the full stop," blathers Jane.

"Will you shut up, you stupid creature." Wriothesley gives the Fool a shove and drags Dot off down the gallery.

43

Whitehall Palace, August 1546

Dot is nowhere to be found. Katherine paces her rooms; a board creaks each time she treads on it, back and forth, back and forth. It has been two days now and she has barely slept with worry. She can feel Wriothesley and Gardiner at her heels.

Most of her ladies have made some excuse or other to get away from the palace—to go ahead to Hampton Court—to visit new babies in the family, or suddenly ailing parents, or a cousin who is dying, to attend to some sudden urgent business somewhere, anything to escape Wriothesley's orbit.

He has terrified them all with his questioning. Her rooms have emptied. The very stones of the palace seem to hold their breath, waiting for events to unfold.

Who sanctioned those interrogations? Can it be done without the King's permission? She daren't ask Henry. Besides, there is barely a moment with him alone and if he comes to her chamber at night, he is paraded in with his torch-lit retinue, who wait outside to march him away within the half-hour. He still tries for an heir, but she has lost hope of that being her salvation, for more often than not he is incapable, despite her best efforts. And where is Dot? Wriothesley's shadow looms over everything and it is the shape of the Tower.

Only her close circle remains. Her sister, who is nervy as a colt, is standing at the window looking out, biting her nails. Lizzie Tyrwhitt, a safe pair of hands, and ancient Mary Wootten, who has been so long at court she has seen everything, are stitching shirts for the poor on the settle. Cat Brandon is here too, embroidering in the window seat to make the most of the light. She is not the sort to abandon ship. And there is Nan Stanhope at the table playing patience, always playing patience, flying the flag for the Seymour family.

Katherine had given Nan leave to go but she insisted on remaining. "We need to stick together," she'd said, "they are trying to bring down the husbands by getting at the wives."

Of course she is right. If Gardiner and Wriothesley could pull down Hertford's lot, then nothing would stand in their way. These days Hertford, it is generally acknowledged, has more power than all the privy councillors put together. And despite the fact that he's a driven reformer, the King still dotes on him—perhaps Hertford reminds the King of his favorite dead wife, Jane. Gardiner would give his right arm to see Hertford take a tumble. Katherine has to concede to Nan—she has fortitude to stay in this wasps' nest.

Katherine would be glad of her diminished household, if it weren't for the fact that it makes her seem deserted, weakened, like an animal at bay. She must give the impression of being unshaken. Which is why—as she'd explained to Dot—she wears her finest dresses, is laced and buckled and buttoned and clipped into them, and weighs herself down with the Queen's jewels.

But where is Dot? Someone must find her.

Anne is crumbling and in no fit state to help. Will is away, as is Udall, and even Huicke—they have each been sent away on one precept or other. It begins to come clear, when she thinks about it. All her allies are away—the men, anyway.

It is no coincidence.

Gardiner and Wriothesley have chosen their moment well to start this thing, whatever it is. She paces, trying to keep her mind away from the Tower and the block.

But William Savage, William is still here. He may have no influence but he can be trusted. She calls Lizzie Tyrwhitt over to find a page to fetch him.

When he comes, he looks perturbed and pale, twisting his long fingers together, his dark eyes woven with worry. He must know that if Katherine is brought down he'll topple with her—all those books would be enough to condemn him. Someone would tell, or they'd rack him until he broke.

She notices that he wears a black enameled mourning ring and when he takes her hand she touches it. "Your wife?"

He nods. "Childbirth."

"I am sorry. The baby?"

He shakes his head.

She strokes the back of his hand. It is soft as a girl's.

He manages a brief smile. "It is God's will."

"That is true, William. We have to trust God's plan for us."

There is a commotion from the yard and a cheer goes up. It must come from the cocking house or the tennis courts. Life continues as usual at Whitehall, while this silent vacuum reigns in her own chambers.

"I have need of your help."

"You know I will do anything."

"Dorothy Fownten is gone."

His eyes widen with shock.

She realizes he has misunderstood her. "Not dead, William. Or, at least, I think not, hope not. Lost—Dot is lost."

He tilts his head to one side, scrunching his brows. "I don't understand."

"It has been two days since I have seen her. You must find her. She is so very dear to me."

"And to me," he says under his breath.

"I have asked all my ladies, but none have seen her, not in the kitchens, nor in any other place here. Only the Fool Jane claimed she'd seen her, but I could get nothing out of her but a nonsense rhyme."

"What did she say?"

"I can't remember, William. It was nothing but gibberish."

"You must try. It is the only thing we have."

"Something about bells, I think."

She rubs her temples as if trying to massage the memory out of her head, and fragments of a song come to her. She begins to hum the tune and the words drift along with it . . . "*When will you pay me? Say the bells of Old Bailey.*"

"There is no bell at Old Bailey," says William, who has taken up the tune too. "It is the bell of St. Sepulchre that is right behind Newgate." He throws up his hands with a sharp exhalation. "She might have been taken to Newgate? I will go there."

"William, I can't thank you enough." Katherine takes his hands in both of hers and kisses the scrunched tips of their gathered fingers. "You must do all you can. Say you are sent by the palace."

He goes to leave.

She stops him with a hand on his sleeve. "Take care, William. And if you find her, remember she is mine. She is the nearest thing I have to a . . ."

She doesn't say "daughter." She knows how it would sound if said out loud, for Dot is as much a different species from her as that monkey. Or that is how most would have it. But it is true: Dot feels as close as kin, closer sometimes.

"You have broken her heart once and you will not do it again." The steel in her voice surprises her.

He touches his hand to his heart. "You have my word."

44

Newgate Prison, August 1546

Dot has been alone for a long time, forty-five hours. She knows this because she has counted the tolls of a great tenor bell that rings out the hours close by.

She drank the last drops of rancid water, from the ewer that someone had plonked down when she arrived, an age ago. There is nothing here—no bench, no candle, no blanket—just a bucket in the corner, a slit for a window, too high to look out of, which throws a little square of light onto the floor, and a nest of mice for company.

She had spent the hours of darkness petrified, huddled into a corner on a heap of piss-ridden straw she had scraped together, listening to the shouts and wails of the other inmates.

She tries to keep her mind off things.

When she arrived she had battered at the door ferociously, shouting, desperate for someone to come and tell her what was happening, but the hours passed and her voice turned hoarse. No one was going to come, that was clear. Her shouts became whimpers and eventually died altogether, leaving her with her thoughts.

When she thinks about the bare fact that she will not survive, it is too much: never feeling the sun on her skin, never crushing a stalk of rosemary between her fingers to release the scent, never again feeling a man's hands on her, never knowing what it is to give birth.

She breaks into a cold sweat and has to clutch at the rough stones of the walls for fear of falling into a dark place. In her mind it is like the pictures of Hell on the walls of the church in Stanstead Abbotts that put the frights up her as a girl—foul demons half bird and half man, ripping sinners limb from limb. She makes herself conjure up an image of Christ on the cross and whispers over and over, "Jesus died for us, Jesus died and was risen."

She tries to think back to that church and the towering crucifix behind the altar, but she cannot fix the image of it in her mind, it is too long ago. Her mind keeps wandering to a statue of the Virgin there that used to cry. People came from far and wide to wonder at those holy tears.

It turned out that they were not tears at all. They were nothing but drips of rainwater from a series of pipes leading to a gutter that someone had rigged up. No one had thought to question why it was that she only cried when it was raining. No wonder people turned to reform. Her own faith is worn thin as spring ice on a pond.

She distracts herself with the words of love songs she remembers from years ago, humming the tunes to push the other thoughts out of her head, but the love songs bring thoughts of William Savage.

Just to see William one more time.

If she thinks hard enough she can feel his fingers burrowing, the heave of him, his breath on her neck. She finds herself awash with tears, gasping, choking on them. And then her thoughts return to the present. If she knew what was on that paper she might at least have an idea of how to save herself, but Wriothesley had given nothing away.

He had marched her out of the palace, one dry claw gripping at her upper arm, his mouth drawn tight like a miser's purse. She had wanted desperately to shout out to someone to tell the Queen, but didn't dare, for now she was Nelly Dent who had nothing to do with the Queen.

Jane the Fool followed them, chanting, "*Ding dong bell, pussy's in the well,*" over and over until Wriothesley turned and kicked her on the ankle, making her yelp like a dog and scuttle off. In the yard he handed Dot over to a man who tied a sack over her head, bundled her into a cart and brought her to this place.

A hatch opens in the door and a hand proffers a cup.

"Where am I?" she asks. "Is this the Tower?"

She hears a snort of laughter. "I don't know who you think you are, gel. You may 'ave a decent wool dress and be brought from the palace, but you ain't one of them duchesses what gets took to the Tower to get 'er 'ead tidily sliced off, that's clear as day."

"Then where am I?"

"This is Newgate, and a pretty palace it is too, for the likes of you."

"But what will happen to me here?"

"Don't ask me. But I do know if you don't take this cup 'ere, you won't be getting another."

She takes the cup. It is half filled with a thin tepid broth. He passes her a hunk of coarse bread and slams the hatch. She finds the curled body of a dead weevil in the bread and a slick of oil floating on the broth, but the smell of it has set off hunger pangs in her gut and her mouth is watering. She wolfs it down and then regrets it, wishing she'd saved some, for she has no idea when more will come.

She has no idea of anything. And nothing to do but pray and wait and try not to think about her fate.

45

It is Anne who unravels first. Her mouth is a dark hole and a terrible animal howl comes out of it, a crazed hollow noise that reverberates around the walls of the chamber, out of the door, into the gallery and beyond. It sounds like a birthing.

The women are silenced, and as one—as if choreographed in some strange dance—they bring their hands to their mouths and step back, watching Anne drop to the floor in a stream of anguished sobs. Her skirts crumple stiffly around her and she looks almost comical, as if she's in costume for a masque. But the distress on her face is not pretend.

The women begin to shuffle, their hands fluttering uselessly, uncomfortable at this display, unsure whether or not she is fitting and they should grab her flailing arms and hold her down.

None of them are looking at Katherine, who barely registers her sister's performance. She is half turned away and holds a paper between the tapered fingers of her left hand, reading what is on it over and over, hoping each time that it might say something different.

Her face is a tired gray and a collection of tiny droplets gathers on her forehead. She stands like this, absolutely still, for some time, just her eyes darting over the text, quick as spring flies, until Anne's wailing reaches a crescendo.

"Anne, there's no need for this." Her voice is straight as an arrow. "Pull yourself together."

She is the big sister back in the nursery, and Anne the fretting toddler.

Katherine crouches to hold her around the shoulders. Anne tucks her face into the hollow of Katherine's neck, leaving a trail of damp tears there. As she does this, the paper falls from Katherine's fingers and slides along the floor, flying like a magic carpet, on a current of air.

It is Nan Stanhope who dives on it, swift as a hawk. She reads it carefully, mouth pursed, eyes enlarging. "Oh God, no!"

Katherine thinks she can see a tiny upward tilt in her lips. But she can't trust what she sees any more. Her situation has rendered her suspicious of everything.

"This is a warrant for your arrest. Signed by the King."

A gasp goes up from the group, each one of them wondering, she supposes, how far they might be implicated in this, whatever it is—how far they might fall. Katherine can almost see their minds whirring, working out how they will save themselves.

A black word that travels around the room—heresy. There can be no other reason to arrest the Queen, though a few have been around the court long enough to know that charges don't necessarily correspond to anything in particular.

Lizzie Tyrwhitt wrings her hands as if trying to wash ink from them. Mary Wootten threads a ring off and on her finger. Anne, still wailing, clutches at her sister's girdle like a child as they both rise from the floor.

"This has Gardiner's stench on it." Cat Brandon's dog jumps up, hearing his name. "No, not you." She pats the animal's head absently. "How did it come to you, Katherine?" She moves in close, talking quietly so the others can't hear.

"Huicke brought it to me. He found it in the corridor outside the King's privy chamber. It must have been dropped."

"Does this not make you think the Lord is on our side," says Cat, "that you should have been warned like this?" They fall into silence.

Katherine wonders why, if the Lord is on their side, his plan for her has led to this. Is her faith being tested? Or is it punishment for her sins? All those old sins are catching up with her. How can you be human and be in this place and not sin?

"What will you do?" asks Cat. "You know I will do anything—"

Anne's wails will not let up.

"I'm more than a match for those snakes. Don't imagine I will be brought down so easily."

Her voice is the only steady thing in the room, but her mind flits about. How thankful she is that they got rid of all those books. How thankful that Huicke is returned. She must get word to her brother—God only knows what he has lying about his rooms—but Will is at the Borders, fighting the Scots.

She would send Dot to check his chambers but Dot is still gone. There are many ways to disappear a person in London, especially a low-born girl like Dot. She feels as if her head is in a vise and it's hard to get her thoughts in a straight line.

She has heard of a torture—a knotted rope around the temples, twisted tighter and tighter with a cudgel. But she *must* get her thoughts straight. She *must* stay calm and hold this whole carnival together. She will not be brought down. They are all looking at her for direction.

"Sister, hush!" She is sharper than she intends. "If any of you still have books, pamphlets—"

But a noise in the corridor stops her. They all turn. Fear thins the air. The door is flung open with a squeal of hinges to reveal Henry, flanked by a couple of his guards.

The women drop into deep curtsies, eyes glued to the floor. He lumbers into the room, standing in his ermine and his armor of intricately embellished robes, the quilting and gilding and embroidery, and the embarrassingly large codpiece peeking out from the folds of his gown like some monstrous pet.

"What's all this?" The flesh of his cheeks quivers like bone marrow. "Wife?"

"Your Majesty." She addresses his white slippers, reaching out to take his hand and kiss the ring.

Her own hand, suspended there, is as still as stone. If she is afraid—and how could she not be?—she will not show it, not to the King, not to anyone, barely even to herself. The ruby is a blob of blood. Her lips touch it. She imagines she is floating high in the beams of the ceiling, looking down on herself stooped before her husband, in her scarlet gown.

"Up, up!" He lifts his hand, palm up.

She rises, as if on a string. The others remain crouched.

"Explain to us what has been going on in here. This dreadful commotion. Are you ill?"

"No, Your Majesty, not I—"

"Look at us!" He showers her with spit.

"It is Anne who is unwell."

She looks up into his pebble eyes, which seem to have sunk further than ever into the folds of his lids.

"Ah, not you then. We had thought it was our wife baying like a stuck pig." He looks towards the red-eyed Anne, rolling his eyes to the roof, and slaps Katherine firmly on her behind.

She forces out a small laugh.

"Go on," he gestures towards the women, inducing a scuffle of brocade as they unfold themselves. "Bugger off, the lot of you."

They disappear like extinguished flames.

It is only then that Katherine is aware of Gardiner lurking behind the King, his waxy face hardly able to conceal the air of triumph. An excited twitch starts up at the corner of his eye. He clears his throat to say something.

The King, seeming to have forgotten he was there, turns and hisses, "You too, Bishop . . . Shoo! I have no need of you here."

Gardiner moves backwards slowly, black-capped head bobbing up and down like a moorhen's. The King gives him a little push in the chest with the palm of his hand before slamming the doors shut.

He draws her over to the settle by the fire.

"Your Majesty"—she strokes the back of his swollen hand—"I fear I have displeased you." She looks up, widening her eyes briefly, sufficiently, before casting them down.

"You fear you have displeased us?" He seems on the brink of laughter.

He is toying with her. She has seen him do this to others. A wasp buzzes frantically in the casement, colliding repeatedly against the glass. Tap, tap, tap.

"I want to be a good wife." Her voice is light as beaten egg-white.

He shifts, wincing as he uncrosses his legs.

"Your leg pains you?"

"What do you think?" His anger is quick and blunt.

"Can I do something to take your mind off it?"

"Now that's more like it." He grabs at her partlet, pulling it open and shoving a paw in, as a bear might look for honey in a hole in a tree, kneading her breast, half tugging it out, so it is painfully trapped by the tight edge of her bodice like a squelch of white clay. "Not the paps of a bitch in whelp, are they?"

She shakes her head.

Her mind teems with thoughts of survival.

She has survived before. She will manage this, like the best of Udall's actors, for she will not burn, neither will she lose her head like those other Queens, even if it means playing the part of a harlot.

She draws her hands towards the oversized codpiece, noticing it is embroidered in red silk thread with the words HENRICUS REX. In case anyone might forget to whom it belongs.

He begins to help her unlace the thing with clumsy fingers. "Down. On your knees. We can silence you, woman. We want a quiet wife."

Tap, tap, tap, goes the wasp.

46

Dot sits at a bare wooden table with both palms face down, as she was instructed with a rap over her knuckles. The papers she found under the Queen's mattress are lying face down in front of her. She wants desperately to turn them over, read what is written on them, but a guard watches her and she doesn't dare even so much as twitch a muscle.

The constant dead weight in her belly, the fear pricking up her spine, the jump at every sound, are now so familiar as to be normal. She is caught in a thicket of brambles, each slightest movement tangling her tighter.

This room at least does not have the foul stench of the other.

The bell tolls one o'clock.

The guard scratches at his neck.

A fly circles the room.

Voices outside, the sounds of comings and goings, seep into the space. The regular creak and slam of a heavy wooden door and a guard asking questions suggests they must be close to the entrance. She can no longer hear the tortured shouts and complaints of the other inmates, which have kept her from her uneasy sleep these last few nights. She lost count of the hours long ago—has no idea if she's been here a week or a month.

Someone arrives. A guard outside asks his business.

"I come from the palace," says the voice.

It is a voice she could never forget. The sound of it is scored into her secret places.

Her heart jabbers.

It is William Savage.

She wills him to open this door, so close, and find her, watches the latch for signs of movement, listens for the soft shuffle of his footsteps nearing.

"Are you the Lord Chancellor's man?" says the guard.

"No, no, I'm looking for Dorothy Fownten, lately gone missing from Whitehall Palace."

He has come for her.

Her heart shouts, now.

She imagines the guard opening a ledger and looking down a list of names. Her hands are trembling now, not with fear but with anticipation. She presses them into the table to hide the shake. William will save her from this place—dear, dear William Savage.

Her guard snaps a sudden fist in the air. She starts. He has caught the fly and lets it drop to the straw.

"There is no one of that name here," comes the voice beyond the door.

It hits her like a slug in the gut that she is not Dorothy Fownten. She is Nelly Dent. She can feel him slipping away, can feel herself slipping away, wants to rush to the door, bang on it till her hands are raw, shout to him that she is here. But she sits, still as stone—she cannot betray the Queen. But neither can she help herself willing him to fling the door open, to see her for himself.

Open the door, open the door, find me, find me. It is I, your full stop.

She hears the outside door squeal shut.

William is gone.

Her breath is shallow, barely reaches her lungs, and she feels the press of tears, forcing them back. She will not give any of these people, these brutes, the satisfaction of seeing her cry.

It seems an age that she waits. She tries to herd her thoughts away from despair but those papers sit in front of her and her mind keeps turning to the word Wriothesley had used—"heresy." With that word comes the heat and the flames and the screams of martyrs. But she is no martyr. She can hardly think of what to say to God when she prays.

Prayer has never been much more than the usual routine of things, and she has barely given a thought to the state of her soul. But now she thinks of it, thinks of her lack of prayer, stretching back for years and years, all that unbelief. She feels the tangle of thorns tighten around her still further.

The door swings open and Wriothesley stands there holding a pomander to his nose. His clothes are a chaos of different colors and layers. A page follows him in, carrying a large bag and yet another gown over his arm, which she supposes Wriothesley has just taken off.

"Get out," Wriothesley says to her guard, who flashes him an insolent look that only Dot notices.

The page puts the bag on the table and pulls a chair out for his master to sit.

"So!" Wriothesley inhales on his pomander with a loud sniff. "Nelly Dent. Let's get this over and done with. I'm a busy man."

He picks up the papers and thrusts them towards her.

Sniff.

She flinches minutely, which provokes a small smile in him.

"Whose are these?"

"They are mine, my lord." She'd known he'd ask this and was ready with her answer. "From a friend."

"Yours." He sniffs again. "Yours?"

"Yes, my lord." She can smell the citrus tang of his pomander.

"What would a mean-bred girl like you be doing with written papers?" Sniff. "Tell me whose they are." He leans in towards her and pokes a finger into the soft part of her throat.

She gags and struggles for breath but holds still and he pulls back eventually.

Sniff. "Don't think I won't break you, Nelly Dent."

"They are mine, my lord."

"Don't take me for a fool, Nelly. A rough little thing like you has no use for . . . How can I say it?" Sniff. "I should think the Queen's monkey reads more easily than a girl . . . a girl who has the smell of the gutter on her. I'm surprised the Countess of Hertford would take on a thing like you."

The page lets out a snort of laughter from where he is standing by the door.

"Remember Catherine Howard? She could barely sign her own name and she was Queen. Tell me, Alfred"—he turns to the page—"can your sisters read?"

"Hardly, my lord." Alfred's shoulders are heaving now.

"You see." He waves the papers at her so she can feel the breeze of them on her face. "And *his* sisters are ladies, are they not, Alfred?"

"They are, my lord."

"For your father is an earl, I believe." Sniff.

"That is right, my lord."

"So, if the daughters of an earl can *hardly* read, where does that leave scum like you, Nelly Dent?"

She imagines that she can see a forked tongue flick out from between his lips.

"I don't know, my lord."

"Go on then." Sniff. "Prove it." He thrusts the sheaf of papers at her. "Read to me."

Alfred is now openly laughing, Wriothesley sneering.

Dot takes the papers, gathering herself. "Would you like me to read all of it?"

"Do you hear that, Alfred?"

The page is now almost bent double with laughter.

"She asks if she should read it all." He comes round to her side of the table and points out a few lines. "This."

The writing is a scrawl and smudged in places but she has already skimmed over the first page. *Last testimony of Anne Askew*, it says at the top. She begins to read the lines he's pointed out. "'I have read in the Bible that God made man . . .'"

Both men are gawking as if she's a performing ape.

"'. . . but nowhere does it say that man can make God.'"

Neither of them utters a word. They still stare at her as if she has two heads or four arms, so she continues reading aloud.

Finally Wriothesley finds his forked tongue. "Enough! You have proved your point. But why do you have such heretic materials? Who gave them to you?"

She thinks fast. "It was from Anne Askew herself, from her maid, when I brought her the victuals."

"From Anne Askew?" His eyes are suddenly bright.

"Yes, my lord, she thought to turn me to the new faith."

"And were you turned?" Sniff.

"I think not, my lord."

"This is heresy, Nelly Dent, and you should burn for possessing it." His lips are gathered tightly, like a dog's arsehole. But the fire in him is doused, his voice and his words are empty. Dot feels a small triumphal thrill run up her spine. "You know we have racked better born women than you—the Askew woman was one of them."

The menace has gone from him. He has not got what he needed, whatever that was.

She heard what he said: "you should burn"—*should*, not *shall*, nor *will*.

"You can rot in here for all I care." Wriothesley rises in a single swift movement, his layers of clothing swinging, leaving a breeze, as he exits.

Alfred gathers up his things to follow him out.

"Take her back to her cell. I will send word of what to do with her," Wriothesley says to the guard and is gone.

47

William Savage is shown into Katherine's rooms. His beleaguered look is indication enough that he has no good news to tell.

She holds a small lavender bag to her face. The sweet aroma competes with the strong frankincense scent emitting from the burner—her attempt to erase the stench of the King's visit.

In the window Cat Brandon is retying the Fool Jane's coif that has become unraveled. Jane is muttering to herself, her own kind of nonsense. Mary Wootten and Lizzie Tyrwhitt are folding gowns and laying them into a big trunk, preparing for the move upriver to Hampton Court tomorrow.

Katherine wonders if she won't be journeying in the opposite direction. The thought of that great gray fortress haunts her.

The King had left in an improved mood. He had said nothing of the warrant, and she had not dared mention it. But he had asked that she come to his rooms that evening, giving her the finest of threads to cling on to—unless he means the guards to come there to arrest her.

That is not the usual way, though. Anne has seen it twice before, Mary Wootten too. The King removes himself first, they say, disappears to another palace. Next someone is sent for the jewels. The Queen's jewels do not belong to the Queen. (Katherine has waited for the arrival of someone—it would probably be Wriothesley with a vicious smirk—to ask for the coffer, but no one has come.)

When the jewels are gone, the Queen—whichever one it is, an Anne or a Catherine—is made to wait for excruciating hours, wondering about her fate, the panic fizzling in her like acid. And when she is well simmered and reduced—then, they come for her.

She beckons William Savage over. The look in his eyes would make her cry were it not for the fact that she has cauterized her tears. She will not be seen to be weak. She knows the King well enough. If word got to him of her weakness, he would stamp on her all the harder.

Anne bursts in from the wardrobe, her face aghast. "Mother's cross. It is gone."

"I have it, Anne." Katherine opens her hand to show her the necklace. The largest pearl has made a deep hollow imprint in her palm. "They will *not* get their hands on this."

"Oh, Mister Savage"—Anne notices him hovering nearby. "Have you news of Dot?"

"Sadly, no, my lady." Distress is etched into him.

"The full stop," calls the Fool Jane from the other side of the room. Cat bids her shush.

"What was that you said?" asks William Savage.

"The full stop. The speck, the dot on the horizon."

The women look from one to the other, bewildered.

"That is my name for her," William Savage explains. "Full stop."

"Come, Jane," says Katherine.

Cat leads her over by the hand, as one might a small child.

"What do you know of Dot? You *must* say."

Jane's one eye wanders frantically, the other fixes on her hands. She picks at her nails.

"Jane," says William in the softest of voices. "Please . . ."

The girl begins to chant quietly, half singing, half speaking: "*Nelly Bligh caught a fly and tied it to some string. Let it go a little way and pulled it back again.*"

Katherine takes hold of Jane's sleeve, saying, "But what does this mean?"

The girl simply begins a new song: "*Deborah Dent had a donkey so fine, marrowbones, cherrystones, bundle 'em jig . . .*" Her wild eye fixes itself momentarily in the same direction as the other, meeting Katherine's expectant gaze briefly, before roaming off again. Another rhyme starts up: "*When will you pay me? Say the bells of Old Bailey.*"

"Not that again," says Anne. "This is getting us nowhere."

The door to the bedchamber creaks open slightly, making Jane gasp and cling to Cat as if she's seen the Devil himself. Rig comes bursting in and skids over to his mistress.

"There there, Jane. There's nothing to worry about." Katherine strokes the girl's shoulder. "Why don't you go and find Will Sommers? He will tuck you under his wing. Mister Savage will take you to him."

William Savage dips into a bow as he takes his leave. "I shall keep searching. I will not rest until she is found."

"Those infernal rhymes," says Anne when they have left. "Some say she is wiser than Methuselah. I find that very hard to believe."

"Poor dear Dot." Katherine seems to speak to herself. "She has no family to look after her interests. She has been nothing but loyal to me and I have brought her only adversity." The guilt of it presses heavily, but she must hold herself together to visit the King.

She turns to her sister. "Anne, will you help me dress for the King? I must wear my finest things tonight. I must be impeccable."

Katherine sails down the long gallery, flanked by Cat Brandon and Anne—three exotic birds, brilliant with color. Their clothes were hastily pulled out of the trunks that had been packed ready for the move to Hampton Court tomorrow.

Their three veils spill out down their backs, and their trains drag behind them picking up a thin layer of grime at the edges and sending little whorls of dust swirling towards the skirtings. A pair of ushers walks before them, occasionally turning for a glimpse of these splendid creatures in their fine plumage heading for the King's chambers.

The usual melee of courtiers mills about in the great watching room, parting like the Red Sea as they pass. The whispers have circulated, carried between mouth and ear on invisible gusts of air. They will all have heard that His Majesty was displeased with his wife. They all know how the King likes rare birds for his table, one way or another.

Katherine is thinking of her husband's signature scored into the warrant in black ink. It was his own hand, not stamped by the great seal that has been used for many of the official documents of late.

She pictures him taking up the pen himself to sign her life away with a flourish. It frightens her. He may as well have etched his mark on her body.

She had thrown the warrant on the fire.

Which version of her husband awaits her?

She tries to reassure herself with the fact that he has asked to see her. That is surely a good sign. Maybe he has grown tired of getting rid of his wives. Still, though, she pulses with dread at the thought that she will arrive in his rooms to find him gone and a troop of guards waiting to convey her downriver.

Jane's infernal rhymes circulate her head: *Nelly Bligh caught a fly and tied it to some string.* The worry of Dot prods at her, poor, poor disappeared Dot.

An arm links through hers. It is Nan Stanhope, in rustling satin and a ruby as big as a rosehip, swinging on a chain. She has come to join them. Katherine wonders, as they exchange a smile, whether she has come in solidarity or if she wants to gloat.

Huicke's words are on her mind: "Be meek, Kit, and for God's sake keep your opinions to yourself. Your life depends on it."

How will she ever thank him for everything he has done, bringing her the warrant, risking his own life for hers? There are some things too great for plain gratitude. He had come back early from Ashridge, having found little wrong with Elizabeth.

He had been pushed out of the way, that is clear. It was Paget who sent him. But he is back now and has bolstered her for this. He wondered about the warrant, if someone had let it drop deliberately for him to find, hoping it would serve as a warning to her, or if it had been a fortuitous mistake on the part of her enemies. Or was it God's work? They would probably never know.

"Dress like the Queen, Kit," he had said, "and remember, docile."

"Biddable," she'd added.

"Acquiescent."

"Yielding."

"Silent."

They had laughed at that, in spite of everything.

Huicke had taken his leave with a light kiss on her cheek and the words, "The meek shall inherit the earth." He wore a smile but his face was tight with worry.

They come to a halt at the door to the King's privy chamber. Cat gives her a little nod of encouragement.

Someone within is playing a lute, another sings ... "*Who shall have my lady fair, when the leaves are green?*" It is familiar but Katherine can't remember where from. There is a general low hubbub of male conversation and Katherine is sure she can hear, with a pang of relief, the King's sonorous tone.

He wouldn't remain to witness her arrest, would he?

A series of whispers is exchanged between the King's ushers and her own before the doors are swung open.

They are all there: Gardiner, Rich, Paget, as well as the usual chamberers and toadies, gathered about the mountainous shape of Henry. But not Wriothesley—is Wriothesley awaiting her at the Tower with his thumbscrews?

A blanket of silence falls over the room as the women glide in. There is a moment of paralysis before the men remember themselves, grappling to their knees and lifting their caps.

Henry is unreadable, splayed across his seat, like a bullfrog.

"Ah! It is my Queen. Come, sit with me, my dear." He pats his lap.

So, I shall be reduced to dandling on his knee like an infant, Katherine thinks, perching herself there and pecking his damp mouth with her own. As she sits the men move to accommodate her companions.

She catches the barely concealed grimace on Gardiner's face. He is like a dog hoping for a bone.

Paget, still curled into an obsequious crouch, says, "I'm sure that even the court of King François himself has not such beauties to adorn it."

"We were talking of God, were we not, Gardiner?" Henry ignores Paget and waves a meaty hand towards the Bishop.

They all know she cannot hold her tongue when it comes to religion. That is the trap. They think they have her.

"We were indeed, Your Majesty." Gardiner's eye flicks towards her.

"We were discussing justification by faith alone. What think you to that, my dear?" He shuffles at the fabric of her gown to feel the shape of her leg beneath, gripping at her thigh.

She can sense all the eyes in the room on her. Her skin feels tight as if it has shrunk and become too small to accommodate her. They mean to have her talking blindly of Calvin. Huicke's words circle her head: *docile, acquiescent, biddable*. It is not so funny now.

"Your Majesty," she says, "I only know that God made me as nothing more than a foolish woman. I could not suppose to know more than you. I must . . ." She pauses. "I will refer my judgment to Your Majesty's wisdom, as my only anchor here on earth, next to God."

His grip tightens on her thigh. "But if this were the case you would not constantly seek to instruct us with your opinions."

A million thoughts are roaring in Katherine's head and the room seems to recede, distorting everyone in it, rendering their features grotesque as they watch and wait for her reply.

She has to rein in the part of herself that wants to leap off her husband's lap and defend herself, to reply to him that she *would* seek to instruct him for he is dense and narrow-minded, tell him that her thoughts and interrogations are more subtle by far than his.

A coal falls from the hearth, rolling red-hot onto the floorboards. A page jumps forward, gathering it with the fire tongs, scuffing at the sooty mark it has left with his slipper.

The room hangs in suspension.

Nan Stanhope fiddles with her preposterous ruby, running it up and down its chain.

Anne grips tightly at her cup of ale.

Gardiner twitches, still awaiting that bone.

"I think it unseemly and preposterous for a woman to take it upon herself to instruct her husband." She keeps her eyes down, her voice low and unwavering but not so low as to prevent the assembled company from hearing her.

"If I have ever given the impression of doing so, it was not to maintain my own opinion but more in the hope of distracting Your Majesty from the terrible pain of your infirmities. My hope was that Your Majesty would reap some ease thereby but also"—she strokes the back of his hand, looking up at him then, widening her eyes like a pet kitten—"that I might profit from your great knowledge of such matters."

The King hugs her to him, saying with a wet whisper in her ear, "That's more like it, sweetheart. Now we are truly friends again."

Relief washes over her. She is reprieved—for now. But she is struck more than ever by the knowledge that her safety hangs on the whims of a volatile old man.

The haste of Henry's about-turn makes her wonder if this was more some kind of devious test than a trap. She wouldn't put it past him. And what, anyway, is true friendship, in someone as mercurial as the King?

Gardiner is convulsing with disappointment.

Katherine smiles at him. "Bishop, your cup is empty. Perhaps you would like more ale."

He holds out the cup to be filled but cannot bring himself to smile back at her.

She has won, but the triumph feels fragile as a spider's web.

48

The Queen's Barge

They time their departure just as the early tide is rising so it doesn't take long to travel to Hampton Court. Katherine had tried to delay, couldn't bear the idea of leaving without Dot. But Dot is still nowhere to be found and she no longer knows where to look or whom to ask. Her diminishing hopes lie with William Savage.

Meanwhile, the King's barge floats placidly alongside hers at the center of the flotilla that conveys the court's inner circle. He waves to her with that look on his face that he used to have, the same look on the faces of the Kings around the manger in the great Magi painting that she remembers hanging at Croyland—a benign adoration. She wonders where that painting is now—adorning some earl's privy chambers, no doubt. It is the look he had for her before they were married.

If last night was a test, then she has passed. But it is no reason for her to drop her guard, for if it took so little to change him it will take less to change him back.

Surrey sits in the King's barge and catches her eye with a nod of solidarity. He, too, knows what it is like to hang by a thread, to be in and out of favor with the King.

As they round the bend in the river, the red molded chimneys and crenellated towers of Hampton Court appear suddenly, banners dancing in the breeze. Soon the rest of the building reveals itself from behind the riverbank vegetation. The sight never fails to surprise her, the vastness of the place, its newness, its audacity.

When they disembark Henry takes her hand, leading her off into the gardens, though he has Paget hovering like an unwanted fly and brandishing a set of papers that need his attention.

Henry swats him away. "Not now, Paget, not now." He turns to Katherine then, saying, "Let's see what the gardeners have been busy planting."

They walk hand in hand, while he chats blithely about this and that. She stoops to pick up the perfect half sphere of a fallen finch's nest. In it, nestled among a drift of fluff and feathers is a late clutch of small, speckled eggs. The sight of them makes her feel quite bereft and she whispers, "How sad."

The King takes the nest from her. "Don't worry, my dear, those little finches will survive." And he tucks it safely back into the branches of a nearby tree.

But the empty broken feeling will not leave her.

She wonders when she stopped wanting a child for the pure sake of it and started wanting one for the sake of her own safety. She has given up hoping now. And what of Dot? She dares not mention Dot to the King for fear of igniting some new suspicion.

They walk a little more and finally sit on a bench beside a pond, in a shady knot garden enclosed by high walls of privet, where he pulls her into him with his arm so that she can rest her head against him. He hums, she can feel the sound reverberating in his chest, and he strokes the softest part of her temple—the place, her brother told her once, you could kill a man if you pressed hard enough.

Katherine begins to become aware, beyond her husband's soft humming and occasional splosh of a fish, of a metallic rattle and the unmistakable sound of marching feet.

The noise approaches, becoming louder, and the King's tune dies as Wriothesley appears in the privet archway at the head of a small army, twenty strong, of yeoman guards, armed and kitted out in the King's own livery.

"Oh, God save me," murmurs Katherine. "I thought it was done with." She has come to the end of her resistance and thinks, just take me now. Take me and do what you will. Of all the ways she had thought it would happen, this was not it. It is Henry's cruelest game yet, to let her believe herself reprieved and then—

But the King is on his feet, black-faced and screaming at his Chancellor. "Knave! Arrant knave! You beast! You blasted fool! Be gone!"

Wriothesley, with a visibly trembling hand, signals the guard to stop.

He seems unsure of how to respond.

The King quivers with rage and seems unable to curb his shouting. "Out of my sight, varlet."

Bewildered and white-eyed, Wriothesley turns tail and scuttles off, hunched and humiliated, under the gaze of the guards. He knows, as she does, that it will be round the whole palace by suppertime—that he came to arrest the Queen and the King sent him packing, calling him a fool and a varlet before a score of halberdiers.

Wriothesley has played the wrong move—so very unlike him. Did no one get word to him of last night's events? Perhaps the King was testing him too—only Wriothesley has failed *his* test.

"That man," Henry growls, "is pissing close to the wind."

"I think only that he is mistaken, Your Majesty, I'm sure he meant no harm. I shall call him back to make amends with you."

"Oh, my sweetheart, how little you know." He strokes her cheek, running his hand over the tender part of her throat. "This man has been an arrant knave to you. He would have had you tumble like the others, my dear. Let him go, devil that he is, to his own comeuppance."

49

Time has lost all meaning for Dot, the days have merged one into the other and she wonders if the world has forgotten she exists. She barely thinks she exists herself any more.

She has stopped counting out the strokes of the bell or watching the sliver of window for signs of day or night. She sleeps when she's tired, wakes when she's not and eats the miserable victuals that are brought to her without complaint.

Each Monday at the toll of nine, the condemned prisoners are taken out to meet their ends. She knows this because the scaffold is outside her cell and she hears their final words, confessing their guilt and begging for the Lord's mercy, or pleading their innocence to the last.

They usually make a prayer or spill out their love to their families, whose choked witterings and wails she can hear too. Then comes the rattle as the trap opens, and with it the curdling fear that pierces through her gut, forcing thoughts of her own fate to the front of her mind.

She has never seen an execution. Nothing like that ever happened in Stanstead Abbotts, only the occasional thief put in the stocks for stealing a loaf or a cut of meat. She always felt sorry for them, whatever their crime, because by her reckoning they only ever stole when they were starving with hunger. She was never one of the ones to chuck rotten cabbages at them.

She has seen some violent things, has felt her share of fear, but the idea of stepping up to the scaffold—or worse, the stake—is too much to think of.

Yet she cannot help but imagine her own death, the cold earth packed over her. She can't bear to think of it but can't not. It makes her hollow. Twenty years old is too young to die. Meg was only nineteen. But Meg may as well have died when Murgatroyd wrenched all the joy out of her.

Meg's words still echo in the air: "*I am afraid, Dot. I am afraid to die.*" If Meg, with all her belief and praying and reading of the gospels, was afraid to die, then what of Dot, who has thought more of King Arthur and Camelot than God?

She tries to think of God now but her head is too full of fear to put things straight.

She thinks she would have completely lost her mind were it not for Elwyn. He is the guard who keeps an eye on her most days, the one who was guarding her the day Wriothesley came to question her. Elwyn couldn't hide his dislike of the man. When he'd taken her back to her cell that day he'd said so, called him a "blasted Catholic brute" and had given her double rations at suppertime.

The next day he gave her a blanket, full of moth, but a comfort nevertheless, and a couple of days later he slipped her a book. She had seen one like it before, in the Queen's library, though that was tooled in gilt on the finest calf's leather, with leaves as thin as skin. This was nothing in comparison, with crude bindings and coarse paper, but the words were the same.

She read each day until she was better at it than some of those tutor-schooled girls at the palace. It was by Martin Luther and spoke of all the things the Queen and her ladies whisper about.

She thinks about it now. Whether the bread at Mass *actually* becomes Christ's flesh. Whether you need miracles to believe in God or if it is enough to simply have faith—she doesn't really understand that one. It's all the same to her, though she'd never tell that to anyone, and she secretly wishes that Elwyn had given her something else to read— one of the romances, a story of knights and maidens and magic. But what use is reading and dreaming of Camelot when she is nothing more than a caged beast?

She may as well get herself educated and Luther is a place to start, she supposes. When Luther talks of faith, it makes Dot think of Anne

Askew, who would not recant to save her own life. Dot didn't understand at first, but now she can see that if you believe in something, really truly believe, then your life makes sense if you are faithful to it.

Other times she thinks of William Savage. Wonders how things might have been had they not been the way they were, wonders what his wife is like and whether they have a string of little ones, little Savages that she would have given her eye teeth to bear herself.

She'd always known she couldn't marry William, but that didn't stop her thinking of it. She'd hated him until her guts burned with it and hated his wife even more. But now she is just glad that he inhabits the same earth as she. He is forgiven and her heart feels lighter for it. She hangs on to the fact that he was seeking her out. It is the slenderest of strings attaching her to the world outside, allowing her to believe she is not altogether forgotten.

The Queen is never far from Dot's mind. She conjures an image of Katherine kneeling in prayer in her rooms at Whitehall, asking God for her safe return. But she fears that the Queen is no longer at the palace, that she too is held prisoner and awaiting an uncertain fate.

She would be held in the Tower, with the ghosts of Nan Bullen and Catherine Howard for company—but Dot will not think of that. And surely Katherine is too clever to let that happen.

Dot has seen how the King is, though, how he can turn on the tip of a pin. He is like two different men—one lecherous and one raging—and both of them would strike fear into the hearts of most people.

Dot sits thinking for hours and hours, rubbing her thumb over the outline of the silver penny her ma gave her all those years ago.

50

Oatlands Palace, Surrey, September 1546

A gold brooch set with thirty diamonds and twelve pearls arranged around a garnet the size of a robin's egg; a pair of jet black coney fur sleeves; a set of four bracelets in silver set about with sapphires; a dovecote with six pairs of turtle doves; twenty yards of purple velvet; a mechanical clock engraved with the words *love is timeless*; a rare, pure-white Persian falcon; a bejeweled dog collar in crimson leather for Rig; a side of venison; a gross of seed pearls for stitching upon gowns and hoods; a pack of greyhounds; five nightgowns of the finest silk; a female monkey, which she has named Bathsheba, as a wife for François—these are all the gifts Katherine has received from her husband.

They would be meaningless to her were it not for the fact that they signify the end of danger. It is all over, and things are as they were before, with the King besotted and fawning over his wife just as he did when he was courting her.

Everyone has returned, everyone but Dot. Katherine has had to resign herself to the fact that Dot may never return. Her brother Will is back at court, and with him Hertford and Dudley, for all the reformers are in the King's favor again.

Wriothesley hangs from a thread after his botched attempt to topple her. Lord Chancellors have been ousted before, and the members of his company are shuffling about with shifty faces and hanging tails, working out which side to leap to before it's too late. Gardiner is nowhere to be seen, having scuttled back under his stone.

Yes, the reformers are on the rise. Her brother had excelled himself, entertaining the French ambassador on his arrival in England. He'd then conveyed his guest to Hampton Court to meet with the King and the two-hundred-strong entourage that rode out to welcome him. Katherine teases Will that if his head swells any more he will be unable to pass through the great door at Whitehall.

Katherine had sat beside her husband to receive the French envoy, the perfect consort. It is as if nothing has happened, as if there was never a warrant for her arrest, never a guard of twenty strong arriving with Wriothesley to take her to the Tower—as if she never imagined the cold blade falling on her neck, or the heat of the stake. That episode has been erased and the Parrs are basking in the sun again. The King has even put Prince Edward in Katherine's care—an honor indeed.

But the dread still simmers below the surface.

She has rarely seen her husband in such fine humor and even the absence of a Prince in her belly has not been mentioned of late. He has other things to distract him and is puffed up like a pigeon over the ratification of the treaty with France.

The victory at Boulogne has put England at the center of European politics again. Defending Boulogne is sapping the coffers and this treaty returns the city to France. It leaves King François indebted to England for a sum so vast he will never find a way to pay it off. That puts a smile on Henry's face. If it were a game of chess, Henry would have just taken François's queen.

Katherine keeps her opinions to herself, benign or not. She speaks only when spoken to and defers always to her husband. If he said the sky was green she would agree. She does not ask anything of him—not if she may invite Elizabeth to court, not if he will demand an investigation into Dot's disappearance (even though Dot would not be gone if the King had put his foot down to stop Gardiner's witch-hunt, she is sure of that, and blame still burns in her).

She manages to act the part of Henry's devoted wife, doing nothing to reveal her true feelings about anything. She reads only her physic manuals and bland books of little interest, and she no longer writes, though she imagines her *Lamentation* festering away in the dark, unseen, unpublished, eaten by mildew.

A sense of failure washes through her when she thinks of all that new faith buried, when she remembers the fervor she had felt at being a part of the great reformation. But it is staying alive that she must concern herself with now, and protecting those around her—even while she fears the worst for Dot.

5 1

Elwyn bursts into her cell, grinning, hardly able to catch his breath. "I am to let you go, Nelly."

"I don't understand."

It can't be that simple. Is that stoat Wriothesley not to come back to give her another grilling? Is she not to be taken to the gallows?

"If this is a joke, Elwyn, then it is not a funny one."

"No word of a lie, Nelly. I am to release you."

"But—"

"You were here so long without word that the chief warder sent for instructions to the Lord Chancellor's office." He grabs her shoulders to look right at her. "Lucky he did, Nelly, for the man there said you had been forgotten, and might have been left here for ever. I suppose the Lord Chancellor couldn't get what he wanted from you."

"Thank heavens for that. Imagine me festering here for ever."

"Listen to this." Elwyn's eyes are glittering. "Fate has struck a blow to the Lord Chancellor. I have a cousin who works in the stables at Whitehall, who says the Chancellor has been disgraced and hounded from court, that he wronged the Queen and that he's lucky to have his head still attached to his shoulders."

"The Queen is not in the Tower?" Dot is thinking aloud.

"Wherever did you get an idea like that? No Queen has been in the Tower since Catherine Howard."

Dot's head is spinning.

She is to be set free, just like that.

What a place this world is!

Elwyn escorts her to the head guard, who makes her sign her name in a ledger, and then he accompanies her to the gates, where she returns his book of Luther to him.

"I was grateful for this book. It is what kept me from losing my wits altogether." She drops a light little kiss on his cheek, which makes him blush, before bidding him goodbye. "And I sincerely hope never to see you again."

This makes him smile. "I truly feared they'd burn you, Nelly."

Hearing that makes her taste the dread again, but then she looks to the door, saying, "Am I really to leave, just like that?"

He nods.

The open door looks like the gates to paradise. She can see the sunshine falling on the cobbles beyond and hear the calls of the market traders nearby.

"You know," she says, quietly drawing close to him, "I can tell you this now, but my name is not Nelly Dent."

He looks at her, his face a question mark.

"I am Dorothy Fownten, Dot to all who know me, and I serve the Queen of England."

His face is a picture, his eyebrows lost in his hair and his eyes popping out and his mouth like an O, which makes her laugh. Then she turns and walks out, calm as anything.

When the gates clang shut behind, it is as if she's entered another world.

She stands in a churchyard gawking at it all, the busy gathering of starlings pecking about the cobbles, the cat lazing in the sun, the apple tree next to the church wall, the spider's web slung in the angle between two branches, the crouched spider and a fly caught there beside it. She looks up at the sky, white clouds with patches of blue, and takes a great heave of breath, like the first breath she has ever taken. Picking up a windfall, the biggest and rosiest of them, she crunches into it, the sweet, juicy foam pricking at her taste buds—she might as well be in Heaven itself.

She moves on from the church square into a market alive with traders shouting out their wares. A herd of bleating sheep passes through with a boy who can't control them, getting hot under the collar when one of them goes off in the wrong direction. He shouts at his herding dog, who is not much less disobedient or stupid than the sheep.

She sits on a step and watches the world go by, the kitchen lads from the big houses coming down to buy fish and bread and the traders trying to squeeze every last penny out of them. A woman drops a basket of cauliflowers, which roll all over the place sending people diving for them, and the bakers' boys are hawking their loaves, shouting, "Fine fresh bread for your table!" and drawing out the words so they sound like a song. The smell of that bread is enough to flog the loaves without the shouting.

Dot takes it all in, sitting in the sun, relishing her freedom. The only place she won't look is at the butchers' stalls where the hanging carcasses and the chop and thud of the cleavers reminds her too much of where she's just been.

Before she knows it the traders are all packing up and the crowds have thinned out. A young lass offers her a meat pie, too broken to sell. Dot refuses at first, saying she can't pay for it, but the girl presses it on her. She must look a sorry state indeed for a stranger to offer her victuals in the street. Her penny is stitched into her hem, she can feel its shape, but if she's going to get herself to Whitehall she'll need to hang on to it.

She heads for the river. The best way to get to Whitehall is by boat because it would not be wise for a girl to wander alone about the city now the afternoon is nearly over and the streets are emptying. The only boat for hire is one of the pretty painted barges, with a singing boatman, that the ladies and gentlemen are wont to take out for romancing.

The boatman is got up in crimson with all manner of bows and buckles and fripperies attached, and he charges her the whole of her silver penny for the short trip. His isn't just a common-or-garden boat, he says, when she complains—it is a barge fit for a princess. She knows she's being fleeced by the fancily clad nincompoop, but she doesn't give a monkey's. After all, if this isn't the emergency she's been saving her penny for then she doesn't know what is. And besides, she has four whole pounds stashed away somewhere in Katherine's keeping—her inheritance from Meg.

She kisses the penny before handing it over and whispers the words, "Bless you, Ma." God only knew where Ma had got hold of that coin in the first place, because the Fowntens were not the sort of family to have silver pennies lying about.

That gets her wondering, while she's going up the river, about her family and what has become of them, whether her brother has drunk himself into an early grave yet, like Pa always said he would—when he'd come in late every night drunk, whacking his head on the beams, walking into things and making a right old racket, waking them all up. She supposes Little Min must be married, and wonders to whom.

Then she thinks of her other "family," of Katherine. She has butterflies in her gut, thinking of being reunited with her. And now she is out, her longing for William has become a constant throb—even only for his friendship, given that he is already married and probably with a string of babies, a fact she tries not to think of.

It doesn't take long to get to the Whitehall steps, where she bids goodbye to her singing boatman. He had insisted on warbling a tuneless ballad about a cuckold, all the way, which has got itself stuck in her head: "For the zealous *jade*, Ben a true cuckold *made*, And now he's no longer in masquer*ade* . . ."

She mounts the steps, making for the palace gates.

"I am Dorothy Fownten and I serve the Queen. Admit me, if you will," she says to the yeoman guard.

"And I'm the King of England," he replies, the cheeky devil.

"But truly I am."

Her voice wavers as she begins to explain how she comes to be where she is. He must feel sorry for her and her ordeal, as his grim face softens a bit but he still holds his halberd in front of him, barring her way.

"Listen, girly, if the Queen were here, I'd have someone fetch one of her pages to take a look at you—just to shut you up, if nothing else. But she's off on progress with all her household. The Queen's chambers are empty save for the decorators who're in there tarting the place up."

Her heart drops at that. She slumps, not knowing what to do—she is free and yet free to go where? The Queen could be away for months, traipsing from palace to palace. Her silver penny is spent and she has nothing but the filthy clothes she stands up in.

All she can do is wait, and hope that someone will come along who recognizes her. Her fight diminishing, she collapses onto a low wall and ponders the disadvantages of her invisibility, which had once been such a blessing.

52

Oatlands Palace, Surrey, September 1546

It is a fine early autumn day and the park is silent, shrouded in mist, its great trees looming like pale ghosts. Spectral antlers move about around them; the park is teeming with deer.

A great winch has been fabricated to help Henry heave his huge shape onto a horse and he has hunted each day since their arrival at Oatlands. Though it is hardly hunting, for the poor deer are herded into a corner before His Majesty's arrival, to contrive that he may be in at the kill. It is no better than slaughter. The creatures don't stand a chance, and Henry's poor over-burdened horse barely breaks out of a walk all day. Despite all this he returns to the palace each evening full of stories of the chase.

But yesterday he took a sudden turn for the worse, and will not hunt this morning.

Katherine, up early, is walking with her brother. The falconer and his lad follow several yards behind, politely out of earshot, hawks leashed to their arms. No one is about, save the bake-house workers who are preparing the day's bread, stacking the loaves in the racks outside. The scent of it is too much to resist and Will breaks off the end of a fresh warm stick that they munch on as they walk.

It is a simple pleasure, eating fresh bread, out of doors. Such satisfactions are few and far between for Katherine, whose every moment is taken up with the artifice of being Queen. They can hear the rustle and scuffle of creatures going about their business under cover of the fog. The hawks flap and strain at their jesses, keen to fly out, but the mist is too dense to send them. Will is in good spirits, gleefully recounting how Gardiner has fallen from favor.

"The old goat refused to gift the King a tract of land. Now he's denied admittance and waits about outside in the halls day after day, hoping to catch the King's eye."

"I can't say I'm not happy for that."

"Kit, you should see him. He waits for privy councillors to leave and tags along with them, to walk out through the watching chamber, so as to give the impression out there that nothing has changed."

"I would have thought he could manage a little more dignity but I can't muster any sympathy. He wished me ill, Bishop Gardiner."

"Lord Denny and our own brother-in-law, Will Herbert," he goes on, "are tipped for the top posts in the privy chamber. Out with the old." He slaps his thigh with a laugh.

"I had heard as much." Anne had mentioned the previous evening that her husband was to be given a new position.

"Kit," says Will, in that lowered tone that means he is about to say something that could compromise them both.

She knows her brother well—too well, she sometimes thinks. "Yes—what schemes now?"

"No schemes, sister." He hesitates and throws a sideways smile at her, glancing behind to be sure that the falconer is too far away to hear what he is about to say. "It is just that the King is . . . well, how to say it. He is not a young man."

"Stop, Will. You know it is treason to talk of such things." She says it, but she cannot deny that she has often thought of the King's demise and her own freedom.

"Who is there to hear? Only the squirrels and the deer."

"And the falconers." She suddenly feels sick of it all, tired of having always to take care not to be overheard, of never being able to simply say what she is thinking. "I shall say this but it is never to be mentioned again. Understood?" Her tone has become impatient. "When Henry went to France he made a new will and in it I was to be Regent, whatever occurred. And now he has given the Prince into my care. Is that enough to satisfy your ambition, brother?"

"Is that true? I knew of the Prince, but the will." He has jumped in front of her and turned to walk backwards, facing her, unable to quash his grin. "Why did you never tell me?"

She is not smiling. She is teetering on the edge of anger and can't stop herself from snapping. "It's not enough that your sister should whore herself to raise you up, but you would be the most powerful man in the land, would you? Do you not understand the danger I have been in? Do you not understand how little I care for power and how much I care for my life?"

Will is chastened and stumbles over a clumsy apology, waxing on about the respect he has for her as not only his Queen but his elder sister, and how he would lay down his life for hers, which she roundly doubts. But the whole stuttering ream of it lightens her mood. He *is* her brother, after all.

"It is hard, is it not, for your pride to shrink sufficiently that you can be sorry?" She laughs.

They walk some more, with Will talking lightly of privy chamber gossip. The mist is lifting and soon the hawks will be able to fly. They stop on a ridge with the rolling hills of Surrey before them, and the falconer's lad helps Katherine strap on her leather cladding so she can take her bird on her arm.

She unhoods it, feeling how it trembles with anticipation of the kill, then loosens its jesses, flinging it out. She watches its great wings spread as it skims and wheels into the distance, seeking out its quarry, then, spotting movement, hangs a moment before making its dive.

"The King has a mind to marry off Mary Howard, had you heard of it?" says Will.

"The Duchess of Richmond? I had not. Which is surprising given how my ladies can sniff out a marriage proposal in the next county."

The falcon rises talons empty and swoops around to hover, preparing to dive again.

"Norfolk is not happy about it."

"Why is that? I'd have thought he'd want to see his daughter wed again. She's been a widow for so long now and has barely two pennies to rub together. Marriage would take her off his hands."

"Ah, but the suitor is Thomas Seymour."

Katherine's fragile world begins to splinter—the equilibrium she thought she'd found is nothing more than a sham. Will talks on, and on, about the endless feuding between the Seymours and the Howards, but Katherine cannot hear him for the torrent of blood rushing through her ears.

"She turned him down once, years ago, but things are different now ... She could do a good deal worse than Tom. He's a hero ... attacked by pirates ... rowed himself to safety ... the comeliest man at court ..."

The world is whirling about her and she holds out a hand to the trunk of a tree to steady herself.

Will, seeing the color drain from his sister's face, reaches out to prop her up. "What ails you?"

"I am just a little dizzy."

She has forgotten her hawk, which plunges silently towards her, dropping a small rabbit with a thud at her feet, making her start. Finding her bearings, she puts out an arm and the hawk takes its cue, settling onto her, seeming so much heavier now. She is suddenly exhausted and drops to her haunches, leaning back against the tree.

"What is it?" Will squats beside her. "What ails you?" He places a hand to her forehead.

"It's nothing, I'm just ..." She hesitates, not knowing what to say. "I'm just feeling a little weak."

"You're with child?" Will can barely suppress his eagerness, his eyes dancing, betraying the inner machinations of his thoughts.

She can see him calculating how much further up the pecking order *that* would put him. "For pity's sake, Will, I am not."

"I'll take you back. You are in no fit state for hawking."

He moves to take her hawk, but the bird is spooked by something and flails about, catching Will's cheek with its talons, leaving a trio of blooded stripes. The falconer and his boy rush forward, apologizing, groveling, as if it had been their fault.

"Take them," says Will. "That one is still in the mood for killing and I must return the Queen to the palace."

They walk back in silence. Will hooks an arm through hers, and with his other hand he presses a handkerchief up to his bleeding cheek. Katherine's thoughts are spiraling and she wonders how she will fare if Thomas is back and paraded beneath her nose.

She had thought it all—the longing, the boiling desire—consigned to the past, buried. After all, it has been more than three years since he took his leave. But it is not over, and the notion of him marrying knots itself up inside her, her inner world thrown so far off kilter that she wonders how she will go about her business without visibly listing.

The palace gardens are bustling with people passing busily through into the courtyard. Pages rush through the cloisters and maids gad back and forth. A lad passes with a box of cabbages on his shoulder and a couple of women, gabbing to each other, carry between them a basket of fish. Everyone has some kind of duty to perform before the first serving of dinner in the hall.

As they notice that the Queen is among them they stop and drop to their knees, though she waves to them to carry on with their business and not mind her. But none notice that she is moving with difficulty through a world that is tipped on its side or see that she fears falling from its edge.

"Thomas Seymour," says Katherine quietly without looking her brother in the eye, "is he back at court then?" The name makes her tongue smart, as if it were too hot and has burned her.

He offers up that impudent grin of his that most girls find so irresistible. "You are not still sweet on my friend Seymour, are you?"

She draws herself together, gathering in her disparate fragments. "No, brother, I am not." She brings his ear to her mouth, hissing in an angry whisper, "And in case you'd forgotten, I am wed to the King of England."

"Yes, yes, sis." He pulls away. "And your answer is over there." He waves an arm to the far corner of the court.

Not understanding what he means, Katherine follows the movement with her eyes. There is Thomas, dismounting from his horse, oblivious to them watching him. A jewel in his cap is caught in a shaft of sunlight, glittering like a fallen star, and Katherine's heart tumbles.

"Seymour!" shouts Will.

Without a word, Katherine slips up the back steps and away before she is seen.

53

Southwark, September 1546

Huicke has been traipsing the Southwark streets in the drizzle for some time now, searching for Udall. When he disappears like this he can usually be found in one of the stews this side of the river.

His lover's insatiable appetite for the young renters who ply their trade around these parts makes Huicke wonder if he will succumb to the pox. God knows where the whore lads have been. But that's all part of it for Udall, or so he says—the danger. Huicke well knows about Udall's proclivity for beating young boys and there are plenty here who would suffer a caning in return for a few pennies *and* walk away with a smile on their grubby faces.

What worries Huicke more is that Udall will find himself on the wrong end of someone's blade—a fancy fellow such as he, slumming it in the stews for days on end. He half expects to turn the corner and find Udall's corpse, stripped of its finery and kicked into the gutter.

As the light fades, the alleys become more menacing and Huicke feels a buzz of apprehension in his belly. The mizzle turns to rain and he skirts the muck-filled puddles in his deerskin shoes, wishing he'd worn something more robust, unable to shake off his annoyance at being led here to pick his way through the maze of heaved-together houses to search for his lover. But Udall is like that. He knows Huicke will follow in his wake, and Huicke is angry with himself for being so predictable.

So he wanders the darkening alleys, fuming and itching—his skin doesn't like the damp weather. He presses a bunch of rosemary tightly to his nose against the reek, poking his head around doorways and looking into windows, following the odd gust of raucous laughter, or a waft of music seeping from the mean casements.

A beggar stands on the corner—a young woman in a torn dress and covered in dirt. Her filthy hands are cupped and Huicke considers tossing her a coin, but he knows only too well that if you stop and take your purse out around these parts, it will be conjured away in an instant. He also knows that there are gangs of thieves who are in the habit of using sorry girls like this as a decoy for their nefarious ends. So he strides on past, still furious with Udall for leading him to this godforsaken place.

When he has rounded the corner he hears a shout. Looking back, he sees the beggar girl approaching apace. He breaks into a run, speeding down an alley towards the river, splashing into a puddle, drenching his hose and cursing under his breath. He can hear her footsteps and the swish of her skirts close behind him. He speeds up, panting with the effort.

"Doctor Huicke," the creature calls. "Please stop!"

A shiver runs through him. How in God's name does she know what he is called? What kind of dirty ruse has he found himself the victim of? Her accomplices must be close by. If he can only get himself to the water where his boat is waiting.

"Doctor Huicke . . ."

She has quite a pair of legs on her for a girl and is closing in on him at speed. He tries to pick up his pace. A stitch stabs at his side, so he turns a corner, seeking a niche in which to hide, but is confronted by a solid wall, far too high to climb. Heart hammering, he turns, expecting a gang of thugs close at her tail. But the girl stands alone before him.

He leaps forward, grabbing her arms, twisting one of them behind her back and clasping her firmly about the waist, gagging on her rancid stink.

"I beg of you, loose me." She kicks out like a wild colt.

"Where are the others?" He tightens his grip.

"There are no others, Doctor Huicke."

"How do you know my name?" He fears himself caught in an elaborate trap, fears that it might be he, not Udall, who ends up on the wrong end of a blade this night.

"But do you not recognize me, Doctor Huicke? It is I, Dorothy Fownten, who serves the Queen."

He looks at her dress, noticing, even in the dimming light, that beneath the dirt it is cut from good wool. She is struggling to unloose his clasp on her wrist, plucking at his fingers with her free hand. It is then that he sees something familiar in the deep set of her eyes, the swell of her mouth. Releasing his hold a little, he allows her to turn and face him.

"You see, it is I," she says with a disarming smile.

"Dot?"

She nods and smiles. "Thank God!"

"And how did you come to be scampering the back alleys of this hell-hole?"

"It would take me some time to tell you my story but I am in danger in this place." She casts her eyes nervously about. "There is a man who has set me to beg for him and he will be seeking me out for his takings—" She stops, with a sharp intake of breath, and the color leaves her face as she appears to notice something at the entrance of the alley.

He turns to see the outline of a hulking fellow with a mutt tugging on a string.

"That is not he," she says with a sigh of relief, "but I must get away from here."

He takes her by the hand and they rush to the river. The boatman grumbles about the time he has waited, demanding double the payment. As they step in, Huicke is thinking of Katherine, imagining her delight at being reunited with this girl. Dot is shivering and Huicke removes his gown to wrap about her, feeling her body, beneath his hands, as insubstantial as a bird's.

"You need a good square meal, Dot Fownten."

"And a new dress."

They both manage a laugh at this, and as the little craft pushes slowly against the tide he presses her to recount what happened during her time in Southwark.

"Suffice to say, I have seen things I never thought to see in this life, and about which my lips are forever sealed." She runs a grubby finger over her mouth, the light from the riverman's torch flickering over her face. "Each of us has a talent, Doctor Huicke. And mine is for keeping a secret."

54

Dot is back, worryingly thin and silent as the grave. Beyond a brief mention of Newgate, she will not speak of how she came to disappear for such a long time.

Katherine knows not to press her. She is just glad to have her returned in one piece and that she is sleeping safely on the truckle bed beside her own. In the dark, Katherine listens to the even rasp of the girl's breath, her heart dilating at the sound of it. She can only imagine Dot has suffered greatly on her account, and it pains her deeply.

She had so wanted to make her position account for something, to set an example by following God in the simplest and most pure way and drive the new faith forward. But now she sees how much danger she has visited on those about her through it, and poor, poor dearest Dot the most innocent of them all.

She has long rid her chambers of any incriminating material. The books, the prayers, the papers, all are gone. There are no more whispered conversations, no thrilling interchanges imagining a new world, no pinning down the vagaries of translation, of interpreting the texts. She censors every thought that enters her head, every word that passes her lips.

Her household is taken up with sewing these days, fingers busy with needles rather than quills, embroidering great swathes of fabric with intricate stitching, a meaningless text.

The King visits and she listens, attaching her tongue to the roof of her mouth so it doesn't betray her by forwarding an opinion. She simpers, she scrapes, she smiles, she agrees, and she endures the nights she must spend in that grotesque carved bed, with its mahogany gargoyles gazing down on her humiliating antics. The King is content with her, even though he ails and cannot hunt, which is eroding his good humor little by little. Nevertheless, for the moment, he is happy to see his sweet Katherine behaving, and the gifts continue to arrive daily with a glorious monotony.

She may be able to hem in her outer self, but the hidden parts of her are running awry. It is the presence of Seymour, whom she glimpses constantly. He is everywhere, as if duplicated a thousand fold. When she takes a walk in the long gallery, he is there. When she strolls in the gardens, he is there. When she rides in the park, he is there, always at the edge of her vision: the flicker of his feather, the glimmer of iridescent satin, the chestnut fur of his beard, grown long in their years apart. And she dare not so much as glance his way, for fear of what might be unleashed.

Will and he are thick as thieves once more and she would give anything to exchange places with her brother, to not be the Queen, to not be a woman, and to be able to sit beside him, thigh against thigh, simply. It would be enough. It fills her with fear, the strength of feeling she has for this man. She can't believe that it is not visible on her, this untrammeled longing. But she must not think of him, or it, or anything—only benign things—and she keeps her eyes down, out of trouble, for they will betray her first.

Dot is a much welcome distraction. Katherine has had a West Country manor made over to her, as a way of showing thanks, but she knows what Dot wants more than anything in the world, and that is William Savage. She witnessed their reunion, how they rushed into each other's arms as if no one were there to see. He had dropped to his knees and asked that he might explain himself.

"My own full stop," he had said. "I know you have suffered at my hands and am sorry from the base of my heart."

"There is no need for that," Dot had replied. "I have long forgiven you, William Savage. I have learned many things about life these last months."

"But you must know, Dot, that though I am deeply ashamed for it,

I didn't tell you of my wife for fear that you would no longer allow me near you, and that was a thought I couldn't bear. We were married so young and I came straight to court, I barely knew her . . . I was foolish and—"

She had hushed him and looked directly into his eyes. "And what of your wife now?"

"She passed away a year since."

"I am sorry for that," she had said. "I mean . . . sorry for *her*."

Dot now goes about with her old glow, which brings Katherine more joy than she has had in a long time. And she has a plan: anything for Dot's happiness and anything, too, to take her own mind off her thoughts of Thomas.

She calls William Savage into her privy chamber, asking him if he has thought about another marriage.

A wistful look passes across his face which makes him seem heavy with resignation.

"If I commanded you to marry, what would you think of it?"

He mumbles, stalling, making sounds that don't fully form themselves into words, his face flushing, finally stringing something together. "If you commanded . . ." And then it is as if he is gripped with a desire to speak his mind. "I would not wish to marry again, madam."

"Is that so, William?" Katherine does not mean to tease but cannot quite help it, for she knows when she says what she plans to say, the moment will be all the more sweet for it.

"I love someone," he says, quite clearly now. "But it is not possible . . . We come from—"

"Hush, William." She places a hand on his sleeve. "The one I want you to wed is Dorothy Fownten."

He is suddenly animated, his skin glowing, a broad smile invades his face and his eyes are dewy. "My Dot . . . You would allow . . . I don't know what to say."

"Yes," she says, "I *would* allow it. Indeed, I can think of nothing I would rather allow."

"Madam, I . . . I . . ." He drops to his knee and takes her hand, kissing it with a fervor that suggests he is already thinking of Dot.

"But you *must* do as I say."

"Anything, anything at all."

"Firstly, if I ever discover that Dot has suffered on your account I will string you up, William Savage, and feed your heart to my hounds. She is never to be hurt."

He nods with a solemnity usually reserved for God.

"You will go to her and ask her yourself, quietly. Let it just be between the two of you. I don't want all my ladies sticking their noses in, for some will not approve. *I* shall write to your family. They will surely not mind if it is the Queen's wish."

Dot no longer sleeps on a truckle bed in the Queen's rooms, nor in the drafty anterooms outside the chamber that Katherine shares, less and less often, with the King. There are others to do that, for now she is a married woman. She sometimes has to pinch herself to believe that she, plain Dot Fownten, is wed to a man who can write poems and play the virginals and that she wears a ring from the Queen on her finger—her very own happy ending.

It was the Queen's doing, William had said, when he had come to her at Windsor, not long after her return. He had taken her hand and they had gazed into each other's eyes like daft lovers in one of the old stories.

He had fumbled in a pocket, patting down his doublet, and looking like he'd lost something important. Eventually, he had produced the ring. She recognized it immediately. It was Katherine's water ring (Dot had always called it that, as she didn't know the name of the stone) and he slipped it onto her finger.

"What are you doing, William Savage? That is the Queen's ring."

"No, my love, it is yours. It is your wedding ring."

It was as if her heart were a flower opening in her breast.

Later Katherine had called them into her chamber, where her chaplain was waiting, and Cat Brandon, who was to be the other witness.

"Imagine," she had nudged William, "to have the Queen of England and the Duchess of Suffolk to witness our wedding."

William had gripped her hand all the while as the chaplain spoke the service. When called to make her vows, she felt almost too breathless to speak. It was as if every event of her life had brought her to that moment and she thought she might explode with joy like one of Udall's fireworks.

They have lodgings now, near Whitehall Palace. It is just a single room the size of a cupboard, squeezed in by the undercroft. But the size of the room is of no consequence, nor even is the fact of the room, for she has her William Savage, and they can spend whole nights in each other's arms, not talking about the past, but being in their perfect now, and only occasionally imagining an indistinct future and the children they will have.

Finally, Dot feels safe and contained after all she has gone through. She tries not to think of all that and when William seeks to draw her out about it, she says, "Let sleeping dogs lie, husband," rolling the "husband" around her mouth as if it were one of the Queen's sugar confections.

55

Nonsuch Palace, Surrey, December 1546

The Earl of Surrey is in the Tower. Henry means to be rid of him. Everyone is reeling with shock at how quickly and how absolutely he has fallen—there was no warning.

Katherine is distraught. Impetuous Surrey, Will's great friend, her own friend, has been in and out of favor for years, but this time it is different. She thinks of him scribbling desperate poems in his cell but dares not write to him with support for fear of toppling with him. Rumor has it that Surrey's father, Norfolk, is detained too—or shall be soon.

The Queen's ladies talk of little else, for Surrey's wife is popular with them. There are Howard girls, cousins and daughters, scurrying about with that hunted look a family gets when the King is in the mood for killing and it is one of theirs at bay.

Katherine can feel the court shifting, everyone vying for position. Anne Bassett has returned from Calais, her family pushing her forward again—hoping for what? Katherine prefers not to ponder on that. But when things are in flux opportunities open up.

Nothing is safe.

She is not safe—but then she never has been.

And there have been rumors circulating that the King seeks a new Queen. But there are always rumors. Even Cat Brandon has been named, for she is recently widowed. Cat had breezed about and made a joke of it, but Katherine couldn't even find a sliver of mirth in the whole wretched business.

They all know, if it comes to it, the King will have what he wants and who he wants and will get rid of anything and anyone who stands in his way. To make matters worse, Henry is in an almost permanent ill temper from the excruciating pain in his leg. He barely leaves his chambers, barking commands to his councillors who creep around him, trying to be invisible—for when he snaps at them it is truly terrifying.

Katherine gently applies a poultice that she had made with Huicke. It is a new concoction designed to help draw out the infection. The King will not have the maggots any more, says they wriggle too much and irritate him. She barely even notices the reek of his ulcer, so accustomed has she become to it. She makes soothing noises and hums a favorite tune of his, but he is sullen and wordless and she tries to think of other things.

She longs for Christmas when at last they can have meat again. She has had enough of fish—fish, endless fish, carp, eel, pike, picking tiny bones out from between her teeth, the bland taste of it, and if not bland then too salty, for all the sea fish—the cod, the ling, the saithe—are packed in salt and make for a terrible thirst. Besides, it is always overcooked and dry and cold by the time it has been brought up from the kitchens. But there are still two more weeks of Advent fasting.

She lets her mind wander as she tends her husband, thinking of the feast they will have at Christmas, the sides of venison, the swans, the geese, the suckling pigs. Poor Surrey will not be so gay. Henry's lawyers are circling about the Howards like vultures, trying to find a plausible reason to butcher him.

The King has always feared that the Howards might become too powerful. She can see her husband is looking death in the face, for she knows only too well a dying man's demeanor. He fears for the aftermath with the Prince still so young. It is she who will be Regent until Edward reaches his majority, or so the will says.

She imagines rising to it, pushing through the reforms, becoming a great Queen remembered for bringing England firmly to the true faith. But a part of her would like nothing more than to live out her life in a small palace such as this, in obscurity—to be rid of the crushing weight of queenship.

She drops the poultice into a bowl, taking a muslin square and pressing it to the ulcer. Henry groans and bangs his hand on the arm of his chair. She asks one of the pages to light some candles. It is dark so early and the nights are endless.

She is glad to be in this pretty palace with a smaller entourage. Nonsuch is a wonder of turrets and plasterwork—like the best of the Florentine palaces, they say—and she is glad of the newness of the place, the stone grates that don't smoke, her very own bath with piped water. She bathes every day here. Why not, she is Queen after all.

She takes a fresh bandage and begins to wrap it around Henry's leg, thinking about the repeating pattern of her life, wondering how many more hours will be spent wrapping and unwrapping the King's bandages with her head down, three and a half years of it.

If she ever has the chance to marry again, it will not be to another old man. She pulls herself up with that thought—the brutal reminder that she, too, is a fruit on the brink of turning, and that old men may be all there is. The yearning for a child has not left her, as many had said it would, with age. She is in her thirty-sixth year now and still feels that gaping emptiness.

She loves the girls as if they were her own, and perhaps that is why: Dot, blessed Dot who would have died for her, and Elizabeth, with that resilience, that determination. There is something about Elizabeth that is hard to quantify, a steely allure that Katherine cannot resist. And then there is Mary, more a sister than a daughter, carrying the woes of her mother on her slight frame. Mary's very fabric is stitched through with tragedy. And Katherine cannot forget poor blighted Meg, misses her quiet presence. Finally, there is Edward too. For all his frosty demeanor in public, he is a sweet little thing underneath, just a child, and what a burden he will inherit.

All these children, who come and go, on the whim of the King, and none really hers. Even Dot is given to William Savage now, though willingly. She smiles to think of them together—her lovebirds. The King gave her a pair of lovebirds once. She wonders what has become of them.

She ties the bandage and the page returns with a carton of candles, which slips from his hands, spilling with a clatter.

"For pity's sake, Robin. Are your fingers made of lard?" Henry's rage doesn't match the smallness of the incident.

She waits silently while Robin collects the candles up and lights them, and when Henry has calmed, she helps him into his hose. That done, he pats the stool beside him.

"Come, Kit. Sit with us a little. We know we are bad-tempered but we are grateful that you do all this for us, when you could as easily leave it to our doctors."

She tells him how she would rather be doing this than anything. "What else is there for a wife to want, than to serve her husband?" Silently she asks God's forgiveness for her lie.

There is a hushed shuffling among the pages and ushers, who had been going about their business invisibly. "Majesty," says one of them, "my Lord Hertford is waiting."

"You'd better send him in."

Hertford enters. He has developed a new swagger of late and a new look to go with it. His beard is carefully fashioned into two points that sit against his white satin doublet like foxtails in the snow. His hose are white too, like the King's, and spotless—a pair of swans' necks—and his outer gown is lined in palest cream rabbit. The doublet is notched and slashed and stitched with pearls. Hertford is fond of pearls. Katherine touches a fingertip to the little bag on her girdle where her own pearl-dropped cross lies—more precious to her than any of the Queen's jewels.

A couple of men move into the chamber behind Hertford but Katherine is too distracted to notice them, by Hertford's sheeny pearls, the gloss of the pale satin, the flawlessness of the white hose, the downy rabbit, the very glow of this man, dripping with confidence, while all the others creep and scuttle—a man on the rise.

It is a few moments before she notices that it is Thomas who stands, in the gloom, behind his brother. She emits an almost imperceptible gasp and can feel heat rise up her face like steam from a bowl of piping soup.

Thomas glances her way and their eyes meet for a fraction of a moment. Her whole being invisibly sighs. She is entirely lost in the place where the memories of all their moments together reside—the feel of his fingers, his lips, the weight of his body, the musky cedar smell of him, the susurration of his voice, whispering nothings.

It is but the briefest moment, a nothing, a no time, but it is also an eternity, and she is turned inside out with longing. She drags her eyes away and on to her husband, whose own flint eyes are flicking back and forth between her and Thomas.

She presses her fingernails into her palm.

Hertford is speaking but she doesn't hear what he says and the King is not listening either.

"Go, wife," he says quietly. Then he erupts: "GET OUT OF HERE, WOMAN!"

As if a cannon has been fired in the room, they all stand stock-still, uncomprehending. Katherine rises, scattering with a misplaced foot all her medicinal paraphernalia. She tries to gather it up, but her hands dither and fluster and things drop out of them.

"GO, I SAID!"

She makes for the door, as fast as she can backwards, afraid to turn away from His Majesty and incur further wrath.

"Not again, not again," she mutters as she rushes away through the empty corridors. She had feared just this. That she would not be able to control her eyes, that her feelings would seep out through her ill-stitched seams. She thinks then of the speed of Surrey's fall and feels sick to the core.

Huicke approaches. His face is creased in concern.

She must be wearing her fear like a gown.

"What is it?"

"The King has sent me away . . . again. But this time it is . . ." She wants to tell him everything, describe the moment, Thomas's dear face, his eyes. "Not here," she whispers.

He understands, nodding and squeezing her upper arm. "You're shaking."

"Go. Are you going to him?" She taps at the jar he holds in his hand. "A tincture?"

"Yes, it is for pain. It is the one you used to make for Latymer. The King thinks it better than magic."

"He likes you more than his own physicians, Huicke."

"Is that a blessing or a curse?"

"It's hard to say, but go carefully . . ." She hesitates before adding, "If you have to distance yourself from me, I will understand."

He brings her hand to his lips and they part.

56

Katherine's words swill about Huicke's head and he wonders what could have triggered this latest incident.

A pair of pages exits the King's chambers as Huicke approaches. One carries an empty coal scuttle, swinging it by the handle, the other a large ewer. They chat casually, laughing about something. He stops briefly to watch them, indulging in the fresh bloom of their skin, the slender lines of their stockinged legs, not quite yet men, but not boys either, imagining them, momentarily, unclothed, how their muscles would be emerging from the soft layers of boyhood, the down on them still soft. One prances and struts, exaggerating his movements, tucking the ewer beneath his arm to remove his cap and wave it about with a flourish of feather.

"It is Roister Doister himself," laughs the other. "Master of the high seas, seducer of ladies."

"Did you know he escaped from pirates once, rowed himself to safety?"

"Yes, yes, everyone's heard that one. As it happens, I like the fellow, for all his fancy posturing. He once paid me a penny to drop a tray of tarts on the palace steps."

"Why?"

"He never said. *And* he helped me pick them up."

Their voices fade as they turn the corner of the corridor and Huicke continues to the door, waiting for the guard to announce him. He has the feeling that this incident must have something to do with Thomas Seymour, and a horrible memory comes to him of Catherine Howard's lover, the beautiful Thomas Culpepper, green with fear, being dragged away by the guards.

As he enters the King's chambers from the chill of the corridor, it is like walking into a wall of heat. The fire blazes, lighting the scattering of men like a Van Eyck he once saw in Bruges. The room has a male smell to it, leather and horse, and a lingering, rancid something.

Thomas Seymour is there, just as Huicke thought. The King must loathe the man for his splendid looks alone. There is a small gathering clustered around His Majesty. Stoatish Wriothesley is there, apparently returned from his exile, looking flustered as if he's just arrived. Hertford is in attendance too, dressed absurdly in white, like a Christmas angel, as well as a couple of ushers lurking at the edges. They stop the conversation as he approaches, so the quiet click of his boots rings out around the space.

"Ah, Huicke, what potions have you for us?"

"I have something to relieve your pain, Your Majesty."

There is a buzz of tension in the silence.

"Well, get it ready then." The King's impatience is clear. He turns to Hertford to say, "This physician is the best of them. His cures are the only ones that soothe me."

Hertford makes a mumble of agreement. He's basking in the King's favor. His timing is perfect, thinks Huicke. With the King deteriorating fast Hertford is rising to the top at exactly the right moment. Huicke has watched the nobles vying to position themselves in these last weeks, and with the Howards on the run the field has been left clear for the Seymours, who, as the Prince's uncles, have the advantage.

Huicke takes his jar to a side table and a page is dispatched to bring a clean cup. Hertford takes his leave with a bow, followed by his brother and one of the ushers. Wriothesley sidles up towards the King; he is making a plea for one of his relatives, couching it in compliments. The King seems to be only half listening. Wriothesley doesn't have the influence he used to.

"What think you of Thomas Seymour, Wriothesley?" The King interrupts the man's oily drawl.

"Seymour, Your Majesty? Did he not court the Queen once?" Wriothesley is slowly kneading his palms together as if rubbing salve into them, and the ghost of a smile appears at the corner of his mouth.

"Is he honest?" The King's eyes reflect the firelight.

"Honest, Your Majesty?"

"Honest, yes. Honest."

"Your Majesty, my opinion is not worth . . ."

"We ask you, what do you think?" The King's hands curl into fists, one on each knee.

"Think, Your Majesty?"

"Yes." His voice is raised now, enough to make most shrink, but not Wriothesley. "Do you think Seymour is honest?"

Wriothesley pauses, drawing his lips together and looking down to his shoes as if pondering deeply on the question. "I *think* he is honest."

The King emits an impatient huff. He, too, must have heard the slight emphasis Wriothesley placed on "think," infusing his statement with doubt, yet still managing to appear the loyal courtier. Huicke, even in his loathing of the fellow, is impressed at the subtlety of his game.

But this is no game.

Wriothesley is attempting to oust Katherine once more, and this time Seymour is his tool.

57

Dot is packing things up quickly with the other maids of the chamber, stuffing gowns into chests, wrapping the mirrors in among the linens, pushing furs into their satin bags, the ties left undone for haste.

There has been a change of plan. The Queen is to go to Greenwich Palace for Christmas and the King will go tomorrow to Whitehall. There wasn't the time to light a fire this morning and it's so cold in the room they can see their breath.

Earlier, Dot had found Katherine alone in her chamber, sitting on the corner of the bed, a blank face on her, running the chain of her mother's cross through her fingers as if it were a rosary. She had barely seemed to notice Dot coming in, as if in some kind of a trance, and Dot had asked her if something was troubling her.

"Yes, Dot," she had replied. "I think this is the beginning of the end." The skin of her face looked stretched with worry, her eyes glassy and unsettled. She has always feared being sent away from the King—she had said as much once. *Dot, as long as he will see me, all will be well.* And now he will not see her.

"If you don't mind me saying, madam, things often have a way of turning out as you least expect them. Look at me, how I festered in Newgate, sure to be burned, and here I am, right as rain."

"Bless you, Dot." Katherine did not look reassured at all.

"And there are no books here. All the books are long gone. There is nothing."

"Ah, but there is something. Not a book. But I will not tell you, for it is better you do not know. And look, I am as good as banished." She tugged at the pearls until Dot thought she would break them. "This is not good, Dot." And then she said something Dot didn't understand: "When it comes to it, save yourself. Save yourself, go to Devon and live a happy life with William."

Dot dressed her in silence, not knowing what to say and wondering all the while what it was that happened at the palace during her time in Newgate, for something happened, there is no doubt about that. What was it Elwyn had said—that Wriothesley had wronged the Queen?

Katherine stood like a puppet, stepping listlessly into her skirts and lifting one arm and then the other for her sleeves to be drawn up and tied. Dot chose what she wore. She didn't even bother to say which gown or which hood, so lost was she in her own world.

"What are the ladies saying of it?" Katherine asked finally.

"Most say the King is unwell and wishes to be alone."

"Most? And the others?"

"One or two have said that the King is displeased with you."

"And one of those is Nan Stanhope, I suppose."

"Not her, no. She left last evening for Syon."

"A rat leaving a sinking ship. Then who?"

"It is just your sister and Cat Brandon, and they only spoke out of concern for you."

"Those two I can trust, at least." She had heaved out a great sigh.

"Go to Devon with William. Promise me that . . ." She paused before adding, "I don't want anything more on my conscience."

Now Katherine is huddled in a corner with Huicke, murmuring, gesturing with her hands as she speaks, her head slowly turning from side to side. Huicke is to stay with the King and Katherine is not happy about that. The rest of them continue to scurry about, packing up.

The Fool Jane wanders around in a flap, getting in the way. She's never happy on the move. Her hood has slipped right back and beneath it she is as bald as a coot—someone must have shaved her to get the nits off. Dot gives her a pile of dustsheets and sets her to covering the furniture. She seems happier having something to do.

Dot can hear the horses being prepared in the courtyard, the jangle of their bridles and the shouts of the stable lads as they call out to each other. Some of the younger maids are fidgety with excitement at the surprise move to Greenwich, but they have not understood that there is something wrong with this arrangement and do not feel the heaviness in the air.

One by one the trunks are heaved down and loaded onto the waiting carts. Dot makes a final round, checking for forgotten things, looking under the beds and behind the doors, finding nothing but clumps of dust. She does it out of habit, forgetting she is no longer a servant maid.

William comes to join her. They will travel together, riding with the Queen.

He holds her hand as they go down the painted staircase and whispers to her not to worry, pressing a finger to the knotted spot on her brow and circling it. "Worrying won't help anything, Dorothy Savage. And things have a way—"

"That is what I said to her."

"And it is true, Full Stop. I would never have thought it possible that we could be married, and yet look at us."

It is bitterly cold in the yard and once Dot is up on her pony she pulls her wool cloak tightly around her and slips on her fur-lined mittens.

Katherine is mounted already and they begin to move away towards the gates, but then she stops—"We cannot leave those poor monkeys"—and calls over one of the boys, telling him to get the creatures.

They all wait for François and Bathsheba to be fetched from the outhouse where the King had banished them in a temper, some days ago. The horses get impatient, grunting and shuffling and throwing their heads about. The cold seeps through Dot's clothes.

Finally, the boy appears with a cage. The monkeys screech horribly as if they're facing execution. They are put in with the little dogs, but the dogs are disturbed by their cries and begin to bark crazily, so François and Bathsheba are found a place elsewhere.

When they do eventually set off from Nonsuch, they move at such a slow pace it seems like a funeral procession. But the group separates out soon enough with the carts trundling at their own pace behind.

They would normally take to the river near Hampton Court, but parts of it are frozen solid, so they will travel further across country to Richmond and join the river there.

The Queen rides ahead with her sister, Lady Mary and her Master of the Horse, and just behind them is a group of her ladies, who seem to fall naturally into the correct order, though none of that matters today.

Dot worries that nothing will be ready when they arrive.

Usually she is sent on a day ahead, after the harbingers, to prepare things. And they would not normally be traveling in such a great unwieldy train. But this is all so last minute. The harbingers themselves only left a couple of hours ago to announce their arrival, and the ushers are traveling with them now, so Lord only knows what chaos it will be when they get to Greenwhich, with no rooms assigned and everybody needing to be fed.

They ride up along the ridge from where, on a clear day, it is said you can see the spire of St. Paul's Cathedral—though Dot has never seen it from here, and certainly won't today for there is a dense mist. The sky is thick and white and low and can hardly be separated from the ground.

Everything is covered in a layer of frost. On the tree trunks and the barn roofs it is like the bloom on a plum, but where the tall grasses grow unprotected at the verge they are densely covered, prickling and glistening, as if they have crystals at their tips. It is pretty as anything but no one is in the mood for prettiness today.

The ground is iron hard and nothing alive has been seen for miles, not a rabbit, not even a bird, only their trudging train that stretches back now, gathered into groups, farther than Dot can see. William rides beside her. He hums some tune or other, which mingles with the sound of the hooves clopping against the ground. The horses grow warm and the heat rises from them in clouds.

When they pass through the villages—Long Ditton, Surbiton, Ham—there are people lining the streets, wanting to see the Queen and Lady Mary. They must have seen the harbingers ride through. News flies fast when it has to do with the royal family and everyone wants a glimpse of Katherine, who waves and smiles.

She occasionally stops and leans down to take a gift from one or other of them—a pot of honey, a dried bunch of lavender, an apple—or to kiss the children's cheeks when they are held up, shivering, by their mothers. None of them have a clue about the worry the Queen is harboring.

These places remind Dot of her own village. Her attachments to Stanstead Abbotts are worn so thin they wouldn't hold anything together. She had wanted to write to Ma to tell her of her marriage but as Ma cannot read, and few she knows can either, Dot hadn't written. When Katherine had heard of it she had sent a letter herself to someone at Rye House, who was to pass on the news to the Fownten family. News had come back from there that all were well, that Little Min had married her father's old apprentice, Hugh Parker, and that her mother had a position as a laundress at Rye House. Dot wondered if the Queen had had a hand in that.

When they get to Richmond Palace, dinner is served in the Great Hall, where they toast themselves by the fire, thawing out their frozen hands and feet, but they do not stay long, for the days are short and they need to get to Greenwich before dark. So as soon as the barges have been loaded, they set off down the river, passing right through London and past all the royal palaces. Southwark glowers against the darkening sky on the opposite bank and Dot thinks of the twists of fate that have brought her to this barge, on this river, in this moment and wonders what lies in store for them all next.

Katherine sits beside her, pale-faced, bundled in furs, her fingers agitating at the pouch containing her mother's cross. She has never appeared so fragile and Dot is aware that, for all the secrets she holds, there is much about the Queen and the court that lies beyond her comprehension.

58

Greenwich Palace, January 1547

Katherine stands in the window, watching the rain pitter onto the glass, drops of it trailing down the panes, each chasing the other, racing to the leaded edges where it trickles along, spilling, re-forming, rolling down the next diamond of glass, joining others to become a little stream.

These last weeks have been a hell.

She has smiled through the Christmas celebrations, twelve days of forced merriment, until she felt her face paralyzed with pretending. The Prince and his sisters were with her for the festivities, the girls oblivious entirely, so used to being banished by their father that nothing seemed unusual to them.

Katherine has watched Mary unfurl like a moth from a chrysalis—she likes to believe that it is her doing—and Elizabeth, the defiant tilt of her head masking the vulnerability that lies beneath her skin. Her family feels as fragile as Venetian crystal.

Katherine plays the part but is sick to the core with her own hidden unworthiness. Elizabeth is a bottomless well and Katherine is the only mother she has had—save her nurse, Mistress Astley, who clucks around her, unable ever to say no, tending her as if she were a golden egg.

She has gone now, to Hatfield, where Astley can cluck undisturbed. Her brother has gone with her, poor little boy. It will not be long before the weight of England is sitting on those nine-year-old shoulders. An armorer came to fit him with a new suit the other day. He was like a toy soldier in it, a sight that compressed her heart with the thought of what lies ahead for him.

"Mother," he'd said. "Will I make a good King?"

"You will, dearest. You will," she had replied, but wondered what would become of him if she were got rid of.

A spider descends from the casement on its filament, appearing suspended in thin air, legs waving slowly. Katherine feels herself hanging on an ever-thinning thread too.

She is no longer herself, has done something that makes her other sins seem like mere trifles. Up the river meanwhile is the Tower, and Surrey, who will be executed today. She thinks of him there, wonders if he's writing poems as he used to do, to distract himself, remembering how in their youth he and Wyatt would compete to impress the ladies with their decorated words.

He had been one of Will's dearest friends. And Will had been commanded to lead the trial. The King's idea of a joke? Or testing Will's loyalty? She had been fond of Surrey. She is riveted by the conviction that she will follow Surrey to the scaffold, has been since she was expelled from Nonsuch.

The King's anger, then his refusal to see her, the rumors of a new wife—what next? They will come and take her jewels, then remove her to the Tower. They will make a pretense of a trial, based on a single look. She will watch from a window as poor dear doomed Thomas is dragged to his death. Then she herself will make her own death speech, desperately seeking a droplet of courage so she doesn't collapse and disgrace herself on the scaffold. Even little Catherine Howard had gone to her death with grace. Katherine wonders if she would too. No, not would, will—if she will. It doesn't bear scrutiny.

That is why she did what she did.

She is too ashamed even to pray, for she knows the Lord will not listen to a sinner. Her sin is pitch black, a darkness that presses up against her. She has made a pact with something ungodly and will be damned for it.

When she remembers what she did for Latymer she wonders if that was the beginning of it all, if the Devil had got to her then and has schooled her since, preparing her, slowly molding her, teaching her how to rid herself of a husband and think it an act of mercy. Yet she is glad she had the courage to do that, for to end Latymer's suffering was a blessing.

But this now—this latest deed—is not an act of mercy, whatever prism she inspects it through: an act of fear, yes, but not mercy.

There are ways to kill and not be damned—oh, she has thought of it all, hoping to find a way to salvage the disparate fragments of her soul. God doesn't consider it a sin to kill on the battlefield, to kill or be killed. She has tried to imagine herself a warrior, a crusader for the New Religion, but she is not. She has never had the courage to die for her beliefs. Yet the brief flames of the stake would be nothing compared to the eternal damnation that looms before her. And while she is no warrior and the court is not a battlefield, the King *has* become her enemy. And she his, though he won't know it.

She goes over and over the whispered conversation she had with Huicke as they were leaving Nonsuch, poor loyal Huicke whom she has dragged down to Hell with her. She remembers sitting away from her ladies in a drafty corner, his gloved hand resting lightly on her wrist, feeling so very choked with fear she could barely speak.

"He will have me, Huicke. For his jealousy is greater by far than his reason—greater than his faith, even."

"No, Kit, no!" He had grabbed her hands in his.

She remembers the softness of his kid gloves, softer by far than a child's skin, and remembers thinking of the red raised welts beneath, angry as if his body were attacking itself.

"I will not let it happen to you. I will do anything."

"Anything?"

She had thought about it all night, praying, waiting for a sign from God, for permission. None came—God was silent—but she knew she would step into sin rather than face the scaffold.

She had had enough of the relentless, clinging dread and having to divine the King's whims, mold herself into whatever shape fitted, the permanent holding of her tongue for fear of something slipping out unbidden. Though in the end it was not her tongue but her eyes that betrayed her: that eternal moment in the King's chambers haunts her still, when she slipped for an instant into Thomas's gaze and gave her innermost world away.

Now either she will survive, or the King.

"Anything, Kit. I mean it."

"He will not get rid of me. I will get rid of him first." Her words had sounded like the hiss of a cat and she wondered then if she was possessed, part of her horrified to the core by the sound and shape of her own utterings.

"I said anything, Kit."

"The poultice."

Huicke nodded.

"Foxglove, henbane, hemlock. Add them all. You know what will do it and the quantities." She felt cold to the bones just saying it. It is a chill that has settled in, filled her veins with ice. "But take great care, that it doesn't touch your own skin."

"You know what this means?"

"I know." She had had the sense then of having passed over an invisible line, beyond which she was no longer herself and where deeds could not be measured by the normal scale of things. She was no longer the person she had always been. "It is he or I."

She had gripped dear Huicke then, as if she were clinging on to the broken strands of her lost self. "Just add a little, so it smells the same, and its effects will be gradual." She appalled herself at the way the words slipped out of her mouth so easily, and the care she had taken to think it all through, even down to Huicke's gloves that would protect him. And knowing that he, of all people, would do it for her, this terrible thing.

It is that which horrifies her now—the premeditated nature of her act, the ease with which she has dispatched with God. She no longer knows herself, can barely look even her closest ladies in the eye. She lingers alone, pondering on what she has set in motion, entertaining her own personal furies that will never leave her now. Each time she hears news of the King's deterioration they flap about her head like night-bats that peck at her soul, ripping it open, emptying its last shreds of goodness.

This is the soul she must live with for eternity.

The monkeys sit by the fire. François quietly picks a nit from Bathsheba's fur, tutting and murmuring to her in their monkey tongue. It is a gesture of such tenderness it makes Katherine feel the sharp stab of tears deep behind her eyes and the tug, like a fish hook in her gut, of the love she still has for Thomas. François strokes his monkey wife now, the little ape, with his odd hand, so much like a man's but longer, made for clinging to branches. Seeing them, she clucking with pleasure, he running his elongated finger behind her furred ear, sends a wave of longing through her.

And she had felt it again, in that moment when her eyes had met Thomas's, the moment that stretched into a little lifetime. The King was right, she supposes, for that instant was a whole, entire betrayal: Thomas may as well have been her lover then, and the King may as well have been a cuckold, for the merging of their eyes was more intimate by far than any night she has passed in the King's bed.

The thought is as good as the deed, some churchmen will tell you. Her insides are plucked at by a longing for tenderness, just a moment of it, like the monkey moment she has witnessed. And she has put herself, like those little beasts, in a godless place with all this.

She wonders where Thomas is now, fears for him, hopes he has spirited himself away from court. Or perhaps not, for that would make him seem culpable. He should stay there under the King's nose, proving his innocence, for he is not guilty, and his brother Hertford is rising so fast now, Thomas will surely be taken up in his wake. He cannot be condemned for inspiring such a love. But he can. She knows that.

And now she has damned herself and Huicke.

But the thing she has started cannot be stopped.

She struggles for breath, feeling faint, holding the wall for fear that she will fall, dragging herself to the escritoire. She pulls the cork from the ink. It tumbles to the floor, leaving a black trail on the pale flags. Taking a quill, she dips it and begins to write, the nib scratching its way over the paper. She must tell Huicke to stop.

Her letter is brief and oblique, she does not want to raise suspicion. *What we discussed*, she writes, *will not be necessary*. She sprinkles sand onto the wet ink, shaking it away, folding the thick paper, dropping a glob of red wax to the join, pressing her seal into it—the Queen's seal.

She calls the usher and the letter is dispatched in an instant, but it is futile to think she can undo the secret poisonous ministrations of the past weeks.

A letter arrives from Westminster—a summons.

Katherine is to prepare to leave with just a few of her ladies. Her gut tightens. This is it—the start of her journey to the Tower.

They pack again and travel towards the city in bitter, driving sleet, struggling upwind, barely moving against the invisible currents. It takes an age. Time is governed by its own laws. Katherine is unable to erase the memory of that minuscule instant when she met Thomas's eyes, how it had stretched out into a thousand lifetimes.

The Tower looms ahead, iron gray against the grim sky.

She cannot look at Surrey's bloodless ghoul head on the bridge. Cat Brandon chokes back a sob. Katherine had forgotten that they'd been close once. Cat had confided it, told of the poems he'd written for her. But that was an age ago, before they became who they are— who he *was*.

The Tower is above them now.

Katherine steels herself, but the barge struggles on past the water-gate, upriver. She feels relief but will not allow herself to imagine that this is a reprieve.

They pull up to the Westminster steps. No troop of yeoman guards awaits her, halberds brandished. Their small party crosses the courtyard, blown about by the bitter wind that makes the ribbons of their gowns fly and snap and their hoods flap like flags, as they rush to the steps and the warm hall beyond. A few people are gathered there, a somber bunch who bow as the Queen passes. There is no music, no gaming, everything is muted and still as if they are in the eye of a storm.

In her chambers a fire has been lit and candles, for though it is still early it is quite dark. She sits with Rig curled in her lap, unable to put her mind to anything, while Dot and the others go about arranging things. There is some noise beyond the door and her usher announces

Hertford. The time has come, she thinks, they are here to take me. She remembers Hertford coming to deliver her to Henry on the day she learned she was to marry him. It was not a proposal but an order wrapped in velvet.

The King had surprised her then with his tenderness, the way they had looked together at his book of hours, seen his father's words scratched there, the pressed primrose. She had seen a glimpse of the man he was, but she has not seen that man often enough of late—just the other one, his terrifying double. She can hear the sad tinkle of those beautiful glasses smashing against the hearth surround, the little fragments of crystal flying out, catching the light like sparks.

Hertford is alone save for a page who carries his effects for him. He drops onto his knee and makes a fuss of removing his cap without looking at her directly. There is something of his brother in his posture—she has always seen it. It makes her eyes smart.

"There's no need for all that, Hertford. Come and sit beside me. What news do you bring?" She surprises herself by the steadiness of her voice, as if nothing had occurred, as if she is the same Katherine, the same Queen she always was, and not frozen to the core and jumping with fear at every sound.

Hertford settles on the bench next to her and, looking anywhere but at her, murmurs, "He has not long to live."

Her throat chokes up and she wants to ask how long, but no words come out. Hertford takes it for tears rather than the guilt that is silting her up, making her struggle for breath.

"It is a matter of days."

She finds a small voice at last. "Did *he* send you?"

Hertford nods. "He thought you should know. He would like you to go to him in the morning."

The relief washes over her in a warm wave but it cannot draw the frost from her bones.

She may be safe from the King's wrath but God's is far greater.

59

Whitehall Palace, January 1547

The royal bedchamber is stuffy and fetid with death. Huicke has Katherine's letter tucked inside his shirt where it chafes, irritating his skin.

He would like to see her—or get word to her, at least—to let her know that God is taking the King's life himself, without their help. He knows she has arrived at Whitehall, as Hertford was sent to greet her, but dares not leave the King's sickbed without permission.

Dr. Owen and Dr. Wendy have their heads together. They are discussing whether to lance the King's lesion again or to cauterize it—they don't include Huicke. He is not one of them, never has been. He is the Queen's physician and they fear that he will take a slice of their pie, for the King favors him and his novel remedies.

They all circle like vultures, maneuvering themselves into position. None dare tell him he is dying. It is treason to talk of the King's death. Huicke is glad not to be important enough for such a task.

It is the meek Lord Denny who is the one to finally muster up the guts to tell His Majesty he must prepare for death. Denny leans in towards the great wheezing man in the bed, his head almost on the pillow, whispering to him and listening carefully to his rasping responses. Huicke, who had never thought much of the man, is impressed by his courage.

Behind him are Wriothesley and Paget, taking notes. It is the will they discuss—the new will. The vultures have played on the King's fundamental disdain of women, quietly suggesting one thing and another. Snippets of what has been said about the fairer sex buzz about the room like flies: intellectual weakness; lack of moral fiber; preoccupation with the flesh.

In the end it was something that Wriothesley suggested that ended the king's vacillation: "Women's judgment with regard to marriage can be so flawed."

The King had slapped a huge hand down on the bed. "We want a council to govern the country until the Prince reaches his majority."

So, they had ousted Katherine in the end, and with such ease. Names were tossed about for their council, which shall, it seems, be made up of them and their cronies. Huicke is glad to hear that Will Herbert has been nominated—as Katherine's brother-in-law he will stand up for her—but Will Parr has not been mentioned.

They are all at sea without someone to look to for direction and naturally turn to the decisive and strategic Hertford, who blooms with confidence. Despite this, it seems he is still capable of misjudgment. As Huicke watched, he had moved to the King's bedside and knelt there to ask, "And Thomas, my brother Thomas, shall he have a seat, Your Majesty?"

The King had given an almighty roar—"NO!"—the loudest thing he had uttered since his arrival at Whitehall. So, it wasn't Katherine's imagination. Huicke pondered on the irony of the King finally being dispatched by his own jealousy: that single shout had precipitated a terrible fit of coughing that they'd all feared would put an end to him that instant, and he has barely been able to speak since.

Huicke pours out a dose of opium, which he administers, watching as the black eyes lose their hardness and begin to swim into delirium.

Hertford returns, saying that the Queen is well and awaits her summons, but the King is elsewhere, beyond comprehension.

Owen and Wendy cluck about, dripping tinctures into the gaping mouth.

The vultures take their positions.

The Archbishop is called for, climbing onto the bed beside the great hulk, to smudge the oil onto his forehead with a thumb, quietly incanting, as the last drops of life leak out of the King.

The very stones of the palace heave a sigh of relief.

60

Katherine awaits her summons.

No one comes.

Time passes.

Dinner is put before her but she struggles to eat. Her ladies are quiet, barely speaking above a whisper, and fidget as they sit with her. They are all in a limbo of waiting.

The iron clock chimes each time it passes the hour.

Supper is served.

Nothing.

They retire for the night. Katherine doesn't sleep, not even for a moment. She thinks of the will, of becoming Regent, wonders if she has the strength. She will have to tighten her bonds with Hertford. Questions fly about her head. Has Henry rallied? Is she forgiven? What of the poison? Where is Thomas? She listens to the pelting rain and watches dawn break through a crack in the bed hangings, a bruised morning sky struggling to assert itself over the darkness.

She rises first and walks out along the gallery. Save for the relentless thrum of rain, the place is deathly quiet, as if the plague has taken everyone in a single night.

She sits in a window embrasure, wrapping her gown about her against the draft. Looks down at her hands, she sees her nails are bitten to the quick. When did she start biting her nails? From there she has a view of the door to the King's rooms and the two scarlet-liveried yeomen outside. They seem to pretend she is not there, if they see her at all, and her mind drifts, wondering if she is not perhaps already a ghost.

The King's ushers and chamberers begin to gather at the door and a parade of kitchen servants appears with breakfast. The guards open up and she sees Wriothesley's ferret face. No one is admitted, not even the ushers, and the platters are handed to him through the half-open door. It puzzles her, it being so unlike Wriothesley to perform such a lowly task.

One of the King's gentlemen passes, seeing her, stopping with a deep bow.

"Madam." He kisses her hand, making no comment on the fact that she is sitting alone, virtually hiding, in the gallery window—not the behavior of a Queen.

"Why are the ushers not admitted, Sir John?"

"No one has been admitted these last four days, save for the closest councillors and the King's physicians."

"And Huicke?"

"He's in there."

"My brother?"

"Not he, madam." So, whatever is happening behind those doors, it would seem the Parrs have been pushed aside.

And Thomas Seymour? she wants to ask, though says, "Thank you, Sir John," as if all this is perfectly normal. And seeing he is unsure how to behave—when the Queen, who is supposed to be the first to know everything, knows nothing—she bids him take his leave.

She wonders if Huicke received her letter, hopes to God he did.

In her rooms her ladies have risen and are preparing to breakfast. She takes her place. They talk of the rain and who will take the dogs out to the gardens and whether more logs need to be fetched, anything not to talk of the thing that is on all their minds. As the lids are lifted from the platters the monkeys begin to squeal. Dot gives them a handful of fruit. Katherine's mouth is too dry to eat but she knows she must and forces down a few spoonfuls of rennet.

At mid-morning Will Herbert is announced—news at last.

Anne rushes to her husband. "What's happening?"

It is the question on all their lips.

"No news." He drops to his knee before Katherine. "But I am asked to tell you, madam, that the King is indisposed and cannot be visited."

He keeps his eyes down. Why will he not look at her?

"Will?" she says. "Will, it is I. Get up off the floor and talk to me like the kinsman you are."

He rises to stand awkwardly before her. "I'm sorry." He picks at the edging on his doublet, still not meeting her eye.

She hides her bitten nails behind her back. "Go on, return to him."

As he leaves, Anne holds on to his arm, pressing him further, but he shakes her off with the words, "I can say nothing."

Katherine is hollow.

She fears the not knowing will make her lose her mind altogether.

After interminable hours she dresses in her finest gown and, taking her sister and Cat Brandon, goes herself, demanding to be let in, but the guards refuse her.

Wriothesley comes out with a pretend smile, wringing hands that are dry and veined as dead leaves. He says, "I'm sorry."

She wants to scream at him, shake him by his frilled collar, pull the truth out of him.

But all she can do is go back and wait.

61

Two more days pass, and Katherine can barely tell if she has lost her mind or not, before Hertford comes to announce that the King is dead.

"Good Lord!" is all she manages to say.

There are a few quiet murmurs among the ladies.

Hertford has a tiny spot of gravy or something on his snow-white doublet. She fixes her gaze on it.

"He did not suffer too greatly."

She nods. Language has deserted her, all she can think of is the poisoned poultice, that she may as well have poisoned herself, that she will never be free of it.

Eventually, she pulls the drifting parts of herself back together. "What of the will?"

"A new one is made." Hertford is formal, as if making a public announcement. "A council will govern . . ." He hesitates. "I am to be the King's protector."

She is momentarily confused. "The King," she says, only then realizing that he means Prince Edward, that Henry is no more. "Edward."

"King Edward the Sixth." Hertford looks shifty.

Does he feel guilty that he has taken her regency for himself?

She searches for her feelings, finding nothing but ambivalence. Hertford seems lost for words too. She wonders if she is supposed to curtsy to him, the order of things has been turned about so—but she is still Queen.

"Your jointure is generous," he says. "As befits a Dowager Queen."

He begins to list off the names of the manors and estates she is to inherit. The Old Manor at Chelsea is one of them.

"Chelsea?" she says.

"Yes, the King . . ." He corrects himself, "The old King thought you fond of the place."

It is true. Chelsea is a pretty manor on the river. She can imagine herself there.

"Lady Elizabeth is to join your household."

"I am glad of that." The thought takes hold in her, of a happy life, with Elizabeth and her own household, away from the machinations of court. She draws herself up to her full height to dismiss him. "You may leave."

But her heart is no longer in this game and her voice lacks authority. Nevertheless, he bows and turns to the door.

But then she stops him. "I should like to see him."

As she waits for her black damask to be fetched, Huicke is admitted. She dismisses all but Dot, who continues packing up the Queen's jewels to be sent to the Tower for safekeeping. Until things are fixed and the boy is crowned, no one can be sure what will happen.

"I have never been so glad to see you." She opens her arms to embrace her friend.

It is good to feel another body close to hers. No one has touched her in weeks, save for Dot helping her into her clothes. They have all reeled about her at a distance, even her sister.

"And I you." He slips a fold of paper into her hand. "I had no need."

She looks at it, seeing her own broken seal.

It is her letter.

"You mean . . ."

"I didn't do as you asked . . . the poultice."

She sighs. "Thank God for you, dear Huicke."

"I felt you were mad with fear, back at Nonsuch, and knew not what you were asking of me."

"You know me better than I know myself." She begins to laugh. She thought she'd forgotten how. "Sometimes I wonder if you are not an angel." She hadn't realized how great her fear had been until this moment, when it drops away and her body feels light as air. She is giddy with relief. "You, at least, will not be damned."

"Nor you, Kit. You are good at heart. God knows it."

She wishes it were true but she can feel God's judgment still—it pricks the back of her neck.

He drops his voice. "It is three days since the King passed."

"Good grief. I have been utterly beside myself."

"We were forbidden to leave the chambers, no one was admitted."

"Why?"

"They wanted time to wrangle over the new will. Dividing up the power . . . Getting things straight." He puts his arm around her shoulder. "You know you are not to be Regent?"

"Hertford at least had the decency to tell me himself. And I find I have never been so glad of anything."

There is a gentle knock on the door. It is Lizzie Tyrwhitt with her black gown. She slips it on over her kirtle. Dot and Lizzie cinch her into it, one on each side of her, pulling tight.

She takes Huicke's gloved hand in hers. "Take me to him."

The chamber is misted with incense and they all drop to their knees as she enters: Hertford, Denny, Paget, Wriothesley, the Archbishop. Habit or courtesy, she wonders, unable to stop herself from casting her eyes about for Thomas. He is not there.

She moves to the bed. Henry has been dressed in his most elaborate outfit, fur-lined purple velvet, stitched with gold thread and jewels. His swollen face has lost its shape, making him seem unfamiliar, and for an instant she thinks this is not her husband at all, but an impostor.

Then she sees his fat hands linked together over his vast belly and catches the gangrene stench of his ulcer beneath the fog of incense. She kneels, shutting her eyes, but she is lost for words, can't form a prayer, doesn't know what to say to God.

She beckons the Archbishop over.

"I'd like to pray together."

A faint smile appears on his face as he kneels beside her, beginning, "Dearest Father—"

She puts up a hand to stop him. "In Latin. He would have preferred that."

As she is about to leave, little King Edward is brought in. He is decked in ermine and stands with his legs apart, arms crossed. So like his father. She sinks to her knees before him.

Hertford makes a nod of approval, like a puppet master pleased with his show.

"Your Majesty," she says. "I give you my heartfelt commiserations."

"You may rise, Mother."

His voice has not yet broken and that makes her sad, to think of this solemn little boy and the colossal weight of his future.

She stands, smiling. But his pinched face remains set. He nods, moving on, Hertford at his side.

She realizes he is lost to her.

62

Windsor Castle, Berkshire, February 1547

Katherine watches the swaying bier, the mourners shuffling beside it. The King's effigy, clad in red, crowned in gold, lies at its top, so like him sleeping, more like him even than his own corpse.

The sight of it forces her heart into her throat.

She feels like a perched bird where she sits in the gallery, the Queen's gallery, glad that her dry eyes cannot be seen, except by her sister who sits beside her. She cannot muster up a shred of sorrow and when she kneels to pray she doesn't pray for her husband's soul but her own, begging God to forgive her—all those sins accumulated around her like a bank of cloud.

She leans forward to watch. She can see Thomas below, his velvet gown so very black, more deeply black than even his brother's, and lined in inky sable. Even darkly clad as he is, he manages to resonate with a brilliance as if he's haloed, like one of the saints.

He glances briefly up towards her. A glimmer of a smile passes over his face and he ruffles his fingers in a wave so discreet he could be brushing away a fly. She feels the grip of anticipation.

She thinks about the manor house at Chelsea being prepared for her—her own haven. It seems strange, foreign, to have an opportunity at last, after all those husbands, to be her own woman, to answer to no one. The thought percolates in her.

The choir start a Te Deum, the sound of it soaring up, but it is not quite as it should be. The boy soprano is only almost making the highest notes and there is something a little off in the timing of it, a dissonance. She wonders if it is only she who can hear it, wonders if the state of her soul has rendered her incapable of appreciating something truly holy. Her necklace sits heavily at her throat. It is the ugliest of them, the gems crowded on to it, vying for space, though it is probably the most valuable of the lot. It will join the rest of the jewels at the Tower after the service.

She absently feels for the pouch at her girdle, forgetting her mother's cross had mistakenly found its way, in the aftermath of the distress, into the casket of jewels that had gone to the Tower for safe-keeping. Her fingers are lost without it.

She *is* still the Queen—or the Dowager Queen, at least—until little Edward finds a wife, so by rights all those jewels are hers. But since Hertford has grabbed the reins of England—calls himself the Lord Protector and has taken the title Duke of Somerset—it may be diffi-cult to prize anything out of him now. Nan Stanhope will like being a duchess, wife of the Lord Protector of England, near enough Queen—it will make her insufferable. *She'd* love to get her hands on some of those monstrous gems.

Titles are being handed out like sweetmeats at Christmas. Thomas will be Baron Sudeley and Lord High Admiral. She won-ders if he is peeved that his brother will be a duke and he a mere baron. Probably!

She glances back down at him, only able to see the top of his cap. His feather is black today but as ebullient as ever. Will is close by. He glances up occasionally to where his sisters sit above. He had been shaken by Surrey's death, was distraught at having to officiate at the trial—another of the King's tests, Katherine supposes.

He was angry, too, about the King's will, the fact that there was no position for him on the council. She imagines he'd got above him-self, fantasizing about his sister becoming Regent and wielding all the power. It is said that he will be made Marquis of Northampton, which must be a consolation. He will be one of only two marquises in the land—and that should mean something to him, at least.

Will has never really thought of her *happiness*; not because he is unkind, it has just never occurred to him that happiness could ever come through anything other than influence.

She watches him whisper something to Thomas, who taps his shoulder with a slender hand. She wonders if Will's ambition will be his downfall, if he is an Icarus. The court is full of them. But, anyway, he must be content with his long-awaited divorce. That will be done, now the King is not standing in the way, she assumes. And he has his new title.

Katherine has the sense that of all the finery she has amassed, the dresses, the plate, the linens, the gems, all the things that have shored up her position, there is little that means anything to her. She will be happy, she fancies, at Chelsea with a few good dresses, her books and her mother's cross. More than that, it is only people who are precious.

While the Archbishop delivers his sermon, she runs silently through the household she will take with her—Elizabeth, Dot, Anne, Cat, Lizzie Tyrwhitt—they will all be close by, even the ones who will not live there, for Chelsea is just a short trip upriver from London. She will bring William Savage and dear Huicke.

The more she thinks of it the more of a paradise her future seems, and she wonders about the possibility that God might have forgiven her already, to have put all this her way.

She touches her sister's hand and they exchange a smile. She has the glow of pregnancy on her again, like a perfectly ripe apple. Katherine examines her heart for the familiar twinge of envy, but there is nothing. She has resigned herself to the fact that she will not bear fruit herself.

She must be happy with the windfalls that have landed near her—and the orphaned Elizabeth is one such fruit.

PART FOUR

Those that be about me careth nothing for me, but standeth
laughing at my grief.

Katherine Parr

63

The Old Manor, Chelsea, March 1547

Katherine sits with Elizabeth in her presence chamber at Chelsea. They are looking at one of Surrey's sonnets, a rendition of Petrarch, comparing it to Thomas Wyatt's version of the same poem.

"Do you see here, Elizabeth, how Wyatt has used Petrarch's rhyme scheme and Surrey has not? Think of how this affects the meaning," Katherine explains.

"But Wyatt has used an entirely new metaphor. See this." Elizabeth speaks fast, as if she must get her ideas out before she forgets them. "Look," she points to the page, "'. . . therein campeth, spreading his banner,' and, 'In the field with him to live and die.' He makes a war of love."

Katherine never fails to be impressed by the girl's fine-tuned intelligence. She is just thirteen and already understands the subtleties of translation better than most. But today Katherine cannot fully concentrate, for her brother is coming to Chelsea and with him Thomas Seymour. She imagines the Seymour barge gliding up the river towards them.

"Yes," she replies. "And see what Surrey has done."

"Though his rhyme scheme's altered, his meaning is more faithful to the original."

She imagines the rhythm of the oars spooning the water, the pat and skim, the synchronized breath of the oarsmen, the push and pull. It occurs to her that the sensations she has now are so much akin to the feelings of dread she had not so long ago: a heightened sense of her body's workings, as if she can feel the blood pumping to the far

347

reaches of her, her heart palpitating with anticipation. She has not seen Thomas yet, except in public. She glances towards the casement, thinks she hears a sound, a splash.

"What hour is it?" she asks Anne, who is sewing with Dot, Lizzie Tyrwhitt and Mary Odell, the newest of her maids, each embroidering a different part of the same piece. It is a cloth of state for the new King.

"It must be eleven of the clock, at least."

Katherine rises, walking to the window. The barge is there in the distance. It is close enough, though, for her to make out the conjoined wings on the banner. She swallows, taking a breath before turning to Elizabeth.

"That is enough for today."

She says it as if nothing is different, as if her heart is not in her mouth. It is all she can do not to rush down to the river steps. She helps Elizabeth collect her books together, choosing the poem they will look at tomorrow. There is a slight tremor in her finger as she points it out.

It seems a lifetime before the usher raps at the door, announcing them.

"The Marquis of Northampton and Baron Sudeley, Lord High Admiral of the Fleet."

They enter, dressed up to the nines, Will in ermine, which he is allowed now he is a marquis, Thomas spilling gold silk from the slashes on his doublet.

"Marquis!" She smirks at Will, who she knows must love the sound of his new title. "Lord Admiral!" Her voice cracks slightly.

Thomas bows. She doesn't dare offer him her hand, fears if his skin touches hers she will lose control altogether.

The men greet the rest of the company and they all gather around the hearth. She cannot look at him but feels his eyes on her. They make conversation. Katherine's tongue is in knots. Elizabeth reads Surrey's sonnet—poor dead Surrey. But all Katherine can really think about is how to conspire to be alone with Thomas. The air is thick and sticky as honey with her longing.

As they move through to the hall to dine, his fingers brush hers and she feels she might faint. She cannot eat. Nor can he. The food comes and goes. Then Will, dear Will, wants to see the new plans for her physic garden. Could she show him the place she has chosen? he asks. And as they wrap themselves against the March cold he says, "Will you join us, Seymour?" as if it means nothing.

She walks arm in arm with Will along the avenue of saplings she has planted. Thomas is at her other side, inches away. Their breath makes clouds. They inspect her herb garden, enclosed in its hedges. Will unhooks his arm, drifting away without a word, and when he is gone they grasp at each other wordlessly, like a pair of animals.

"I have waited an eternity for this," he murmurs.

His cap falls to the ground. She presses her nose to his neck to breathe him in and she finds she has lost touch with the boundaries of her body—where she ends and he begins.

It is as if her entire life, each moment, each experience, has conspired towards this. *This* is what love feels like, she tells herself. She thinks of those carefully organized love sonnets—but this is not carefully organized, this is perfect chaos.

"My love. I have wanted you. I want you." He grapples at her, pulling her partlet aside, pressing kisses onto her breast.

"Come tonight." She has forgotten she is recently widowed, forgotten any sense of seemliness or correct behavior, abandoning herself to him, wanting him to un-civilize her entirely. "I will have the meadow gate left open."

Katherine watches the ripples of Thomas's back as he pulls his shirt over his head, and the way the flicker of candlelight plays on his skin. The feeling, as if her heart will burst, has not diminished in the last month—a month of secret visits.

He is sulking. He always sulks when he has to leave before the household wakes. He wants to marry her, has pushed and wheedled for it. She would be content to remain lovers, enjoys the clandestine thrill. And then there is the scandal it would cause, a new marriage with the King barely cold.

"But you married the King just two months after Latymer was gone," he'd reminded her.

"Thomas, that was different, and you know it."

"Why different?" He scowls. "Am I not a man, as *he* was?"

She reminds him that marriage would likely be construed as treason, that she is the Dowager Queen and he is the King's uncle, and neither are at liberty to marry whom they choose—they are bound by the council and by Hertford.

"Your brother would not be pleased."

"The Lord Protector." He makes a face as if his brother's title tastes bitter. "The King wouldn't mind. I am the favorite uncle. I shall get *his* permission."

"Mind not to put your brother's nose out of joint. He could make trouble for us."

"*My brother* made even *your brother* a marquis. And all I have is a paltry baronetcy and some castle in the middle of the country, miles from anywhere."

She would have thought that his petulance would make him seem less attractive, but the effect is the opposite. He reminds her of her brother, she supposes.

"You are Lord Admiral too, and that is a great office."

"And so I should be. There is no one more suited for the job in the whole of England."

It isn't the danger of angering the Lord Protector that holds Katherine back from agreeing to marriage. It is something intangible, a feeling, the sense that she has tasted freedom at last, has unfurled her wings, and that marriage would clip them again.

But then there is the undeniable fact of *him*, his very man-ness, the irresistibility of him, and the things he does to her, the excess of pleasure. And a part of her wants to pin that down, to own it, box it, treasure it.

"*You* may be content to have me for a lover but *I* want this to mean something in the eyes of God." He goes on and on, slowly eroding her with the hyperbole of romance. "I want you all for myself, Katherine. I can't bear the thought of another man even looking upon you."

He talks of how long he has waited and asks her what she thought it felt like for him to be maneuvered out of the way, forced to watch his own true love married off to the elderly King. He'd watched her from afar, dying inside, he said.

Somehow, slowly, he rubs off on to her, in the way not-quite-dry ink leaves its ghost print on the back of the previous page. The lure of freedom begins to shrink in the face of him, seeming eventually small and inconvenient. And with all her secret sins weighing down on her, if she is to be damned for eternity, then why *not* fill her time on earth with pleasure?

"Do you not feel as I do, Katherine?"

Nothing she says convinces him that she loves him equally.

"Imagine spending the whole night together."

They laugh about that, remembering that tale from Chaucer's miller, with the lovers who want to do just that. He had read it aloud to her the other night, acting out all the parts, playing the cuckold and the young lover and piping his voice into a high-pitched squeak to play the wife, until she'd laughed so hard she couldn't catch her breath. Mary Odell had rushed in, thinking she was choking to death, and Thomas had had to hide beneath the bed.

"See what a man will do to spend the whole night with his love?" he'd said when Mary was gone. And then he'd become angry, his feathers ruffling. "Think of how it is for me, lurking about in the darkness like a thief."

And then there is the undeniable fact that this is a man who turns grown women into giggling wrecks, who blows through legions of girls, leaving them flattened like young wheat stalks after hail. He could have any of them, but it is *her* he has chosen. She is rendered weak in the face of that, and though she is aware it is driven by vanity, she barely cares.

Deep down she knows herself to be changed, that the events of the last months have broken her down and remade her. She questions everything, wonders about her beliefs, about God. It has lent an intense urgency to the business of living and this man infuses every pore of her with vitality. When she is with him she is alive, more alive than she can ever remember.

Her normal cares have paled. She doesn't mind that Nan Stanhope swans about like the Queen now. She'd refused to take her place behind Katherine in the procession at the coronation, but Katherine couldn't have cared less, for her mind was elsewhere, back at Chelsea in the arms of Thomas. Let Nan Stanhope worry about precedence and who goes where in the line.

The woman has somehow got her hands on the Queen's jewels, had worn the best of them that day, and all Katherine had thought was how glad she was not to have those heavy necklaces pinching and rubbing at her skin. Her only sadness is that her own mother's cross is among those jewels, though Nan Stanhope wouldn't deign to wear anything so understated. It is the single thing Katherine would like to have returned.

She runs a hand over his shoulders, pressing her fingers into his firm flesh. The thought lurks that if he doesn't marry her he will attach himself to another, as sure as night follows day, for that is the way of things. At the bottom of it she can refuse this man nothing, for just the slightest brush of his fingers against her skin makes her irresistibly alive.

"I *will* marry you," she says, just as he has pulled on his boots and is about to leave.

He jumps onto her, pushing her back down onto the bed. "You will not regret it."

"I do not intend to." She smiles and runs her fingers through his hair.

"I will write to the King today." He rises, touching a kiss onto the thin skin of her inner wrist, then stroking it softly with a finger. "I see your vessel here, blue with your blood. We shall mingle yours and mine and make an infant out of the parts of us."

She hasn't dared think of a baby—it is too tender a thought—and says nothing in reply, for she wonders if it is possible to have so much of what she desires, if it would be asking too much of fortune to give her a child as well. She can't help remembering her dead baby, its withered little face and the tiny scribble of veins on its closed eyelids.

"Write and ask the King's favor for our marriage. Visit the King, tease him into it. *You* are his favorite uncle, make him play Cupid for us."

"That is a plan indeed. My brother will be stuck with it if it is *the King's* wish to see us wed."

He opens the door but she beckons him back, wanting to feel his skin beneath her fingers one more time. "Remember, the King is still a boy and your brother holds all the power. Better have him with you, than against."

"I would be lost without your good counsel, my love."

"And tell your brother," she says as he's almost out of the door, "I want my mother's cross back. It is all I want. His wife can keep the rest, if it means so much to her to have the Queen's gewgaws. I had my turn with them."

He catches her eye and she sees a flash of something—anger, ambition, she's not sure what—but it gives her a pang of unease.

"Not just the cross, Katherine. Those jewels are worth a fortune and they are yours."

Then he is gone. What he meant by that, she realizes, is that he will get his hands on those jewels. Everything will be his when they marry.

She doesn't care, has never really cared about *things*, but she wants him more than anything.

64

"Dot, bring your husband and follow me," Katherine says.

"Let me fetch him, madam. He is in the music room."

"Hurry, and not a word."

When she returns with William, Seymour is there.

He hustles them into his barge, saying, "You didn't tell anyone?"

"Not a soul, my lord," says William.

"Not 'my lord,' Savage," he snaps. "It is 'Lord Admiral' and don't forget it."

"Begging your pardon, Lord Admiral." William only just manages to hide the resentment in his voice.

But Seymour wouldn't notice—William Savage is too far beneath him. Dot knows what her husband thinks of the man—that he's an arrogant so-and-so. But he is Katherine's arrogant so-and-so and that is enough for Dot to think he must have some good in him, even though he has a shiftiness that puts the creeps up her, something hollow about him, as if he's all shining surface but there is nothing beneath.

The barge slinks downriver. Dot watches Katherine, snuggling up to Seymour like a love-struck maid. Dot has never seen her so besotted and carefree. And if any woman in this world can handle a tricky fellow, it is Katherine Parr. He *is* handsome, she'll give him that. She remembers him back at Charterhouse, making waves with all the girls when he visited, and poor Meg petrified she would have to marry him. And that time in the orchard—how could she forget?

He always had a way of sizing up the lasses that makes them swoon. Not Dot, though—she'd got the measure of those types back when she'd had a hankering for Harry Dent. Harry Dent was a handsome one too, with the same kind of twinkle in his eye, making a girl think she's better than the Queen of Sheba. But when it came to it, Harry Dent was only interested in Harry Dent. And this one's not so different, Dot would wager her last penny on it.

She'd seen Harry Dent when she visited Stanstead Abbotts, just the other week, to see her ma. He'd run to fat and lost his hair and his looks with it, which made Dot chuckle inside for the merry dance he'd led her all that time ago. It had been nearly ten years since she left, and everything was changed, not just Harry's girth.

She found her ma in the laundry at Rye House. Standing beside her, even in her plain gown and not the taffeta one the Queen had offered her for her wedding, Dot felt distant from her, as if she were a foreigner and a great ocean separated them. Her ma's dress was clean but patched at the elbows, and her skirts were hitched up and tucked into her pinny. Her coif was of coarse Holland, just like Dot used to wear when she was a girl.

She had brought a gift—three yards of fine satin—but handing it over felt silly, for what would her ma do with a stretch of satin the color of apricots?

Ma's hands were red raw and rough from all the washing and Dot hid her own hands in her sleeves, as they had become soft and white of late—ladies' hands—and adorned with the Queen's aquamarine so big she would have had her finger cut off for it in Southwark.

Their greeting was stilted and Dot's voice sounded all wrong.

"Look at you," her ma had said. "My own little Dotty grown up and wed, and quite the lady you've become." She stood back to admire her daughter.

They talked awhile, reminiscing. Dot noticed her mother's skin had become wrinkled as crumpled linen and her eyes were glossy with tears. "William and I have a manor in Devon and I thought you might want to live there. I am bound to fill it with little ones before long."

Ma stroked her daughter's cheek with a finger rough as carpenter's card. "Oh pet, I think I'm too old to get used to a new place, and wherever is Devon? It sounds far away. Besides, I couldn't leave Stanstead Abbotts in case your brother returns. He went off, see. Got himself into debt and scarpered. Left his missus and the little ones."

"But, Ma . . ." Dot had tried to speak, but her mother was determined to say her piece.

"And I like it here, see."

"If you're sure of that, Ma?" A little knot was tightening in her throat. She felt separate again, as if her mother were slipping into an unreachable place. "I thought to ask Little Min and her husband to come too. He could run the farm." She saw her mother's eyes droop at this and heard a catch in her breath. "But that would leave you here alone."

"I am happy enough here, Dotty, I have friends, see. Your brother's wife has her hands full with a brood of six and needs my help more than you do. But Little Min must go with you. See, you can make a lady out of her and I would not stand in the way of that. They have a couple of little ones themselves, see, who'd be raised with yours. Imagine, Dotty, my own grandchildren proper educated."

Dot felt a surge of love then for her mother and swallowed away the lump in her throat. "Would you like to meet my William?"

"I don't think so, pet, I wouldn't know what to say to him, see, what with him being so well-born and that."

"But, Ma, he's not like that, you shall—"

"No, Dorothy," her mother cut in firmly. "You cannot see how much you are changed. I would rather we left it like this."

As Dot was leaving, Ma pressed the bundle of satin back into her hands. "Give it to Little Min. She will have more use for it than me, if she's to go to Devon."

"Will you take this then?" Dot had fumbled to untie her purse from her girdle.

She held it out, dangling in the air between them with both their eyes fastened on it. Then, simultaneously, they looked at each other and began to laugh.

"That I will not refuse," said Ma.

"There is more where that came from. I shall make sure you want for nothing."

"Hoy!" cries the boatman, jolting Dot back to the present.

The barge draws against a small wooden pier and they bundle out, following Seymour, striding ahead, pulling Katherine along by the hand.

Soon they arrive at a chapel, sitting alone, away from the gathering of cottages by the water. Just as Dot is wondering what they are doing here, Seymour announces that they are to witness Katherine's wedding to him.

And before Dot has even had the chance to work out what she feels about this, a chaplain appears as if from nowhere.

"Ah, the happy couple." He smiles broadly, opening his arms, welcoming them into his little church, which smells more of damp than incense.

He starts up about the sanctity of marriage, and children raised in the new faith.

But Seymour stops him. "Let's just get on with it, shall we?"

Katherine barely notices the dankness of the chapel, nor the bag of coin that Thomas slips the chaplain for his silence, nor the way the service is rushed through.

She remembers her previous wedding—the carefully selected nobles, the magnificent feast, the entertainment, the dancing—and she is glad of the simplicity of this one, and glad too that she has her dear Dot and William Savage to bear witness. She would have liked her brother and sister there, but Thomas had insisted it was kept quiet.

He has not yet asked the permission of the King, nor the council, nor his own brother. She doesn't think of that, but rather looks over at Thomas, drinking in the sight of him as he repeats his vows.

There are swallows nesting somewhere up in the rafters, occasionally swooping down and out of one of the windows. It amuses her that she, the Dowager Queen of England, is marrying in a chapel with no glass in its windows. One of the altar candles sputters in a draft and dies.

". . . in sickness and in health," she says. "To be buxom in bed and in board . . ." She cannot help but remember Meg reading from "The Wife of Bath," put up to it by Cat Brandon. How they had laughed. She is truly thrice widowed now, and on to her fourth. She wonders what God thinks of that.

"Till death us do part."

It is as if the years have collapsed, that she was never wed to Henry.

"I plight thee my troth."

He leans down to kiss her, pushing his tongue between her teeth, pressing himself up to her. The chaplain doesn't know where to look, pretending to busy himself with clearing the altar, but she doesn't care.

Her head is spinning.

She is hustled out through the hamlet and into the barge in a blissful daze. They saunter back upriver against the tide. It is a fine day, the sun glistening on the surface of the water and a flotilla of swans gliding by. Her new husband draws her towards him. His eyes catch her and he kisses her tenderly on her forehead.

"I am the happiest man alive."

"You *will* tell the King?" she says.

"Sweetheart, don't worry. I will deal with it all. Nothing can go wrong. I shall get his permission and then tell him it is done."

She wonders how the young King will take it, to discover that they are already wed. She feels uncomfortable with the deceit and worried, too, about Thomas's brother. But her love draws her into the lie. Besides, it is such a little sin compared to what she might have done to the young King's father, were it not for Huicke's intervention.

"You are in my hands now," Thomas says. "You are mine to look after."

She feels the firmness of his grip on her shoulder. The young King would never allow them to be charged with treason—not his favorite uncle and his stepmother, surely.

"You *will* take care of me, won't you?" she finds herself saying.

"Of course I will, sweetheart, of course I will. I live to look after you. I will square things with the King and council, I will get your jewels back and"—he draws her tight—"I will put a baby in you."

She breathes out a deep sigh, and her anxieties dissolve. She has been so used to the dread, she's forgotten how to be without it.

65

Seymour Place, July 1547

Seymour's new ward, Lady Jane Gray, arrived yesterday. She is practically a Princess and Elizabeth, who is her cousin, circles her like a cat getting the measure of a mouse.

Jane Gray is a skinny little thing with a long neck. Definitely not one of those plump-cheeked ten-year-olds all rounded with puppy fat, she is made up of angles, sharp elbows, jutting shoulders. She reminds Dot of a bird with her fluttering hands and far-apart eyes so pale they look white in the sunlight. She wouldn't be surprised if the girl has feathers beneath her hood instead of hair.

There has been a lot of talk about Jane making a match with the King. The gossips say that Seymour paid a fortune for her wardship and that if he can make that marriage happen, he will be the one to reap the rewards.

Whenever the idea of Jane wedding the King is mentioned Elizabeth huffs loudly like an ancient aunt. Jane is a scholar too, probably a better one than her cousin, or so Dot had heard Katherine say to Seymour earlier, when Jane had recited a poem in Greek. (At least, Dot had thought it a poem, as it seemed to have verses. And she had only known it was Greek because Elizabeth had spat, "So she knows Greek, does she?" under her breath.)

Now Jane sits beside William at the virginals, playing the high notes of a tune for him. It is a complicated piece of music and she tries it several times, stumbling repeatedly at the same spot, but never giving up. When she does get to the end of it without fault and William says, "Yes, that's right," her whole face breaks into a smile so instant and natural Dot can't help smiling too.

Dot realizes in that moment, when they are all basking in Jane's beam, that Elizabeth rarely ever smiles—and when she does, she is cautious about it as if smiles are as expensive as gemstones and not to be wasted. Dot is surprised by the little sprout of sympathy she senses growing in her.

Dot sits with Anne's three-year-old at her feet, sorting wooden beads. She has been charged with the care of Ned, who has come to live with them for a few months. It is gentlewoman's work and that is what she is now, if she could ever believe it—a gentlewoman.

She is embroidering a partlet for Katherine, stitching small red flowers in silk thread, each one with a seed pearl at its heart. Bright light floods in from the window, casting shapes over the floor and into the grate, which needs sweeping. Dot resists picking up the brush and giving it a good going-over. She can't get used to this new life, to not being the invisible girl who sweeps the hearth and beats the dust out of the rugs. Sometimes she finds herself not missing it exactly, but missing the way it made her feel useful, the way she always had something to do.

Sometimes she even misses the work itself, the way it made her body feel strong, the heaving and carrying and running up and down stairs, the scrubbing and sweeping and plumping and folding. It made her feel alive. The embroidering and reading and card playing and reciting of poetry, which is what gentlewomen seem to do a lot of, have the opposite effect. And though she is meant to care for little Ned, there is a maid to wash his napkins and clean up after him, and another to make sure he is fed; her job is simply to occupy him, teach him his prayers and scold him if he is naughty, which is rarely.

This is what it is to be a woman in the world she has risen into—to be still and silent and pretty, in public at least. The others dance daily, with an Italian dance master who comes to teach, bossing the girls into submission. Mary Odell, one of the new girls in the household, is usually a bit of a lump but when she dances she is light on her feet and quite changed. Elizabeth is the one who dances best. She makes it her business to be best at everything. Dot is afraid of drawing attention to herself, so doesn't join in, just sits watching with Lizzie Tyrwhitt, who says her dancing days are over.

Dot can hear Katherine talking with Seymour in the garden under the open window. She is thankful the marriage is no longer a secret. It had seeped out anyway, though she had not breathed a word of it to anyone and neither had William. Seymour was probably spotted coming and going at night.

Elizabeth's nurse, Mistress Astley, had accosted Dot about it in the kitchens at Chelsea, not a week after the wedding.

"Tell me, Dorothy Savage, about the Queen's new peacock." She had made a lewd gesture with her hand. Dot hasn't warmed to Mistress Ashley.

"I don't know what you mean." Dot had tried to leave.

But the woman had planted her sturdy form in the way so she couldn't pass.

"Don't get high and mighty with me. You may serve the Dowager Queen but I serve the Lady Elizabeth, who is a Princess of the blood, and yours is only Queen by marriage."

Dot hadn't known what to say to that, and had been tempted to give her a shove, but in the end said, and did, nothing. Dot has learned the value of keeping her gob shut.

"And," the Astley woman went on, "don't imagine I'm fooled by *you*, Dorothy Savage, in your fine dress that was a gift from the Queen. I know what kind of place you come from." She said it with a scowl.

"I have nothing to hide about my impoverished roots, Mistress Astley. My father may have been low born but he was a good man." Dot had drawn herself up to tower over the squat woman. "Besides, a thimbleful of good blood doesn't necessarily make for a good person." She could hardly believe such a fine riposte had come out of her, but she's learned a good deal by listening all those years at court.

Astley had harrumphed and fumbled for a response.

But Dot had turned, quick as anything, and skipped away into the yard, calling back over her shoulder, "As I recollect, Christ was not more than a carpenter . . ."

Elizabeth has seated herself at the virginals now, with Jane Gray perched on the very edge of the stool beside her. She's playing a popular ditty, a love song that has been going around and that they have all been humming for weeks. Elizabeth's long white fingers flit over the keys and she adds her own little flourishes to the tune, then begins to sing in her thin, high voice, eyes shut mostly, but sneaking the occasional glimpse to be sure everyone's looking, which they are. Jane is all agog.

At a break in the verse Elizabeth turns to William briefly, who stands behind her, throwing him a wink. He looks away and over at Dot, raising his eyebrows. Elizabeth can't bear to think any man wouldn't desire her and Dot has seen her play up to even the lowest servant boys. William, though, seems immune to her charms, has confessed to Dot that he finds her tiresome. But Katherine has asked him to instruct the girl in music, which he hasn't been able to refuse.

It is warm in the sun by the window and Dot drops her head back onto the frame, drifting off. She can still hear the Queen and Seymour talking in the garden below, their voices floating up to her. Katherine sounds agitated and Seymour is calming her but with the music she can't quite make out the words, just the tone.

His voice is velvety, hers shrill.

"Kit," she hears him say, in a break in the singing, "we will get them back." He sounds angry, now. "This is a slight against me as much as you."

It occurs to Dot that, like Elizabeth, Seymour wants to be admired by everyone.

"But my cross, Thomas. My mother's cross is among those things and Nan Stanhope well knows it." Katherine scrunches her handkerchief into an ever-tighter ball.

It has been three months since he promised he would have her mother's cross returned to her. Three months of marriage.

"That cross is nothing but a trinket, sweetheart. I shall give you jewels far more beautiful than that. What I can't bear is the idea of that brother of mine and his monstrous wife doing this to me. She, strutting about the palace dripping in the Queen's jewels when *you* are Queen. Until my nephew marries, you are still the Queen and you are *my* wife. This is a slight against me, Katherine." He bangs his hand against his thigh.

She says nothing. There is little point trying to convince him of the worth of that so-called trinket to her, or what it means. And she has *him* now. She thinks of all those hours spent running the pearls beneath her fingers and thinking of him, wondering where he was and who he was with, seething inside at the thought that he might love another.

Now he is hers and she his, and what they have is like nothing she has ever known, as if he has brought her to life. She is consumed by her desire for him. She'd never thought herself capable of that: pragmatic, sensible Katherine Parr driven to wild abandon.

But already she can feel him slipping away in tiny incremental steps. At first the intrigue had kept him in her thrall. The Lord Protector was incandescent with rage about the marriage and the King hadn't been happy, either, to discover that his permission had been asked and granted for a marriage that had already taken place.

Thomas had squared it, though, just as he promised he would, working his charms on the young King. Next to the Lord Protector, who barely lets the poor boy breathe without his wherewithal, Thomas must be like fresh air. Thomas gives him pocket money, for the Lord Protector leaves him poorer than a church mouse. And the child may be distant now but he cannot have forgotten that she cared for him when he was barely out of skirts. But she feels she has lost his trust with this secret marriage. Mary's too. Mary does not approve, thinks it shows disrespect for her father that his widow would marry so soon, and she no longer replies to Katherine's letters.

And then there was the scandal. When news of the marriage got out, pamphlets were printed making spurious suggestions about Katherine's virtue, with terrible lewd drawings—or so Huicke had said. He had refused to show them to her, said she could do without seeing such things.

She had felt so deeply and horribly ashamed. Thomas had been a rock to her, helped her hold her head high, even in the face of the scathing comments from Nan Stanhope about how she had diminished herself by marrying a younger brother when she had once been the wife of the King. Nan had always been like that, her fingers gripping firmly on to the ladder, knowing exactly who should stand on each rung at any given moment and scrambling up and over people to pull herself higher—how she must love being the Duchess of Somerset. Thomas, meanwhile, was charged up by the adversity, the defense of his wife.

But now that he has her and the world accepts it, she senses a separation, as if his fascination has diminished minutely. It is not apparent enough for anyone else to notice as he fawns over her in public in a way that borders on indecent. Sometimes, though, she knows it is a performance, this love of his, and she feels its dwindling like a thin current of cool air. While his seeps away, hers burgeons, swallowing her up.

One of the gardeners walks past them and she calls out to him, beckoning him over. "Would you cut some lavender, Walter? A good quantity, enough for strewing in my chamber?"

He removes his cap, fumbling as he has a fistful of bulbs.

"What are those?" she asks.

"They are hyacinths, madam."

Katherine can feel her husband's eyes burrowing into her, and hears his impatient little snort.

"I shall store them, then we can enjoy them early next year. They are the fragrant ones you liked so much."

"I shall look forward to them, Walter."

"That'll be all," barks Seymour.

Walter moves away, head down.

"Why ever do you call him Walter?" His lips draw tight.

"It is his name." She strokes the coarse hair of his beard with a smile.

"I will not have you be so forward with the servants."

"Oh Thomas, I knew his father. I saw the lad grow up."

"I will not have it." He grips her wrist hard, as if to emphasize what he says.

She opens her mouth to speak.

But he continues, "And all that about the hyacinths. He is too familiar. I should get rid of him."

"As you wish." She knows that if she defends the man it will only be worse. Seymour cannot bring himself to meet her gaze and is sulking like a little boy.

His desire may be waning but his jealousy knows no bounds. He will not allow her to be alone with any man, barely even Huicke, and she wonders if somewhere inside him he believes those pamphlets that talk of her corrupted virtue.

She is reassured by his jealousy, though, clings on to it as proof of his continued love, thinks it part of his boyish pride—but at the bottom of it she knows he doesn't trust her.

She can hear Elizabeth singing in the music room, her unmistakable voice, high and clear, drifting through the summer afternoon.

"That girl has a voice," she says.

"I must go." He plants a perfunctory kiss on her hand before striding away across the garden.

I love him too much, she thinks, watching the way his gown flips up at the edges and swirls about his thighs as he moves. She thinks of those thighs slapping up against her skin, the grip of his fingers around her waist, and feels sick with desire. Surely, she can't help thinking, a child will come of this passion—how could it not? But time is ticking away.

She feels the years on her. At thirty-five most women have stopped their birthing. But then again, at thirty-five most women have been all used up and stretched out of shape by dozens of babies and, as Thomas said once, ripping her shift from her, she still has the body of a maid.

"Will you be back tonight?" she calls after him.

But he doesn't hear, or at least doesn't react.

She hears the clatter of hooves on the stable cobbles—the sound of him leaving. He will come back around to her, she is sure of it, for theirs is a love match. He is only sulking.

"Are you sad?" The small voice comes from nowhere, making her jump.

"Oh!" she cries. "You surprised me, Jane, I thought you were in the music room with the others."

"Are you crying?"

"No, Jane, it is just that my eyes itch and I have rubbed them."

"You have a sad air about you."

"How could I be sad when I have everything I ever desired?"

Jane smiles at this in a puzzled way, as if the notion of having one's desires met is incomprehensible.

"Let's find Rig and walk him in the orchard."

They call for the dog and head to the orchard gate, arm in arm.

Jane has such poise, thinks Katherine, for a girl so young, already shaped for her future, like the espaliered trees that grow along the orchard wall, contrived into intertwining obedient forms. It is a future that will not be hers to choose, for she, like her singing cousin, has royal blood in her veins.

Thomas is conniving to make a match between Jane and the King, which would not be such a bad thing. But the Lord Protector continues to hope he will lure the five-year-old Scottish Queen into his pocket before the French get their hands on her. All these girls being moved around like pawns in a game of chess.

It's time someone was lined up for Elizabeth—she is fourteen now, but no one is sure whether she's a good bet or not, legitimate or not, a Princess or not—poor child.

66

Hounslow Heath is bitter and a low sky, thick as gruel, hangs over them. The storm of a few nights ago has blown the last of the leaves from the trees, giving the place a bleak, unforgiving air. Sweat striates the horses, who have run themselves out and now walk sedately towards the house with the mud-covered hounds lolloping after them. It has been a good day's hunting and a quartet of men follows behind with the carcass of a great stag strung between them, while another leads a mule with two smaller bucks slung like a pair of sacks over its back.

Katherine will send one of them to Nan Stanhope in a gesture of goodwill that she hopes might promote the return of her mother's cross—though she doubts it, for the whole issue has become a battle between Thomas and his brother.

Nan has been intolerable, swanning about at court, throwing her weight around. She is with child again—number eight—and Katherine can't help but ponder on the injustice of a world that can send eight children to one woman and none to another. But she is accustomed to the feeling, which is no longer the intense longing it once was—it is more a vague sense of something lacking, that is all. And she has Jane Gray now and her sister's boy, little Ned Herbert, in the nursery—and of course there is dear Elizabeth, so they make a satisfactory family.

Elizabeth is up ahead, riding beside Thomas. Her escaped hair blows behind her in a fiery comet's trail. Katherine watches them closely. They chat easily. Elizabeth says something, making Thomas laugh, and he draws his horse up next to hers, leaning over to remove a twig from her hair. She holds his wrist with her long pale hand, smiling at him, saying something, whereupon he pulls his arm free and gives her a slap on the thigh, trotting off ahead.

Katherine's jealousy is a tangle of snakes, and she tries to persuade herself that he is just being a good stepfather to the girl, but knowing, dreading, there is more to it.

There has been gossip among the servants, but only snippets had reached her. It was Dot eventually who said something, told her that Thomas had been visiting Elizabeth in the maid's chamber in the morning, when she was still abed. Katherine hadn't wanted to believe it. Dot had never got on with Elizabeth. Katherine had seen that for years, the way Dot watched her with a frown, and Elizabeth had not been kind to her, that is true. This, she had supposed, was Dot's little revenge.

"Everyone is talking of it," she'd said.

Katherine told herself it was simply his innocent affection for the girl, and servants *will* gossip. But she had taken to accompanying Thomas on his morning visits. She had discussed it with Huicke, who had suggested sending the girl away. But that would mean breaking up her fragile family, and she will not do that.

This little scene she has just witnessed, though, smacks of a particular kind of intimacy. She is reminded of that look between herself and Thomas, the fatal moment that had inspired such wrath in the King and had precipitated what she thinks of as her fall from grace. She knows how much meaning can be carried in a moment like that.

"But we are just married and ours is a love match," she'd said to Huicke.

He had sighed, a long, exasperated sound. "A man's love is never exclusive. It is only women who truly love with their hearts. I know that, for I am both." He had confided in her once of Udall's excessive promiscuity, and she had asked if it didn't make him jealous. "No," he had replied, "for I know he can't help it."

But *her* jealousy writhes up inside her and will not settle. I will not break up my family, she says to herself. She wonders, beneath all her other thoughts, if God has finally chosen his punishment for her—in this man who pulls her heart in every which way.

She cannot even find inspiration for her writing. Huicke persuaded her to send her *Lamentation* to the printers. If it weren't for him she would never even have thought of it, so taken up has she been with Thomas. She feels lost to this love, is drowning in it, and all the things that mattered before have shrunk away to almost nothing. She wonders where that woman has gone who would have been the beacon for the new religion.

But her *Lamentation* will be published, thanks to dear Huicke, and it will be a memorial to that ambitious woman—but the thought of it leaves her empty. Reform is happening anyway without her—the Archbishop and the Lord Protector are driving it.

New statutes are announced monthly, banning the candles, the ashes, the incense, prayers in Latin—altar stones are transformed into paving slabs. It is taking shape, just as she had dreamed, but she is no longer moved by it as she once was. Her beliefs still stand, but the dreams of bearing the torch are gone. Her sins are too great. "Justification by faith alone," she murmurs with a dry little huff, remembering her excitement about the eclipse ringing in the changes and Copernicus revolutionizing the heavens. She'd seen herself as an intrinsic part of it, had even believed for a moment that it couldn't happen without her. "How proud I must have been, and how fickle."

Elizabeth has caught up with Thomas again now and Katherine gathers herself, finding her fight, pushing Pewter into a canter to join them. She touches her crop to the rump of Elizabeth's horse, calling out, "Hoy!" It skits to the side and she nudges Pewter's flanks, forcing him forward between the two of them.

"My darling." Thomas kisses the tips of his fingers, touching them to her cheek.

Elizabeth is suppressing giggles, her shoulders heaving, so very young and girlish. It suddenly seems quite innocent and Katherine feels silly for having let her imagination run away with her.

"We have a surprise for you," Elizabeth says.

"What is it?" Katherine's fears abate.

"That would be telling," Thomas laughs, "and then it wouldn't be a surprise."

The turmoil inside her subsides, her world settles back to its usual rhythm and they ride together through the gates into the yard, dismounting and handing over their horses, slipping off their muddy gowns and stamping their feet to get some heat back into them.

"Come, Mother." Elizabeth takes her by the hand, leading her into the squillery. "We must be very quiet."

She tiptoes over to a niche by the fireplace, beckoning Katherine to follow her. Elizabeth's cheeks are flushed with a high color. In the cranny lies François's monkey bride, Bathsheba, curled up asleep with a tiny pink baby snuggled into the curve of her, its miniature hand clenched to a tuft of its mother's fur.

"There is your surprise," Elizabeth whispers.

Katherine's heart feels light as air and the only sound that comes out of her is an "oh" that is more a sigh than anything.

67

The Old Manor, Chelsea, March 1548

It is March already but still cold. Huicke is impatient for the warm weather as the damp chill makes his skin feel tight and uncomfortable. There is a light mist of drizzle in the garden at Chelsea, and despite the weather he walks with Katherine on the riverbank.

She has him firmly by the arm and Rig trots ahead, occasionally stopping to sniff at one thing or another. Katherine's manner is loose and easy, she laughs and tells him funny stories about her household, demanding he feed her snippets of gossip from court.

Huicke has never seen her so well: the tension is all gone from her and her edges have softened. Perhaps this marriage has been good for her after all. Huicke had advised her against it, suggested she keep Thomas as a lover, and it still pains him to see her with someone so shallow. But after all those nights with the gross and reeking King she has earned the right to something beautiful in her bed. She stops to pick up a flat stone, which she skims into the water, and they watch its arc as it kisses the surface six . . . seven times.

"When did you learn to do that?" Huicke is impressed.

"My brother and I used to have competitions. He could never beat me."

She stoops suddenly, scooping something from the riverbank into her hand.

"What is it?"

She opens her cupped hands slightly and he can see a frog crouched there, its tiny body palpitating.

"Kiss him," teases Huicke, "he may turn into a handsome prince." He is struck by the memory of the King's frog pie at Hampton Court—the King's first test.

"I already have a handsome prince." She releases the little creature, letting it hop away to the edge of the water.

He can see how besotted she is. Huicke wishes she weren't, as he feels he's losing her, bit by bit. Besides, Seymour won't sanction her being alone with another man, not even him, and they have had to steal this time together while he is at court.

"Do you not mind that he won't let you alone with a man?"

"What, his jealousy? Not a bit."

"*I* couldn't bear it."

"But don't you see?" she says with no hint of irony. "It is proof of his love."

"But *I* am hardly a threat."

They laugh together about this.

"He is not very perceptive about such things."

This provokes another gust of laughter.

"He can't imagine how it is possible for any man not to want what is his."

There it is, her ruthless humor. It is good to see Katherine so carefree, so much herself despite the new husband. Huicke can't help but hate him a little. He has known men—men like Seymour—whose sole aim is not to love, but to be loved. And, more than that, to be the most loved of all.

"You like it here, don't you?" he says.

"I find I am happy away from the court and its . . ."

She doesn't need to finish—they both know what she means.

"Your book is circulating there. You should be proud. There are no more copies to be had and everyone wants one."

She bends to pick up a stick from the ground, throwing it for Rig. "I shall instruct Bertelet to print some more then."

Huicke notices a lack of interest, as if that intellectual fire in her, which had once burned so strongly, has been quenched. They walk on in silence. He picks a stem of rosemary, rubbing it between his fingers, bringing it to his nose and breathing in the heady smell. He wonders if she ever allows herself to think about the old King's death, what she requested of him in her desperation, if it weighs on her conscience. He wouldn't ask. It is a buried thing, a dark thing that joins them, something that cannot be put into words. Seymour can't intrude upon *that* secret.

The rain begins to fall more heavily, the sound of it pattering and rustling through the leaves above.

"I am glad you are here," she says out of the blue, pulling him under the cover of an arbor where there is a stone bench.

The wet brings new smells, grassy and earthy.

"Tell me—how does Udall? Is he inventing wondrous masques for the young King?"

They talk a little about Udall and how his star continues to rise, but Huicke has the idea that there is something she is not telling him. The cold damp from the stone seeps through his hose. Katherine chatters on, not seeming to notice or care. She is reminiscing about Udall's play, *Roister Doister*, laughing about it, "his audacity" as she says. But he remembers how forced her laughter was on the day it was presented to her at court.

"There *is* something." She suddenly becomes serious. "If you wouldn't mind putting your physician's hat on."

She seems a little embarrassed, and he squeezes her arm.

"What is it?"

"It is women's stuff really, but I wanted to ask you about the change, you see . . ." She hesitates. "Oh, you may as well be a woman, Huicke. I don't know why I'm so shy about it. It's just that my courses have stopped these past three months and I think things may be finished for me. I am not yet of such a great age but how can I know if the change has begun?"

It all makes sense to him now, the bloom on her, the ripeness.

"You are with child, I'd wager my last sou on it." He clutches her hands.

Tears have sprung in her eyes. "I thought it was over for me." She wipes her cheek with the back of her hand. "I am to have a baby? I

hadn't dared think ... I mean ... Oh Huicke, I am lost for words."
She is laughing now between sobs. "And now you mention it, I *have*
been a little nauseous. I put it down to a bad oyster."

Her happiness touches him, but he feels that he is losing her a little
more. He quashes the thought with a silent admonishment for his selfish-
ness, for wanting her all for himself.

"I am to have a child! I can barely believe it. Wait till I tell Thomas.
He will be beside himself with joy."

68

The Old Manor, Chelsea, May 1548

Katherine lies stretched out on her bed. She had dreamed of Henry, that she was still married to him, and had woken with a jolt, confused and steeped in that familiar pervasive fear, before realizing after a few moments, with a sigh of relief, where she is.

If she lies very still she can feel, minutely, the stirrings of her baby, barely there, a vague oscillation, like a moth trapped inside her. A feeling of utter joy washes through her as if the world at last makes sense.

There is a dip in the pillow where Thomas had lain beside her. She had returned from court utterly exhausted, barely able to keep her eyes open in the barge, and they had lain down together. Thomas was angry with his brother as usual and hadn't stopped talking of it, but she had let his words drift over her as she sank into sleep. She didn't care about any of that now, the jewels, the nonsense about who should go first, whether Thomas had a position on the council.

The only thing that matters to her is the infant forming miraculously in her belly.

Thomas's face was a picture when she told him—the wide beam of his grin, as if it had never been done before, as if he were the first man to have ever made a baby. She had teased him, called him Adam, and she felt his attention falling back onto her. She could almost hear the wheeling of his mind, building great dynasties on the head of this tiny seed inside her.

"You will give birth at Sudeley," he'd said. "For this fellow must begin his life in his own castle. I shall have the place prepared. Make it fit for a Queen, for my child will be the son of a Queen."

She has an overwhelming sense of fecundity, feeling more woman than she ever has before, and her desire for her husband's touch increases daily as the infant develops deep in her belly. But Thomas, for all his adoration, won't touch her for fear of doing damage. She feels she might go quite mad with wanting, but he will only take her in his arms and stroke her hair, whispering sweet things. She has never felt so adored, nor so frustrated.

A faint knock at the door stirs her.

Dot appears. Her coif is on inside out with the selvedge showing. Katherine can see that something is wrong, for her face is flushed and her eyes skip about. Dot is rarely perturbed.

"Is something wrong?" Katherine pats the bed beside her.

But Dot doesn't sit. She makes a dark shape with the bright afternoon light from the west window behind her, pressing her hands together. She is moving her mouth to speak but saying nothing.

"Dot, what is it? Has something happened to William?"

At last she finds her voice. "There is no way to tell you this, madam. But I will show you."

Katherine sits up, feeling a rush of blood to her head. Dot's face is so very grave she wonders what it could be. Her insides shrink.

"You must gird yourself for this, madam."

Katherine follows her down the long corridor, through the gallery and up the single flight of stairs into the eastern wing of the house. She wonders where everyone is, then remembers it is time for prayers and that they must all be in the chapel. As if on cue she hears a faint sound, a psalm being chanted, wending its way up through the floor . . . *the Lord is my shepherd, I shall not want. He makes me to lie down* . . . There is the Astley woman bustling towards them. Why is she not at prayers? Something is wrong. Someone is ill . . . She stands between Dot and the door.

"I don't think—" Astley seems to hiss.

"Let us pass, if you please, Mistress Astley," says Dot.

But the woman has her hand on the latch, her fingers curled tightly around it, though she seems unable to explain herself. Her mouth opens and shuts trout-like but no words emerge ... *he leadeth me in the paths of righteousness for his name's sake ...*

"Step aside." Katherine finds herself whispering too, without knowing why, confused by all this and losing her patience.

But the Astley woman still holds the latch in one hand and has now taken hold of Katherine's sleeve with the other, is trying to tug her away from the door ... *Yea though I walk through the valley of the shadow of death, I fear no evil ...*

Katherine shakes her arm free and Astley seems to realize what she has done, as she lets go and drops to her knees. "Forgive me, madam, please forgive me."

"For goodness' sake," snaps Katherine, "get up."

The door slowly swings open, revealing the big tester bed, partly curtained, its covers disarranged. A long pale leg protrudes from the sheets and above it an arm, palm up, inner elbow exposed, a gray vein running down its length. *For thou art with me, thy rod and thy staff they comfort me ...* There is a clamminess about the skin and a hot damp smell in the chamber that is horribly familiar.

"It is Elizabeth, she is sick?" Katherine's head fills with thoughts of the sweating sickness and the stories that are told of how quickly it can kill, remembering those she's known who were taken by it.

Then she realizes that Elizabeth, who seems to be stirring now, is not alone. There is another leg, darker, bigger, half concealed beneath the coverlet.

Her mind takes a moment to adjust and all she can think of is that it was she who embroidered the pattern of hollyhocks on that coverlet. She remembers working on it one long-ago summer at Hampton Court. She focuses on this—each stitch, each flower, each knot of thread—so that she does not think about the second leg, for it is a leg she knows intimately, each blemish, each contour, the scar from a Turkish sword, the little hollow on his shin from where he fell on a stone step.

Someone flings the bed hangings back. It must be Dot.

But Katherine is struggling to stay upright, clinging to the bedpost ...

goodness and mercy shall follow me all the days of my life . . . A flood of black seeps up her, spinning towards her head.

She feels herself drop, then nothing.

Katherine falls.

Her head cracks sickeningly against the floor.

Everything slows down. Dot sinks down beside her. She is out cold but breathing.

Seymour leaps from the bed, his thingy swinging, grabbing a pillow, pushing Dot brusquely aside. He crouches, lifting Katherine's head and sliding the pillow under it, stroking her face. "My love, my love."

Katherine gives a little moan. Dot rinses a cloth in the ewer and places it over her forehead.

"Latch the door." Seymour is barking at the Astley woman, who is standing with one hand over her gob, staring, useless.

Squatted like that on the floor, naked and hairy, he looks half man, half beast. Dot grabs Elizabeth's clothes, which are scattered about the floor, and flings them to the girl. Elizabeth doesn't move. She looks horrified, clutching the blanket up to her chin. Without a word to her, Dot swipes shut the bed curtains.

"Cover yourself," she says to Seymour, not caring about her curt tone nor whom she is addressing. "And you'd better leave before anyone comes. I shall see to the Queen."

Seymour, mute with shame, gathers his things, pulling his hose up and slinging his doublet on, unable to look at Dot or Mistress Astley, who are busy anyway with Katherine. Finally, he slinks from the room like a punished dog.

Katherine doesn't stir, seeming just to sleep peacefully, but a dark swollen bruise has begun to appear on her forehead where she hit the floor.

Dot is struck by the awful fact that she brought Katherine to this. The whole household had been gossiping for months about the goings-on between Seymour and Elizabeth. Dot had tried to tell her, more than once, but Katherine had refused to accept it.

"He is just being a tender stepfather, Dot," she had said. "It is nothing but harmless play."

Dot knew there was no one else, with Anne away, who would tell Katherine the truth of it—only Huicke, perhaps. But she wishes now she had been more measured, curses her impetuous nature. Though she had never imagined, bringing Katherine to this room, that they would find anything worse than Elizabeth on Seymour's lap on the window seat, canoodling—she had never imagined *this*.

Elizabeth appears, dressed but disheveled, pulling back the bed curtains and straightening the plummet, replacing the pillows—something she has likely never done in her entire life.

"Help me," Dot says. "We must get her off the floor." Dot takes her shoulders and Mistress Astley her feet. She weighs little. Even with child there is nothing of her and they heave her easily onto the bed, covering her with a blanket. Dot opens a window to get some fresh air to her and let the stink of their coupling out. There is a stench of urine, too, and a dark, wet tell-tale patch in the hearth. Men, like dogs, will piss anywhere they please. Dot can hear the clatter of everyone leaving chapel downstairs.

"Fetch Huicke," she says to Elizabeth.

The girl looks at Dot peevishly, waiting for her to remember her rank, but then glances at the unconscious Queen and makes for the door.

"Wait, my lady," calls Mistress Astley, grabbing Elizabeth's shoulder. "Your hood." She places it on the girl's head, tying it beneath the chin, stuffing her hair underneath it. "That will have to do, Bess."

Dot sits beside Katherine, stroking her hand, whispering to her. "Madam, wake up. Please, wake up."

Katherine's eyelids begin to flicker and roll, and she heaves in a deep breath that seems to bring her back to life. "What happened?" She touches her fingers to the bruise. "That hurts." She looks puzzled for a moment, furrowing her brow and wincing. "Tell me it is not true, Dot. Tell me I was dreaming." She croaks, as if the words hurt her.

"It is not a dream, madam. I am very, very sorry but it is not a dream."

"Oh Dot," seems to be all she can manage to say. Her shoulders slump back and her eyes close again; she looks like a flower that is over.

Huicke enters, and with him Seymour.

"What happened?" asks Huicke.

"I told you," says Seymour. "She fell and cracked her head on the floor."

Huicke sees the bruise, making a tutting noise with his teeth. He looks at Dot for confirmation.

She nods.

"Right—give me some space."

Dot stands aside.

"How long was she out?"

"No more than ten minutes," she replies. "She has just come round."

"Kit, tell me how you feel."

"It is nothing," she says, "just a little bump. But the baby. Is my baby harmed?"

The doctor asks Seymour to leave for modesty's sake while he examines her.

But Seymour refuses. "She is *my* wife, there is *nothing* I have not seen."

Huicke draws the bed hangings, and Dot can hear his hushed voice asking questions, "Any cramps, any strangeness of vision?" and eventually saying, "No lasting harm has been done. It will take more than a fall to unlodge this baby, it seems." He emerges, saying to Seymour, "Someone must stay up beside her for the night to be sure all is well."

"I shall—" starts Seymour.

But Katherine interrupts him. "I should like Dot to sit with me. Would you mind, Dot?"

"Yes, yes"—Seymour steps back—"of course, it is women's business."

Eventually, after making a deal of feeling his wife's forehead and stroking her hair and fluffing up her pillows, Seymour leaves, and with him Mistress Astley and Elizabeth too, who's been standing in the doorway like a lemon, not knowing what to do.

Just Huicke and Dot are left with the Queen.

Dot tidies a heap of Elizabeth's hastily removed jewelry—a tangle of rings, a couple of bracelets, a necklace with a few strands of hair caught in its clasp—and beside them, open, face down, is Katherine's new book. The sight of it makes Dot feel another great surge of anger at the girl.

Katherine is saying, "What a fool I have been. I should have listened to you, Huicke. You were right, my husband is not what he appears and never was." She drops her head to her hand. "Such a fool."

"You're no fool, Kit. We're all susceptible to the pull of desire. It can blind us to the truth and monsters come in all guises." Huicke whispers something to her. They look like sweethearts and Dot thinks what a shame it is that Huicke is one of those. (She knows it, for she saw him once embracing that playwright behind the Whitehall cockpit.)

"What should I do?" Katherine says.

"You know it. The girl must go—to salvage her reputation, if nothing else. As for your husband . . ." Huicke leaves the words unsaid.

But the truth in his silence hangs in the chamber—there is nothing she can do about her husband.

Elizabeth stands before her, looking more than ever like a small child, deserted entirely by her confidence.

"Sit." Katherine pats the seat beside her.

Confronted with her, she cannot find it in herself to hate the girl— it is Seymour who must carry the blame for this. But still she finds her forgiveness does not easily rise to the surface.

Elizabeth sits, but can't look Katherine in the eye and fiddles with the pearl edging on her robe. "Mother, I don't know . . ." she begins in a barely audible voice.

But Katherine stops her. She can't face having to talk about the details yet. "I have arranged for you to go to Lord Denny's house at Cheshunt. Lady Denny is Mistress Astley's sister, but I suppose you must know that."

Elizabeth nods. "I will do whatever you ask of me." All of a sudden she drops to the floor and buries her head in Katherine's lap. "I cannot begin to describe how much I hate myself for what I have done to you."

"Get up," Katherine says. "Stop hiding. What is done is done. You must accept that." She is surprised at her anger, thought she could hide it better.

Elizabeth begins to get to her feet. "I will do anything to make amends."

"I do not blame you, though you have been foolish. He took advantage of you. But what you must do, Elizabeth, is take my advice. I have been many years on this earth and there are things I have learned. It would please me if I thought you could learn those things also before you ruin yourself."

"I will, I promise."

"You must understand that passion is transient. It means little in the scheme of things. You are too much governed by your passions. You need to rein them in."

Elizabeth is nodding.

Katherine barely recognizes this biddable girl.

"You have a fickle nature and you must find a way to curb it—find some constancy, it will stand you in good stead." Katherine feels a wave of sadness wash over her. Her family is fragmenting, but her anger simmers and she has to hold tightly to it so it doesn't escape. "This thing that has happened—this . . ." Katherine doesn't know how to form it into words, can't bring herself to call it what it is—a betrayal. "There are events in life from which we learn our most profound lessons and sometimes those events are the ones of which we are most ashamed. It could be the pivot upon which you turn, Elizabeth. It could be the making of you. Think on that."

Elizabeth seems deflated, truly chastened, and Katherine is glad she is not weeping crocodile tears and begging forgiveness or trying to find ways to excuse her behavior.

"You do not want people to call you your mother's daughter. That would be the end of you. It is all his doing but it is you who will be called a whore."

"My . . . My mother was—" Elizabeth begins to say something but then seems to change her mind. "I never knew her."

"No, nor I." But Katherine has heard enough about Anne Boleyn. "I only know what people have said of her, and whatever she was truly like, that is how she is remembered. You do not want to be re-membered for this, for it will stick to you and never be got off."

"I only wish it had not happened. I have destroyed the love you gave me." Her eyes are dark with regret, their usual spark doused.

"I am sending you away for your own good, not mine. Now, come," and she holds out a hand to beckon the girl closer. "Kiss me, for I will not see you again before you leave."

As Elizabeth plants a kiss on her cheek, she can't help but think she would rather be rid of Thomas. Her upset with Elizabeth will soon wane, but her husband she will never forgive.

When the girl makes to go, Katherine says as an afterthought, "Be careful whom you agree to marry, Elizabeth, for once the ring is on your finger you lose everything. And you are a girl who likes to hold the reins."

When the door closes, tears well up in Katherine's eyes and she wonders if she had been wrong all along about Elizabeth. She had believed her so very misunderstood. Anne had always had her reservations about the girl—Dot too. She wonders if she had simply fallen for the Elizabeth charm, as Meg had.

After all, she was fallible to the Seymour charm—it withers her to think of it—so why not also Elizabeth's?

69

The Old Manor, Chelsea, June 1548

Elizabeth leaves tomorrow, and good riddance. Dot can't wait to see the back of her.

Katherine goes about as if nothing has happened, making her plans for the move to Sudeley Castle where her baby is to be born. But Dot can see the brittleness beneath the surface that she's seen before. Katherine talks often about her baby—that softens her edges. Dot had dreamed of being nurse to the infant but it will not happen, for Dot is with child too. She hadn't told anyone until she started to show—only William, who was daft with joy. She had cradled her secret but it has been five months now and there is no hiding it.

"You must go and set up your own household. You have a baby in your belly to think of, and your husband too." Katherine hadn't quite been able to hide the sadness behind her words. It will be a wrench for her too. Dot was distraught at the idea of their separation, had protested but Katherine had been firm. Dot knows well enough that when Katherine is decided on something there is no use in trying to change her mind. But the idea of leaving her with that man makes her feel sick inside.

Katherine had said once, on the eve of her wedding to the King, that things often turn out the way you least expect, and Dot has thought about how true this is. Both Katherine and Dot had married for love. A daft thing to do, really—and by rights they should both be reaping the regrets of that. But Dot has never been happier than she is with her William Savage.

384

She reminds herself of how she used to repeat his name over and over, adding it to hers: Dorothy Savage. It was never more than a story she made up about her future and was not something that was ever actually going to happen. But it *has* happened—she *is* Dorothy Savage. Just the thought of her husband makes her belly turn over with desire, even now, after more than a year of marriage.

She has her happy ending. Who would have thought, after all that time thinking William Savage was a bad penny, that he's turned out to be the kindest, sweetest creature who ever walked the earth? It is Seymour who has turned out to be the bad lot.

So, they are moving on. Katherine and her household are going to Sudeley, Dot to her manor, Coombe Bottom, in Devon—to think of it, she in her very own manor and a gentlewoman to boot. Elizabeth has already gone to Cheshunt and Lady Denny, who is very strict by all accounts. Dot is helping Katherine pack her valuables. After so much packing and unpacking, it will most likely be the last time.

"There is no way of telling," Katherine says, "with men, which one is a rotten apple. Anyway, Dot, I am happy that you have your William Savage."

"But what of you?" Dot asks.

"One thing I have learned is that you can never know what fate has in store for you."

There was a time when she would have said something more like, "You can never know God's plan." She has changed. But then they have all changed.

Dot thinks about visiting Ma and how she felt like she didn't belong in her own family any more, that she'd left them behind, without even knowing it. She has wondered if it was being able to read that changed her most, or the weeks in Newgate, or all that time spent in the royal palaces and seeing so much.

She sometimes thinks about how, as a girl, she'd imagined the King and his court to be like Camelot, and how she's since come to see for herself that it is not one little bit like that. Camelot is nothing but a place in her imagination, for the court may be beautiful on the outside but inside it is as ugly as sin.

She wonders if perhaps those stories of knights and maidens are just tales for children and that she has grown out of them. One day, hundreds of years from now, people will tell stories about the court of King Henry and the romance of it all—the Eighth King Henry and his Six Wives. Will they tell of the terror that came with it, or will it be made to seem a golden age?

They are sorting a pile of jeweled gloves into pairs and there is one left partnerless.

"Where do all those single gloves go?" Katherine smiles, placing the rest of them in a box. Then, leaning back she brings her hands to her stomach. "Dot, feel this." She takes Dot's hand and places it on her round belly.

Dot can feel the movement under her fingers, like a fish is wriggling in there. "Oh," she sighs, thinking of her own little fish wriggling away inside her, a whole new life that will be lived one way or another. "He's a busy little lad."

They've always talked of him as a boy, never even imagined he might not be.

"I have this little one to think of now," says Katherine. "He makes me happier than I could ever have believed, and though I'm losing you, I have many true friends around me. And I have had a letter from Mary." She takes a fold of paper from her purse, opening it out, waving it as if to prove to herself that it exists. "We are reconciled. It is this one," she taps her belly, "who has rekindled our friendship. He is already doing good for us all, even before he is born. What a blessing he is."

"I wonder how I will fare without your wisdom." Dot feels then the painful drag deep inside her, like the pulling of a tooth, marking the beginning of their separation.

"Wisdom, pah!" Katherine says with a tight little laugh.

Dot isn't sure what she means by that, whether wisdom is not all it's cracked up to be, or if she is not as wise as Dot has always believed.

"Here." Katherine picks up a bracelet, gold with garnets. Taking Dot's hand, she slips it onto her wrist. "Have this for luck with your baby."

Dot holds up her arm to admire it. "Thank you. Not just for this . . . I mean thank you for everything."

"No need for thanks." Katherine is suddenly brusque, seems embarrassed.

Dot wonders if she, too, is feeling that painful tug of separation.

"I do miss my mother's cross. I wonder if that woman will ever return it."

Dot circles the bracelet on her wrist and considers her future. Little Min and her family are already installed at Coombe Bottom and she wonders how it will be, living with her sister. She knows so little of her, for Little Min was barely four years old when Dot left Stanstead Abbotts.

She thinks of the life taking form in her and of her dear William Savage and imagines their future stretched out like a garden on the brink of blooming, each bed differently planted, lavender here and roses there, irises and hollyhocks and all the herbs that she will make into remedies, as the Queen has shown her, so she can care for her family. In the distance, vague and unformed, as she does not really know what it looks like, is the sea. William says that you can see the sea from the gardens at Coombe Bottom.

"I suppose, in time"—Katherine seems to be thinking out loud—"I will find a way to forgive Elizabeth."

"But *how* will you forgive her?" Dot can't imagine that it could be possible. She stops what she is doing—folding linens—and looks to Katherine, waiting for her answer.

"Elizabeth was exploited just as I was. It is not she who made Seymour the way he is. He was ever thus." She meets Dot's gaze. "It was *I* who did not see it."

"But—" Dot begins.

The Queen raises a hand to hush her. "Elizabeth is . . ." She pauses with a sigh. "She is only fourteen." She stretches her arms up to unclasp her necklace. Dot passes over her coffer, which she opens, tipping the chain into one of its silk pockets. "Elizabeth suffers more than I for her deeds. It is easier to be betrayed than to betray, Dot."

But Dot cannot forgive Elizabeth. She was horrified by what she had walked in on that day. It was as if she herself had been betrayed. Regret eats at her still for the way she led Katherine to Elizabeth's chamber. William had always said that no good came from meddling, and he was right. But Dot couldn't help herself, and in her mind it was her loyalty to Katherine she was thinking of.

If she searches her soul, though, she'd also done it for her loathing of Elizabeth. Only it ended up being Katherine who was hurt. Would it have been better if Katherine had never known?

Dot wishes she could be more like Katherine, forgiving, instead of the type to harbor a grudge. But she still blames Elizabeth for Meg's misery, even more than she blames Murgatroyd. How to explain that? Meg would have said that God was testing her faith, like Job. Dot can't see it like that. She never did understand the story of Job—why God made all those terrible things happen to him, just so he could prove his faith.

Elizabeth is a puzzle. The day before she left, Dot had overheard her talking with Jane Gray in the long grass at the bottom of the orchard. It had reminded her of how she and Meg used to hide in the orchard at Whitehall and share their secrets.

Dot was by the pond with little Ned Herbert, counting the fish. Elizabeth had strolled by arm in arm with Jane Gray, without even so much as a look Dot's way—nothing new in that. But Jane had waved and called out a greeting with one of her bright smiles. Dot is glad that Jane Gray will go to Sudeley with Katherine. She is a sweet girl, if rather serious and always has her nose in a book—usually the Bible. In that way she is a little like Meg, but she is a smiler and much sunnier than poor Meg ever was.

Dot couldn't help but overhear Jane ask Elizabeth about her— what family did she come from?—and had crept closer to listen better, bringing Ned with her, telling him it was a spying game.

"She is the daughter of a *thatcher*, would you believe it," Elizabeth had said, throwing off her hood, unlacing her gown and falling into the grass with a laugh.

Jane had shrugged. "Her husband plays like an angel. And besides, I like her."

"Is that so?"

Jane had said nothing. Sometimes there is no way to respond to Elizabeth.

Elizabeth pulled up a blade of grass, putting it between her thumbs, blowing through it to make it sing. "If you were a man for a day, what would you do?"

"I cannot imagine such a thing."

"Think of the power. I would like the feeling of that, to have all the women in the world do your bidding. I would make a good man, I think."

They were silent then for a while. Dot was thinking about how everyone did what Elizabeth said anyway.

"The Queen will not see me," Elizabeth suddenly blurted out. "Do you know what it is that I have done, Jane?"

Jane shook her head, saying nothing.

"I have betrayed her, and she won't see me now before I leave."

"Is there some message you would like me to pass to her?"

"There is," said Elizabeth. "Will you tell her that I have taken to heart everything she said and that I hope one day she will be able to forgive me?"

"I'm sure she will do that. She is one of the most forgiving people I have ever come across."

"Perhaps. But Jane, you don't know the extent of my betrayal." She paused to pluck a daisy, twisting it in her fingers. "She told me I am a girl who likes to hold the reins. Do you think that, Jane? That I am someone who likes to hold the reins?"

Jane picked another daisy and passed it to her. "I suppose so. You do not like to be ruled."

"Does that make me more man than woman then?" Elizabeth had laughed bitterly, not waiting for an answer, and then suddenly confessed, "You know I lay with her husband."

Jane gasped loudly at this, covering her mouth, embarrassment flushing over her face.

"I cannot explain why. I have tried to understand it but I can't. Sometimes, though, there are things I cannot find a way of resisting, though they are terrible things." She rolled onto her front, propping herself on her elbows, resting her chin in her hands. She had broken the daisy chain and let it drop. "I do things to make myself feel alive but then I end up feeling more dead than ever."

There were tears welling in Elizabeth's dark eyes, something Dot had not thought possible. She had always imagined Elizabeth was made of dry, hard resilient things and had not a drop of liquid in her.

"I *hate* that man, more than I hate the Devil."

"Seymour?"

"Yes, him. And I am so filled with regret I don't know what to do with myself. She is the only mother I have known. I am like a boy who pulls the wings off flies to watch them suffer." She blinked back her tears, taking a breath before continuing. "You know he made a suit for my sister Mary, and when she sent him packing he tried it with *me*. He must have thought me stupid if he imagined I would wed him without the council's permission and risk losing my head for it." Her voice was hot with anger. "Then he married the Queen."

"Seymour tried to marry Lady Mary *and* you? But I thought it was a love match with the Queen, that they had been in love—"

"Love!" Elizabeth spat, not letting Jane finish. "What is love? Ambition, more like. That man couldn't manage to get himself a Princess of the blood, so the Queen was the next best thing. What do you think to that, Jane?"

"I . . . I don't know what to think."

"He would have had *you*, Jane Gray, if he could have. You have a fair dose of royal blood in you."

Jane wore an expression of horror.

"Jest, Jane, jest," Elizabeth laughed bitterly. "I think at nine you would have been too young even for Seymour."

"But . . ."

"No buts, Jane. I wager you all the gold in Christendom that if the Queen dropped dead tomorrow, Seymour would be knocking at *my* door."

Jane let out a shocked little gasp.

"If you want one piece of advice from me," Elizabeth went on, "do not marry any man . . ." She drifted off, letting her words hang.

Dot supposed she was thinking how empty that advice was, for those girls would be hitched to someone whether they liked it or not.

"And you know what else the Queen said to me? She said that the things that bring us the greatest shame can also bring us the greatest lessons. Do you believe that, Jane?"

"If you heed the parables, it is true." Jane's eyes were following a bumblebee that dithered from flower to flower, not wanting to look at Elizabeth.

"You are quite the good little God-fearer, aren't you?"

There was her sting, but Elizabeth is like that, can't help herself.

Dot thinks she will never understand the girl—but then, perhaps even Elizabeth herself cannot solve her own puzzle.

70

Sudeley Castle, Gloucestershire, August 1548

Katherine lies in a quiet, shaded chamber awaiting the birth of her baby. They say the curtains should be drawn and the windows shut tight for a lying-in, but each time Katherine is left alone with Mary Odell they draw everything back, opening it all wide, luxuriating in the summer light and the warm breeze.

Spread below the window is the knot garden, intricate as an Oriental carpet, and at its far end lies an ornamental fishpond, which reminds Katherine of her little nephew Ned, who so loved to watch the carp in the pond at Chelsea. This in turn reminds her, with a sweet longing, of Dot, who could always be seen with him there at the water's edge, pointing out the fish.

Mary Odell is nice enough and willing, if a little slow, but she is not Dot, who, for all her daydreaming and scattiness, had a way of knowing what Katherine wanted before even she did herself. Closer than kin, that is how she will always think of dear Dot. She would welcome a visit from Anne, but her husband holds a place on the new Privy Council and likes her at court by his side. Anne will come when the baby is born, though.

Katherine can just see the gold stone crenellations of St. Mary's chapel, and beyond them the parched park rolling into the distance, scattered with ancient trees and clusters of deer. Of all the great palaces and castles Katherine has lived in over the years, this is the one that feels most like a home, and she itches to be out exploring the place. But she must stay incarcerated in her tomb-dark chambers until the infant comes.

When Lizzie Tyrwhitt returns, she makes a great huffing of complaint as she shuts all the windows up again and draws the drapes, demanding that Mary Odell help her, which she does, though her shoulders are heaving with the giggles for she knows the minute Lizzie is gone Katherine will want them open again.

Katherine is fond of Lizzie. She has spent much time with her over the years. Indeed, they were sisters-in-law from Katherine's first marriage to Edward Borough and lived at Gainsborough Hall together for a short while. But Lizzie can be insufferably truculent when it comes to anything to do with a birth.

Each afternoon Jane Gray comes, and Levina Teerlinc too, who arrived recently to paint a likeness of Jane for the King. She often sits sketching them all going about their quiet business, with her hound, Hero, beside her, his head resting on her lap, the rasp of charcoal on vellum lulling them.

Levina has a gift for capturing things: the way Mary Odell swipes at her hair with the back of her hand; Lizzie's bustling demeanor; the serious crease on Jane's brow as she reads out loud from *Paraphrases*. Jane has an appetite for learning and often likes to compare the Latin and English versions of Erasmus. Katherine still feels a bristle of pride at her part in the translating of Erasmus and is reminded, too, of the husbands she has read that book to—not Thomas, though. Thomas can barely sit still long enough to pray for the safe delivery of his infant.

Now that Thomas has returned from London to await the birth, no man is allowed in these rooms, save for Huicke and Parkhurst the chaplain. And he only allows those two because he cannot refuse her her physician, nor her cleric, but he always remains, glowering over them, when they are here: his jealousy has reached an excessive degree. So, the gardener no longer comes daily with fresh flowers from the gardens, nor even her chamberlain or clerk, for Thomas will not have it. Katherine remembers how, not so long ago, she saw his jealousy as proof of his love. How wrong she was.

Seymour is like the boy in the Greek myth doomed to look ceaselessly at his own reflection. What is it he is called? She seems not to be able to remember anything these days. Lizzie Tyrwhitt says it is because she is with child. She hopes that is the case, because she can barely get to the end of a sentence and remember the beginning of it.

Thomas is more attentive than ever, though, charming the maids into fetching and carrying, bringing fresh fruit from the garden, tonic wines from the cellar, sweetmeats from the kitchens, and he himself brings gifts daily, a jeweled fan, a book of poems, a posy of violets, sitting beside her for hours, reading aloud and sharing gossip from London, still adamant that he will negotiate Jane's marriage to the King.

He is even more hopeful now that the little six-year-old Scottish Queen Mary is out of the running. She is betrothed to the Dauphin and will travel to France soon, to live with the French royal family. One day she will be Queen of France as well as Scotland, poor child. Meanwhile, Thomas continues to vent his anger at his brother about Katherine's jewels. The situation between them deteriorates and he scribbles angry letters that are ignored.

All that has ceased to interest Katherine, who lets it all drift over her, only half listening, disengaged. Her feelings for Thomas altered irretrievably on that day at Chelsea—her love disappeared like water down a hole. Exploring her heart now, she finds Elizabeth is forgiven and the letters she has sent, tentative and apologetic, sorrowful, are touching. Katherine is sure that her mistake will have been the making of her and can only think tenderly of that lost girl.

As for her own marriage: she thinks of it as nothing more than an arrangement, the kind most have. The only good to come of it is this child.

She thinks incessantly of her baby and imagines herself forgiven by God—for this blessing, after all those years of emptiness, is surely a gift from him. She has picked up *Lamentation* and is revisiting her own writings, surprised by the passion and fervor she had once felt—when everything was different. She thinks of it as her "before" period—like Eve before the fall.

Since then, she has changed irrevocably, has lost her certainty about things, about faith—but with this miraculous gift forming inside her she can feel herself drawn on the current of it to a better place. So, she writes to Elizabeth, her dear black sheep, encouraging her to read the book, to learn from it how to set aside her frailty and vanity.

"Katherine," says Thomas, "are you listening to me?"

"I was drifting. Thinking."

They are alone and she is lying on the bed in just a loose gown, flushed with the heat and breathless. She is so very huge now, there is little space for air in her lungs and she feels the constant press of something—a tiny foot or hand, she supposes—under her ribs. Comfort is elusive, her feet are numb and her back aches. She must lie on her side, propped with pillows, for if she lies on her back she passes out.

"What were you thinking?"

His eyes flash in that way that she used to find irresistible but no longer does—she sees them now for the counterfeit gems they are. She wants to say she was thinking what a disappointment he has been to her, but she doesn't. "I was thinking about our child."

"Our boy. We will call him Edward, after the King. He will do great things, our boy. Son of a Queen, cousin of a King, he will inhabit the highest places."

"Yes," she murmurs, "the highest places." Secretly she longs for a daughter but she can barely admit it even to herself, for everyone is supposed to want a son.

Huicke enters, slipping into the room quietly, waiting for Seymour's nod of permission, saying, "I have brought a tonic for the Queen."

"What is in it?" demands her husband.

"Oh, some health-giving herbs." He pours out a measure from a jar, handing it to her.

But Thomas stops him, taking hold of his arm. "What exactly?" He sniffs at the cup's contents. "I want to know what you are giving my wife." He is being overbearing, as usual.

Although Seymour only does it to feel a measure of control, thinks Huicke. "It is an infusion of raspberry leaf, meadowsweet and nettle."

"And they are for?" Seymour adds pressure to his grip around Huicke's arm.

"The raspberry leaf aids an easy delivery and the meadowsweet relieves heartburn."

"And the other, what was it . . . ?" His mouth is downturned in distaste.

"The nettle, my lord, promotes strength."

Seymour drops his arm with a tut and passes the cup to Katherine, who drinks it down. "From now on *I* shall give the Queen her tonic, Huicke. Understood?"

Huicke imagines slapping the man clean across his face, punching him even, or sticking him with a blade and watching the blood drain from him.

"Huicke," Katherine says, handing back the empty vessel. "My feet feel completely numb."

"I will massage them for you." He sits at the base of the bed, taking her small feet onto his lap, rubbing them between his gloved palms.

"I will do that." Seymour gives him a little shove. "Shift yourself!"

"As you wish, Lord Admiral." Huicke moves aside, watching Seymour handle his wife's feet gingerly, as if holding a brace of dead pheasant that needs plucking and gutting.

"A little more firmly, my dear," says Katherine, meeting Huicke's glance and rolling her eyes upwards with a wry smile.

That's my Katherine, he thinks, still not lost her sense of humor.

"That will be all." Seymour waves an arm to dismiss him.

But Katherine cries out then, a low kind of animal sound, and her waters break with a slosh. Seymour jumps up, flapping his arms, his face etched with a kind of fearful disgust.

"I will fetch the midwife," says Huicke, laughing inwardly at Seymour, known for his bravery, panicking so.

The waters drip, drip, drip onto the floor.

"No, no," Seymour is almost shouting. "I will go. You stay with her, Huicke." And he runs from the room.

When the door slams, Katherine and Huicke both burst out laughing.

Huicke says, "Men!" busying himself with straightening her cushions and making her comfortable.

"Huicke," she says in a small voice. "I am afraid of this birth. I am not young . . ."

He draws his hand over her brow. "Hush, many women are safely delivered at your age. Thirty-six is not so old and you are strong. Submit to it, let the birth take its course."

Lizzie Tyrwhitt bustles in with a small army of ladies including the midwife, aproned and armed with towels and sheets and basins of water.

"If you please, Doctor, no men in here for now."

He kisses Katherine on the top of her head, breathing in her dried-violet scent, before leaving.

Jane Gray is outside the door, her face the image of concern. She is too young to attend a birthing. He leads her to a bench by the window and they talk for a while, listening to Seymour pacing up and down the hall below, his feet clicking on the stone flags. The moans from within the chamber become more frequent and insistent, and with each one Jane winces quietly.

"You are fond of the Queen, are you not?" he says.

"Oh yes, I have grown to love her dearly."

"I too, Jane, I too. She is one of those rare creatures that no one can help but love."

"Dr. Huicke," she says, looking up at him with her round pale eyes, "do you believe in the new map of the universe?"

"I do," he says, thinking how much older she seems than her ten years.

"Well, I think of the Queen as the Sun, around which we are all in orbit."

"I couldn't have put it better myself."

He sends her away not long after, though she doesn't want to go, but Katherine's cries have become urgent and unsettling and he doesn't want the girl terrified.

There is nothing he can do, but he can't bring himself to leave, so he waits and waits, through the night and into the morning. Each time someone leaves the room, for clean sheets or to change the water or to fetch victuals for the ladies, he starts up, meeting their eyes. But always it is a little shake of the head.

Poor Kit, this is a long one.

He waits on, feeling powerless, knowing that for all his physician's knowledge there is nothing he can do to help her.

Another day passes, torturously slow.

It is hot and close as if there is a storm gathering. Night falls and he realizes he hasn't eaten, thinks he can't.

The minutes creep. Katherine's moans sear through him. He wonders, for the first time, if she will survive this.

Just as he begins to hear the first birds sing in the dawn, Lizzie Tyrwhitt bursts from the chamber, wan with exhaustion but smiling.

"Doctor, the Queen is delivered of a daughter. I will fetch the Lord Admiral."

In that moment he feels that he might be overcome with tears, only then realizing quite how great his anxiety had been.

Katherine has a daughter.

She is a mother.

People move about the chamber like shadows. There are whisperings and shufflings and the gentle tinkling of liquid being poured. Something is held to her lips. It is cool and slips down her throat. Katherine's mind wanders and flits. She feels herself slipping and sliding at the edges of consciousness. She is hot, burning, and fears she is already in the fires of Hell, then remembers the cloying summer heat.

"Where is Huicke?" she murmurs. "I must see my doctor."

She cannot hold on to anything, thoughts fall out of her mind like petals from a dead rose. She throws the covers off her body. The place is a furnace.

"Open a window," she croaks, but isn't entirely sure if any sound leaves her mouth.

A girl waves a fan—the cool air chills her skin, where she is damp with perspiration, and suddenly she is cold to the bones.

"Meg?"

"I am Jane," says the girl.

And she can see it now—the pale round eyes, the swan's neck, not Meg at all.

She hears snippets of murmured conversation. Mary Seymour—she remembers naming her baby Mary after her stepdaughter, who is back in the fold of her family. My *own* daughter, she thinks, still barely able to believe it.

"Jane," she is suddenly afraid for her child, "Jane, is little Mary well?"

"Yes, she is. She is feeding with the wet nurse."

"I should like to hold her." She wants to press her face up to the soft fuzz of her baby's crown, breathe in her brand-new scent.

"A week-old infant cannot be disturbed at her feed." It is bossy Lizzie Tyrwhitt.

Katherine's need becomes desperate, to touch her little girl, to feel the clench of her tiny fist around her finger, to see her little bud mouth, swollen from sucking. It is unbearable to be separated. She tries to sit, to heave herself out of the bed, but her body is a dead weight.

"There, there." She feels Lizzie's capable hands coaxing her back to the pillows. "You will have her when she is fed."

"Where is Dot? And Elizabeth? Where are my girls?"

"Dot is not here," says Jane. "She is at Coombe Bottom in Devon, do you not remember?"

But Katherine cannot hold on to her memories. They are like wet fish and slip from her fingers just as she thinks she has a hold on them.

"But Elizabeth is here . . ?"

"Elizabeth is at Cheshunt with Lord and Lady Denny."

Jane's face moves in and out of focus, as if seen through water. Katherine closes her eyes and allows herself to drift.

"Childbed fever," she hears Lizzie say, in a hushed voice to someone. Is it Seymour or is it Henry? No, it must be Seymour, for Henry is no more.

So, I am dying, she thinks then with a grip of dread, wondering, as she used to, which husband she will accompany in paradise—if that is where she is going. She can't think about the other place. Will it be the greatest of her husbands? No, Henry will have Jane Seymour at his side. Will it be most recent then, the father of her daughter?

She silently begs God not to give her Seymour for the whole of eternity. She hopes it will be Latymer, for he was the one she was with the longest. Dear Latymer, the one she killed—the thought intensifies her dread.

Latymer's face drifts before her and she wonders if he has come to meet her.

But it is Huicke. His eyes are clouded with grief.

She wonders why, realizing then that it is for her, remembering she is dying. She takes his arm and pulls him towards her, holding her hand to cup his ear close to her mouth.

"Huicke, he has poisoned me."

She doesn't know why she has whispered that, where it came from. But she feels something in her, something wrong that has got into her. Her husband's words float back to her—*I want to know what you are giving my wife.*

"He wants rid of me so he may wed Eliz—"

No, she says to herself, stopping the words. I am thinking of what I did to Henry, to Latymer. But something has got inside her and is sapping her. Who put it there? She can feel, with a clench in her belly, the blackness of the other place like a cold shadow to the side of her eye.

"Huicke," she whispers to his ear, "did I poison the King?"

"No, Kit, you did not."

She can feel him stroking her hair. She is floating, slipping, falling.

"I am going, Huicke. Fetch me the chaplain. It is time."

Then Seymour is beside her on the bed, clasping her hand. She feels she might suffocate, tries to shake herself free. Lizzie is there, wiping a cool cloth over her face. The cold damp is soothing.

"I am not well handled," she says to Lizzie. She can hear the trickling sound of her rinsing the cloth in a basin. "Those about me do not take care of me." She tries to nod in the direction of her husband, for it is him she is talking of. "They laugh at my misfortune . . ."

"Why, sweetheart," comes a well-oiled voice, "I would do you no harm."

It is Seymour. He has wrapped an arm around her. It is heavy like a great limb of iron pressing down onto her. She pushes it off, rolling away, exhausting herself with the effort.

"No, Thomas, I think *so*," she hears herself say.

There is a muffled sobbing. Who is crying? She can feel tears on her cheek from where Seymour has just pressed a kiss.

"I would have given a thousand marks to see Huicke before now, but dared not ask for fear of displeasing you." She is surprised at how clear her voice sounds. "Your tears are for guilt, I think, not grief."

"Sweetheart . . ." He seems lost for words.

A waft of cedar and musk seeps into her—his smell. It cloys unbearably. She doesn't want this to be the last earthly thing she smells.

"Go," she says, feeling lighter as he moves away—lighter and lighter, blowing away like a dandelion clock.

There is the chaplain looming, his wooden cross dangling from his neck. She fixes her gaze on it, the still point in a spinning world. He has hold of her hand, to prevent her from drifting away.

"Will God forgive me? I have so much to be forgiven."

His habit smells of just-blown-out candles. She hears him administer the rites, feels the soft brush of his hand on her forehead.

"You will surely be forgiven."

She sighs and floats, exhaling.

Epilogue

Dot watches Little Min down on the beach below the house with the baby in her arms and Min's own three children trotting behind her along the side of the water. Dot's baby girl is four months old now.

She is in the garden trimming back her physic bed. Her bracelet glints in the sun. It is the one Katherine gave her before they parted. She never takes it off. When she first heard of Katherine's death it was like a punch in the gut—she thought she might go mad with grief. Just the idea of her no longer being somewhere on the earth was too much to bear. She thought about the people she'd lost: first her pa falling from the roof and sweet Letty, her childhood friend, then Meg and now Katherine, each one of them taken at the wrong time. Everyone said to her, "You will be together again one day."

But what if Heaven and Hell are just stories people tell each other, like the stories of Camelot? The thought of it is too unwieldy for her head.

It was the birth of her own child, her dear little daughter Baby Meg—that was the thing that helped her hold on to her sanity. And William, of course—her own William Savage has been her rock and Baby Meg the thread attaching her to him.

"You must not think so much, Dot," William would say to her. "If you let those thoughts run wild they will pull you over the edge of things."

He is right, of course; there are some things that don't bear thinking of.

Little Min and the children are all swaddled up against the brisk wind. The tide is coming in and the shingle will be under water in an hour.

Dot has grown to love the sea, the constant heave and suck of it, its sound, like wind blowing through leaves. Little Min is running in a circle and the children are chasing her. Snippets of their laughter can be heard between gusts. Little Min is not little any more—she is a good two inches taller than Dot, who is already tall enough—but the name has stuck.

Dot has enjoyed getting to know her sister. She had never thought about how much family could leave its print on you, like the way Min sits with her head in the clouds half the time and the way she is not afraid of anything much and sometimes acts before thinking.

"The impetuous pair," is what William calls them, for they like to throw off their shoes and stockings and search for clams in the shallows with their skirts tucked up like farm girls, not caring a jot that they are getting drenched in saltwater, and when it snowed last winter they took the biggest platters from the kitchens and slid on their behinds down the hill to the beach—things that ladies should never, ever do.

But in lots of ways Min is different too. She has no interest in learning to read, doesn't care a fig for stories. It is singing she likes and she will often accompany William with a song in the evenings when he plays the virginals. It is Dot who teaches the children to read, sitting with them, going over their books, correcting their mistakes, helping them sound out the letters—it always reminds her of Katherine, doing the same with Meg and Elizabeth.

They are not so remote here in Devon that they don't have news from court, for William is often summoned there to play for the King and carry out various other duties, returning full of gossip. Seymour is in the Tower for conspiring to marry Lady Elizabeth without the permission of the council, which is treason.

"Now *there* is a man who let his ambition get the better of him." That was what William had said of it.

Dot remembers overhearing Elizabeth in the orchard at Chelsea . . . *I wager you all the gold in Christendom that if the Queen dropped dead tomorrow, Seymour would be knocking at my door.*

He will go to the block for it, so William says. Elizabeth was questioned, came close to losing her head too. Dot feels almost sorry for the girl in spite of everything, pushed as she was from pillar to post, raised to be this and that, bowed and scraped to, lifted up, thrown down, then criticized for becoming who she became—and never a moment of innocence in her whole life. In fact, when Dot really thinks about it, she believes she might have forgiven Elizabeth after all. But she doesn't think so very often of it.

She wonders what will become of Katherine's daughter, little Mary Seymour, with her mother gone and her father in the Tower, facing his comeuppance. William says she is to go into Cat Brandon's care, as hers is a household befitting Mary's rank.

Dot wishes Mary Seymour could come to Coombe Bottom and be raised here, learn to milk a cow and ride a pony bareback and pick cockles off the beach at low tide, imagining her with the children below, whose laughter trickles up through the wind. But Mary Seymour is the daughter of a Queen and must be raised as such.

Dot gazes out to the water, taking comfort from the notion that Katherine lives on, in a way, through that infant daughter, and how even when they are all turned to dust the stories will continue on through time—as endless as the sea.

Acknowledgments

There are many I would like to thank and without whom *Queen's Gambit* may never have come to fruition: Katie Green, Stephanie Glencross and Diana Beaumont for their editorial help; my publishers, in particular Sam Humphreys and also Trish Todd, who has published it in the USA; my agent Jane Gregory; Catherine Eccles; the BAFTA Writers' and Georgina Goodman, who inspired the initial idea.

As *Firebrand*, my novel has had a second life and I owe gratitude to the team behind the film: producer—Gabrielle Tana; director—Karim Aïnouz; and screenwriters—Henrietta and Jessica Ashworth. I also want to acknowledge my publishers once more for giving me the opportunity to produce a new edit of my novel, but mostly I thank my editor, the ever-patient Jillian Taylor.

Characters

(Characters are listed alphabetically using the
name most often used in the novel)

Anne Askew	Outspoken religious evangelist, with suspected links to the Queen's household; burned for heresy. (*c*1520–1546)
Anne Boleyn	Also Nan Bullen. Second wife of Henry VIII; mother of Elizabeth Tudor; a religious reformer; executed for suspected incest with her brother and adultery with a number of other courtiers, deemed as treason, though the charges are unlikely to have been valid. (*c*1504–1536)
Anne of Cleves	Fourth wife of Henry VIII; marriage annulled due to non-consummation. (1515–1557)
The Archbishop	Thomas Cranmer, Archbishop of Canterbury; confirmed religious reformer; burned for heresy during Mary Tudor's reign. (1489–1556)
Cat Brandon	Duchess of Suffolk (née Willoughby de Eresby); fervent religious reformer and great friend to Katherine Parr; stepmother to Frances Brandon and step-aunt to Lady Jane Gray. (1520–1580)

Catherine Howard	Fifth wife of Henry VIII; executed aged about seventeen, for adultery, deemed as treason. (c1525–1542)
Catherine of Aragon	First wife of Henry VIII; formerly the wife of his elder brother Arthur, Prince of Wales, who died before ascending the throne; mother of Mary Tudor; marriage annulled, though this was never accepted by the Catholic contingent. (1485–1536)
Denny	Anthony, Lord Denny; confidant of Henry VIII and Privy Council member; brother-in-law to Mistress Astley. (1501–1549)
Dot Fownten	Dorothy Fountain; maid to Margaret Neville as a child; chamberer to Katherine Parr as Queen; married William Savage. (Dates not known)
Edward Borough	Of Gainsborough Old Hall; first husband of Katherine Parr. (Died before 1533)
Edward Tudor	Only son of Henry VIII; came to the throne as Edward VI, aged only nine. (1537–1553)
Elizabeth Tudor	Younger daughter of Henry VIII; deemed illegitimate when Henry divorced her mother, Anne Boleyn; became Elizabeth I. (1533–1603)
Frances Brandon	Lady Frances Gray, Countess of Dorset; wife of the Marquis of Dorset; niece of Henry VIII; daughter of the Duke of Suffolk and the King's sister, Mary Tudor; mother of Lady Jane Gray; religious reformer. (c1519–1559)

Gardiner	Bishop of Winchester; Privy Council member to Henry VIII; fervent Catholic; attempted, with Wriothesley, to bring down Katherine Parr, resulting in his own political demise. $c1497–1555$)
Henry VIII	King of England; ascended the throne in 1509. (1491–1547)
Hertford	Edward Seymour, Earl of Hertford; later Duke of Somerset and Lord Protector of England; oldest uncle of Prince Edward, later Edward VI; brother of Thomas and Jane Seymour; brother-in-law of Henry VIII; husband of Anne Stanhope; religious reformer; executed for treason. ($c1506–1552$)
Huicke	Dr. Robert Huicke; physician to Henry VIII and Katherine Parr; witnessed Katherine Parr's will. (Died $c1581$)
Jane Gray	Lady Jane Gray; daughter of Frances Brandon and the Marquis of Dorset; ward of Thomas Seymour; later Queen of England for under two weeks; executed, aged about seventeen, by Mary Tudor; a fervent religious reformer. (1536/37–1554)
Jane Seymour	Third wife of Henry VIII; mother of Prince Edward, later Edward VI; died in childbed; Henry chose to be buried with her as the only wife that had given him a son. ($c1508–1537$)

Jane the Fool	A fool named Jane is recorded in Privy Purse accounts during the reigns for Henry, Mary and Elizabeth; almost nothing is known of her except she may have had the surname Beddes or Bede. (Dates not known)
Katherine Parr	Sixth wife of Henry VIII; sister of William Parr and Anne Herbert; mother of Mary Seymour; died in childbed; religious reformer. (c1512–1548)
Latymer	John Neville, Lord Latymer; second husband of Katherine Parr; father of Meg Neville; controversially and perhaps reluctantly involved in the Catholic uprising the Pilgrimage of Grace; pardoned by Henry VIII. (1493–1543)
Lizzie Tyrwhitt	Lady Elizabeth Tyrwhitt; gentlewoman of the privy chamber to Katherine Parr and attended her deathbed. (Died c1587)
Margaret Douglas	Countess of Lennox; niece of Henry VIII; daughter of Margaret Tudor, Queen of Scotland, and her second husband, Archibald Douglas; half-sister of James V of Scotland and aunt of Mary Queen of Scots; imprisoned for her liaison with Thomas Howard, half-brother of the Duke of Norfolk, and caused scandal with an affair with Charles Howard, Catherine Howard's brother; married the Earl of Lennox, second in line to the Scottish throne, a political coup and figurative foothold in Scotland for Henry VIII. (1515–1578)
Mary Odell	Maid of the chamber to Katherine Parr as Dowager Queen. (c1528–1558+)

Mary Seymour	Daughter of Katherine Parr and Thomas Seymour; raised in Cat Brandon's household after her father's execution. (1548–no record of her after 1550)
Mary Tudor	Daughter of Henry VIII and Catherine of Aragon; committed Catholic; deemed illegitimate; later Queen Mary I, known in history as Bloody Mary. (1516–1558)
Meg Neville	Margaret Neville; daughter of Lord Latymer; stepdaughter of Katherine Parr. (c1526–1546)
Mistress Astley	Katherine Astley (née Champernowne); governess to Elizabeth Tudor; attempted to negotiate marriage between Elizabeth and Thomas Seymour, nearly losing her life for it. (1519–1594)
Paget	Sir William Paget; clerk of the Privy Council; ally to Bishop Gardiner. (1506–1563)
Robert Dudley	Later Earl of Leicester; favorite of Elizabeth I. (1532–1588)
Anne	Anne Herbert (née Parr); later Countess of Pembroke; younger sister of Katherine Parr; married to William Herbert; served all Henry VIII's Queens; religious reformer. (c1515–1552)
Nan Stanhope	Countess of Hertford; later Duchess of Somerset; married to Hertford and therefore sister-in-law of Thomas and Jane Seymour; reputedly unpleasant and ambitious; confirmed religious reformer who was thought to have given Anne Askew gunpowder to speed her demise at the stake. (c1510–1587)

Surrey	Henry Howard, Earl of Surrey; heir to the Duke of Norfolk; poet thought to have been responsible, with Thomas Wyatt, for introducing the sonnet form to England; executed on trumped-up charges relating to his right to bear certain royal arms but most likely because, in his final days, Henry VIII feared the power of the Howard family was too far-reaching. (1516–1547)
Thomas Seymour	Later Baron Seymour of Sudeley and Lord High Admiral; famed for his good looks; fourth husband of Katherine Parr; brother of Hertford and Jane Seymour and therefore brother-in-law to Henry VIII; executed for, among other charges, attempting to marry Elizabeth Tudor. (c1509–1549)
Udall	Nicholas Udall; playwright and intellectual; author of *Ralph Roister Doister*, thought to be the first English comedy; provost of Eton, a job he lost for unspecified "immoral" reasons; friend of Katherine Parr; a religious reformer. (1504–1556)
Will Herbert	"Wild" Will Herbert; later Earl of Pembroke; husband of Anne Parr and brother-in-law to Katherine Parr; known as a brilliant military tactician and brave soldier; member of the Privy Council; religious reformer. (1501–1570)
Will Parr	Eventually Earl of Essex, then Marquis of Northampton; member of the Privy Council; brother of Katherine Parr; spent many years trying to divorce his wife Anne Bourchier for adultery in order to marry Elisabeth Brooke; religious reformer. (1513–1571)

Will Sommers	Court Jester to Henry VIII. (Died 1560)
William Savage	Musician at the courts of both Henry VIII and Edward VI; married Dorothy Fountain. (Dates not known)
Wriothesley	Sir Thomas Wriothesley; later Earl of Southampton; Lord Chancellor to Henry VIII; had been an ally of Thomas Cromwell but aligned himself to Gardiner on Cromwell's demise; became a fervent Catholic conservative; joined Gardiner in the failed plot to bring down Katherine Parr. (1505–1550)

I have endeavored, where possible, to remain faithful to the known facts, events and people of the period and to this end turned to the work of a great number of excellent historians. Only the most minor characters, grooms, stewards and the filthy-mouthed Betty Melcher are entirely of my own invention. Though Katherine's ordeal at Snape is documented, Murgatroyd too is an imagined figure.

My greatest liberties were taken with the characters of Dot and Huicke. Almost nothing is known about Dorothy Fountain save for what is written above. She was almost certainly more gently born than I have made her. There is no evidence whatsoever that Dr. Robert Huicke was homosexual. Having said that, *Queen's Gambit* is a novel and as such all my characters are fictions.

From this distance in time even much historical "fact" is based on misapprehension and conjecture and people's thoughts and feelings can only be imagined.

For those seeking to discover more about the life of Katherine Parr, I can recommend both Linda Porter's and Elizabeth Norton's biographies:

Norton, Elizabeth. 2010. *Catherine Parr*. Stroud: Amberley Publishing.
Porter, Linda. 2010. *Katherine the Queen: The Remarkable Life of Katherine Parr*. London: Macmillan.

A Tudor Timeline

1509   Henry VIII proclaimed King (24th April).
       Henry VIII marries his brother's widow Catherine of
       Aragon (11th June).
       Thomas Seymour born.

1512   Katherine Parr born.

1513   William Parr born.

1515   Anne Parr born.

1516   Mary Tudor born (18th February).

1527   Henry VIII begins to seek annulment from Catherine
       of Aragon, claiming her prior marriage to his brother
       invalidated their union in the eyes of God; known as "The
       King's Great Matter."

1529   Katherine Parr marries Edward Borough.

1533   Henry VIII marries Anne Boleyn (25th January).
       Edward Borough dies (spring).
       Elizabeth Tudor born (7th September).

1534   Henry VIII declared Supreme Head of the Church of
       England, in the Act of Succession (23rd March).
       Catherine of Aragon's title changed to Dowager Princess
       of Wales.
       Mary Tudor declared illegitimate.
       Katherine Parr marries Lord Latymer (summer).

1535 Thomas Cromwell recognized as the King's principal
secretary and chief minister.
Commencement of the dissolution of the monasteries.
Thomas More executed for refusing to accept the Act of
Succession and Henry VIII as Head of the Church (6th July).

1536 Katherine of Aragon dies (7th January).
Anne Boleyn executed (19th May).
Elizabeth Tudor declared illegitimate.
Henry VIII marries Jane Seymour (30th May).
Pilgrimage of Grace; the North rises up in protest against
religious reform (September–December).
Katherine Parr (then Lady Latymer) taken hostage at
Snape Castle.

1537 216 Northern rebels put to death.
Lord Latymer pardoned.
Edward Tudor, heir to the throne, born (12th October).
Jane Seymour dies of puerperal fever (24th October).

1538 Cromwell's Act for the Dissolution of the Greater
Monasteries passed.
Henry VIII excommunicated by the Pope (December).

1539 First edition of the English Great Bible published (April).

1540 Henry VIII marries Anne of Cleves (6th January).
Marriage to Anne of Cleves annulled, due to non-
consummation (29th June).
Henry VIII marries Catherine Howard (28th July).
Thomas Cromwell executed (28th July).

1541 Catherine Howard executed (13th February).

1542 Scots routed at Solway Moss (24th November).
Mary Stuart born (8th December).
James V of Scotland dies, leaving the week-old Mary
Stuart as Queen of Scots (14th December).

1543 Lord Latymer dies (March).
Henry VIII marries Katherine Parr (12th July).
Anglo-Imperial treaty signed; pledge to attack France.
Religious conservatives, including Gardiner, Bishop of
Winchester, on the rise; statute declared restricting the
reading of the English Bible to the wealthy classes.
Three Lutheran preachers burned (4th August).

1544 Elizabeth and Mary Tudor restored to the succession
though neither legitimized.
Thomas Wriothesley appointed Lord Chancellor
(3rd May).
Victory in Scotland; Edward Seymour, Earl of Hertford,
burns Edinburgh (3rd–15th May).
Anglo-Imperial war against France; siege of Boulogne;
Katherine Parr rules as regent (19th July–18th September).
Emperor makes a secret treaty with François I, thereby
leaving England to fight France alone.

1545 French and English fleets engage near Portsmouth; the
Mary Rose is sunk (19th July).

1546 Anne Askew burned for heresy (6th July).
Gardiner and Wriothesley attempt to bring down
Katherine Parr (July).

1547 The Earl of Surrey executed (19th January).
Henry VIII dies (28th January).
The King's death announced three days later.
Edward VI proclaimed King, with Edward Seymour (soon
to be Duke of Somerset) as Lord Protector (31st January).
Thomas Wriothesley (now Earl of Southampton) dismissed
as Lord Chancellor (6th March).
Katherine Parr marries Thomas Seymour (now Lord
Seymour of Sudeley and Lord Admiral of England) in a
secret ceremony (spring).
Bishop Gardiner imprisoned (5th September).

1548 Elizabeth Tudor sent to Cheshunt to avoid scandal of
sexual misconduct with Thomas Seymour (May).
Mary Seymour (daughter of Katherine Parr and Thomas
Seymour) born (30th August).
Katherine Parr dies of puerperal fever (5th September).

1549 Thomas Seymour executed (20th March).